HIS ARMS WRAPPED AROUND HER WAIST, CRUSHING HER SOFT LENGTH AGAINST HIS STEELY ONE . . .

Hallie's mind ... it her traitorous b... own, undulating ag... that sent shivers o... Fear of Jake Parrish... masculinity . . . of his almost hyp... sensuality . . . and, most of all, fear of her own uncontrollable response to his beckoning. Her mind battled with her quickly surrendering body, desperately scrambling for the solution that could save her from succumbing to her own fierce desires.

"Saltpeter!" she gasped.

That stopped him short. He tipped his head back to peer into her flushed face. "What?"

"Saltpeter," she mumbled, putting a safe distance between them. "That should take care of your problem with these uncontrollable urges."

His eyes narrowed dangerously. "That might take care of my problem, Doctor," he retorted coolly. "But what do you intend to do about your own . . . ?"

"A wonderful, brooding hero and an innocent, spirited heroine make this richly detailed, suspense-filled romance an excellent debut book for Heather Cullman. I was enchanted."

—Jane Bonander, *Dancing on Snowflakes*

ANNOUNCING THE

TOPAZ FREQUENT READERS CLUB

COMMEMORATING TOPAZ'S 1 YEAR ANNIVERSARY!

THE MORE YOU BUY, THE MORE YOU GET

Redeem coupons found here and in the back of all new Topaz titles for FREE Topaz gifts:

Send in:

 2 coupons for a free TOPAZ novel (choose from the list below);

- ☐ THE KISSING BANDIT, Margaret Brownley
- ☐ BY LOVE UNVEILED, Deborah Martin
- ☐ TOUCH THE DAWN, Chelley Kitzmiller
- ☐ WILD EMBRACE, Cassie Edwards

4 coupons for an "I Love the Topaz Man" on-board sign

6 coupons for a TOPAZ compact mirror

8 coupons for a Topaz Man T-shirt

Just fill out this certificate and send with original sales receipts to:

TOPAZ FREQUENT READERS CLUB-1ST ANNIVERSARY
Penguin USA • Mass Market Promotion; Dept. H.U.G.
375 Hudson St., NY, NY 10014

Name____________________

Address____________________

City____________ State________ Zip__________

Offer expires 5/31/1995

This certificate must accompany your request. No duplicates accepted. Void where prohibited, taxed or restricted. Allow 4-6 weeks for receipt of merchandise. Offer good only in U.S., its territories, and Canada.

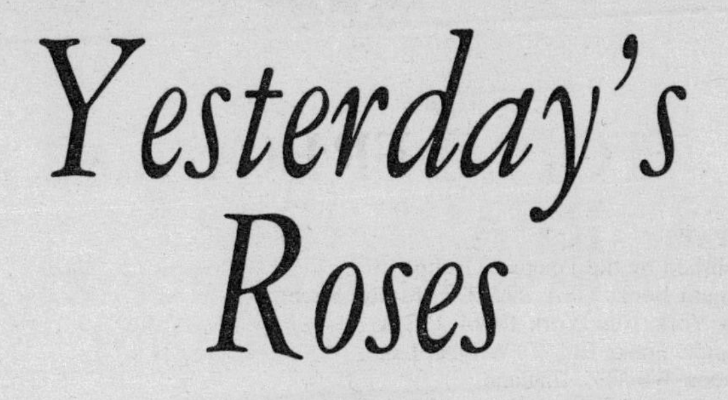

by

Heather Cullman

A TOPAZ BOOK

TOPAZ
Published by the Penguin Group
Penguin Books USA Inc., 375 Hudson Street,
New York, New York 10014, U.S.A.
Penguin Books Ltd, 27 Wrights Lane,
London W8 5TZ, England
Penguin Books Australia Ltd, Ringwood,
Victoria, Australia
Penguin Books Canada Ltd, 10 Alcorn Avenue,
Toronto, Ontario, Canada M4V 3B2
Penguin Books (N.Z.) Ltd, 182–190 Wairau Road,
Auckland 10, New Zealand

Penguin Books Ltd, Registered Offices:
Harmondsworth, Middlesex, England

First published by Topaz, an imprint of Dutton Signet,
a division of Penguin Books USA Inc.

First Printing, April, 1995
10 9 8 7 6 5 4 3 2 1

Printed in the United States of America

For my husband, Chip,
who taught me that the key
to making my dreams come true
is finding the courage to follow
them. Thanks for the wisdom.
I love you.

Chapter 1

San Francisco, 1865

They called him "Young Midas."

Lord! she thought, *the man certainly looks to be living up to his nickname.* Never in her travels—and Dr. Hallie Gardiner prided herself on having seen a good portion of the world—had she seen anything quite like this house.

House? she asked herself wryly. Somehow, that word seemed to be a bit of an understatement. This *house* was a grand, castlelike structure with all the homeyness of the Tower of London. Not that the building wasn't lovely. Hallie had to admit there was an overblown sort of charm to the steeply pitched gable roof and jutting towers, rather like something the Brothers Grimm might have dreamed up in a fit of grandiose madness.

At odds with the simple yet stylish London-type brick mansions that composed the rest of the South Park square, the impressive fortress seemed to lord over those lesser residences. Hallie prayed that the man wasn't as overbearing as his home.

For the first time that day, she felt her optimism flag. Even if the size and ornateness of the structure hadn't set it apart, the fact that it was completely surrounded by a stone wall did. It was clear that Jake Parrish was a man who jealously protected his privacy, and that was not a thought she found particularly comforting.

But what choice did she have? The Mission Infirmary for Chinese Women was in desperate need of funds, and she was sure this man could help. She had learned from her ledgers that he had been generous with his past donations. Surely that was a fair indicator of his benevolent nature, wasn't it?

Besides, Hallie reminded herself, she didn't intend to ask him for anything except his financial advice. If she could convince him to help her devise a plan to make the infirmary self-sufficient, she wouldn't have to depend on him—or the goodness of society's fickle hearts—for support. And from the dismal state of the ledgers, the people of San Francisco had been none too charitable of late.

Except for Jake Parrish. That fact and his impressive reputation for having a golden touch were what had brought her here today. He was her last hope to save the floundering clinic. If the Mission Infirmary failed, Hallie would be forced to return to her life in Philadelphia and—

No! She simply couldn't afford to fail!

Ignoring how cold the wrought iron felt beneath her gloved hands, Hallie clutched at the intricately twisted gate bars. Silently, she willed her resolve to be as strong as the metal beneath her trembling grip.

He's just a man, she reminded herself. *If he's smug, pompous, and condescending, well, you've dealt with that type before. Just smile into his overfed face and try to ignore his jiggling belly.*

Hallie gave a nervous laugh at the picture of a toad-like little man all puffed up with self-importance. With humor strengthening her resolve, she gave the gate a fierce tug, determined to take the castle by storm. But, alas, her plan for siege was foiled; the gate was locked.

Puzzled, she consulted the watch pinned to her Zouave jacket. Mr. Parrish's note had told her to call at four o'clock, and it was five of the hour. She stared at the gate for a moment, uncertain as to what to do next. Her plans hadn't included scaling walls and breaching a fortress.

Fighting back her irritation, Hallie waited by the gate, sure that someone would be along to let her in. No one came. When her watch read a quarter after the hour, her patience snapped.

The rudeness of the man! she raged silently. How dare he keep her waiting at the gate like some kind of beggar! With determination born of desperation, she marched around the perimeter of the wall looking for another entrance. By God, she would find a way in, even if it meant climbing that wall!

Her search was rewarded by the discovery of a wooden servants' gate at the back of the property, which she promptly gave a vicious yank. It didn't budge. Wanting to scream her frustration, she pulled on it again. It was locked.

Wonderful! Now what? Heaving a long-suffering sigh, Hallie studied the gate. It wasn't really that high, and the horizontal supports looked sturdy enough to provide adequate footholds. Perhaps if she—

Oh, no, Hallie! she lectured herself sternly. *You are not going to climb that wall. You will return to the mission like a proper lady and send His Royal Rudeness a proper note which only hints at your annoyance. You will then wait for another invitation, which you will accept with proper gratitude.*

Hallie let out a short laugh at her own absurdity. Since when had she ever done anything that could be considered even remotely proper? Propriety be damned! And before she could talk herself out of it, she was halfway over the gate, her plum merino skirts hiked scandalously high above her knees.

As she straddled the top, fully prepared to plunge to the other side, she was stopped cold by a dreadful thought: What if Mr. High and Mighty kept dogs? The big, mean kind with beady eyes and sharp teeth, the kind people kept to ensure their privacy? Visions of enormous, salivating hounds from hell flitted through her mind, and for a dreadful second she was certain she could hear an unholy baying.

Hallie froze with horror as she visualized the fate sure to befall her should she dare to enter the devil's lair. Anxiously she scanned the grounds for any sign of the dreaded hounds. Except for an occasional rustle of leaves from a nearby eucalyptus tree, all was quiet.

Slowly she let out the breath she'd been holding, feeling foolish for letting her imagination run away with her. Scolding herself for acting like a featherbrained schoolgirl, Hallie stiffened her spine and squared her shoulders, more determined than ever to reach the house with some semblance of dignity.

Unfortunately, the forcefulness of her motions served only to upset her precarious balance. She wavered unsteadily for a moment, flailing the air wildly for something solid to hold on to before tumbling over the gate to land in an undignified heap.

Hallie lay motionless for several seconds, winded from her fall. Gasping for breath, she cautiously began testing her limbs for injury, wiggling first her arms and then her legs. When she was convinced that she had survived the fall unharmed, she eased herself to her feet, muttering a string of unladylike adjectives directed at the occupant of the house.

Her relief at escaping unscathed soon turned to dismay as she surveyed the damages to her appearance. There was a large rip where her skirt had caught on something sharp, and weren't those grass stains on her—well, where she sat? With an exasperated sigh, she pushed her tumbling hair out of her eyes, succeeding only in scattering her hairpins in the process.

Great. Now I look like a wharfside doxy after a barroom brawl.

Well, there was no help for it. She'd gone to too much trouble to turn back now. Cursing herself for an impetuous fool, Hallie twisted her hair up and viciously stabbed it into an untidy heap atop her head with her few remaining pins.

It's all Mr. Jake Parrish's fault, she thought, sniffing for emphasis as she slapped at the dirt on her skirts. And if he was offended by her appearance—well, too bad! With that thought boiling in her head, she stormed through the heavy foliage, belligerently set on keeping her appointment.

"You no ring bell!" exclaimed the Chinese houseboy.

Hallie stared at the little man, momentarily caught off guard by his unprovoked rudeness.

Braced at the door like the sentry at a citadel gate, the man fixed the trespasser with a menacing stare. "How you get in if you no ring bell?"

"Excuse me?" If she hadn't been so taken aback by his unorthodox greeting, Hallie probably would have been hard-pressed to stifle a giggle. At ridiculous odds with his fierce bearing and threatening scowl, the man was diminutive in stature, at least a head shorter than herself.

He favored her with a long-suffering look and rolled his eyes toward the heavens. "Bell go ding dong. Man come. He unlock gate. Ver-ry simple." His manner was insultingly like that which one used when speaking to a very young or very stupid person.

An embarrassed flush stained Hallie's cheeks as the meaning of his words became clear. Of course there would have been a bell. Why hadn't she realized that?

"What you want?"

"I'm here to see Mr. Parrish. If you'll—"

"No see Mr. Jake! He no see anyone." The man began to inch the door closed, obviously considering the matter settled. "You go now!"

"Wait!" Hallie cried, becoming panicked by the very real possibility that she might not get to appeal to Mr. Parrish. "I have an appointment." To her relief, the houseboy paused.

" 'pointment?" He looked at her dubiously.

Unable to stifle her annoyance, she snapped, "Yes. You know—Mr. Par-rish send note. I come?"

His scowl wavered at that, and he seemed almost amused by her perfect imitation of his pidgin English. "Hop not told of 'pointment," he replied, apparently not amused enough to put aside his suspicions. "You go. Come later."

As he made to slam the door in her face, Hallie's temper flared. "No!" She thrust her booted foot in the door to prevent it from being closed. "I'm Dr. Hallie Gardiner. Mr. Parrish told me to be here at four. *He* invited *me*. Do you understand? I've gone through a lot of trouble to get here, and I intend to see that he honors our appointment."

The man stopped tugging at the door. "You doctor?"

Hallie could have sworn that relief flooded his face. "Yes. I just told you so. I'm Dr. Hallie Gardiner."

"You late. Mr. Jake ver-ry mean-headed."

"I know I'm late. I already explained about the gate."

"Yes. You no—"

"—ring bell," she finished for him with irritation. "You've already pointed that fact out to me. Mean-headed? Are you trying to tell me that Mr. Parrish is suffering from a head ailment?"

The houseboy looked at Hallie as if she were the one with a head ailment. Sighing over what he viewed as her lack of mastery of the English language, he flung the door open and motioned for her to enter. "You come now. Hop Yung show you to Mr. Jake."

The foyer into which Hallie was shown was impressive in size and content. Twin stairways curved into a graceful horseshoe shape, leading to a balustraded second-floor balcony. It was a design calculated to draw the eye upward and ultimately capture the observer in the breathtaking glory of the frescoes adorning the high, vaulted ceiling. Cut-crystal lamps gleamed from the chandeliers high above, capturing the kaleidoscope of light streaming through the stained-glass windows and casting playful rainbows of color on the white walls.

While stunning in appearance, Hallie secretly thought, the design would have been better suited for a theater lobby or a museum entry. The only homey touch was the expensive Axminster carpet in muted shades of blue, rose, green, and ivory, which served to add warmth to the white marble floor.

"Hop Yung, who is that with you?" demanded a strident female voice. There was a no-nonsense sort of tyranny to the utterance that called to mind Miss Dibell, Hallie's first and most domineering governess.

Hallie snapped her head around, fully expecting to encounter a hard-faced shrew who would perfectly match the voice. The only other person in the foyer was a woman who was not only young but ethereally beautiful. Hallie stared in disbelief for several seconds before shifting her gaze to the empty space behind the woman. She half expected the true possessor of that voice to step out of the shadows and resume her verbal barrage.

"Hop Yung! When I ask you a question, I expect an answer. Is that too difficult for you to understand?" The woman turned from Hop Yung and speared Hallie with her cold green gaze. "Just who is this person?" She practically spat the word "person."

Hallie was caught off guard by the viciousness of the unwarranted attack. For a moment she seriously considered telling these people exactly what she thought of their rudeness and trying to find another way to save the infirmary. But, of course, there was no other way. She'd already determined that dismal fact.

As the women studied each other for a long moment, each sizing up her adversary, Hallie found herself becoming shamefully conscious of her own shortcomings. Faced with this perfect example of one of Mr. Godey's ladies, she, who never gave the mirror more than a passing glance, suddenly found herself wishing that the cut of her visiting gown was a bit more modish and that she had taken the time to properly pomade her wildly haloing hair. Oh, and what she wouldn't have given at that moment to have her hair mellow from its bright autumn-leaves red to a softer hue of auburn or chestnut.

With a sinking feeling Hallie also noted that, from the top of her perfectly coiffed black curls to the toes of her green kid slippers, the other woman's appearance was flawless. Just when her bravery was about to wave a white flag of surrender in the face of such an intimidating foe, the woman shattered the illusion of perfection by snapping, "Just who are you and what do you want?"

"She doctor!" answered Hop Yung brightly, still unfazed by the woman's apparent displeasure. "Mr. Jake send for doctor."

The woman gave him a look of undisguised contempt. "Jake sent for Dr. Barnes. Does this person look like Dr. Barnes to you?"

"She say she doctor," he insisted mulishly.

Hallie was about to interrupt and explain her purpose, but the woman's frigid expression warned her that her efforts would be futile. *Who is this shrew, anyway?* she wondered. *Could this miserable person be Mrs. Parrish?*

If that was the case, Hallie could only pity the poor man for being saddled with such an ill-tempered wife. Undoubtedly "mean-headed" meant hung over, for this creature would be enough to drive even the most temperate of men to drunkenness!

"And you believed her?" retorted the young woman, expelling a short and thoroughly unpleasant laugh. "How many times have I told you not to believe everything you're told?"

"She say she have 'pointment with Mr. Jake."

The woman snorted in an unladylike fashion. "I thoroughly doubt that." Rounding on Hallie, the color high in her cheeks, she spat out, "I don't know who you are and I don't care. I just want you out of this house!"

"Mrs. Parrish?" inquired Hallie.

"No," she snapped, rudely refraining from any introduction.

Hallie relaxed visibly at her retort. Thank God for small favors! She could only imagine the futility of her task if this termagant were Jake Parrish's wife. She was undoubtedly the type of woman who would browbeat her husband until he was a mewling Milquetoast unable to make any decisions without deferring to his wife's superior approval.

So if she wasn't his wife, who was she? A mistress, perhaps? That would certainly explain the woman's animosity at the mention of a wife. Hallie had had enough distasteful encounters with her adulterous father's mistresses to know the effect the word "wife" had on them.

The woman didn't miss Hallie's look of obvious relief. She crossed her arms tightly across her breast, a wary expression masking her rigid features. "I would suggest you state your business promptly. I have little time or patience with uninvited visitors."

A hundred tart retorts sprang to the tip of Hallie's tongue, but she diplomatically suppressed them and answered politely, "I'm not an uninvited visitor. I really do have an appointment with Mr. Parrish. If you would be kind enough to inform him of my presence, I'd be most grateful."

"I can't imagine what business a dreary creature such as yourself could possibly have with Jake. Obviously you're lying about your appointment—or it was too unimportant for Jake to mention to me. Besides, he happens to be indisposed and isn't seeing anyone. Hop!" She glanced furiously about, muttering beneath her breath, "Now where has he gone? Worthless Chinese heathen." But the houseboy was nowhere to be seen.

Dreary creature, indeed! Hallie would show this awful person what lay beneath her "dreary" exterior! Looking down her nose at the woman and adopting the pompous demeanor she had perfected to use on recalcitrant patients, she announced coolly, "I don't feel obligated to state my intentions to you. And I would suggest you let

Mr. Parrish decide whether or not my business is important. By your own admission, you aren't his wife, and by your appalling lack of common civility I'd venture to guess that you're not his social secretary either. If Mr. Parrish is truly indisposed, then I suggest you find a more reliable doctor than this Barnes person. If there isn't one, I happen to be a doctor of excellent repute and would be willing to examine him myself."

The girl looked appalled by her suggestion and when she looked to protest, Hallie effectively cut her off. "Be advised, I was invited here, and whether you like it or not, I will speak to Mr. Parrish. You can tell him that Dr. Hallie Gardiner from the Mission Infirmary has arrived and that he has kept me waiting long enough."

Hallie was pleased to see the woman pale at her words. *Good,* she thought. It seemed that rudeness was the only thing these people understood, and by the look on the other woman's face, Hallie had made her point abundantly clear.

"You're from the mission?"

Hallie nodded. She was finally getting somewhere.

That somewhere wasn't exactly where she had expected. Whereas the woman had been merely hostile before, she now smoldered with hatred. "I knew it! You're one of Lavinia Donahue's spies! Come to collect more malicious gossip to spread to your petty little group of social reformers, have you? Well, you've wasted your time. If you think—"

Her tirade was interrupted by a short, sharp scream, immediately followed by a longer shriek. The shriek was quickly muffled, leaving both women frozen in their tracks. Being intimately acquainted with the sounds of human suffering, Hallie could tell that the person making those sounds was not only in pain but frightened as well.

The woman seemed to wilt as she cast a distressed glance toward the staircase, and for the first time Hallie noticed how young she was. Why, if you looked past the sophisticated attire and elaborate hairstyle, she was really nothing more than a jaded schoolgirl—one who could have benefited from a switch to the backside. She couldn't have been more than eighteen or nineteen, though her demeanor was that of a woman much older.

Mr. Parrish certainly likes them young, Hallie thought sourly. Fighting back her disgust, she reminded herself that as much as she disliked this girl, there was someone upstairs who sounded badly in need of her help. And as a doctor Hallie had taken an oath never to forsake those who were suffering. She was about to offer her assistance when the girl resumed her assault.

"Haven't you people done enough damage to this family?" There was a growing note of desperation in the girl's voice. "I might have been naive enough to believe the lies about your noble intentions in the past, but I know better now. You go back to Lavinia and tell her that I'll do anything necessary to protect my brother from her viciousness! Tell her—"

Another sobbing scream from upstairs crescendoed into a series of louder ones and served to deflate what was left of the girl's waning confidence. "Just leave," she choked out.

She looked on the verge of tears, and against her will Hallie found herself feeling sorry for the girl and seeking to reassure her. "I would be glad to give this Lavinia your message—if I knew her." She gave a self-deprecating shrug. "But I've only been in the city for a little more than a week and have met very few people. I definitely haven't met anyone named Lavinia. From the sounds of her, I doubt we would have much in common."

The girl didn't look at all reassured by Hallie's words. As another cry rent the silence and both women jumped in surprise at the crash of glass being forcefully broken, a tear rolled down the girl's cheek. She rubbed it away with her balled-up fist, a gesture childishly at odds with her adult appearance. Indistinct sounds of an argument seemed to agitate the girl even more, and when the argument was abruptly cut short by the slam of a door, she firmly grasped Hallie's arm and started to drag her toward the door.

"Look here, Miss—?" Hallie shook off the girl's hand impatiently. "You've got me at a disadvantage. You have my name, but I haven't the slightest idea who you are."

A harsh grate of laughter forced the women to break the glower they had been exchanging and transfer it toward the tall, dark-haired figure slowly descending the stairs.

"Always keep your adversary at a disadvantage. Isn't that right, Penelope?" the man quipped as he came to a stop at the bottom step. He swept Hallie with a quick but all-encompassing look before asking drily, "It seems as if I'm also at a disadvantage. Who are you?"

"You've already decided that I'm your adversary." Hallie didn't like the way his silvery-green eyes seemed to bore into her, and she definitely didn't like his handsome face. A man that good-looking was bound to be selfish, vain, and as past experience had taught her, cruel. If it hadn't been for his aura of raw masculine power, Hallie would have been inclined to call him beautiful. But she sensed that no one except a fool would dare call him that within earshot. And Dr. Hallie Gardiner was no fool.

She certainly wasn't fool enough to have her head turned by that face or, for that matter, by his tall, athletic physique. She'd seen how miserable a man like this could make a woman. Her own mother had been reduced to an unhappy shadow by such a man. Hallie had always believed there was no man on the face of the earth who could match her father's good looks, but this man was twice as handsome, and that made him twice as dangerous. So perhaps he had been right after all, for that pretty face was enough to make him her adversary.

It was Penelope who finally answered the man's question, her tone damning. "She's from the mission."

"Ah. Well, that would explain a lot," he replied, staring pointedly at Hallie's drab gown and unkempt hair. "What brings you here, Mission Lady? Undoubtedly Penelope has already given you her opinion of the Bible-thumping brethren of the Mission Society."

"I have an appointment with Jake Parrish and unless you're he, which I doubt, I—"

"Why would you doubt it?" he interrupted lazily, amusement stealing into his cold eyes.

"Well, everyone knows that Mr. Parrish is a genius."

"A genius, you say?"

"Yes. And rich."

"Of course."

Hallie's mind raced to think of something that would

wipe the arrogant smirk off the man's face. "From what I can surmise, he's inclined toward a charitable nature. And renowned for his . . . kindness. So you see, you couldn't possibly be Mr. Parrish. You obviously possess none of the aforementioned virtues!"

The last part, about Jake Parrish being kind, was pure fabrication. Hallie had certainly heard no such thing and doubted that it was true, but it had seemed an inspired touch. She stole a glance at the man through her lowered lashes, expecting him to look thoroughly chastised. He was staring back at her, thunderstruck.

Kind? he thought wryly. *She has imagination, I'll give her that. And rich? Since when is that considered such a virtue? Convenient, yes. But virtuous?* He threw back his head and howled with laughter.

"I don't see that any of this is funny in the least!" exclaimed Penelope in a querulous voice.

Ignoring her protest, he pointed out to Hallie, "It seems as if you're the one at a disadvantage. I am Jake Parrish, and it's been a long time since anyone has added kindness to my list of virtues. If that's what those crows at the mission are saying these days, I'm going to have to remind them that lying is a sin."

Hallie had the good grace to blush at his words. *Oh! Good show! Now you've really done it! First you insult the man and then resort to lies. He'll never help you now. Never in a hundred—no, a MILLION—years! I definitely see a trip back to Philadelphia looming in your near future, Hallie . . . unless you think of something—and quick!*

But what?

Ever heard of an apology?

But one look at his hard face told her that probably nothing short of groveling on her hands and knees would do to pacify him. Damned if she would stoop that low! Oh, Lord! Why couldn't he have been the pompous little toad she had imagined? Him she could have handled. Without thinking, she murmured, "You're not quite what I was expecting."

"And what were you expecting?"

"Don't encourage her, Jake! Dr. Barnes should be here any time now, and we don't want her around prying into our affairs." Penelope cast a meaningful glance toward the stairs, and Jake nodded in agreement.

"Well, Miss—" he began brusquely.

"Doctor," she corrected him. "I'm Dr. Hallie Gardiner from the Mission Infirmary. You asked me to be here at four o'clock."

"Really?" He pulled out a pocket watch and snapped open the case. A tune that Hallie recognized, but couldn't quite place, began to play. He raised his eyes to hers. "You're late."

"I know, but the gate was locked."

He clicked the case closed again, abruptly cutting off the music. "Why didn't you just ring the bell?" As he watched the heat rise in her cheeks, it suddenly dawned on him how she'd come by her unkempt appearance. A mocking smile twisted his mouth, and he asked with feigned innocence, "Just how did you get in, if not through the gate?"

"I found a back way," she answered truthfully, unable to meet his cynical gaze. She would die before she admitted to climbing his fence.

"You obviously went to a lot of trouble to see me," he said with pointed emphasis on the word "trouble." When she didn't deny it, he admitted, "To be honest, I had completely forgotten our appointment. I'm afraid you've wasted your time and trouble. I can't see anyone today."

"I told you he was indisposed," Penelope crowed.

"Really?" Hallie swept him from head to toe with her skeptical gaze. "He looks healthy enough to me."

"See, Penelope? You have a doctor's word on it." Smiling slyly at Hallie, he added, "I'm glad someone agrees with me on that score. My overbearing little sister insists on treating me like an invalid."

The challenging look he threw at Penelope forced her to protest, "Jake! You know what Dr. Barnes says about exciting yourself."

"Proves my point that doctors are a pack of charlatans and butchers, doesn't it!"

Color infused Hallie's face as she pointed out, "I'm a doctor, and I am neither a charlatan nor a butcher!"

He snorted. "No. You're something worse."

"Oh?"

"Yes. You're a straitlaced little spinster who is so afraid of your own femininity that you'd rather compete with men than admit to your failure as a woman."

Her face darkened to an unbecoming shade of crimson in her anger. "And you're a typical narrow-minded ass of a man if you're stupid enough to believe that!" she retorted. "Could it be that you're actually intimidated by a woman who can do more than play the spinet, do needlework, and simper adoringly every time you stoop to grace her with your inane conversation? Why is it that every time a man—"

Her tirade was cut short by another loud scream, punctuated by several heavy crashes.

As the wailing continued, a tall, reed-thin black woman scampered down the stairs. Ignoring Hallie's presence, she blurted out, "She be bad, Mista' Jake, real bad! I done all I can, but the Missus, well, she ain't havin' nothin' to do with me. Won't let no one close! The Missus be needin' a docta' real soon! I cain't do no more!"

"Damn it!" Jake bellowed. "Hop Yung! You get your yellow ass—" He whipped around, only to find Hop Yung right behind him. A muscle worked in his jaw as he skewered the houseboy with his angry glare. "Where the hell is Dr. Barnes? I sent you for him more than an hour ago! So help me, Hop, if you forgot to fetch the doctor—"

"Hop talk to doctor assistant," the Chinese man cut in defensively. "He say doctor come r-right way!" At his employer's quelling expression, the houseboy swallowed hard and sidled toward the door. "Hop go. See what keep doctor." With that, he sprang out the door, slamming it behind him with a loud *bang*!

"Celine? How much time do you think we have?" Jake asked the black woman, distractedly raking his fingers through his hair.

"Don' know, Mista Jake. She seems real bad off. Don' know what else to do."

"Excuse me," Hallie interrupted. All three people jerked around, obviously having forgotten her presence. "Maybe I can help?" When they just stared at her as if she had suddenly mutated into a three-headed monster with cloven hoofs and a forked tail, she proceeded urgently, "There is someone who needs a doctor's services, and this Dr. Barnes doesn't seem to be in any kind of a hurry to get here. Perhaps I should have a look at the patient."

It was Penelope who finally broke the stunned silence. "Absolutely not! Dr. Barnes will be here any time. We know and *trust* him!"

"Are you so sure he's coming? God knows, I've been in enough situations where I couldn't leave a patient, not even if President Johnson himself had demanded my services."

Jake ran his thumb across his jaw and studied her thoughtfully for a moment. "Are you a good doctor?"

She answered without the slightest hesitation, "Very good." And the words rang true.

"You've got conviction, I'll grant you that. I'm almost inclined to believe you."

"Jake!" Penelope shrieked, trying to be heard above the raucous cries, which had resumed with a vengeance. "You're not actually considering engaging this woman, are you? I'm not at all convinced that she's not a fraud."

Fraud. Charlatan. Butcher. That did it! Hallie had had enough, thank you kindly. She'd been gracious enough to offer her services, and they'd been insulting in their refusal.

"Fine!" she snapped. "Then I don't see any point in continuing this interview. I'll be returning to the mission now, and leaving you to the tender mercies of this Dr. Barnes—if he shows."

As she turned to leave, Jake Parrish's hand shot out and grasped her arm in a bruising grip. When he turned her to face him, Hallie could have sworn that she read a fleeting anguish in his expression. Visibly wincing at the sound of another heartrending wail, he nodded.

Penelope's face distorted into a study of horror as she realized her brother's intent. "Jake, if you engage this woman and something goes wrong, well, don't say I didn't warn you!" Lifting her skirts, she ran up the stairs, her shoulders shaking with soundless sobs.

Jake's eyes narrowed as he met Hallie's indignant glare. "You say you're a good doctor and you want to help?" His punishing grasp tightened on her arm. "Then pray for strength, Dr. Gardiner. You're hired!"

Chapter 2

"Fine." Hallie nodded at Jake Parrish, picking up the gauntlet he'd defiantly thrown. "Of course, I'll require the use of *both* my arms in order to provide my best services. That is, if you haven't permanently impaired my circulation."

Jake glanced down, genuinely startled by her remark. He was clutching her arm so tightly that the veins in his hand were standing out in tense relief. Murmuring an apology, he loosened his grip and deftly eased his hand into a gentle, massaging motion.

A burning tingle raced down Hallie's arm as her blood resumed its flow. Surprised at the tenderness of his ministrations, she quickly glanced up from his long-fingered hand to his face. As their eyes met, she could have sworn that he looked . . . kind.

Confusion and hallucinations are common symptoms of a head injury, she told herself, suddenly wondering if she'd suffered a worse fall from the gate than she had previously thought. After all, as Mr. Parrish had already pointed out, he wasn't kind.

"Doc?"

Hallie jumped at the sound of his voice.

"Your arm? I take it you've suffered no permanent damage?"

"Uh? Oh . . . no."

He smirked at her confusion in a manner that made Hallie long to kick him. Arrogant beast! She would have thoroughly enjoyed watching His Supreme Smugness's face dissolve into a mask of pain and outrage as he howled at the indignity of it all.

"The patient?" he prompted with mock helpfulness.

"Of course." She gave the arm he was massaging an impatient tug. "Will you please stop prodding at my arm in that annoying fashion? Must I remind you that I'm hardly a delicate young miss and am not likely to fall into a fit of vapors at a little rough handling?"

"Yes to your first question." Jake abruptly dropped her arm. "And no to your second."

To Hallie's mortification, he leaned forward to examine her face critically, making it clear that he was searching for signs of her impending fossilization. As if in confirmation of some insulting conclusion, he nodded and actually had the nerve to chuckle.

Uppity bastard! Hallie's foot began to twitch. *I know exactly where I'd like to kick him.*

Arching his brows in feigned astonishment, his voice dripping with sarcasm, Jake said, "Let's see now . . . one . . . two. I count two arms and both in your possession. Are you ready to begin your duties?" His handsome face became the picture of solicitude. "Of course, I realize that you're no longer a young miss and your circulation might not be what it once was. If you need more time—"

"I'm fine," she snapped. The gall of the man, alluding to her age. Good Lord! She was only twenty-six years old, hardly ready for a shawl and cane. With an indignant sniff, she said, "If you're finished wasting my time with your pleasantries, I'd like to do the job you've hired me for."

His only response was another of his superior snorts. As he turned on his heel, he nodded over his shoulder, apparently expecting her to follow.

The man must be suffering from a nasal condition, she thought spitefully. And hadn't Penelope snorted in much the same manner? *Must be a family defect.* Well, she had just the treatment for their condition. One that involved a big, sharp hook.

So caught up was Hallie in her delightful pictures of treating Mr. High and Mighty's nose to the agonies of the hook that she was completely robbed of her breath, more from surprise than impact, when she slammed into something solid. An explosive curse told her that the "something solid" was Jake Parrish's back.

Instinctively she grabbed at him for support but soon realized her mistake. He, too, appeared to be fighting for his balance. For one dreadful instant, Hallie was certain they were about to go tumbling down the stairs to land in an ignominious pile in the foyer below.

To her eternal relief, Mr. Parrish quickly mastered the situation. Crushing Hallie against his side with one steely arm, he grabbed the oak banister and managed to haul them both to a more stable perch. As Hallie went hurling into his hard chest, she heard something clatter down the stairs.

They stood frozen in that position, Hallie clutched against the strength of his tall form, his arm wrapped protectively around her waist, both fighting to catch their breath. The impropriety of their closeness was forgotten in favor of mutual relief, but only for a moment.

All too quickly, Hallie became all too aware of the muscles rippling beneath the fine linen of his shirt. There was something about the way his powerful torso pressed against her soft curves that made it impossible for her to breathe. Pointedly ignoring the spicy, masculine scent that clung to his waistcoat, Hallie turned her face from where it had been buried against his wide shoulder, suddenly overwhelmed by his disconcerting proximity.

She raised her eyes to see if their closeness was having the same electrifying effect on her rescuer as it did on herself. If the strange expression on his face was any indication of his feelings, then Jake Parrish was definitely disturbed by something. But it clearly wasn't Hallie's person doing the disturbing. Swallowing something that felt suspiciously like disappointment, Hallie pushed away from his slackening hold and followed his troubled gaze to the object at the bottom of the steep stairway.

It was just a cane. A black one with a gold top, to be exact. As Jake Parrish uttered a soft but graphic oath, Hallie cast him a questioning look. Pointedly ignoring her stare, he cursed again and struggled to brace himself more firmly against the banister, holding on to the gleaming wood as if it were a lifeline in a storm-swept ocean.

Hallie was puzzled by the expression of frustrated helplessness that spread across his face. He looked so . . . lost, as he seemed to mentally gauge the distance between himself and his cane. It was then that she realized the truth, and it stunned her: the cane wasn't an affectation. Jake Parrish was a cripple.

And she was a doctor, for God's sake! Why hadn't she noticed such an obvious infirmity before now?

Because you couldn't get past that pretty face of his, she admitted to herself.

Cautiously, he took a halting step down, never once looking at Hallie. It was almost as if he was afraid of what he would see in her eyes. At his next step, his left leg gave out, and as he stumbled, his hissing intake of breath told her of his pain. Hallie impulsively reached forward to offer him support, but snatched her arm away before he could see it. She could only guess at how galling such a handicap was to a man as proud as Jake Parrish and knew that by offering her assistance she would only be adding to his indignity.

Politely, she pretended not to hear him as he drew deep, ragged breaths, or to watch him when he pressed his hand hard against his left thigh as if to ease a nagging ache. She even managed to avoid staring at the way his knuckles had bleached to a bloodless white with the tension of his grasp on the handrail. But when she saw a quicksilver flash of vulnerability burst across his previously blank face, Hallie knew she didn't have the heart to subject him to any further humiliation.

Acting quickly, she sighed, "Oh, clumsy me! If I'm not tripping over my own two feet, I'm dropping or breaking something. 'Hide all the breakables!' my father would always shout. 'Here comes the most graceless creature on the face of the earth!' " She illustrated her point by tripping down the stairs like a hell-bent hoyden to retrieve his cane.

As she handed it to him in a brisk, matter-of-fact manner, he gifted her, for the first time, with a genuine smile. Hallie swallowed hard as she stared at the dimple provocatively creasing his left cheek. She had realized that he was an extraordinarily handsome man, but when he smiled like that, he was more beautiful than the archangel in the church window back home. And she'd had more than her share of romantic fancies about that angel.

"Did your father really call you graceless?"

Hallie forcibly composed herself and nodded.

"Then his definition of grace differs from mine." Jake expertly positioned the cane and with an incline of his head said, "If you'll follow me, Dr. Gardiner, I believe I hear your patient clamoring for your services."

Indeed, the din had resumed with a vengeance. Without further comment, he began his tedious, self-conscious trek up the stairs, leaving Hallie to pace herself behind his awkward gait.

Though the stairs had been an ordeal for Mr. Parrish, he proved to be adept at maneuvering through the halls, and Hallie found herself almost running to keep up. As they rounded a corner, the wails grew deafening.

Suppressing the urge to clamp her hands over her ears, Hallie studied the corridor in which they had paused. There were two doors on either side of the hall, which ended at a pair of leaded-glass doors opening onto a spacious balcony. Shafts of late-afternoon sunlight glittered through the diamondlike windowpanes, infusing the entire area with a warm glow. Hallie would have found the effect enchanting had it not been for the heavy ironwork barring the doors—and the screaming.

Hallie looked to Jake Parrish with mute inquiry. Her question was not *why* he needed those bars, for the animalistic howls were answer enough, but for *whom*?

As if in answer to her unasked question, he shoved open the second door on the right, a motion which elicited a battery of garbled screeches from the occupant within.

"Dr. Gardiner," he drawled, keeping his face rigidly void of expression. "Allow me to introduce you to my charming wife, Serena."

The woman strapped to the functional iron bed struggled against her bonds at Hallie's approach. Serena Parrish had once been a beautiful woman, that much was apparent, even in the semidarkness of the room. Traces of her former glory were still visible in the white-gold iridescence of her matted hair, and in the amazing eyes that shocked the senses with their blaze of cerulean fire burning against the contrasting chalky white canvas of her face.

Though her face had that pinched, drawn look which Hallie associated with wasting illness, the well-bred elegance of the woman's bone structure had defied the ravaging forces of her ailment. Her screams had ceased when she'd caught sight of the stranger with her husband, and she now lay quietly, her lips still trembling. Hypnotically, Hallie was reminded of a moonlight nymph startled by the unexpected presence of a lowly mortal.

The silence also made Hallie twice as conscious of the crunch of broken glass beneath her boots. Drawing her attention away from the spell cast by Serena's compelling face, she peered down at the floor in disgust. Nasty, viscous-looking liquids congealed with multicolored powders amid the shattered remains of glass vials, staining the rich Aubusson carpet. The once beautiful parquet floor beneath the carpet was badly scarred, as if it had been subjected to violent and frequent blows; the spartan furnishings were bolted to the floor. All in all, the room bore evidence of a recent conflict, as well as the marks of past battles.

Though Serena's belly was heavily swollen with child, Hallie could tell by the size of her hands and feet that she was a small woman, and she had trouble visualizing her wreaking such havoc. Yet how else would one explain those thick leather straps binding her ankles and wrists?

Serena lay still for a moment, her expression angelic as she surveyed Hallie. "How very kind of you to visit," she drawled in a voice thick with the echoes of Dixie. "Shall I ring Bosworth for refreshments? Yes, I do believe lemonade and . . . some of Mammy Celine's blackberry pound cake would be wonderful." She pursed her lips for a moment, her gaze sweeping Hallie from head to toe. Smiling cordially, she added, "Why, I'm green with envy over that gown of yours. Is that one of Monsieur Worth's new creations?"

Jake snorted at his wife's remark. "As you can tell from that particular comment, our Serena is somewhat deluded."

The clicking of his cane against the wooden floor warned Hallie that he had abandoned his relaxed stance against the door frame and was now stalking toward them. When the clicking came to a halt, Hallie could feel his presence at her back. Just as she was about to question him about his wife's condition, he hissed, "Damn it to hell!"

The explosiveness of his curse made Hallie jerk her head around in wonder. To her discomfort, she found her face scant inches from his chest. Hallie Gardiner was considered tall for a woman—an Amazon, according to her father. Yet next to Mr. Parrish she felt almost petite. For the first time in her life she was forced to tip her head back to peer into a man's face.

What she saw in this particular man's face was an anger so palpable that it would have burned her with its intensity had it been trained in her direction. Which it wasn't, thank God.

Hallie traced his fury-sparked gaze to the woman on the bed. Surely he didn't blame this pathetic creature for her condition, did he? Nervously chewing the inside of her cheek, she stole another glance at his face. She wasn't particularly comforted by the stony mask which had descended over his blazing features.

"Has the doctor finally arrived then, sir?" inquired a brusque voice tinged with a trace of an Irish accent.

Hallie didn't miss the way Serena flinched at the sound of the connecting door slamming shut.

A large, rawboned woman carrying a broom trudged to the bedside. Pausing to bestow a rancorous glare on Serena, she snapped, "Made quite a mess, did we? Always makin' extra work with never a thought for us poor souls havin' to clean up."

Serena began to shake, her mouth working soundlessly, as the woman's bulky form loomed against the foot of the bed. Violently she twisted from side to side, her body arching rhythmically. It was almost as if she were seeking to escape some great torment. Whimpering like a frightened child, she jerked her head up and stared past Hallie. When her gaze touched her husband's, she started to wail.

Never in her life had Hallie heard such a soul-rending sound. The visceral terror in the cry chilled her very soul, and she could only wonder at what past evil had served to provoke such a response.

"Screechin' like a banshee again, are we?" the woman chastised as she advanced steadily toward her charge. "Can't you see you're disturbin' your husband with your squallin', girl? Can't say as I've much patience with it myself."

When Serena failed to quiet, the woman bent closer to the bed. "Bein' stubborn? Well, I'll put a stop to this nonsense quick enough, or my name isn't Maggie O'Shea."

In a lightning-quick motion that would have done a wrestler proud, she grasped Serena by the neck and pressed her head brutally against the mattress. Serena struggled frantically, her eyes rolling with animal terror. Producing a length of rough, none-too-clean fabric from her apron pocket, Maggie callously shoved the cloth between Serena's teeth.

Hallie was appalled by the inhumanity of such treatment and as she opened her mouth to protest, Mr. Parrish snarled, "Damn it, Maggie! I will not stand back and watch this abuse. I've told you that under no circumstances are you to bind my wife."

He shoved the nurse aside and knelt, with much difficulty, beside Serena.

"And what would you be suggestin' I do, sir?" The woman's snide tone belied her courteous words.

Jake fixed the nurse with a formidable look, one that never failed to quell even the most stalwart of men. "You were hired with the specific understanding that you were to use no abusive tactics against your patient," he barked. "I distinctly recall your agreement to the terms."

Maggie crossed her meaty arms over her bosom. "Beggin' your pardon, Mr. Parrish, but what experience have you had with crazed folks that makes you such an authority?"

"None with so-called crazed folks. But I have had the shaming experience of being bound and forced to submit to unspeakable treatment against my will. By virtue of such experience, I feel as if I speak with the greatest of authority!" He practically shouted the last few syllables.

The anguish behind his words tore at Hallie's heart, moving her to reach down and give his shoulder a reassuring squeeze.

Jake tensed sharply beneath her hand, and jerked his head up to slant her a probing look. There was no pity in her expression, only gentle understanding. Almost imperceptibly, his features softened and he gave her a slight nod in acknowledgment.

"Well, speak up, woman." His face hardened again as he turned his glare on Maggie O'Shea. "What have you to say for yourself?"

"Not a thing. What I did was right and proper, and I'll not be apologizin' for it. Not to anyone, you hear! Nobody tells Maggie O'Shea that she's not knowin' her job."

"Well, someone is now!" he snapped. "Get out!"

"You'll be regrettin' your decision soon enough. And when you do, don't expect me to come runnin'. It's glad I am to be getting away from that crazy woman. Gives me the willies, she does." With that parting shot she stamped out of the room, slamming the door behind her.

Jake watched the nurse's retreat with a weary sigh. As the bang from the door reverberated through the room, he carefully turned Serena's face from the mattress, against which it was pressed. She struggled at his touch, and the savage fear in her expression made him pause for a moment.

"It's all right," Jake murmured. "You know I'd never hurt you." Gently grasping his wife's chin to still the frantic jerking motion of her head, he pulled the cloth out of her mouth.

Serena beamed up at her husband in a caricature of goodwill, then viciously sank her teeth into the vulnerable fleshy part of his hand.

Jake's breath exploded from his lungs at the suddenness and intensity of the pain. Reflexively, he tried to wrench his hand free from her piercing bite, but her teeth clamped further into his flesh, widening the already deep lacerations. He could see his blood welling up around the wounds to flow copiously from her lips, and it chilled him to his very core to see that she was smiling. Then she laughed.

As Serena opened her mouth wide to issue hysterical peals of distorted mirth, Jake snatched his damaged hand out of harm's way. He could only stare in shock at his palm, from which she had savagely bitten a good-sized piece of flesh.

"God!" he muttered thickly as he transferred his gaze back to his wife. He felt his gorge rise at the macabre sight of her merrily laughing face, her lips stained with his blood. As he stared at her, the horror of her words the day he had left for the war echoed through his brain:

Remember my laughter as you lie bleeding on your precious battlefield. I'll be laughing with joy at the news of your death. I just hope that you suffer the torments of hell before you die!

She'd gotten half her wish, for he had indeed suffered the torments of hell.

Jake turned to look at Hallie as she took his injured hand in hers and carefully examined the wound. Her face was a study of concern as she gently probed the area. When she finally looked up, Jake was stunned by the depth of compassion in her eyes. It had been forever since anyone had offered him the simple gift of solace. Yet here was a virtual stranger offering just that.

"It's a nasty wound," she whispered. "It should be cleansed and stitched. I'm always careful with human bites, for I've seen them produce the most awful infections. If you'll send someone to the mission for my bag, I'll care for it properly."

"I've survived much worse wounds than this one," he replied, drawing his hand away. "There's no need for you to bother with it."

"But it's deep and it could become infected. If—" Hallie's words were cut off abruptly by Serena's shouting a string of graphic oaths.

Jake was taken aback by the foulness of her language, but he quickly regained his composure to comment, "It seems my loving wife has been working on expanding her vocabulary."

"Mr. Parrish," Hallie began, resolutely ignoring Serena's obscenity and the fact that her own face was burning with embarrassment at the woman's words. "About your hand—"

"Good God!" Jake interjected as Serena uttered a few words that Hallie had never heard before. "I can't imagine where she could have learned that one! Look, Mission Lady, I promise to clean my hand properly. I'll even have Hop or Celine bandage it if it'll make you feel better—"

"God?" Serena shrieked, a crafty smile looping across her face. "God? Oh, yes. Pray for your sins, my dears, lest you be plunged into the depths of hell! Can't you see how the devil is punishing me?" She jerked her head toward her rounded belly.

"She doesn't understand." Jake rubbed his eyes wearily with his undamaged hand and then lurched to his feet, half pulling himself up by the iron headboard.

Hallie rose to stand beside him. "Mr. Parrish?"

If ever a man looked haunted by a deep, unrelenting sorrow, that man was Jake Parrish. "She thinks her pain is caused by the demons of hell." He smiled at that, but in a way that made her ache at his unhappiness. "Seeing as how she considers me to be the devil incarnate, perhaps, in her demented way, she is correct. At any rate, Dr. Gardiner, my wife has been in labor for several hours, and it is up to you to find some way to deliver the child."

Jake closed the door to Serena's room, cutting off the hushed tones of Hallie's coaxing voice. It was only then that he allowed his shoulders to slump beneath the crushing weight of his weariness. Leaning against the wall of the corridor, he suddenly felt too weak to brace himself against the overwhelming despair which had haunted him since that day all those months ago.

"No hope." That's what the specialists had said about the condition of Serena's mind. They had meant that never again would she be the witty, lively woman of the early days of their marriage, nor would she ever resume her reign as a queen of society.

But to Jake, the words "no hope" had a far different meaning. For him, the words carried a damning verdict that condemned him to a life sentence, with no hope for peace or happiness. There would be only the dark, hate-filled purgatory of her mind for Serena and the lonely years marked by regret for himself. And, of course, there would be the child.

But Jake didn't want to think about the child.

Pushing the disturbing thoughts out of his mind, he shoved away from the supporting wall and straightened to his full height. To the world, he would continue to be the man with the golden touch—the man who had everything.

They called him "Young Midas." Only Jake himself knew the emptiness that lay within the grandeur of his title.

Chapter 3

He's beautiful, you know," whispered Serena.

"Hmmm?" A frown creased Hallie's forehead as she pulled Serena's sticklike arm through the sleeve of the clean nightgown. The fight had gone out of the woman, and she had remained as limp as a loosely stuffed rag doll while Hallie changed her wet gown for a dry one.

Not that it was such a difficult task. Aside from her swollen belly, Serena was as insubstantial as the mythical nymph she resembled. Hallie had almost been moved to tears when she had removed her patient's voluminous gown, revealing a pathetically emaciated body.

Before leaving the room, Jake had curtly ordered Hallie to release Serena from her bonds. With much trepidation, and not without a quick prayer for strength, she had complied. To her frustration, she found the knots in the leather restraints so tight from Serena's constant tugging that it took her a good half hour to untie them.

While she worked, Hallie struggled to keep up a steady stream of conversation in hopes of calming the woman's agitation. She tried her best to imitate drawing room banter, but having never actually participated in such vague chitchat, she became uncomfortably aware of entering into uncharted territory.

To her surprise, she did quite well, managing to prattle on subjects ranging from popular music to the latest fashion trends, all while unsnarling the tangled puzzle of her patient's bindings. At one point during Hallie's enthusiastic, albeit one-sided, discussion on the trend toward smaller crinolines, Serena surprised her by nodding her agreement.

Though Serena remained docile during Hallie's ministrations, when all was said and done, and the last of the bonds had fallen loose, Hallie braced herself for an onslaught of violence. To her relief, her crooning nonsense had worked its magic, and Serena was perfectly willing to follow her lead—so much so that she allowed herself to be led to the chair where she now sat.

"There, now. Isn't that better?" Hallie inquired, buttoning up the last of the nightgown's tiny mother-of-pearl buttons. Not that she really expected a response. The woman barely seemed aware of her presence, and the question had been asked more from force of habit than anything else.

A frown creased Hallie's brow as she moved toward the bed. What she really needed to do, and only God knew how, was to gain enough of Serena's trust to make a proper examination. Provided that her patient's periodic moans and belly clutching were an accurate gauge of the frequency of her pains, it would be several hours yet before she gave birth. Hallie could only pray that she could keep the woman calm enough to do what was necessary.

Serena sat in silence for several moments, staring into space as if hypnotized. Suddenly she cocked her head to one side and shifted her gaze in Hallie's direction.

"The devil," she announced in a strangely flat voice.

"Excuse me?" Hallie paused in her task of stripping the soiled sheets from the bed. She'd been appalled by the discovery that Serena had been allowed to lie in a gown and bedding soaked with her own birthing waters, and in her typically efficient way, she had set about to remedy the situation.

"He's very beautiful, you know. The devil, that is."

"The devil?" Hallie grimaced. *Beautiful?* At once the breathtaking picture of Jake Parrish's smiling face flashed through her mind. *Jake Parrish was a bit of a devil, and he certainly was beautiful.* Assuming that Serena was referring to her husband, Hallie agreed, "Oh, yes. Very handsome."

Serena stared at her unblinking for a moment, and Hallie had the uncanny feeling that the woman was reading her thoughts.

"Don't be fooled by his beauty," Serena hissed. "Some of his faces are quite ugly. And he can be . . .

crude. I hate it most when he's crude." She shuddered as she imparted that last piece of information.

Expertly tucking the corners of the bottom sheet beneath the mattress, Hallie replied, "I expect that all men are prone to ugly moods from time to time. And I daresay most have moments of crudeness. I've always suspected that it has something to do with the way they're made." She paused to frown at the sheet, which had come untucked at the far corner of the bed, before asking, "Have you ever noticed that men just don't seem to have the same degree of restraint as women do?"

Ignoring Hallie's diatribe, Serena shifted her gaze to the far corner, her expression dreamy. "But sometimes he's ever so gentle. I love him when he strokes me . . . teases me."

Gasping out a string of breathless little moans, Serena closed her eyes and threw back her head. "He tortures me until I beg him to touch me . . ." With a rapturous sigh, she pressed her hand between her legs. ". . . here."

Hallie dropped the corner of the sheet she had been tucking and stared at the woman, shocked. Nothing between the pages of the textbooks had prepared her for this type of situation.

"And when he finally . . . takes me . . . I can't help screaming my pleasure." Serena uttered a strangled groan as a look of ecstasy burst across her face.

Hallie glanced away in confused embarrassment. Whatever was she supposed to do now? Should she just ignore the woman's behavior and pretend it wasn't happening? Or should she do something to put a stop to it?

Serena herself saved Hallie from having to make a decision. Expelling a crescendo of explosive gasps which escalated into a shrieking moan, she jerked twice and then abruptly fell motionless.

What do you say to that, Miss Know-it-all? Hallie asked herself, giving the bed a clumsy smoothing with trembling hands. *That's one area where your education is definitely deficient.*

She stole a peek at Serena, who sat slumped in her chair. A smile of supreme satisfaction twisted the woman's lips, and her breath was coming in ragged spurts.

Sounds like Jake Parrish is quite the lover, doesn't it?

There was something about that thought which Hallie found profoundly disturbing.

Resolutely turning her mind back to her present task, Hallie murmured, "I'll be finished with the bed in a few minutes. Then we can get you settled all tight and cozy."

But Serena didn't appear to hear her. She was staring into the deep shadows in the far corner of the room, her mouth opening and closing soundlessly. Cringing against the chairback, her face deathly white, the woman wore an expression of unbridled terror.

Hallie followed her patient's gaze, puzzled. The only thing against the far wall was a plain wooden chair with a scarlet glove draped over its back—hardly a sight to provoke such horror.

Whimpering softly, Serena shook her head, her expression imploring. Then, with a suddenness that made Hallie's heart jump to her throat, she screamed,

"Make him stop!" In one erratic motion, Serena hurled herself from her chair to land huddled in the corner. As she lay on her side trembling, clutching her arms and legs tightly against her chest, she shrieked, "Please don't let him hit me again!" Flinching violently, she threw her hands in front of her face as if to ward off a blow.

Hallie dropped the pillow she had been plumping and rushed to where Serena lay, horrified by the woman's pantomime of terror. Sinking to her knees, she tentatively reached out to stroke her patient's trembling back.

Serena jerked away as though she'd been struck. "I try so hard to please him . . . so very hard. But when I don't . . . dear God! He's so ugly when he hits me!" She cowered deeper into the corner, her body recoiling in vivid response to an imaginary assault. "Don't let him hurt me!"

"Hush now," Hallie crooned, at a loss for a way to handle the situation. "No one's going to hurt you."

Tears streaming down her cheeks, Serena clamped her hands over her ears as if struggling to shut out an offensive noise. "Please! Make him stop saying those awful, crude words!" she pleaded. "He knows I can't bear it!"

Hallie froze, feeling utterly helpless. *Dear God, what has been done to the poor woman? And by whom?* For all his faults, Jake Parrish didn't seem like the type of man who would abuse his wife. Grudgingly, she had to admit that she'd been touched by his patience with her. Why, he hadn't even raised his voice when the woman had bitten him.

She glanced down at Serena's stricken face, troubled. Had Jake Parrish's tolerant behavior all been an act played for her benefit? Hallie knew from experience that as far as husbands were concerned, Public Lambs were often Private Wolves.

Hadn't all of Philadelphia society marveled over how doting a husband and father Ambrose Gardiner had appeared to be? Hallie had learned at an early age that appearances could be deceptive and that her father was a master at the game. In a den of wolves, he had always been the leader of the pack. Was Jake Parrish, too, a wolf in a lamb's disguise?

Serena rolled over to crouch defensively on her elbows and knees. Peering wildly through the gossamer tangle of her hair, she moaned, "He says he can't take his pleasure unless I cry and beg. He blames me if his man's part can't—" She burst into tears and began a terrible keening.

"Serena," Hallie crooned in a soothing manner, gently trying to ease the woman from her huddled position. "You're safe with me. I won't let him hurt you. Never again! Do you hear me?"

Serena fell limp beneath Hallie's hands, her body heaving with strangled sobs.

"There now, there's my good girl," Hallie whispered. "You're safe. I'll—"

Suddenly Serena reared up on her knees, snarling like a rabid animal, and with a strength that was amazing for her size, she threw Hallie viciously against the wall.

For the first time in her life, Hallie was grateful for her crinoline and layers of petticoats. As she was flung, the mountain of her skirts swayed back and up, effectively pillowing her body from the bruising contact with wall. Stunned, she lay against the wall, struggling to regain her senses.

Hallie recovered quickly and lunged after her patient, who was crawling away, seemingly intent on reaching the area beneath the bed. In a quicksilver motion, she tackled Serena, careful not to crush her belly.

As gently as possible, she rolled Serena onto her back. Serena howled and began flailing wildly at her captor.

Ignoring the blitz of stinging blows, Hallie drew Serena into her embrace and hugged her close. They remained in that position for a long while, Hallie whispering words of comfort as she rocked the sobbing woman. Gradually, Serena calmed.

Her fury spent, Serena raised her head from Hallie's damp shoulder and wiped her face with her sleeve. "Dear God," she whispered in an anguished voice. "What have I done?"

Pulling herself from her companion's grasp, she moved to sit a few feet away, her arms wrapped around her belly and her legs crossed. She stared at the red-haired stranger curiously for a moment before murmuring, "I'm sorry. I don't think I know you, do I?" She shook her head in a bemused fashion. "Of course, I don't seem to know much these days."

Hallie was stunned. If this woman had been properly groomed, sipping tea in the parlor, her tone couldn't have been more cordial or her expression more normal. Hallie smiled and held out her hand. "I'm Dr. Hallie Gardiner."

"My pleasure." Serena took her hand and gave it a squeeze. "A lady doctor—imagine that! I didn't know there was such a thing." She looked at Hallie expectantly. "Is someone sick?"

Then her face clouded. "Oh," she sighed. "It must be Jake. He's been so terribly ill—the war and all, you understand. Is he dying, then?"

Hallie shook her head and gave the woman a calm smile. "Nothing so awful as that. I'm here for a happy reason. I'm here to help you deliver your baby."

Serena looked down at where the soft white gown billowed over her abdomen. "The baby. I had forgotten, I'm afraid," she whispered, tears beginning to cut an uneven course down her cheeks. "My poor little baby. How could I forget it?"

"That doesn't matter now." Hallie clasped the woman's cold hand between both of her warm ones. "Just think about the baby who wants to be born. Will you let me help you?"

Serena studied the woman in front of her for a moment. She looked clean, and her expression was kind. "I-I g-guess so."

"Good." Hallie hesitated, and then proceeded in a delicate tone, "If I'm going to help you, it'll be necessary for me to make an examination. Do you know what that means?"

Serena looked panicked by the idea.

"Won't you trust me?" Hallie pleaded, her tone gentle.

She watched indecision rage across Serena's face and when the woman finally nodded her consent, Hallie heaved a sigh of relief. "Good girl!" She gave her a quick hug. "Now I'm not going to lie and say that giving birth won't hurt. It will, perhaps a great deal. But I promise I'll do everything in my power to make it as easy for you as possible. Do you understand?"

Serena nodded again.

"Fine. Then let's get you into bed, where you'll be more comfortable." Hallie looped her arm around Serena's waist and helped her to her feet. "Everything's going to be all right now."

As they came to a stop by the bed, Serena turned abruptly and clutched at Hallie's waist. "You won't let him touch me, will you?"

"Who? Your husband?"

Serena shook her head. "Not just him. Any man!" The madness had crept back into her eyes and hysteria tinged her voice. "Promise me you won't let any man touch me! Promise!"

"Nobody will touch you but me," Hallie vowed, prying Serena's fingers from where they were biting into her uncorseted waist. With a reassuring smile, she helped the woman recline on the bed and then sat beside her.

Serena sighed once and closed her eyes, leaving a troubled Hallie to stare at her now calm face.

What has been done to this poor woman to make her so fearful? And by whom?

Despite herself, Hallie thought of Jake Parrish and her mind screamed its accusations: *Guilty of wife beating. Guilty of unspeakable perversion.*

Guilty!

Yet, though her mind condemned him on every count,

her heart pleaded eloquently in his defense and every beat proclaimed him innocent.

After two hours of blessed silence, the racket had resumed. Jake groaned and cast a weary glance toward the ceiling, wincing at the all-too-familiar sound of his wife's shrieks. Judging by the high-pitched timbre of her screams, he guessed that Dr. Gardiner had done something to displease her and was now being treated to one of her infamous tantrums.

Glancing up at the mantel clock, he mentally marked the time. If Dr. Gardiner was anything like her long line of predecessors, it would be only a matter of minutes before she abandoned her efforts to tend his wife and fled in horror.

Jake shrugged. Well, there was always Dr. Barnes. In one swift gulp he drained his glass of whiskey and turned his attention to shutting out the noise. After spending months in the army hospital confined to his bed, he'd developed a talent for mentally blocking out the never-ending screams and sobs of his fellow patients, a talent which he had put to good use during these last few weeks.

Now Jake immersed himself in the soothing inner silence of his mind, relaxing slightly as the heat from the whiskey sent a jolt of bracing warmth through his body. The chill of the damp evening fog was rising from the bay, making his leg ache unbearably.

Damn San Francisco and her contrary climate. Here it was, late May, and Jake wondered if he would ever feel warm again. Shivering, he glanced at the imposing marble fireplace. Though the flames were valiantly trying to chase away the chill, the room still felt cold.

Restlessly tapping his finger against the rim of his glass, he gazed around his library, wondering why it no longer seemed as inviting as it had before the war. Aside from Serena's clamoring, to which he'd grown accustomed, nothing appeared to have changed. Frowning, Jake took a mental inventory, searching for something—anything—that would account for his sudden feeling of disquiet.

In front of the hearth were his favorite, age-softened cordovan leather wing chairs. With their casual, time-worn comfort, they were like a pair of old friends, and Jake had spent many happy hours curled up in their familiar depths, often with Serena on his lap.

Lining the mahogany-shelved walls were his scores of books. Unlike many of the fashionable libraries of the wealthy, who bought their books by the yard for decorative purposes, Jake's library was filled with volumes that had all been thoughtfully selected. A number of them were even showing signs of wear from frequent use.

The imposing oval Hepplewhite desk at which he now sat and where he had made hundreds of decisions, as well as millions of dollars, was still positioned where he could pause to admire the manicured expanse of lawn through the beveled-glass doors. He could remember all the times he had been pulled from deep concentration by the sound of Serena's happy laughter floating on the wind as she entertained her friends from the Wednesday Afternoon Ladies' Mission Society.

Jake stared down at the face reflected in the highly polished surface beneath his hands. The features were familiar, though the expression was foreign. He bent nearer. Were those really his eyes, so haunted and filled with despair? And when had he begun to look so grim . . . so bitter?

With a groan, Jake buried his face in his hand. *The room hadn't changed; he had.*

"Thought you might need some company," announced a pleasant voice from the doorway. "Looks like I was right."

Jake didn't bother to look up at the sound of his best friend and business partner's voice. "What makes you say that, Seth?"

"Call me psychic. That gypsy down on Dupont Street told me I was possessed of great powers," he quipped, squiggling his fingers in the air in a comic imitation of a divining seer. When his friend failed to rise to the bait and continued to stare morosely into the fire, he sighed. "I ran into that incorrigible houseboy of yours down on Sacramento Street. He was hauling an enormous doctor's bag, so I put two and two together. I can't imagine why you keep the man. He's a regular menace."

"He keeps out the riffraff," Jake replied. Closing his

eyes and wearily tipping his head back against the chair, he amended, "Well, usually."

Seth Tyler's only reply was a deep chuckle. Unperturbed by his friend's surly mood, he closed the door and strode over to the sideboard, where he paused to study the contents of several cut-crystal decanters. After a moment of serious deliberation, he settled on the same fine, perfectly aged Kentucky whiskey that Jake had been abusing earlier. At home in his surroundings, Seth poured himself a liberal portion of the strong liquid. He took an experimental sip and then grinned, satisfied with his selection.

Throwing an appreciative look in Jake's direction, he proceeded to drape himself casually onto the butter-soft black leather sofa, propping his long legs comfortably over the arm.

The men sat in silence for several minutes, Jake unnerved by Serena's relentless wailing and Seth groping for something to say that would distract his friend from his troubles.

It was Seth who spoke first. "When I met Hop on the street, he was mumbling something about a lady doctor."

"I have engaged a lady doctor to deliver Serena's baby," Jake replied, not bothering to open his eyes. "Judging from the infernal racket upstairs, it would seem that she isn't having any better luck with Serena than her male predecessors did."

Serena Parrish was notorious among the members of San Francisco's medical profession. So violently had she resisted various doctors' efforts to examine her during her pregnancy that, with the exception of the pompous Dr. Barnes, all had refused to tend her a second time.

Jake snorted as a particularly earsplitting howl penetrated the thick library walls. "It sounds like my wife is in rare form this evening. I expect that lady doctor to come flying down the stairs and out the front door any minute now."

Finally opening his eyes, he glanced despairingly toward his friend, only to exclaim, "Good God, Seth! What the hell is that you're wearing?" His eyes widened incredulously at the intense hue of Seth's modish attire.

Seth picked an imaginary piece of lint from his Chinese blue kerseymere coat. "You like it? I'm told it's the latest thing from London."

"And you believed it?" exclaimed Jake with genuine disbelief. His friend had become somewhat of a peacock of late, but this was extreme even by Seth Tyler's rather excessive standards. At first his rebellion had been confined to his hair. His belligerent refusal to conform to the neat styles of the day had resulted in the thick, leonine mane that now fell below his wide shoulders. And bad had quickly gone to worse.

If it weren't for Seth's blatant masculinity and the hard, dangerous glint behind his hazel eyes, there probably would have been serious questions raised about his sexual preferences. Still, despite his affected mode of dress, Seth remained a favorite among the ladies. Though he lacked Jake's breathtaking good looks, he had a rugged appeal which had quickened many a heart. It was rare to see Seth without at least one beautiful woman clinging to his arm, and any social event would find him surrounded by a bevy of beauties, listening to his outrageous tales with big, worshipful eyes.

"Wouldn't hurt you to add a dash of color to your own dull wardrobe, you know," Seth offered amiably, pleased that his colorful attire had temporarily distracted Jake from the situation upstairs. Deciding that a bit of good-natured jesting was in order, he added, "You might be surprised to find how far a few bright garments could go in improving that foul disposition of yours."

"I hardly think that blue-and-red checkered trousers would do much to bolster my spirits," groaned Jake, contemplating the article in question with a jaundiced eye.

"Tsk, tsk, Jake. You may have become dull in your old age, but I've never known you to be close-minded." Seth critically examined Jake's understated yet fashionably cut garments for a moment. Then he teased slyly, "My tailor has a bolt of violet broadcloth that would be just perfect for you."

"Hmm. Violet broadcloth? Does he have a nice roll of Valenciennes lace for trim?"

"I thought alençon lace would be more appropriate, but if you insist on Valenciennes . . ." Seth grinned broadly at the thought of the supremely virile Jake Parrish parading around San Francisco decked out in violet broadcloth and lace frills. At the sound of Jake's rich baritone laugh joining him in his merriment, Seth realized with a sudden tinge of poignancy how much he missed the quick humor of the old Jake.

"Do my ears deceive me?" Seth lightly cuffed the side of his head in mock disbelief. "The somber Jake Parrish actually letting a laugh cross his dour lips?" He sat up and bent forward to peer into his friend's face with feigned concern. "Perhaps I should take it easier on you next time we spar. I gave you a couple of masterful blows to the head last week. It seems as if I might have cracked that thick skull of yours after all."

Jake smiled at Seth's friendly baiting. Both men knew that before the war, Jake had reigned supreme as the boxing champion at the Olympic Club and Seth had never had a prayer of tumbling him from his throne.

But that was before Jake had been wounded. Now it took almost all his effort just to remain on his feet, much less inflict any real damage. Still, Seth's good-natured heckling was contagious, and Jake laughed. "It would take more than your paltry efforts to crack this stubborn head. Speaking of heads, how did yours feel the next morning?"

"Enlightened."

"Enlightened? Such as the kind of enlightenment that comes from finally succeeding in luring the luscious Mary Ellen Palmer into your bed?" asked Jake with great interest.

"Enlightenment such as to why Reverend DeYoung is so persistent in his railings against the evils of alcohol. I felt like hell!" The memory was enough to make Seth regard his glass of whiskey with less enthusiasm.

Jake laughed at his friend's pained expression. "Too bad. I was almost looking forward to hearing the tasteless details of your amorous adventures with Mary Ellen."

"What's this about Mary Ellen?"

"Well, you did mention Miss Palmer during the course of the evening." A wicked gleam entered Jake's eyes as Seth's face paled. "Actually, you did more than mention her. It seems as if you were intent on banging at her door and dragging her off to your bed. Not, mind you, that she probably would have protested too loudly. I'd guess it would be just the opportunity she's been waiting for. Everyone knows that there is nothing she would like better than to have a reason to trap you in her marriage-hungry grasp."

Seth groaned. "Lord, I hope you talked some sense into me! The last thing I need is to have Mary Ellen sobbing over her lost virtue and demanding marriage."

"Rather like the scene she played for Frank Wilson last month?"

"Or the one she so dramatically portrayed for Michael Burris the month before that," added Seth with a whimsical smirk.

"Thankfully, you were too drunk to drag anyone off to bed—yourself included. The last I saw of you was when you were being led rather unsteadily up to bed by that long-suffering manservant of yours." Jake grinned at the memory of his friend being hauled up the stairs while singing snatches from a filthy ditty.

"Well, then, let's hear it for the intoxicating effects of fine brandy!" suggested Seth, raising his glass in a mock salute. "And to equally intoxicating women. Speaking of which, what's this about a woman doctor?"

Jake stared at Seth blankly for a second. True to form, Seth had distracted him from his troubles. His friend had a great talent for making him laugh, even in the worst situations. Jake would always be in debt to Seth for the way he had stayed by him in those agonizing days after he had been wounded. When the pain had been wrenching and Jake was sure he couldn't endure another second of the torment, Seth would invariably say or do something outrageous that would draw his mind away from his misery.

"Well? Is she a delectable piece?" A mischievous grin twisted Seth's lips. "Say, you might have her take a look at that leg of yours. Considering where the scar is located, it could turn into a pretty interesting experience. Now that I think about it, I've been having a few pains—"

"She's from the mission," Jake interjected with a significant lift of his brows.

The loopy grin disappeared from Seth's face, replaced by a look of horrified fascination. "Just what San Francisco needs, another pious, prune-faced old soul-saver to make all our lives hell on earth."

Jake laughed at Seth's distaste. "Not so bad as all that. She's one of Davinia Loomis's flock and didn't appear to be particularly righteous. She didn't thump her Bible or preach, if that's what you're worried about."

"But she's prune-faced. Am I right?"

Jake opened his mouth to deny Hallie's prune-faced status, but before he had the chance, Mammy Celine came charging into the library like a bull elephant on a rampage.

"We's got trouble, Mista' Jake. Big trouble," she blurted out, twisting her apron in agitation.

"What is it this time, Celine? Did Hop steal one of your voodoo charms again?" Jake asked with feigned seriousness. Celine generally reserved the term "big trouble" to apply to Hop Yung's frequent misdemeanors.

"Ain't nothin' like that. It's that Docta' Barnes. He be talkin' to that lady docta' real mean-like. And after she done so good! She done had the Missus actin' all tame. She be brushin' the Missus's hair, talkin' as if everythin' was normal and that Docta' Barnes come chargin' in and starts hollerin'. The Missus, she starts whimperin' and beggin' the lady not ta leave her. There be lots of arguin' up there! The lady be callin' Docta' Barnes a Charlotte Butcher. He be spittin' mad over that!" She chuckled, making it clear which of the opponents she favored.

"Charlotte Butcher?" Jake asked, a frown creasing his forehead. Then he laughed. "I believe you mean a 'charlatan' and a 'butcher.'" He could just imagine the puffed-up Dr. Barnes's reaction to a female doctor calling him that.

Celine put both her hands on her bony hips and stared at her employer severely. "That be what I jus' say. That Miz Penelope, she done tell the lady docta' to leave, that the real docta' come. That didn't sit none too good with the lady docta'. What you gonna be doin' about this, Mista Jake?"

Jake sighed. "I guess it's time for me to go upstairs and perform a gallant rescue."

"Now there's something I don't want to miss," Seth quipped. "Jake Parrish rescuing a Mission Lady."

"Who said anything about the Mission Lady? If my hunch is correct, it's Doctor Barnes who's going to need rescuing!"

Chapter 4

"You stay right there!" Hallie warned, brandishing Maggie O'Shea's hastily abandoned broom.

"This just goes to prove my point that females don't have the temperament for the medical profession, doesn't it?" barked Dr. Barnes, eyeballing his two strapping apprentices expectantly. Like automated French puppets, the young whelps bobbed their heads in practiced unions, eliciting a smug smile of approval from their mentor.

"I can just imagine what *that* point would be, seeing what an open-minded, progressive individual you are," Hallie snapped, still smarting from the man's attacks on what he saw as the mental and emotional inferiority of the female sex. What irked her most was that he honestly believed that women were to be viewed like half-witted children and to be treated accordingly. It chilled her to the core to imagine the kind of medical treatment a woman would receive at his hand.

Turning to pry her arm free from the numbing effects of Serena's constant clench, Hallie tried to reassure her patient. "It's all right, dear. There's no need for you to be frightened."

Serena was clearly terrified by the appearance of the men, and all of Hallie's efforts to calm her were meeting with dismal failure. Every time she managed to free herself from Serena's convulsive grip, the woman simply reattached herself to whichever limb happened to be within her reach.

"Make them go away!" Serena shrieked, peering around Hallie's shoulder at the burly, red-faced man and his companions. Dr. Barnes glared at the pregnant woman impatiently, the menacing promise in his eyes making her shrink against Hallie with a frightened little whimper.

"You promised you wouldn't let anyone else touch me," she wailed childishly. "You promised!"

Hallie patted the woman's pale cheek. "Hush, now, Serena. No one's going to hurt you." Why wouldn't these idiot men just go away and let her do her job?

Without warning, Serena let out a long, strangled scream. Dropping her hands from Hallie's arm, she fell to her knees, clutching at her belly with a sobbing chant. "Hurts! Hurts! Hurts!"

"Damn it, woman! Can't you see that Mrs. Parrish is about to deliver a child?" Dr. Barnes snapped his fingers at one of his apprentices, who sprang into action and began stalking toward the women.

"Smart of you to have noticed," Hallie ground out. "What was that, the second pain in the last five minutes?" With that, she swung the broom, bringing it down on the head of the apprentice who had edged too close to Serena.

He howled as the broom made whumping contact with his skull, cowering like a mangy cur beneath Hallie's threatening scowl.

"Mr. Parrish engaged me to deliver his wife's baby," Hallie said, "and I intend to do just that."

"I have been attending the Parrish family for many years, and let me tell you this: I don't intend to stand by while some excitable female with pretensions of being a doctor murders one of my best patients! Do I make myself clear?"

"Yes. It's clear that you're a narrow-minded fool. As for pretending—just where *did* you receive your medical education, Dr. Barnes? I'd be interested to hear." Tossing the man a challenging glare, Hallie stooped down to stroke Serena's trembling back.

"That wouldn't be as interesting as hearing about the training that makes you consider yourself qualified to call yourself a doctor. That is, if you have any training at all."

Hallie met Dr. Barnes's impervious gaze with a shrug and then proceeded to tick off an impressive list of European hospitals where she had received training in addition to her degree from the Woman's Medical College of Pennsylvania.

When she finished, the man stared at her in red-faced silence. With his double chins quivering beneath his luxuriant graying whiskers and his mouth working like that of a grounded carp, he was the very picture of outraged dignity.

Regaining his composure with admirable speed, the doctor cleared his throat several times before replying with galling condescension, "That all sounds very well and good, but everyone knows that females are incapable of retaining knowledge for any reasonable length of time. I'm afraid, my dear, that your poor parents threw their money away. Better they had spent it on a dowry instead." With a nasty smile, he added, "Even the most undesirable of females is rendered desirable in the presence of a large marriage portion."

"Yes. But only to undesirable males," Hallie replied flippantly as she tried to pull Serena toward the bed. As if she didn't have enough problems already, the woman had decided that she was having none of Hallie's coaxing and refused to budge from her crouched position on the floor.

With a sigh, Hallie decided to try to reason with her. "Now Serena—"

"Hurts!" wailed Serena as another contraction rocked her body.

Hallie made some quick calculations. Gauging from her last examination of her patient, the birth was critically near. Damn it! She had to find some way to get rid of these men. Only then would she have any hope of delivering the child successfully.

"Dear God!" exclaimed Dr. Barnes when yet another cry was wrenched from Serena. "I've wasted enough valuable time trying to reason with this irrational female. Claude! Benedict! I want Mrs. Parrish bound to that bed! Now!" he ordered, and the three of them advanced on the women.

Hallie leaped into action. Wildly she swung the broom, first catching Claude in the back of the head with a blow that brought him to his knees, and then backhanding Dr. Barnes in his considerable belly, making him double up with pain. Defensively, she spun around to face the apprentice, Benedict, but it was too late.

With an agility Hallie hadn't counted on, he easily caught hold of the flailing broom and wrenched it out of her hands. Tossing the weapon aside, he pulled her into an immobilizing grip that made her fight for breath.

"Stop that! Can't you see she's terrified?" demanded Hallie as Dr. Barnes and Claude dragged the screaming Serena to the bed. They wrestled with her roughly, trying to still her arms long enough to bind them.

"You promised!" cried Serena, frantically struggling against the restraining strength of the two men. "You promised you wouldn't let them touch me! You promised! You promised!" The desperation of the words tore at Hallie's heart, spurring her to renew her battle with a vengeance. Twisting and pulling until she gained enough distance from her captor to move her legs, she called forth all of her waning strength to give him one sharp kick. As the pointed toe of her boot made bruising contact with his shin, Benedict let out a yowl loud enough to drown out Serena's hysterical shrieks. Instantly, his arms dropped from Hallie's waist and he slithered to the floor, clutching at his leg.

Satisfied that her captor was preoccupied with nursing his abused limb, Hallie lunged into the fray at the bed.

"Looks like a scene from bedlam, doesn't it?" Seth observed, viewing the altercation from the doorway. "Oh, good left on that lady!" he added with admiration as Hallie landed a punch squarely against Claude's chin and effectively eliminated him from the tussle.

As Jake joined his friend on the threshold and stared aghast at the chaos in the room, Seth quipped, "We should probably stop the little hellion before she annihilates San Francisco's finest medical practitioners."

"As if that would be a great loss," Jake muttered, his face tightening with thunderous fury as one of the lumbering apprentices clasped Hallie in an immobilizing hug and wrestled her to the hard floor.

Hallie bellowed with unladylike rage as she was slammed to the floor, face down. Feeling as if she was suffocating beneath the crushing weight of Benedict's body, she struggled frantically to free herself. As she clawed impotently at the wooden floor, kicking her feet in hopes of inflicting damage on a stray body part, her heavy burden was miraculously lifted. Catching a deep, panting breath, she rolled onto her back and braced herself for the counterattack she knew was coming.

Nothing prepared her for the sight of Jake Parrish standing over her prone figure holding the intimidated Benedict by the scruff of his neck like an errant puppy. Nor did she quite know how to respond to the man dressed in a colorful suit of clothes who murmured, "Fine left hook, sweetheart," and then hauled her up against his hard form.

Hallie could only gape with bewilderment as the stranger seized her left hand, lifted it to his lips and kissed her open palm, sighing, "Such a delicate hand to pack such a wicked wallop. I stand in awe of such a lovely and worthy contender."

Jake snorted derisively. "Seth, let go of Dr. Gardiner and stop your nonsense." Without sparing the hapless Benedict so much as a glance, Jake flung him aside as if he were so much rubbish. The youth scrambled to his feet and scampered off to cower behind the indignant Dr. Barnes.

After kissing Hallie's palm one last time, Seth reluctantly released her. As he turned to move toward Jake, he tossed her an impudent wink that brought a half-hearted smile to her lips.

Jake waited until his friend had finished his tomfoolery before turning the full heat of his glare on the brawlers. "What the hell is the meaning of this chaos?" he demanded.

The combatants stood silently accusing one another with their mutinous gazes, no one wanting to be the first to speak up. Then all hell broke loose. Bickering loudly among themselves, arms flinging in broad gestures, each of the guilty parties rushed to lay blame on someone else.

At the sudden onslaught of noise, Serena whimpered and huddled against the mattress, her imploring eyes darting to Hallie. Then she let out a strangled cry and doubled over into a shaking heap of misery.

Spurred by old habit, Jake started toward his wife. He got no further than a few steps before he was stopped short by Serena's expression of repulsed horror. Her silent rebuff only served to add kindling to his already flaring temper. Pinning Dr. Barnes with his glare, Jake barked, "Well?"

"I was just trying to save your wife from the hands of this hysterical female," intoned Dr. Barnes pompously.

"And I was trying to save her from this butcherous charlatan," countered Hallie.

Jake ignored Dr. Barnes's gasp of outrage. Riveting his gaze on Hallie's face, he taunted, "Butcherous charlatan? One of the members of the exalted medical profession? Surely you jest."

Hallie sputtered at that. Must this man always twist everything she said? Straightening her spine to stand tall, Hallie returned Jake Parrish's stare. Ignoring his barb, she asked, "Do you know what this man wants to do to your wife?"

"This should be educational," Seth murmured, leaning against the wall and nonchalantly examining the glossy ends of his hair.

"He was talking about tying Mrs. Parrish down and risking serious damage to her body by pulling the baby out with forceps."

Dr. Barnes harrumphed several times before stating, "Which is a perfectly acceptable course of action—considering the circumstances. As we both know," he paused to give Jake a look of ingratiating conspiracy, "Mrs. Parrish is incapable of taking instructions, and therefore extreme measures must be considered."

"Oh, yes! Why don't we tell Mr. Parrish about your extreme measures, Dr. Barnes? Like how you intend to crush the infant's skull should the head be too large for the forceps to grip?"

"Good God!" Seth dropped the lock of hair he had been studying and stared at Dr. Barnes, appalled.

Jake's eyes narrowed as his gaze moved from Hallie's outraged face to Dr. Barnes's smugly self-righteous one. He considered the man for a second before drawling, "Really?"

"Only in the most extreme situation, mind you. Most probably the forceps will be adequate." The doctor threw Hallie a condescending look.

"And you think it necessary to tie my wife?"

Serena cried out at that suggestion, and Hallie went

to sit on the edge of the bed. With desperation, the woman pushed herself at Hallie, clinging to her tearfully.

Jake watched as Hallie pulled Serena into her arms, rocking her gently and whispering into her ear. Gradually his wife calmed beneath Hallie's soothing ministrations. It was clear that Serena trusted this odd mission doctor.

Strangely enough, so did he.

Jerking his gaze away from the revealing scene, Jake demanded, "Well, Dr. Barnes? I repeat: do you really think it necessary to tie my wife?"

"Of course. How else could you expect me to keep her still and in the proper position?" The man's confidence was unflappable.

"Interesting. And what do you have to say, Dr. Gardiner?"

Hallie slowly raised her face from where it rested against Serena's hair. Meeting Jake's glittering gaze with a steady stare of her own, she replied, "I don't see why this baby can't be delivered just like any other. As for binding Serena, well, up until this man disturbed us, your wife was following my instructions perfectly. I expect she will again once you remove this charlatan and his butchers-in-training from her sight."

Jake rubbed his jaw thoughtfully.

"Jake." Seth walked over to his friend and clasped his shoulder gently. Only he knew how difficult this decision was for Jake; only he understood the pain—and the guilt. "It's up to you to decide what's best for your wife."

Jake glanced from his friend's concerned face to Dr. Barnes, standing stiffly beside his apprentices. Then his gaze moved to the tableau at the bed. Hallie had tied a twisted sheet to the footboard and was encouraging Serena to pull on it as another contraction jerked her body. Miraculously, his wife was cooperating.

With a shrug, Jake replied, "It appears my wife has made the decision for herself."

Chapter 5

Jake looked up from the papers in front of him as a soft rapping at the library door disturbed the stillness of the room. He gave the porcelain mantel clock a quick glance.

Half past one.

Almost an hour since the first thin wails had proclaimed the birth of the child. The better part of an hour which he had spent reading the same paragraph over and over again, tensely waiting for the knock at his door, dreading the moment when it would come.

Almost an hour; it had seemed like an eternity.

He closed his eyes tightly for a moment, searching for a crevice of calm in the seething mass of his tension. But Jake Parrish could find no peace tonight, for the restless phantoms of a thousand regrets lurked in the shadows of his thoughts, haunting him with the infinite litany of his failures.

Drawing a deep, shuddering breath, he pressed his palms against his throbbing temples and braced himself for the second assault of knocks that he knew would come.

And they came almost immediately, this time with a persistence that was impossible to ignore.

As Jake lowered his hands to the desk in front of him, he noticed distractedly that they were trembling. Clenching them into tight fists to disguise their betraying motion, he barked, "Yes?"

The only response to his query was the sound of the door gliding open and then closing with a soft click.

Pretending to be engrossed in his reading, Jake ignored the unwanted visitor. He could hear the slight rustling of her skirts as she moved to the center of the library. When the sound of her heels tapping sharply against the floor was suddenly muffled as she stepped onto the carpet, Jake knew she was very near. It wasn't until she paused in front of his desk and waited several moments for some sort of acknowledgment that he lifted his head to throw her an annoyed glance.

"Well?" he snapped. Completely disregarding the tiny bundle in the doctor's arms, he returned his gaze to his paperwork.

Hallie felt a flood of disappointment sweep over her at Jake Parrish's indifferent greeting to his newborn child. She always enjoyed the time she shared with a first-time parent, watching as the anxiety of the new father's face was transformed into an expression of fierce, possessive pride. Such scenes had provided some of the finest moments of her professional life.

Nothing brought her more satisfaction than watching a man stare at his offspring with emotional fascination, often declaring that the baby had his eyes or nose as he gingerly counted the miniature fingers and toes. There had even been an occasion or two when Hallie had watched with amusement while an overjoyed father had pulled down his baby's diaper to happily confirm the gender of a long-desired son or daughter.

Hallie sighed inwardly. Well, in all fairness, this could hardly be considered a normal set of circumstances, and Jake Parrish did seem to be one of those men who kept his displays of emotion on a tight rein. Besides, it was late and they were all tired. Hallie hadn't missed the shadows beneath the man's eyes or the way his shoulders were slumped with weariness.

Determined to make the best of the difficult situation, Hallie pasted a smile on her face. "I thought you might be interested in meeting your daughter, Mr. Parrish," she said in what she hoped was a cheerful voice.

"Fine," he replied shortly, giving her an abrupt jerk of his head that Hallie assumed was meant to be a nod.

He didn't look up again until she had moved around the desk and was standing directly beside him. Tossing down the papers he was examining, Jake leaned back in his chair with a heavy sigh. Using one finger, as if trying to avoid touching something repugnant, he pushed the blanket away from the delicate face and gave the baby a cursory glance.

There was no welcoming smile or softening of his rigid features as Jake Parrish viewed his daughter for the first time—only an expression of cool disinterest.

Without comment, he dropped his hand and turned back to his work with an air of dismissal.

Hallie felt a chill as her past whispered of another infant who had been callously disregarded by her father. She would never forget the terrible hurt she had experienced later at overhearing the servants gossiping about her father's unfeeling reaction to her own birth.

Poor, poor child! they had clucked. Why, Ambrose Gardiner didn't care enough about his newborn daughter to see her until almost two weeks after her birth! And if he hadn't been obligated to acknowledge her at her christening, it probably would have been even longer.

Of course, as a man ever conscious of the strictures of society, he had been the picture of the proud papa during the ceremony at the church. He even held his daughter at the party that followed and drank numerous toasts to her health.

But as soon as the last guests had taken their leave, Ambrose shoved Hallie at her nurse with an air of disgust, warning the poor woman that she would be dismissed if she didn't keep that "red-faced, squalling brat" out of his sight—and hearing. Worse yet, he never once bothered to inquire after his wife, who lay near death with childbed fever.

In later years, he had cruelly lamented to Hallie the injustice of fate that his wife, Georgianna, hadn't died in childbirth and taken Hallie with her.

Watching Jake now, as he sat calmly writing on a document, his face as cold and exquisite as that of a mythical god carved in marble, Hallie felt the scar on her soul torn asunder with a violence that released an eruption of long-dormant pain.

And with the pain came anger.

"Aren't you even the least bit interested in how your wife is doing?" snapped Hallie, wanting nothing more than to snatch the pen from his hand and force him to see her fury.

The pen stopped in midstroke.

Lifting his face to level Hallie with a bland stare, he inquired, "And how is my wife?"

As if you care, you unfeeling bastard! fumed Hallie silently.

Ignoring the urge to call him several unflattering names but unable to keep the reproach from her voice, she replied, "It was a difficult birth. Of course, I expected that, considering your wife's deteriorated physical condition. To be honest, it's a miracle your wife and child survived the delivery. Mrs. Parrish became so weakened toward the end of her labor that she could barely find the strength to push the baby into this world."

Hallie lifted her gaze from the baby's face to meet Jake Parrish's emotionless eyes. "Mr. Parrish, your daughter wasn't breathing when she was born, and it's only by the grace of God that she's alive at all."

Jake glanced sharply at the infant resting in the crook of Hallie's arm. As the impact of her words pierced his wall of calm, he was struck by sudden fear. Struggling to keep his voice steady, he asked, "But she's all right now?"

"I'm not going to lie to you. Your child is much too small. Babies in this condition *have* been known to survive and thrive, but only in rare instances. We can only pray that this poor little mite will be one of the lucky ones."

"You'll do everything possible, of course." His words weren't a request but a command.

Hallie nodded. "Of course. I've left instructions with Celine, and with your permission, I'll send a woman from the mission to act as a wet nurse."

"Fine. Do whatever you think is best." With that, he picked up his pen again as if to resume his writing.

But Hallie chose to ignore his signal that their interview was concluded. "I'll come by every day to check on the baby's progress myself. And Mrs. Parrish's, too. Your wife lost more blood than is normal, but, thankfully, there is no sign of hemorrhage. Aside from being exhausted—and barring the possibility of fever—she should be back to normal in no time."

A grim smile twisted Jake's lips. "Back to normal? Isn't that being just a bit optimistic, Dr. Gardiner?"

"You know what I mean," she retorted, shifting the now squirming baby to her other arm.

"Really? I thought it was just another one of your misguided attempts to convince me of the miraculous powers of the almighty medical profession."

Hallie gasped with outrage as her thoughts solidified into words that exploded from her lips before she could stop them.

"Do you know what a heartless bastard you are?"

There was a sizzle in the air as icy green eyes collided with burning amber ones.

"Yes!" he lashed back, his voice snapping like a whip.

Hallie tore her gaze away from his face, infuriated by the look of smugness there that told her just how unworthy an opponent he found her in this duel of wits. Lord! How she would love to think of a retort that would wipe that superior expression off his face!

"Why so angry, Mission Lady? We actually agree on something for a change." His smirk widened as a crimson flush crept up from her chest to infuse her face with color.

The infant picked that moment to let forth a howl of protest.

"My, my. She already sounds just like her mother," Jake observed wryly.

Rocking the now squalling babe in an attempt to calm her, Hallie sputtered, "O-o-o! Now look what you've done!"

"What I've done? I'm not the one tossing that baby around like a sack of rotten potatoes."

Hallie looked down at the red-faced infant, who was, indeed, being subjected to some fairly wild gyrations in her arms.

Damn that Jake Parrish!

Raising the baby to rest against the softness of her breast and patting the small back soothingly, Hallie met Jake's eyes with a glow of intense dislike.

"Are you this rude to everyone, Mr. Parrish?"

Jake's eyes swept her with insulting thoroughness before he drawled, "No. Just to you."

Watching with interest as her face turned from an unattractive red to a mottled purple, he added pointedly, "Most women find me charming. But then, we've already established the fact that you're not a woman, right, *Doctor*?"

"I can't imagine any woman in her right mind finding you the least bit appealing," Hallie shot back with a disdainful sniff.

"Right mind? Interesting choice of words," he pointed out coldly, tapping his fingers against the top of his desk.

"There you go again, deliberately twisting my words around," she ground out, carefully securing the blanket around the whimpering form. "Lord! You've got to be the most maddening man I've ever had the misfortune to meet."

"Probably. Serena is living proof of that, isn't she?"

Not bothering to justify his last remark with an answer, Hallie spun on her heel and stalked toward the door, but not before throwing Jake Parrish a look that told him exactly what she thought of his hard-hearted cynicism.

"What's this, Dr. Gardiner? Not going to stay and try to pick my pocket for services rendered?"

"No," Hallie tossed over her shoulder. "But I will send you a bill and believe me, Mr. Parrish, when you see the size of it, you're going to wish I had merely picked your pockets. What I have in mind right now is more akin to highway robbery!"

And with that parting comment, she slammed the door behind her with resounding emphasis, effectively cutting off the echoes of his mocking laughter.

"Hell and damnation! HELL AND DAMNATION!" gasped Davinia Loomis, the directress of the Mission for Chinese Women, when Hallie had finished recounting her experiences at the Parrish house. "I didn't even know Serena was expecting a child! Of course, that Penelope Parrish is as diligent as a rabid watchdog when it comes to guarding her family's privacy. I imagine she would have introduced you to the street dust quick enough if Jake hadn't intervened when he did. What I can't understand is what could have gotten into that boy to make him behave like such an ill-bred clod."

Hallie shrugged and continued to remove an assortment of boxes and bottles from the makeshift medicine cabinet that stood in the corner of the so-called "surgery." Taking inventory of the Mission Infirmary's assets had proved to be a discouraging, as well as filthy, chore which had encompassed the better part of the morning. Hallie had experienced an awful sinking sensation when she had first seen the contents of the bandage chest, a feeling that plunged deeper with every drawer and cupboard she explored.

Wherever were they going to get the supplies needed to make the infirmary a workable proposition? She pushed an unruly tendril of hair out of her face with dusty fingers, leaving a smudged trail of dirt across her cheek.

The Mission House directress watched as Hallie opened a bottle and sniffed at the contents. Folding her arms across her ample bosom, her handsome, if time-worn, face set in lines of righteous affront, Davinia muttered, "Just you wait until the next time I cross paths with that Parrish rascal. See if I don't give him a lesson or two on the virtues of gratitude. Might even shame him enough to see him in church next Sunday."

Hallie laughed. "Well, if anyone could work such a miracle, it would be you."

"The miracles, I'll be leaving to the Lord," replied Davinia sanctimoniously. "Jake Parrish, however, is an entirely different matter. I've known that boy for over twelve years and don't intend to stand by while he turns into an unprincipled heathen."

Hallie put the bottle she'd been examining into the "save" box and peered suspiciously at the contents of a particularly grubby jar. Holding it up to the dim light filtering through the sooty windows, she grimaced with disgust.

"Good Lord! Didn't your last doctor know that leeches are useless? Especially," Hallie pointed out, tossing the container into the crate at her feet, "dead ones."

"Durned man had buffalo chips for brains and wouldn't have known a dead leech from a live one. Same as with his patients. The nincompoop assured Mrs. Merriman that her husband would make a full recovery from his fit of apoplexy, completely oblivious to the fact that the man was as stiff as a poker and dead as a June bug in July. That bit of business cost us a pretty penny in lost donations, let me tell you!"

"Wherever did you find such a stellar example of the medical profession?" asked Hallie, her voice becoming muffled as she leaned forward and thrust her head deeper into the confines of the cupboard.

"Why, he was one of Dr. Barnes's protégés."

"I should have guessed," came Hallie's barely audible reply.

Davinia watched Hallie for several seconds, her intelligent brown eyes glowing with frank curiosity behind the lenses of her spectacles. "Most women find him charming."

"Ow!" yelped Hallie as her head made bruising contact with the top shelf of the cabinet. She emerged red-faced, with cobwebs clinging to her hair, and gingerly prodded the back of her head.

"Dr. Barnes? Charming? Ha! Not likely."

"Of course not Dr. Barnes. I was referring to Jake Parrish."

"Oh, *him*. Well, he was conceited enough to mention something along those lines," mumbled Hallie, still rubbing her head as she turned to survey the dismally inadequate sum of the infirmary's medical supplies. Things were even worse than she had imagined. "Personally, I found him about as charming as an epidemic of smallpox."

Davinia gave a raucous hoot of laughter. "If that were true, then every woman in San Francisco between the ages of six and sixty would be rushing to contract the disease."

"I guess *some* women are silly enough to have their heads turned by that handsome face of his," Hallie scoffed.

"So you did notice that much, huh? Did you by any chance get a look at that delicious backside of his? Always did have an eye for—"

"Davinia! Surely you know that it's improper to discuss a man's anatomy. Especially that below the waist," exclaimed Hallie, blushing furiously.

"Hell and damnation, Hallie! Stop carrying on like an old maid! You're a doctor. I would think you would be familiar with all of a man's parts—the ones below the belt included. Besides, where's the sin in admiring one of the Lord's more interesting creations? Take my John,

God rest his soul, for example. That man had one of the finest bottoms this side of heaven."

"Davinia, please!" Hallie groaned. "I don't care to discuss Jake Parrish or his assorted parts, thank you."

Davinia threw up her hands in exasperation. "Oh, all right. If you're going to be such a priss about it, we'll change the subject. Too bad, though. The conversation was just getting interesting. I think it's only fair to warn you that I always speak my piece and I don't mince words. Never could abide folks who shilly-shally around and won't say what's on their mind."

She peered at Hallie suspiciously. "You're not a shilly-shallyer, are you?"

"Of course not!"

Davinia looked dubious, but sighed, "In that case, we should get on well enough."

The two women worked in companionable silence for the next half hour, vigorously scrubbing down the grimy countertops and chasing the dust balls from the corners.

"Davinia?"

Davinia poked her head up from beneath the rickety old table that served as an examination couch, her glasses dangling precariously near the end of her nose.

"What happened to Serena?"

The question hung heavily in the air for several seconds while Davinia removed her spectacles and slowly cleaned the lenses with a corner of her apron. Balancing them back on the bridge of her nose, she finally replied, "I'm surprised you didn't ask that question sooner."

Hallie shrugged. "I was hoping I wouldn't have to."

Crossing her legs comfortably beneath her skirts and settling back against the table's leg, Davinia mused, "I guess you have a right to know, seein' as how you're Serena Parrish's doctor now."

Hallie opened her mouth to protest the dubious honor, but Davinia cut her off with a wave of her hand.

"No. I know what you're going to say. What you haven't yet realized is that Serena has chosen you and what Serena wants, Jake makes sure she gets."

"Mr. Parrish didn't strike me as a particularly accommodating husband. At least not one who would go out of his way to satisfy his wife's whims," Hallie remarked incredulously.

Davinia fixed Hallie with a knowing look. "That's because you don't know him. When those two were first married, Jake vowed to anyone who would listen that he would never deny Serena anything her heart desired."

She paused to chuckle. "Never saw a man so besotted in my life. Of course, everyone else loved Serena too. Not only was she eye-poppin' pretty, she had that rare knack of charming everyone she met. Jake used to brag that only the best of everything was good enough for his wife and he set about to provide it."

Staring up at Hallie dreamily, she sighed, "You should have seen the two of them together. They were so beautiful, it almost hurt to look at them. Everything was storybook perfect."

"So, what happened?" asked Hallie, sinking to the floor to sit next to Davinia.

"Jake said no to her."

Hallie stared at her companion in disbelief. "I can't imagine how saying no to a woman could drive her mad!"

Davinia gave her head a quick shake. "Oh, Serena's not exactly mad. The correct word would be . . . damaged."

At Hallie's questioning look, Davinia whispered, "Opium. I've heard rumors that she had degenerated even further and that her downfall involved morphine. Of course, one can't believe everything she hears these days, and the Parrish clan are a notoriously close-mouthed bunch."

Hallie frowned. "But how does Jake's telling her no have anything to do with all that?"

"He told her no when she demanded that he fight for the Confederacy. You see, Hallie, Serena is from an old, powerful Virginia family. After her family's home was razed by the Union army, her parents found themselves destitute. Somehow they made their way to San Francisco and threw themselves on Jake's mercy."

"And Jake told them no?" Hallie leaned forward, caught in the seductive web of Davinia's story.

"Of course not! He was most generous with them. Unfortunately, they were bitter people and filled Serena's head full of all sorts of vile nonsense. They so despised Jake for his support of the Northern cause that they turned their daughter against him. Serena used to complain to the Wednesday Afternoon Ladies' Mission Society that her husband loved the Union more than his own wife. Things finally got so bad that Jake was forced to order her parents to leave the Parrish house."

Davinia paused for a moment, scratching her chin and staring into space reflectively. "How she hated him for that! And when he actually joined the Union army—well, you can imagine the hell that broke loose. It would have been so easy for him to sit out the war, being so far from the fighting and all. But our Jake is a man of strong convictions, and he refused to turn his back while his country was being torn apart. Serena could never forgive him for that. Her problems started shortly thereafter."

Hallie felt a tidal wave of sadness surge over her. Jake and Serena's life together, which had started out as magically as a fairy tale, should have had a happy ending. Yet it hadn't, and the story only served to strengthen Hallie's belief that "happily ever after" was a myth. She was about to comment on the tragedy of it all when a firm knock at the door brought both women scrambling to their feet.

"What!" shouted Davinia rudely, fighting to readjust her skirts over her wide crinolines. As she gave the recalcitrant garments a final tug, she muttered beneath her breath, "Never could abide people who skulk around outside doors."

The door flew open with a wide swing and Jake Parrish stepped in, grinning when he saw the women's disheveled appearances. "Ah, if it isn't Davinia Loomis. And as polite as ever, I see. The housekeeper at the Mission House said I would find you ladies here."

"Well, speak of the devil! If it isn't Mr. Jake Parrish himself," exclaimed Davinia testily.

"The devil, am I?" laughed Jake, arching an eyebrow in inquiry.

"I can't imagine who else could have gotten into you, considering how shabbily you treated poor Dr. Gardiner." Davinia placed her hands on her hips and glared at Jake as if he were an errant child of six instead of a man of thirty-three. "I hope you've come to apologize to her."

Jake fixed his gaze on Hallie, who had picked up a scrub brush and was busily scouring the tabletop. He smiled as he noted the smudge of black grime adorning the end of her nose, making her look a bit like an overgrown chimney sweep. Covered from neck to ankle in a voluminous apron that bore the unmistakable signs of a morning spent doing heavy labor, Hallie was the very picture of a ragamuffin. For some unfathomable reason, Jake found himself charmed by her appearance.

"Well, Jake, we're waiting," Davinia prodded, tapping her foot impatiently.

Jake shrugged. "Fine. I apologize."

He didn't miss the way Hallie's hand tightened on the brush or the way she ground the stiff bristles viciously against the table's wooden surface. Undoubtedly she was wishing it was his hide she was stripping, instead of the greasy film of dirt.

Davinia scowled up at him sternly. "You could have at least tried to sound sincere. Now try again, or I'll personally subject you to a lecture on the evils of pride and arrogance."

Jake groaned theatrically, making Davinia chortle in spite of herself. Sounding much like a chastised schoolboy, he murmured, "Dr. Gardiner, please accept my sincerest apologies for my unforgivable behavior last night. I behaved, as you were quick to point out, like a heartless bastard."

Hallie dropped the brush with a strangled gasp. Leave it to that unprincipled man to throw her hasty words back in her face.

"A heartless bastard, eh?" chuckled Davinia, fixing Hallie with a speculative look. "You might just work out after all, Dr. Gardiner. Got a temper, do you?"

"Got red hair, doesn't she?" quipped Jake, with maddening sarcasm.

Hallie picked up her brush once more. Oh, how she would love to throw it at His Royal Smugness and watch as it left a stain on his immaculate suit. Lord! What was it with that man anyway? Didn't his clothes ever get even the least bit wrinkled, and did he have to look so damned handsome all the time?

Feigning a put-upon air, Hallie resumed her scrubbing and asked, with a calmness she didn't feel, "Was there a reason for your visit, Mr. Parrish? I assume you didn't come all this way just to bait me."

"True. As much as I've enjoyed this little tête-à-tête," he flashed her a wide smile, "my real reason for coming was to discuss a business proposition with you."

Hallie tore her gaze away from the sight of the beguiling dimple creasing his left cheek. "I can't imagine any business we could have."

"Can't you?" His gaze locked into her golden eyes, commanding her full attention. "There's the matter of my wife and child."

"Oh, Lord! Nothing's happened, has it?" choked Hallie, as all sorts of dreadful possibilities raced through her mind.

"Of course not. Don't you think I would have mentioned something like that immediately?"

"Yes . . . of course." Hallie let her breath out in a sigh of relief. "So, what exactly do you want?"

"Not what I want. What's my wife wants," corrected Jake. "And what she wants is—you."

"Hell and damnation, Jake! Will you stop talking in riddles and get to the point?" Davinia exclaimed, looking from Jake to Hallie and back again. "Never could abide people who don't say what they mean."

Jake grinned down at Davinia's glowering face. "It's all quite simple, dear lady. Serena has refused to let anyone save Dr. Gardiner tend her. Amazingly enough, she's even asking for the good doctor by name. So I want to engage the doctor to care for my wife until she is fully recovered from giving birth."

"I already said I would look in on her," pointed out Hallie, tossing the brush into a bucket with a loud splash and wiping her sodden hands on her apron.

Jake shook his head. "Not good enough. What I propose is that you take up residence at Parrish House until Serena is completely recovered. Celine says that she appears to be running a fever and that she's been bleeding quite a bit. Of course, my wife refuses to let anyone touch her and keeps calling for you."

Before Hallie could reply, Davinia cut in, "And how much do you intend to pay for Dr. Gardiner's services?"

"I'm sure you'll tell me," answered Jake with a short laugh.

"You're right about that. Let me see." Davinia frowned slightly as she thought. Suddenly her eyes brightened with inspiration. "We want this infirmary completely outfitted with new equipment and medicines."

Hallie choked out, "Davinia—"

"Done," Jake agreed, ignoring Hallie's grunt of protest. "My carriage is waiting outside. Dr. Gardiner can send for her things later."

"Not so fast, young man!" snapped Davinia. "I'm not finished yet. All the equipment will be the best to be had, and we want plenty of everything."

"Is that all?" There was a definite gleam of amusement in Jake's eyes as he watched Hallie's mouth drop open.

She gasped, "I will not be bartered—"

But Davinia cut her off. "AND, a monthly stipend for the support of the infirmary. A generous stipend, mind you."

"You seem to have a rather high opinion of Dr. Gardiner's worth, Davinia," Jake said, chuckling. "Why should I pay so much?"

"Supply and demand, dear boy. *Supply and demand.* You taught me all about that principle yourself."

"Wait a minute!" protested Hallie. "I have no intention of taking up residence at Mr. Parrish's home. How dare you both even suggest such a thing! I'll be happy to visit on a daily basis, but living in is out of the question!"

Jake seemed about to speak, but Davinia silenced him with a commanding wave of her hand. He nodded and smiled, leaning on his cane in a relaxed stance.

Hallie was uncomfortably reminded of a cat watching a mouse it intended to eat, and she happened to feel like the poor, doomed rodent.

"Now, Hallie. What do you mean 'won't go'? Of course you'll go. How can you even think of turning down such a generous offer?"

"Davinia—"

"Think, Hallie! Without proper medicine, equipment, and funds, the infirmary is doomed to failure. You know that as well as I. And without the infirmary, where will all the poor Chinese women go for medical help? The white hospitals won't touch them, and that's a fact. It seems to me that as a doctor, you have an obligation toward the welfare of those women." Davinia crossed her arms, her foot tapping, as she waited for Hallie's reply.

"Surely there has to be another way?" Hallie looked from Davinia to Jake in wild appeal.

Jake shook his head slowly. "There is no other way. My wife needs constant attention, and there is no one else she will accept. Let's not forget the baby either. She needs you most of all. How can you turn your back on her?"

Hallie sputtered with outrage, "Why, that's—"

"Blackmail?" Jake supplied helpfully, seeing his victory clearly written in the lines of resignation on her face. "You're right, Dr. Gardiner. It's blackmail—pure and simple."

Chapter 6

Oysters?

Scrambled with bacon and eggs?

For breakfast?

Hallie groaned. Wouldn't you just know it? Here she was hungry enough to eat Jake Parrish's foul-tempered thoroughbred stallion—hooves and all—and they serve her this nasty concoction.

She picked up her fork to poke suspiciously at one of the offending little monstrosities. Did Jake Parrish actually enjoy such appalling fare? Or was this supposed to be some subtle form of torture?

Probably the former, she told herself with a disdainful sniff. Not that she had any idea what the man actually ate, for he hadn't deigned to take a meal with her in the two weeks she had been at the house. She sniffed again. Come to think of it, she couldn't recall ever seeing him before noon, or anytime after nine o'clock at night, for that matter.

Ha! The beast must be one of those men who carouses all night and sleeps the morning away.

Suddenly her stomach gave an angry growl, as if to protest its deprived state. What she wouldn't give for *plain* eggs, *plain* bacon, and a thick slice of lightly toasted bread. And while she was indulging in a bit of fantasy, she might as well add some sweet, sticky raspberry preserves to the list. Now those were what dreams were made of!

Clenching her lips into a tight line, Hallie refocused her eyes on the depressing reality of her plate. Not only was she about to die of boredom in this overdone mausoleum of a house, but it appeared she was going to be starved to death as well.

And it was all Jake Parrish's fault! Viciously she

speared an oyster, chortling with glee as she pretended it was Mr. High and Mighty's heart.

Take that, you arrogant cur! Thought you'd gotten the best of me, did you?

Clink! Silver clashed with fine china as the oyster slid from the capturing prongs of her fork and flew off her plate to ricochet off her bodice and into her lap.

Oh! Wonderful! That happened to be your last clean gown.

With a moan of exasperation, she dabbed at the greasy mess trailing down her lilac silk bodice, succeeding only in making matters worse. Damn. And just look at the damage done to her skirts. Expelling her breath forcefully through her nose to produce a noise that sounded suspiciously like one of Jake Parrish's superior little snorts, she attacked her soiled skirts with a violently wielded napkin.

Clunk! Hallie's elbow collided with her fork, which had been properly balanced on the edge of her plate.

Plop! It went spinning beneath the table and came to rest upon the colorfully patterned Kidderminster carpet.

"Oh, damn!" she swore indelicately, bending down to retrieve the utensil from beneath the heavy oak table.

Double damn! If she could just manage to stretch another inch—

"It's called a Hangtown Fry."

Thunk! Hallie emerged rubbing her head and casting a baleful glare in Jake Parrish's direction.

"What did you say?" she muttered crossly, noting the way he was lounging at the other end of the table, grinning at her in his infuriating manner. The sadistic bastard actually seemed to be enjoying her discomfort. And wouldn't you just know it? Her little faux pas had been witnessed by a nastily smirking Penelope as well.

"The dish you appear to be so strenuously enjoying—it's called a Hangtown Fry. It's considered to be quite a delicacy here in San Francisco." Jake moved to seat himself at the head of the table while Penelope hovered at his side.

Hallie couldn't help noticing that he was sporting a black eye and that there was a nasty-looking cut on his full lower lip.

The man probably considers a good barroom brawl a

form of highbrow entertainment, she thought, watching him grimace as he stiffly lowered himself into his chair and eased his bad leg under the table.

Staring pointedly at Jake Parrish's battered features, she said, "And here I thought San Francisco was supposed to be a mecca of civilization. My mistake."

Jake laughed at Hallie's none-too-subtle double entendre. "San Francisco is one wicked lady who happens to thrive on her own raw, untamed energy. She contains scores of sinners who are just ripe for your brand of redemption."

As Penelope reached for his napkin and made as if to place it in his lap, he snapped, "Will you please sit down and stop treating me like a damn invalid?"

Their eyes met—Penelope's sullen and rebellious, Jake's reflecting the heat of his growing temper. Twisting her mouth into an ugly scowl, Penelope shrugged and seated herself on Jake's right. He threw her a final warning glance before refocusing his attention on Hallie.

"Hop thought you might enjoy trying one of the city's more notorious dishes."

"Notorious?" Hallie stared down at her plate skeptically.

"As far as food goes, yes. During the rush of '49, a meal of a Hangtown Fry was a popular last request made by prisoners condemned to hang."

"Probably because one bite was enough to make them wish for a quick death," she replied, making a wry face.

Jake laughed. "Not quite. The real reason was the scarcity of eggs. Requesting a Hangtown Fry could mean a stay of execution for several months while the precious commodity was hunted down. You see, Dr. Gardiner, even in the crudity of the mining camps, there were certain proprieties that couldn't be overlooked, the final request of a condemned prisoner being one."

He paused to jerk his head in an abrupt nod at Hop Yung, who seemed particularly intent on pouring "Mr. Jake" a cup of coffee.

Hallie waited until the houseboy had ceased his fussing—why *did* everyone flutter about Jake Parrish as if he were some sort of imperial deity?—before retorting, "I would rather be hung quickly and cleanly than have to spend months contemplating the unpleasant experience of eating this vile stuff." She glared down at the rubbery mess congealing on her plate as if to punctuate her point.

Jake grinned and took an experimental sip of his coffee, only to wrench the cup away as the hot beverage made stinging contact with his damaged lip. He waited for the pain to subside before replying, "I've never had any fondness for the dish myself, although it's a favorite of Seth's." Picking up his cup again, he took a cautious taste.

Penelope let out one of the famous Parrish snorts. "I always thought there was something criminal about that man. What I can't understand is why you remain friends with such an uncouth creature. He certainly isn't our kind of people." Swinging her cold gaze in Hallie's direction, she added snidely, "You do seem to have an unfortunate tendency to take up with the most questionable sorts of characters."

"Oh? And just what are our kind of people, pray tell?" Jake's stare was unyielding as it pinioned his sister over the gold-edged rim of his cup.

Hallie was instantly grateful that she wasn't the recipient of that particular stare. With his face set in those grim, hard lines and his eyes sparking with emerald fire, he looked like an archangel hell-bent on delivering some awful form of retribution.

But Penelope was a seasoned veteran of her brother's dark glowers, and she simply shrugged. "You know exactly what I mean."

"Do I?" Carefully setting his fragile cup in its saucer, he leaned toward his sister and stated softly, "Penelope, you're a snob."

"One must have one's standards," she replied with a sniff.

"I owe my life and leg to that *uncouth creature*. If it weren't for Seth, I'd probably be one among the thousands of nameless wretches buried in Fredericksburg. You might do well to remember that fact next time you think to measure him against your narrow-minded set of standards."

Noisily toying with her silverware, Penelope sighed. "Really, Jake. I see no reason to spoil the day with an argument. I know you like Seth, and I promise I won't say another word against him." Lowering her eyes, she murmured, "It's just that I love you so much and can't help wanting to protect you."

"I'm hardly in need of protection, and certainly not from a girl barely out of the schoolroom. You say you want what's best for me? Fine. Then you'll stop meddling in my affairs." Ever so gently, Jake covered Penelope's fidgeting hand with his, stilling the metallic clatter of her silver. "And for the record, little sister, I love you too."

Hallie found herself staring at her stained skirts with sudden fascination, feeling as if she were somehow intruding on a private moment between the Parrish siblings. She slanted a glance from beneath the sweep of her lashes at Jake's hand holding that of his sister. Then she smiled to herself. Now here was a chink in perfect Penelope's armor. Each nail on the dainty fingers had been bitten to the very quick.

"What do you say, Dr. Gardiner?"

Hallie jerked her head up to stare at Jake, uncomprehending.

He smiled at her confusion. "I was just suggesting that my sister might find something to do to fill her time constructively. I thought she might help out at the Mission Infirmary, perhaps rolling bandages or doing some sewing."

Penelope gasped, her beautiful face reflecting her distaste. "You know how I feel about the Mission Society! I have no intention of spending my time with a pack of sanctimonious old crows rolling bandages, and you know very well that I don't sew."

"Well, perhaps Dr. Gardiner can teach you a few simple stitches. I assume you sew?" He raised a dark eyebrow in Hallie's direction.

"Not on cloth. However, I have been known to suture wounds quite artistically. Masterpieces of needlework, if I must say so myself. Perhaps someday you might like to test my skills?"

Jake blanched as her words summoned the hideous memory of his own flesh's encounter with the needle. Gritting his teeth, he muttered, "I pray to God that I never find myself the canvas for one of your creations."

"What a tasteless and repulsive conversation!" Penelope

gagged, adding an exaggerated clutching motion toward her throat with great effect. "I hope you're both satisfied. You've managed to completely ruin my appetite." With a melodramatic shudder, she jerked herself away from the table.

"I'm sorry," Hallie murmured, watching as Penelope flounced out of the room. "I can't imagine what could have prompted me to say something so tactless."

Jake waved his hand dismissively. "Don't apologize. There's nothing my sister likes better than causing a scene. In no time at all, she'll be cozily ensconced in her room, drinking chocolate and stuffing herself with sweet rolls." He paused to nod his thanks to Celine, who had set a large platter of buckwheat cakes and honey-glazed ham in front of him.

The heavenly smells assaulted Hallie's senses, drawing her attention back to her own gnawing hunger. Suddenly, and with humiliating volume, her stomach let out a loud growl of protest. She could feel the scalding banners of color unfurl across her cheeks as Jake glanced in her direction and chuckled.

"Celine, I believe I just heard Dr. Gardiner's stomach request a few buckwheat cakes for herself."

"The lady docta' don' like her fry?" Celine peered over Hallie's shoulder with interest. "I tole that worthless yeller man the lady wouldn' be likin' it. Don' you be worryin' none, Miz. Mammy Celine will be bringin' you some of her own good cookin'."

Throwing a triumphant glance at Hop Yung, who was fussing over Jake's half full cup of coffee, she swept away the offending plate and bustled toward the kitchen.

Hop cast his eyes to the ceiling with a long-suffering sigh. As Celine hurried through the door, the houseboy pulled his monkeylike face into a comical mask and wiggled his tongue at her retreating back. When he caught sight of Hallie struggling to stifle her laughter at his antics, he quickly composed himself and sketched a deferential bow in her direction. Bobbing his head in response to Jake's nod of thanks, he raced after his antagonist like a man with a purpose.

A loud crash reverberated from the kitchen, and the rising decibels of a heated debate drifted back to the pair at the table.

"What in the world is that all about?" asked Hallie, turning her wide-eyed gaze on Jake's grinning face.

"You'll get used to the noise. Hop and Celine share a sort of professional rivalry. Hop was a medicine man back in his country and by all reports quite a good one. Mammy Celine is reputedly a 'mambo,' or voodoo priestess. She is much sought after for her healing powers. Of course, the two are always at odds over who is the best at his or her trade, and God knows we've all suffered their questionable remedies at one time or another."

Jake paused to smile at Hallie's melodious laughter. "I can't imagine what those two must make of you."

"They apparently think as little of my skills as you do," she pointed out, the merriment fading from her face. "They're constantly criticizing my ways and bombarding me with advice on how best to care for your wife and daughter."

Jake studied her solemnly for a moment and then sighed. "We got off to a bad start, and I'm sorry for that. As for doubting your skills, I may be many things and most of them not particularly admirable, but I'm no fool. I wouldn't have gone to so much trouble and expense to bring you here unless I thought you were qualified to care for my family. Regardless of what everyone seems to believe, I only want what's best for them."

"I realize that," Hallie replied gently. "And I think you care for them far more than you want anyone to know."

He gave a harsh laugh. "Let's just say I take my responsibility seriously." Looking up as the door opened, Jake commented, "Ah, it looks as if your breakfast has arrived."

Hallie closed her eyes and sniffed blissfully at the buckwheat cakes in front of her while her stomach rumbled a blessing of its own.

Smiling at Hallie's expression of gastronomic ecstasy, Celine inclined her head in mute acknowledgment of Jake's dismissing smile and glided soundlessly from the room.

"Dr. Gardiner?"

"M-m-m?"

"Why haven't you ever asked me about Serena?" The question was asked with deceptive casualness.

Hallie opened her eyes to meet his fathomless gaze. Pausing to consider her words carefully, she replied, "Davinia told me all about your wife's . . . problem."

"All?" he asked, a shaft of bitterness lancing through his voice. "I doubt that."

"I know your wife developed a craving for . . . opium, and Davinia did mention something about morphine," she murmured, pretending not to feel the sudden and inexplicable chill of his stare. "I can't imagine she would have left out any important details."

"Really?" He studied her for an moment with an odd expression on his face. Leaning toward her, he inquired, "Did she, by any chance, mention that my wife became so distraught when I returned from the war alive—barely alive, mind you—that she tried to take her own life?"

"Dear God, n-no!" Hallie stuttered, shocked.

Jake drew back and gave a short bark of harsh laughter. "Oh, yes. She said she would rather be dead than suffer living with a man who was not only a traitor to the Confederate cause but a pathetic cripple as well."

He could still see Serena as she had been that day, unkempt and wraithlike, poised at the top of the stairs, venting her venom in a strange, singsong voice. Her malignant words had hurt him badly, piercing his soul over and over again until he had felt like little more than a bleeding mass of wounds. Yet it was the sight of her tears as she had sunk to her knees keening, "Why didn't you die? Dear God! Why didn't you die?" that had delivered the mortal blow. For each crystalline teardrop had been an irrefutable testimony of her unforgiving hatred of him. It was then that he had wept, mourning, as he watched his dreams die their unfulfilled death.

"Mr. Parrish . . ." Hallie's words faded to stunned silence as she saw his face twist into a mask of heartbreaking agony, and when his eyes grazed hers, she could see the terrible legion of scars gleaming in their naked depths. Like marks tallying the score of a thousand soul-crippling blows dealt by the tragedy that had become his life, they spoke eloquently of a suffering that he was desperate to soothe, yet powerless to escape.

She drew a trembling breath, scrambling to think of

something to say—anything that could ease that awful hopelessness from his eyes. But her mind remained blank, all thought blotted out by a raw surge of emotion that cried to fill his heartrending need.

How she longed to pull him into her arms, to cradle his cheek against her breast as she rocked him gently, crooning all the words of comfort he needed to hear. She wanted to hold him close until, with a sigh of surrender, he yielded to the warmth of her solace. And when the pain had at last drifted from his mind, he would find peace in the enveloping sanctuary of her arms.

But, of course, she could do none of these things. Swallowing convulsively, Hallie somehow managed to murmur something, though only God knew what she said.

Jake dropped his gaze to his hands and carefully traced the rim of his cup with his fingertip. "She drank enough laudanum to kill a man twice her size. I never knew where she got the stuff. I had had her confined to her rooms, hoping to wean her from her addiction. God! What a fool I was! I thought that once I had broken her habit, everything would be all right. I thought—" He broke off raggedly and buried his face in his hands.

Hallie reached across the table and after a moment of indecision, gently stroked his silky hair. She could feel him start beneath her hand, only to relax as he accepted her touch.

Without lifting his head, he continued slowly, "For three days she lay unmoving and barely breathing. There were several times when her heartbeat became so faint that we were sure she was gone. And she was so cold to the touch . . . so cold."

"It was a miracle she survived at all, Mr. Parrish," Hallie whispered, drawing her hand away from his hair as he raised his head.

He leveled her with a cynical stare. "If that's your idea of a miracle, then I would hate to see your definition of a tragedy." Her eyes darkened with hurt at his unprovoked attack, and he instantly regretted the cruelty of his words. He cursed himself virulently for being such a bastard.

"I'm sorry. You didn't deserve that shabby remark." Sighing, Jake rubbed his forehead. The damn thing felt as if it were being constricted by a band of steel. "Please understand that I've heard those same words dozens of times before, only to be told in the next breath that my wife's brain has been damaged beyond all hope and that she will remain little more than a vindictive child for the rest of her days."

His lips twisted in a sad caricature of a smile. "I know that's no excuse for my acting like such a bastard, but I hope you can forgive me anyway."

Impulsively Hallie reached over and clasped his hand. "There is nothing to forgive, Mr. Parrish."

"Jake. Please, call me Jake. I would like for us to be friends."

"I'd like that too . . . Jake. And as friends, I'll expect you to call me Hallie."

Jake gave her hand a firm squeeze. "Pleased to make your acquaintance, Hallie."

And then he smiled that heart-stopping smile.

"Charming the ladies again, eh, Jake?" Seth Tyler strode into the breakfast room, staring at Jake and Hallie's clasped hands with bemused interest.

They both started, snatching their hands apart self-consciously.

Jake threw his friend a look of annoyance. "For your information, Seth, Dr. Gardiner and I have just come to a mutual agreement and were in the process of shaking on it."

"Oh, well, don't let me stop you," he replied breezily, plopping into the chair next to Hallie. Eyeballing Jake's untouched plate with greedy appraisal, he said, "Say, Jake, if you're not going to eat those buckwheat cakes, you might want to slide them in my direction. My cook can't seem to make anything that isn't either dismally underdone or burned to a crisp."

With a snort of good-natured exasperation, Jake pushed his plate toward his friend. Grinning at Hallie's surprised expression, he laughed, "Can't have Seth gnawing on the furniture, can we?"

"Well, I did have my mouth all set for that delectable-looking Sheraton sideboard in the dining room, but Celine's cakes actually look to be easier on the teeth." Presenting Hallie with a toothy grin, he snatched up

Jake's fork and proceeded to eat with unbridled enthusiasm.

Jake watched his friend lazily for a few minutes before inquiring, "Who died, Seth?"

Seth choked on his mouthful of ham, his face turning such an alarming shade of purple that Hallie jumped up and pounded his back furiously.

"A-l-l RIGHT!" Seth managed to gasp, as he attempted to escape Hallie's violent ministrations. "Enough! I'm all right now—thank you!" Tossing Hallie a look that was equal parts pain and admiration, he poked at his abused spine gingerly. "Quite a jab you've got there, sweetheart. Bet I'll be black and blue for days." With that, he reached over and took a quick swig from Jake's coffee cup. Looking at his friend with interest, he asked, "So, who *did* die?"

"That's what I was wondering, seeing as you're so somberly dressed."

Hallie turned to examine Seth Tyler doubtfully. True, his suit was a subdued charcoal gray worsted, but given the fact that the lapels were canary yellow silk, with a knotted tie to match, and his waistcoat was colorfully embroidered with fanciful creatures, his attire could hardly be described as funereal.

Seth hooted at Jake's barbed remark. "Punch him for me, will you, sweetheart? Since you pack such a mighty wallop, you'd be doing me an enormous favor."

He stared at Jake critically for a moment and then, pointing his fork at his friend, remarked, "You might want to aim for his right eye. It seems I failed to blacken it in my preoccupation with the left one. Take it easy on his mouth, though. I was pretty rough on it last night."

Seth winked at Hallie. "Won't be kissing anyone anytime soon, eh, Jake?"

"Damn it, Seth—" Jake sputtered.

"O-o-o! Such language! Maybe you should start with his mouth after all."

"You did that to Jake's face?" Hallie was appalled. "Whatever possessed you to do such an awful thing?"

"Sport!" the two men howled in unison.

Glowering at the guffawing pair as if they were a couple of town idiots caught in the act of baiting the mayor's dog, she exploded, "You consider it sport to try and beat your best friend's face to a pulp?"

Seth shrugged. "Well, that's hardly the point, though that pretty face does occasionally get in the way."

Jake snorted with mock indignation. "You were aiming for my belly and you just happen to be clumsy enough to miss." Rubbing his lip at the painful memory, he explained, "Seth and I occasionally enjoy a round of boxing at our club. And usually," he glared at Seth's unmarked countenance, "this idiot looks as bad—or worse—than I."

Hallie looked from one man to the other doubtfully. "It hardly seems a fair contest. I mean—" She stopped short, not quite sure if it would be proper to mention Jake's bad leg.

"You mean Jake's leg," finished Seth. "Oh, don't let that worry you. Why, if it weren't for our boxing matches and our morning rowing contests, Jake would still be the same self-pitying cripple who passed his days huddled beneath his blankets."

"Seth," Jake growled, looking none too pleased with the direction the conversation had taken.

"Weak and shaky as an infant was our Jake. I'll never forget the first time I dragged him down to the bay and forced him to row that boat—"

"Damn it, Seth!" gritted Jake threateningly. "I don't appreciate—"

Seth deliberately turned his back on his friend and focused all his attention on Hallie. "Yes, he could barely hold the oars, he was shaking so badly with weakness. Why, even that paltry effort was enough to send him vomiting into the bushes."

Jake groaned and looked ready to throttle his friend at any moment, but Seth blithely ignored him.

"I also found out just how creative Jake can be with a colorful phrase."

"Seth," Jake choked out murderously. "If you're finished with your tasteless commentary, I'd like to sign those papers you were supposed to bring. You did remember to bring them, didn't you?"

"Of course. But I haven't had a chance to tell Doc how you upset the boat with your clumsiness and had to be rescued from drowning." His eyes brightened as he warmed to the subject. "You should have seen him! The elegant Jake Parrish thrashing in the water like a duck with a hornet up its backside and looking like a—"

"Enough!" intervened Jake, color darkening his face.

"Too bad. That's one of my favorite stories." Seth paused to take another bite of ham. "Oh, well. Now that Doc is a citizen of our city, I'll have plenty of opportunities to regale her with tales of your past, er, glories."

"I'm sure that thought gladdens Dr. Gardiner's heart to no end. Now, if you don't mind, I'd like to look over those documents."

As the men made to rise and retire to the library, Hop Yung came darting into the breakfast room with obvious agitation.

"Mister King to see Mister Jake. Ver-ry mean-headed. Ver-ry!" he added with mournful emphasis, wringing his hands anxiously.

Seth threw Jake a concerned look. "Serena's father? I wonder what he's doing back in town."

"God only knows," groaned Jake, an uneasy feeling trickling down his spine. Cyrus King could be summed up in one word: trouble. Heaving a sigh of resignation, he added, "The only way to find out is to see what he wants."

"Would you like me to go with you?" asked Seth, worry tainting every line of his handsome face.

Jake shook his head, but smiled at his friend's show of support. "No. I've handled Cyrus before." He rose and balanced himself on his cane, painfully flexing his stiff leg. "Just don't be alarmed if you hear some rather loud . . . conversation. The man is overly fond of shouting."

Seth stared at his friend doubtfully for a moment, and then nodded. "I'm sure you know best."

Jake nodded back. "Since we obviously won't have time to go over those documents this morning, you might want to take them downtown to our solicitor and get his opinion on the legality of the proposed transaction. It'll save us time this afternoon. That is—" he turned to Hallie, "—if Dr. Gardiner will excuse us?"

Hallie nodded her consent, though she felt a strange sense of disappointment at Jake's leaving. "Of course. I'm sure you and Mr. Tyler—"

"It's Seth, sweetheart," Seth interjected. "My father's name was *Mr.* Tyler."

She laughed at his droll expression. "And I'm Hallie."

Jake limped toward the door, smiling at Hallie's laughter. He liked the way it sounded, husky and filled with unbridled joy. Hand on doorknob, he paused to glance in her direction. He liked the way she looked, too. Grinning impishly up at his friend, her eyes sparkling with mirth, she looked almost pretty. His smile broadened . . . until he heard Seth's words.

"Now that we're on a first-name basis, I can tell you about the time Jake got tipsy and decided to serenade cranky old Mrs. Wornley—"

With a beleaguered groan, Jake stepped over the threshold and slammed the door behind him. Clenching his cane in a deathlike grip, he began his slow trek to the parlor. *Cyrus King. Here. Trouble.* His muscles tensed at the disturbing thought.

Once in front of the parlor door, he stopped to ask a passing maid to inform the other servants that he and Cyrus King were not to be disturbed. She bobbed her head and set off to do his bidding.

Privacy ensured, he sucked in a deep, steadying breath and mentally braced himself for the coming conflict.

Chapter 7

The early morning sun danced through the leaded-glass windows of the parlor, igniting a spark of cheer that kindled and blazed until the austerely formal room radiated with a warmth it ordinarily lacked.

The man pacing restlessly within the gilded blue and white confines was feeling many things, but warmth or cheer did not number among them.

No. His emotions seethed darkly, a roiling combination of bitterness, rage, and a soul-consuming hatred—all directed toward the man who had robbed him of his beloved Serena, crushed her spirit, and ultimately destroyed her.

Jake Parrish.

The name sat like a profane curse on the tip of Cyrus King's tongue, and he felt an overwhelming urge to spit, to rid himself of the vile taste it left in his mouth. It was at that moment, with the foulness of his hate overwhelming his senses, that he vowed to himself that someday, somehow, he would find a way to bring his mighty son-in-law down in the dirt where he belonged.

"Cyrus King." Like the flicker of a candle in a cool autumn breeze, the friendly warmth of the parlor seemed to falter and then die, extinguished by the chilly voice that broke the stillness. "And to what do we owe this honor?" inquired Jake, unable to subdue his irony. He moved into the room until he stood in front of the imposing white marble fireplace.

Cyrus's head jerked up at the sound of his son-in-law's voice, and his eyes narrowed with hostility.

"You can cut the pleasantries, Parrish," he snarled, his face becoming a twisted mask of malevolence. "You know damn well that I've come to take my daughter home where she belongs."

Jake leaned casually against the fireplace and issued a harsh bark of laughter. "Really? And where is home these days? Last I heard, you were living in an abandoned tar-paper shack up at the old Devil's Flat Camp, existing off whatever change you happen to earn by working odd jobs at the wharf. I'm sure Serena will thank you for taking her away from all this." He gave a negligent wave at his opulent surroundings. "And reducing her to an existence unfit for even the crudest individual."

"Fine surroundings and wealth can never compensate for the hell my daughter had endured at your hand." Shaking with anger, Cyrus raked his fingers through his thinning, silver-shot blond hair. He had once been an attractive man, but years of bitterness and hard living had taken their toll, leaving his face so deeply lined that it seemed set in a perpetual scowl.

"Jesus!" he expelled vehemently, advancing a step toward Jake. "When I think of all you've done to Serena, I could—well—if I wasn't such a civilized man, I would have killed you long ago."

"The only thing I 'did' to your daughter was to spoil and indulge her in all of her extravagant whims. Perhaps by doing that, I *did* ruin her. If I had told her no more often, she might have learned that the world didn't revolve around her selfish wants, and she might have developed enough integrity to recognize your slanderous lies for what they really were—attempts to estrange her from me."

Jake leaned forward, his eyes boring into Cyrus's. "Tell me, King. How does it feel to know that you've ruined your daughter's life?"

"I did no such thing, and well you know it! Don't try to blame me for your own foul deeds. I love Serena, while you—"

"No, Cyrus," Jake cut him off with a commanding tone. "If you want to lay blame for your daughter's condition, lay it at your own door. It was you who poisoned her mind against me, you bred her dissatisfaction toward our marriage, and you who planted the seeds of unhappiness that led her to attempt suicide." Jake stabbed out the words, punctuating each syllable with biting emphasis.

Cyrus King's hands clenched tightly against his sides as he spat back, "Damn you to hell, Parrish! When are you going to admit to yourself that my daughter came to her senses about you and couldn't stand living with Yankee scum. Your pride couldn't bear the humiliation of losing your wife, so you ensured that she couldn't leave by driving her mad."

He paused to steal a glance at Jake. The miserable bastard! He was staring at Cyrus much the way one watched a clown act at a carnival: with amusement and a touch of pity. Well, he would wipe that superior look off the man's face quickly enough.

"A pack of good it did you! Just look at you now, nothing more than a pathetic cripple. My daughter despises you! Everyone knows she'd rather die than suffer your foul touch. Not that she has to worry about that, eh?"

Cyrus leaned in, his eyes glinting with malicious speculation as he taunted, "Rumor has it that Serena confided in Lavinia Donahue that you came back from the war less than half a man."

Jake let out a snort of derision. "We all know what a creditable source of information Serena is these days. Taking into consideration the baby upstairs in the nursery, it's safe to assume that either your daughter lied or she's taken a lover."

Jake watched with satisfaction as Cyrus's now eggplant purple face slowly bled into a deathly white mask with bulging eyes and gaping mouth. His mouth opened and closed frantically as he tried to speak but couldn't. A vein began to throb in his temple as he finally croaked, "Baby?"

"Yes. Your darling daughter gave birth about two weeks ago. A girl. Unnamed as yet," Jake informed him shortly.

Cyrus closed the gap between them with mind-spinning speed.

"You rutting bastard!" he shrieked, smashing his fist into Jake's mouth, tearing open his already damaged lower lip.

Although at six-four, Jake topped his opponent by several inches, rage propelled Cyrus, giving him an inordinate strength. Fluidly catching his opponent by the lapels of his wool morning coat, Cyrus pushed Jake against the fireplace, stunning him as his head was whipped back and cracked against the hard surface of the mantel with a loud thud.

"You forced her! You forced my Serena! She never would have let you touch her by her own volition! Never!" He slammed his fist into Jake's belly with such nauseating force that the cane slid from Jake's hand and he doubled over, completely incapacitated.

Seeing his victory close at hand, Cyrus seized the heavy Limoges vase from the mantel. He was about to inflict a devastating blow to the back of his opponent's neck when Jake surprised him.

Rearing up and deftly catching Cyrus's arm, Jake twisted it relentlessly until the vase went crashing to the floor. He then jerked the man around to face him and hit him in the jaw.

"Get out, Cyrus! Now! Before I lose control and kill you!" Jake punched him heavily in the kidneys.

Howling with pain, Cyrus swiftly brought his knee up and rammed his opponent in the groin with a viciousness that sent Jake crumpling to the ground, with Cyrus still clutched in his grasp. Like lovers in a frenzied embrace, the two men tumbled to the floor, Jake landing squarely on top of Cyrus.

Cyrus struggled frantically beneath Jake's weight for several moments until he was able to push himself free. With satisfaction, he noted that Jake was still stunned by his punishing blow, his face blanched with agony and sweat beading on his brow. Roughly, King rolled Jake onto his back, fully intent on pummeling him into a state of senselessness. As he raised his fist to continue his assault, he was whomped across the back of his head with a blow that sent him sprawling to the floor.

Cyrus could only stare with disbelief at the avenging red-headed virago bearing down on him, wielding a ridiculously frilly pink parasol as if it were a flaming sword of righteousness. She raised her weapon again, but then paused to cast an anxious glance in Jake's direction, who had begun to chuckle softly.

Thank God she was on his side! Jake thought drolly. That tiny parasol looked positively lethal in her hands. Why, with all that bright hair springing wildly from her chignon and standing to the topmost inch of her considerable height, she was the very picture of a legendary Amazon capable of wiping out whole armies single-handed. Still clutching painfully at his abdomen, Jake pushed himself to a sitting position and grinned up into Hallie's outraged face.

"Jake! Oh, Lord! Look what that beast did to your poor lip!" she exclaimed, peering down at him with concern.

"My lip?" Jake asked, shifting uncomfortably on the hard floor. "That's not what's hurting right now."

Hallie patted his arm. "Well, don't you worry. First, we'll dispose of this trash," she nodded toward Cyrus, who was dazedly pulling himself into an upright position, "and then I'll examine your injuries. Thank God Serena insisted that I look for her lost parasol, or I never would have happened by."

Jake eyed her with mock innocence and feigned an injured moan. "You promise? You'll take care of *all* my injuries?"

"Of course," she retorted soothingly, turning to frown in Cyrus's direction and thus missing the deviltry growing in Jake's eyes.

"So this is the piece who's replaced my daughter in your bed, eh, Parrish?" growled Cyrus, staring back at Hallie with open contempt.

Hallie gasped with shock, her hand tightening instinctively on the parasol.

Cyrus's eyes raked her with distaste. "Can't say much for your taste in women these days. But then again, I don't expect that a gimp like yourself has much of a choice anymore." He gave Hallie a lewd wink. "Well, at least he doesn't keep you awake at night, eh, Missy?"

Hallie flushed with embarrassment as the man made a crude hand motion that left little doubt as to the meaning of his remark.

With a growl of fury, Jake hurled himself at Cyrus, pinning him to the floor. Like a man possessed, he rained blow after brutal blow upon his antagonist in an uncontrollable barrage, unmindful of anything except satisfying his burning rage. The sight of the man's frightened eyes and his desperate struggles to escape only added fuel to Jake's anger.

"Jake, stop! Please stop! You're going to kill him!"

Jake ceased abruptly as Hallie's frantically pleading voice penetrated his bloodthirsty frenzy. As he stared at Hallie's ghostly white face and looked into her amber eyes, large with terror, he dropped his bloodied fist to his side. Then he looked down at Cyrus's battered face. With a foul oath, he released the man, who, now silent, sagged against the carpet.

"Jake," Hallie murmured, her heart contracting at the look of shame and defeat that swept over his features. She bent down to help him to his feet, whispering, "It's all right."

Wrapping her arm around his trim waist and stooping slightly to brace her shoulder beneath his arm, she supported him securely against her softness. He made no protest as she guided him to a chair a few feet away and settled him carefully in it.

She then turned to scowl darkly at Cyrus King. With a little sniff of disgust, she stalked to the door, fully intent on summoning Hop Yung to toss their unwanted visitor into the street.

As she yanked the door open, Hop Yung came tumbling into the room, obviously guilty of eavesdropping. With admirable aplomb, he pulled himself upright and made an energetic bow in her direction.

Hallie couldn't help smiling at the little man's audacity. "Hop Yung, would you be so kind as to see Mr. King to the door? I believe he has expressed a desire to take his leave."

Hallie and Hop turned to stare expectantly at Cyrus King, who hesitated and then nodded, apparently thinking better of voicing his objections.

Jake watched the byplay, smiling to himself and thoroughly enjoying the sight of his father-in-law being forced to defer to Hallie's imperious commands. He chuckled softly. *His Mission Lady certainly was a bossy piece of work.*

As Cyrus King followed Hop out the door, he stopped abruptly, his cold glare striking Jake from across the room. "Don't think this is the end of it, Parrish. I'll be back for Serena, and the next time don't expect to hide behind a woman's skirts."

"Be glad for that woman's skirts. They kept me from killing you."

"Just remember my words when you toss up those same skirts and take your paltry pleasures. Next time it will be you at my mercy, and nothing will stop me from killing you."

With that, Hop Yung slammed the door shut, catching the lagging Cyrus squarely in the back and eliciting a loud howl of pain from him.

"What an awful man," whispered Hallie, sinking to her knees in front of Jake.

"And they say mothers-in-law are the ones to be feared," he joked feebly, smiling as she spat daintily on her handkerchief and lightly dabbed at the blood smearing his chin.

Hallie returned his smile wistfully. Even with that blackened eye, and with blood dripping from his lip, he was still the most wonderfully handsome man she had ever seen.

As gently as possible, she wiped his lip, relieved to see that the wound had stopped bleeding. Unconsciously, she touched the cut, and the texture of his sensuous mouth seemed to burn her fingertips.

Lord! she thought, dropping her hand abruptly. *The man's strong, masculine beauty is making my mind go all mushy and turning me into a witless ninny.* It didn't seem fair, or decent, that every inch of him was so perfect.

Hallie let her gaze slide down to the muscular form correctly attired in a gray morning coat. No, it wasn't fair at all. How was she supposed to keep her wits about her when his jacket hugged his powerful shoulders like that? And the way the white linen of his crisply starched shirt contrasted against the smooth honey tones of his skin? It was positively sinful. She definitely needed to attend a few of Reverend DeYoung's revival meetings, seeing as how her mind was working its way down such a wicked path.

And down was where Hallie's gaze sank. She didn't miss the way the cut of his impeccably tailored trousers snugged against the flat surface of his belly, or how they hinted at the athletic strength of his thighs. She also noted, with unmaidenly interest, how the fit left little doubt as to his masculinity.

Hallie suddenly realized where her eyes were focused and quickly glanced back up at his face. She drew a sigh of relief when she saw that his expression was politely bland. Thank God he hadn't noticed her over enthusiastic inspection of his person. She flushed at the memory of her bold scrutiny, and it was then that he rewarded her with a wickedly charming grin.

"Finished with your examination, Doctor?" Jake quizzed lightly, leaving no doubt in her mind that he had observed her eager perusal. "And have you come to any conclusions?"

He leaned forward as if daring her to reply.

Hallie hastily composed herself and answered in her best doctor-to-patient voice, "I conclude that the nasty-looking cut on your lip should be properly tended."

"My lip?" he asked, a teasing light dancing in his smoky-green eyes. "Is that all you discovered in your rather, ah, lengthy observation?"

"I wouldn't presume to pronounce any further findings without a far more complete, and I might add, intimate, examination," she retorted rather primly. She stole a glance at Jake and saw that he was regarding her with warm interest.

"I can't say I've ever had the unusual privilege of being intimately, or otherwise, examined by a lady physician." He lightly stroked the curve of his jaw, mulling over the notion. "The idea does have some merit, though. Hmm. Come to think of it, I did take some nasty blows from Cyrus King that could benefit from your tender ministrations."

He nodded, and Hallie became mesmerized by the genuine smile that sketched across his lips, a smile that was reflected in the inviting depths of those tip-tilted eyes, beckoning her to move closer.

"What's wrong, Doctor? Afraid to *intimately* examine a man?" he taunted challengingly. "Or could it be that you're not nearly as experienced as you would like me to believe?"

"Of course I've *intimately* examined men before. Hundreds of them!" she lied, half expecting the ceiling to open up and lightning to strike her where she kneeled.

For, in truth, her experience with male anatomy was strictly limited to little boys and one very old cadaver. She'd certainly never treated a man as potently masculine as Jake Parrish.

Nonetheless, not being one to shrink from a challenge, Hallie added brazenly, "I've even been known to dissect a few male cadavers, and if that's not intimate knowledge I don't know what is."

What, indeed! Jake thought, forcibly suppressing his urge to howl with laughter at the naivete of her words. In a choked voice he managed to reply, "I hardly think a dissection will be necessary. However, you did promise to tend my injuries and I'm feeling the need sorely." He closed his eyes, groaning playfully.

Hallie rose to her feet and reached for his face. "If that is what you wish, then it's my sworn duty to aid you in your distress."

Jake almost laughed aloud at Hallie's priggish little speech. Then he felt her cool, work-roughened hand cup itself beneath his chin. He opened his eyes as she gently lifted his face and found himself captured by a most remarkable pair of golden eyes. The color vaguely reminded him of the sun reflecting through amber glass, and they were lit as brightly as a candle, flaming with an intelligence and compassion that sparked his imagination. They were beautiful eyes, exotic with their almond shape and thickly rimmed with inky lashes. Eyes that offered a generosity of spirit, an innate kindness, a caring, that Jake found himself longing to accept.

Hallie tenderly traced the dark swelling beneath his eye, not daring to meet the gaze she could feel trained upon her face. For she knew that to do so would mean to drown in those cool green pools. When Jake at last lowered his lids, his heavy lashes swept against her fingers, startling her with their length. Then he winced, almost imperceptibly, at her gently probing inspection, and her heart wrenched with sympathy.

"I'm sorry," she whispered, for to have spoken in a normal tone would have broken the curious magic of the moment. "I didn't mean to hurt you."

"You didn't." He sighed and then relaxed.

She let her fingers slide in a feather-soft motion down the side of his face, her sensitive touch reveling in the surprisingly silky texture of his skin. She stopped to explore the tempting contour of his high, chiseled cheekbone.

"Jake?"

"Hmm?"

"I would never hurt you," she murmured, overwhelmed with tenderness.

"I know."

And Hallie felt her breath catch in her throat as Jake rested his cheek in her cupped hand, nuzzling gently against her palm in an almost childlike gesture of trust. It was an act of naked vulnerability—an act that made her yearn to enfold him in her embrace and to rest her face against his, an act of such simple faith that it almost undid her.

It was as if Jake Parrish, a man known for his omnipotent strength, had let a chink open in his steely armor and was entrusting her with a revealing glimpse into his sensitive inner soul. Lightly, she stroked his cheek, mutely acknowledging his silent plea for tenderness.

The feel of Hallie's gentle fingers against his face infused Jake with the peace he urgently sought yet rarely found these days. He was held spellbound by the magical solace that radiated from her touch. How natural it felt to rest his cheek in the curve of her palm—how right. It was as if he had waited a lifetime for someone who could still the thundering chaos raging in his head and engulf him with a warm blanket of tranquillity. It seemed like forever since he had been blessed with the priceless gift of a caress.

Yet, somehow, this odd little woman had recognized his aching need and, with the touch of her hand, had made him realize just how much he missed simple human contact.

Jake opened his eyes to study the face that went with the bewitching touch. It was true that Dr. Hallie Gardiner would be considered plain by many, for her face had that square-jawed type of strength that was at odds with the delicate, doll-like features that were so in vogue. Yet her skin was as smooth as an unblemished peach, with a tint every bit as delicate as the fruit it resembled. And though her nose was a bit long, it wasn't unattractive; it didn't hook, bump, or twist. Indeed, it was blade straight and could safely be pronounced unremarkable.

Then Jake's eyes sharpened with interest, caught by a pair of generously curved lips. He had always preferred women with full, succulent mouths, for they seemed to invite a provocative impression of lush promise.

And Hallie Gardiner definitely had the sort of mouth that made a man hunger to tease it with his lips and tongue. Jake could almost picture that mouth swollen and trembling from the assault of his kisses, and his groin tightened uncomfortably in response to his erotic thoughts.

With a violent shudder, he forced his eyes away from the disturbing feature to meet her dreamily longing gaze. Ah, yes. One mustn't forget those wonderful, expressive eyes.

Yet most people would consider it a nondescript face, he mused to himself. But if that were true, then why did he, a man known for his unerring appreciation for beautiful women, feel such an urge to pull those untidy coils of hair from the spinsterish chignon and watch them dance in fire-touched splendor around her face? Why did he long to explore what lay beneath her ugly, ill-fitting clothing, to discover if her magic was in more than just her touch? But most of all, why did he feel such a need to bury himself in her flesh and fill his loneliness with her warmth?

A slash of heat knifed through his loins as he suddenly pictured Hallie naked and in his arms. She was beautiful, her skin the color of melted peaches and cream, touched by the molten copper of her hair as it cascaded around her enraptured face. He could almost feel her heat as he plunged his needful flesh into the core of her fire, forcing a response from her body so sweetly overwhelming that she arched up violently, hungry to receive every inflamed inch of him.

So graphic and unexpected were his thoughts that he was unable to suppress his shuddering moan.

"Jake?"

He opened his eyes at the sound of her anxious voice.

"Are you all right? You look so flushed and . . . strange." She paused to feel his forehead. "You seem to be a trifle warm. I hope you're not getting a fever."

"Warm?" he muttered beneath his breath, shifting in his seat to find a more comfortable position. "Now there's an understatement." The cut of his trousers was definitely on the constricting side at that moment.

"Excuse me?"

"Nothing!" he snapped, far more sharply than he intended. Didn't the woman realize what she had done to him?

Then he laughed. Of course not. She was the Mission Lady, for God's sake. Imagine getting worked up over one of those prudish Bible-thumping fanatics.

He glanced at her highly colored face and remembered the longing he had read in her eyes. *Well, maybe not so prudish,* he amended. Not if her transparent reaction to him had been any indication of her true feelings. A deep chuckle rumbled in his chest as he wondered what Hallie's reaction would be if she could read his thoughts.

Worried. Hallie was worried. Lord! The man was sitting there, laughing like a lunatic, and neither one of them had said anything remotely funny. Perhaps Cyrus King had inflicted some sort of terrible damage on Jake's head when he had hit him.

Unmindful of everything except her growing concern for Jake's condition, she abruptly buried her hands in the sable softness of his hair and began to prod at his skull with sharp, jabbing motions.

Jake's laughter died in his throat at her odd behavior. "What are you doing?"

"Looking for the bump."

"What bump?"

"The one that will be swelling over the crack in your skull. I can't think of anything else that could make you behave in such an unpredictable manner!"

"Ow!"

"Aha!" she crowed triumphantly, poking at the knot rising on the back of his head. "I knew it!"

"My behavior has nothing to do with that particular bump," he growled, removing her hand and rubbing the area with a reproachful look.

Hallie crossed her arms over her chest. "If your head isn't the culprit, then pray tell what is?"

"You really want to know?"

"Of course. I can't make a proper diagnosis if you don't tell me where it hurts," she scolded. "Now why don't you show me the area that's causing you such discomfort so I can make a thorough examination?"

His eyes raked her boldly for a moment before he drawled, "Fine. Do you want me to drop my trousers here, or would you prefer to examine me in the privacy of my chambers?"

At his words, Hallie's gaze flew downward, and her eyes widened with shock as they focused on the bulge of his arousal.

"Well, Doctor? What's it to be?" He grinned lazily. For the first time in their acquaintance, the woman was struck speechless.

Think, Hallie! she commanded herself, wondering at the strange tension that was coiling deep in her belly and trying to ignore the way the thought of Jake Parrish trouserless made her feel curiously flushed all over. She glanced up at his face to see him smiling at her. *Aha! He was bluffing. He had to be. He wouldn't just drop his pants like that . . . would he?* But did she dare to call his bluff?

"Right here will be just fine."

His eyes flared with surprise and then he gave her a very slow, very wicked grin. "As you wish, Doctor." And his hands moved to the buttons on his trousers.

"Wait!" Hallie gasped. *Damn the man. Leave it to Jake Parrish to effectively trump her play. Oh, Lord! Now what?*

"What's this, Doctor? Surely a woman of your vast experience wouldn't be shocked by the sight of a naked man?"

"Of course not." *The bastard! Wait. Oh, yes. She knew how to fix him!* She remembered a woman at the medical college who had been much too pretty for her own good. She had regularly been accosted by such behavior from clodhopping men. After one such episode, in which a swain had become frighteningly persistent, she and Hallie had concocted a method of discouragement which had proved to be 100 percent effective.

"Well, Doctor?" he quizzed in a taunting voice.

"I was just trying to save your modesty until after I had had Hop Yung fetch me a bucket of ice. Of course, if you want to undress now, it makes no difference to me." She stared at his hands on his waistband.

"Ice?" His eyes narrowed with suspicion.

Hallie shrugged and moved toward the door as if she were indeed about to summon Hop Yung. "Yes. Ice. I've found that by packing the area with a cold substance—ice being the most effective—such swellings are reduced in a remarkably short period of time." She watched with satisfaction as he recoiled at her suggestion.

And then he laughed. So hard, in fact, that he doubled over, clutching his sides.

"I don't see what's so funny." This wasn't supposed to be the way he reacted. He should have cringed with horror and beat a hasty retreat.

"Ice?" He snickered again. "Got a remedy for everything, don't you, Doctor?" He leaned forward to fix her with a smoldering stare. "However, in this case, I can think of a cure that's far more interesting and pleasant."

"I'm sure you can. But don't you know you'll grow hair on your palms and go crazy if you abuse yourself in that manner?" she snapped, deliberately misunderstanding his meaning.

Jake threw back his head, shouting with mirth. "Let me assure you that *self-abuse* is hardly what I had in mind."

He rose to his feet and stalked toward her until they were only inches apart. "Shall I explain in detail exactly what I was thinking?" he purred silkily, drawing his face close to hers.

Hallie's breath caught in her throat. He was so near, she could smell the clean scent of shaving soap lingering on his skin, and see the way the moss green irises of his eyes were ringed with smoky gray. As she felt his warm breath caress her cheek, the tension in her belly seemed to explode, sending rivulets of heat shooting through her body, creating a fever so intense that she wanted nothing more than to melt against him. Hallie wavered toward him, and when he reached out to steady her, she gave in to her wanton urges and molded herself against his muscular body, mindlessly intoxicated by his closeness.

His arms wrapped around her waist, crushing her soft length against his steely one. She could feel his muscles ripple beneath his clothing as he pressed his groin against her belly with a moan, and the insistent hardness of his arousal served to remind her of his dangerously potent need.

Hallie's mind sounded a frantic warning, but her traitorous body reacted with a will of its own, undulating against his with an erotic response that sent shivers of fear racing through her brain. Fear of Jake Parrish's overwhelming masculinity, of his almost hypnotic sensuality, and—most of all—of her own uncontrollable response to his silent, carnal beckoning. God help her, she wanted nothing more than to stay in his arms and experience the pleasures at which he had hinted.

But she didn't dare, for to do so would have been madness. Her mind battled with her quickly surrendering body, desperately scrambling for the solution that could save her from succumbing to her own fierce desires.

As her head bent back and his lips began to descend toward hers, she hit upon the answer.

"Saltpeter!" she gasped.

That stopped him short. He tipped his head back to peer into her flushed face. "What?"

She drew a long, shuddering breath. Avoiding his incredulous eyes, she fought to work her way out of his now-slackening embrace.

"Saltpeter," she mumbled, putting a safe distance between them and straightening her skirts with shaking hands. "I'll have Hop Yung dose your food with saltpeter. That should take care of your problem with these uncontrollable urges."

His eyes narrowed dangerously. "That might take care of *my* problem, Doctor," he retorted coolly. "But what do you intend to do about your own?"

Chapter 8

"There's a wild, almost neglected look about this place," observed Hallie as she stopped to sniff the fragrance of a delicate silvery-pink rose. To her delight, she had discovered the rose garden her second day at the house and had since adopted it as her own secret haven.

She loved the overgrown splendor of the garden, with its riotous colors blooming in every imaginable shade of pink, red, yellow, and white, for unlike the people who occupied the house, the roses burst forth with exuberant joy. In untamed glory the flowers had thrived until they embraced every inch of the small area, twining around the arching bowers above her head, spilling over bushes, trees, and hedges, and snaking across the ground like a carpet created by fairies at a midsummer's night ball.

"It does look in need of tending," replied Davinia, peering at her aromatic surroundings thoughtfully. "Can't say I'm surprised, though. After all, this is Serena's garden—or was."

"I don't see what that has to do with anything." Hallie sniffed. "I swear, the rest of the grounds look as if the gardeners grovel on their hands and knees, and hand-trim each blade of grass individually. Why, I'm almost afraid to walk on the lawn for fear of damaging all that green perfection." Frowning, she bent down to pull a weed that was threatening to suffocate a miniature rosebush. "It seems to me those same gardeners could manage a simple task like pruning a few roses."

Davinia merely shrugged. "Probably. But they know better than to touch the garden without Jake or Serena's say-so."

She took out her rumpled, slightly grubby handkerchief and scrubbed at a stone bench which had been placed in a small bower. After pausing for a moment to squint through her glasses, she deemed the seat clean and, with a sigh of foot-weary relief, plopped down. Smiling at her companion, who stood glaring at another patch of weeds as if her glance might wither them, Davinia thumped the space next to her in noisy invitation.

"You see, Hallie, Serena refused to entrust the care of a single petal of her precious roses to anyone except herself." Davinia pushed her beige silk skirts aside to make room for her friend. "Durn stubborn about it, too! Of course, when something was too heavy, too high up, or too dirty, she would simply look at Jake all helpless-like, and he would come running to do her bidding. Him, she trusted."

"Somehow, I have trouble picturing Jake Parrish grubbing around in the dirt," Hallie scoffed. Of course, knowing that man, he could probably have planted the entire garden single-handedly without mussing a hair, breaking a sweat, or wrinkling his clothes.

Davinia guffawed with unladylike volume. "Hell and damnation! I've seen Jake as dirty as a hog wrestler. Serena too, for that matter. I'll never forget finding the pair of them lollygagging in the dirt behind the hedge one afternoon. Judging from the streaks of mud running up the back of Serena's gown, I'd guess if I had happened along any sooner, we'd all have been sporting red faces."

She chuckled at the memory. Then she got that gleam in her eye that Hallie was beginning to identify as trouble. "Can't say as I would have objected to seeing Jake's bare fanny, though." She sighed remorsefully. "Bet he's got haunches like a thoroughbred racehorse—all sleek and muscular. Probably not hairy, either. Never could abide hairy buttocks."

Hallie rolled her eyes in exasperation. Lord! When Davinia got on one of her tangents, nothing short of divine intervention could get her off it. She idly wondered what Davinia would say if she knew that Hallie had recently come all too close to observing unclothed the portion of anatomy in question. Knowing Davinia, she probably would have been disappointed that Hallie hadn't examined him and given her a full report on his level of hairiness.

Hallie couldn't help laughing, and when she caught Davinia's questioning look, she quipped, "God save us from the evils of hairy backsides," and the small garden echoed with their raucous laughter.

"Lord! I've missed you!" Hallie exclaimed, giving Davinia a quick hug. "I can always count on you to lift my spirits."

"Spiritual enlightenment is my duty," stated Davinia, adding a wicked wink that completely negated her puritanical words.

"I don't know how I would have survived these last few weeks without the visits from Reverend DeYoung and you. Sometimes I get so lonely I could scream. Why, I almost miss Penelope and her scathing remarks."

The day after Jake and Penelope had joined Hallie for breakfast, Penelope had declared herself unable to tolerate the presence of "riffraff" in her home and had announced that she was going to stay with her sister in New York until after Hallie had left. Jake had merely shrugged and offered to drive her to the wharf.

Davinia rolled her eyes at the mention of Jake's sister. "Spoiled brat, that girl. Jake should have applied a switch to her backside far more frequently than he did. That boy is too durn softhearted where his sister is concerned."

"Perhaps he's just too busy to notice her bad behavior. Except for breakfast, and an occasional dinner, he's seldom home." And Hallie treasured those precious moments alone with Jake, when they dined companionably, discussing everything from his expansion plans in Panama City to her dreams for the infirmary. Never had she felt quite so comfortable, or attracted, to a man as she was to Jake Parrish.

Davinia patted her friend's arm. "Never fear. Marius and I will make sure you don't succumb to loneliness."

"He's so kind to keep Serena occupied while you fill me in on what's happening in the world outside this prison," Hallie replied. "Besides, she seems to enjoy his ministering."

"Of course she does. Why, those two used to be closer than sweat on a mule," Davinia remarked somewhat wryly. "Not only was Serena the head of the Wednesday

Afternoon Ladies' Mission Society, she never missed the Monday morning Chinese Relief Fund Committee meetings, Tuesday's Stitching Shirts for Saved Souls sewing circle, or Friday's Food for Foreign Friends fund-raising drive. And, of course, her Sunday churchgoing record was sterling. Never missed a single one of Marius DeYoung's inspirational sermons. Spent a lot of time at that big parish house of his, too. Transcribing notes for him, or some such nonsense."

Not only had the woman been rich, beautiful, and charming, thought Hallie dismally, *she had been a veritable saint as well.* And she said as much to Davinia.

Davinia chuckled at that idea. "A saint? Hardly!" she snickered. "When she and Jake were first married, why, you had never seen a bigger pair of heathens. Never attended church once in their first two years together. When I would take Jake to task on the state of his soul, the handsome devil would smile that angelic smile of his, and say how he and his wife had their own way of finding heaven on the Sabbath. Of course, Serena would turn bright red and get all calf-eyed over that mention, leaving little doubt as to the kind of worshiping they really did."

Breathlessly Hallie recalled the way Jake's body had felt pressed against hers. She had to admit that the feelings he'd incited in her had come pretty darn close to her idea of a religious experience, tempting her with a little taste of paradise as surely as the biblical snake had tempted Eve with that apple. How she had longed to taste the sweetness of the forbidden fruit and find her Eden in Jake Parrish's arms! For a moment, Hallie found herself jealous of what Serena had once had. She wondered what it would be like to be so cherished by a man like Jake.

Almost as if she'd read Hallie's mind, Davinia remarked, "Every flower in this garden is a gift from Jake to his wife. He had the captains of his ships comb their exotic ports of call for new and rare species of roses."

Davinia reached out to pluck an odd, pale green bloom and presented it to Hallie. "This one came from the garden of the Emperor of China. The pink damask you were admiring earlier started as a cutting taken from a bush adorning the final resting place of Mumtaz Mahal. Of course, everyone knows that the Taj Mahal was built by her grief-stricken husband as a loving memorial, and what could be more romantic than a rose from such a place?"

"I never took Jake to be a fanciful character," Hallie murmured, a trace of wonder shading her voice.

"That's because you didn't know him before the war. You should have seen the way the ladies sighed over his daring exploits. I heard he almost spent time cooling his heels in an Indian jail over the Taj Mahal escapade. Fortunately, he was saved by his sister, Anne. Never met the girl myself, but I've heard that she's married to some bigwig official of the British Crown and, as luck would have it, her husband happened to be serving in India at the time of the, ah, incident."

Davinia shuddered as she fixed Hallie with a look of horrified fascination. "That boy was damn lucky, if you ask me. *Damn lucky!* I'd hate to think of what might have happened to him otherwise. One hears such lurid stories about those foreign infidels. Nothing more than a pack of godless *sodomites* in those awful jails!" She waved at Marius DeYoung, watching as the man strolled across the lawn with Serena.

Hallie smiled at Serena, who had caught sight of her and was racing across the lawn like a puppy overjoyed at the return of a long-absent master. Dressed in a frilly gown of white muslin, with her hair tied back artlessly in a blue satin ribbon, Serena was the very picture of childlike innocence. She came skidding to a halt in front of Hallie, nervously sucking on her left fist and staring around her with wide eyes. An old, parian-headed doll with a crack snaking across its face was clutched in her right hand.

"Did you have a nice visit, Serena?" Hallie inquired, reaching out to pull the woman toward her.

Serena gave a vague nod of assent and then sank to the ground to sit at Hallie's feet. With her knees in the air and her legs apart, she appeared to be completely indifferent to the fact that she was exposing far more undergarment than was decent. She was so involved with crooning to her doll that she didn't appear to notice when Hallie bent forward to rearrange her skirts in a more modest fashion.

Watching as Serena wrapped an expensive cashmere shawl around the doll, Hallie wondered, not for the first time, where her charge had found the filthy, battered toy.

The doll was truly hideous to behold, with bulbous glass eyes and a smirking, garishly painted mouth that was open to display a set of rather alarming ivory teeth. To add further to its bizarre appearance, the wig had been lost, leaving the top of its hollow head gaping open.

Yet in Serena's warped mind, she had somehow identified the doll as her baby, and she treated the sawdust-stuffed figure to her own confused brand of mothering. Hallie had caught her watching the wet nurse and herself with guarded interest as they tended the infant, though she never attempted to make contact with her child. No, she seemed to content herself with observing and imitating, using her delicate handkerchiefs as diapers, and forcing milk into the doll's open mouth. Which reminded her . . .

Hallie wrinkled her nose with disgust. Serena's "baby" was beginning to smell worse than the milking room floor at a dairy farm on a hot day. The odor of souring milk had permeated the sawdust-stuffed kidskin body of the doll, with nauseating results.

Perhaps a lesson in the fundamentals of infant hygiene would help, she mused, glancing back down at her charge thoughtfully.

Her eyes widened with dismay as she saw Serena fumbling with the hooks at the front of her bodice. Oh, Lord! Serena had been watching the wet nurse suckle the baby again and was apparently about to try it on her doll.

"Uh, Serena, don't you think your baby would prefer a nice sugar teat?" Hallie suggested, relieved that Marius DeYoung was still far enough away not to have caught the exchange.

Serena looked up at her companion solemnly and then back down at the bundle in her arms. She raised the doll to her ear, pausing to listen to an imaginary voice. With a sigh, she nodded her assent to Hallie and lovingly kissed the doll's ugly parian face.

"Now there's a face only a mother could love," commented Davinia, as she glanced down at the monstrosity cradled in Serena's arms.

"I think she takes after her father," the woman replied pensively, holding the doll up for Davinia's closer examination. "What do you think?"

Hallie and Davinia exchanged glances, perplexed.

With a shrug, Davinia agreed, "Well, I have seen Jake bare his teeth like that a few times. Especially when I've suggested that he improve on his church attendance record."

Serena just stared at the woman blankly.

"How did you do today, Marius?" inquired Davinia, looking up as the man came to a stop in front of her.

He cast an approving glance in Serena's direction. "Quite well. We took tea and I gave Serena an uplifting lesson on the importance of returning to the path of righteousness from which she has strayed." Reverend DeYoung turned his penetrating gaze on Serena. "Tell them what you learned, my child."

Serena looked up at him and promptly jammed her fist back in her mouth, making frantic sucking noises.

"Serena? I'm waiting," he commanded in a sonorous yet firm tone, his well-favored face now starkly forbidding.

Marius DeYoung prided himself on the rich, almost seductive beauty of his voice. It was that, and his theatrical flare, that packed the pews at the Ascension Tabernacle every Sunday. He had occasionally reflected that if God hadn't blessed him by setting him on the path of righteousness, he might have made quite a name for himself on the stage. Not that he often indulged in such thoughts, for to do so was vain, and vanity was a sin of such magnitude that it required him to serve penance of daunting severity.

Marius frowned at the woman on the ground. "Well?"

Suddenly Serena dropped her hand from her lips, and a jumble of words rushed out. "I will obey God's word as instructed by Reverend DeYoung, pray for His forgiveness for my terrible sin in attempting wanton self-destruction, and—" She broke off with a desperate little gasp, staring at Marius helplessly.

"And you will—? What else will you do?" he prompted, kneeling next to her and forcing her to meet his unblinking stare.

She gulped convulsively and then broke into a giddy little laugh. "Oh! I remember now! Cleanse my mind by thinking pure thoughts and turn my idle hands to doing good works."

Serena cocked her head to one side, waiting for him to express his approval, but he just continued to look at her with that stony expression.

Her smile faded. "D-d-did I forget s-something?" she asked haltingly, feeling somewhat alarmed. She so hated disappointing Reverend DeYoung.

Then he broke into a smile, beaming at her like the sun upon Noah's ark after forty days of rain, and Serena sighed with relief. She hadn't failed him. No, not this time. She was glad, for she couldn't bear it when she displeased him.

Hallie observed the exchange uncomfortably. Although she attended church faithfully and tried to do the right thing, she wasn't altogether sure that she approved of such religious zeal. Especially where her patient was concerned. Hallie studied Marius for a moment.

He was an attractive man in his late thirties, with a halo of fair curls and deep blue eyes. Although he was of only average height, there was something about him that commanded attention, making him seem larger than life. And he had a way about him that seemed to inspire trust in people. Why, just look at the easy way Serena was babbling to him, even going so far as to tug at his sleeve in her excitement. It was a miracle, considering Serena's apparent distaste for men.

Hallie sighed with resignation. So the man was a bit of a zealot. What did she know about that, anyway? Reverend DeYoung was a friend of the Parrishes' and had been ministering to them for years. Undoubtedly he knew what he was about, for Serena always seemed much calmer after his visits.

Serena abruptly cut into Hallie's thoughts as she began to hum and then burst out chanting in a loud, singsong voice. "There was a crooked man, who walked a crooked mile—"

Hallie jerked her head to follow Serena's gaze. She saw Jake freeze in his tracks and stare coldly at his wife.

Rising to her knees, Serena jabbed her finger in his direction, repeating, "There was a crooked man, who walked a crooked mile—Gimpy Jake! Gimpy Jake!"

"Hush, Serena," chided Hallie, giving Jake an apologetic smile. "You're being unkind, and I'm sure Reverend DeYoung doesn't approve of such behavior any more than I do."

Serena narrowed her eyes, considering Hallie's words and studying Jake as he paused briefly to shake hands with Marius.

"Reverend DeYoung taught me that lying is a sin," Serena replied with a crafty half-smile. "And the truth is, my husband is an impotent gimp."

"Serena!" chorused Hallie, Marius, and Davinia in embarrassed unison. Only Jake remained silent, simply returning his wife's gaze, his face set in rigid lines.

But Serena ignored them all. She bobbed her head up and down, smirking cruelly. "Not a man—Jake. Couldn't rise for me, couldn't be a man. Nothing but a pathetic cripple."

With that taunt, Hallie had heard enough. Roughly, she jerked Serena to her feet and gave the woman a shake that made her teeth clatter. Pulling her charge close enough to whisper in her ear, Hallie warned, "You will cease this disgraceful behavior now. Do you hear me, Serena?" She administered another sharp shake. "I refuse to tolerate such misconduct, and if you can't behave like a lady, I'll be forced to confine you to your room. Do I make myself clear?"

Serena stared at Hallie uncomprehendingly for a second, almost if she wasn't quite sure what she had done wrong. Then, she nodded slowly.

"Good. I—" But Hallie had lost Serena's attention again.

With a crow of delight, the woman spied her abandoned doll, which was lying at their feet in a grotesque sprawl. Swooping down, she seized the toy and fiercely hugged it to her breast, acting as if nothing out of the ordinary had happened.

Hallie glared warningly at Serena for several seconds, but the woman was blithely unaware of her displeasure. Sighing with exasperation, she glanced up at Jake and was relieved to see that he had apparently chosen to ignore the whole incident.

With quiet dignity, he took Davinia's hand in his and murmured something that made her smile. Then he shook Marius's hand, once again speaking in a low voice. Marius nodded and clapped Jake on the back jovially. Without further comment, Jake swung around and began to make his way across the lawn, completely ignoring Hallie and Serena.

As Hallie watched him leave, she noted that even with his painfully awkward gait, he somehow managed to look formidable. Everything about Jake Parrish proclaimed him a success, a man to be reckoned with, the Young Midas. But it wasn't his air of decisiveness or the quiet strength that surrounded him like a warrior's armor that struck her so forcefully—it was the ruined grace of his movements.

Hallie's breath caught in her throat as she felt a strange sense of loss. Once upon a time, Jake Parrish must have run with the fluid beauty of a racehorse and danced as lightly as a fallen leaf on an October wind. She could still see vestiges of his once elegant carriage in the ungainly motion of his retreating figure. Yet, though he walked as straight as a general in a victory parade, there was something self-conscious about the proud set of his shoulders that tugged at her heart.

"Davinia, would you . . . ?" Hallie nodded toward Serena.

Davinia smiled with understanding and nodded her assent.

Muttering a hasty excuse to Reverend DeYoung, Hallie rushed after Jake.

"Jake?"

He made no sign of acknowledgment as she moved to his side.

"I'm sorry. I had no idea your wife would behave in such an appalling manner."

Still, he gave no response to indicate that he had heard her apology.

"Please," Hallie entreated again, hating the grim look that masked his features. "She didn't understand what she was saying. I know she didn't mean it."

Jake stopped abruptly and stared into her face, his eyes narrowing in a way that made Hallie curl her toes uncomfortably. When he finally answered, his voice was soft. Dangerously soft.

"Good try, Doctor. But we both know Serena understood exactly what she was saying, and she meant every damn word of it."

Hallie clutched at his arm desperately, wanting nothing more than to find the words that would melt the wall of ice that had frozen up between them. "Davinia and Marius know how Serena can be. I'm sure they took her words for the nonsense they were."

His gaze slid from hers to stare pointedly at her restraining hand on his arm and then back up into her eyes. With his face utterly devoid of emotion, he turned away.

Wordlessly she dropped her hand to her side.

"Jake."

He paused, but didn't look back.

"I promise it won't happen again," she whispered brokenly, sensing the depth of his anger and humiliation, yet at a loss as to how to help him.

At that he turned, his face darkly sardonic. He even smiled, but in an awful, humorless way.

"You can be sure as hell of that, Doctor Gardiner," he snapped in an uncompromising tone. "I intend to see that it never happens again!"

It would never happen again, he vowed to himself, standing motionless in the shadowy rose garden bower. *Never again would she make her vile accusations. Never again would she remind him of his failure as a man.*

He drew in a hissing breath as the disturbing scene from the previous afternoon flashed through his mind. For the first time since her suicide attempt, Serena had shown signs of rousing from her witless state. True, her lucidity had lasted only a few moments, but in that brief instant she had remembered the very things he'd prayed she would forget.

Like a vicious, half-witted child, she had taunted him with those memories—memories damaging enough to strip away his proud facade and expose the vile weakness he had fought so hard to conceal, memories that could ruin his reputation as a community leader.

He clenched his hands into fists, digging his fingernails painfully into his palms. To his shame, she had remembered every depraved detail of their sexual exploits, laughing as she reminded him of his humiliating inability to satisfy his carnal urges in the conventional manner.

Uttering a tortured moan, he dug his nails deeper. But Serena had known how to take care of his special needs. She had been talented in ways that would have shocked polite society to its shallow core. Just thinking of the way she had pleasured him made him harden with rampant lust.

Sobbing raggedly, he unclenched his fists and snaked his hand down to touch the source of his shame. The ache was more than he could bear.

God help him! How he hated his uncontrollable urges. Loathed them with a vehemence that burned like a fever in his soul. They clouded his mind and possessed his body, driving him to perform acts of unspeakable degradation.

Tears of remorse rolled down his cheeks as he succumbed to the carnal urging of his flesh. As much as he detested himself for his pathetic actions, he was powerless to cease them.

Just as he tottered on the brink of release, he heard Serena approach. In a whisper of fine silk, she appeared, the hem of her diaphanous nightgown trailing behind her like a bridal veil. She was carrying her ugly doll, and she was humming in that strange, toneless way he'd always found so unnerving.

His hand stilled. So he had been right—she was regaining her senses. Just the fact that she had remembered to meet him this morning bore out his suspicions. It also meant she had become a danger to him.

It was time to silence Serena once and for all.

Smiling with a thrill greater than any he'd ever experienced between a woman's thighs, he yanked his hand out of his trousers.

It was all Serena's fault, his disgraceful lapse of control. It was the bitch's inflammatory reminders of his weakness that had driven him to these shameful new depths.

Mentally cursing the woman before him, he stepped out of the concealing shadows of the bower. *It would never happen again.*

Forcing a welcoming smile to his lips, he softly called her name.

She started at the sound of his voice, and when she whirled around to face him, her features were rigid with wariness. To his sardonic glee, she was trembling.

Yet despite her apparent apprehension, she had worn the glove. That well-worn glove, made of red silk and adorned with glittering mock-diamond buttons, was proof positive that she remembered.

He nodded once.

She relaxed visibly and spared him a tiny smile.

Slowly he held out his arms, his deceptively tender gaze coaxing her into the deadly trap of his embrace.

Like a lamb to the slaughter, she followed his lead.

Hallie had always loved this time of day best, when the rising sun peeked into her windows and beckoned her to enjoy its peace, half promising and half teasing her with the unhatched secrets of the coming day.

Like a cat on sun-warmed pavement, she stretched, thoroughly enjoying the luxury of the silence. Serena was an early riser, and it was seldom that she allowed her companion a few private moments before beginning her barrage of ceaseless demands.

Hallie frowned to herself. *Where was Serena, anyway?* She reached for her watch pin and peered at the time. *Five-forty.* Her charge had usually awakened her by now.

Shrugging one shoulder, she returned her watch to the bedside table. It was little wonder that Serena was late in rising this morning; she had been unusually restless the night before.

Restless? Hallie snickered at her own understatement. "Combative" would be a more accurate description of Serena's behavior. Not only had she refused to eat her supper and take a bath, she'd thrown a terrible temper tantrum when Hallie had tried to put her to bed. It had been a long night for everyone in the house. After all, when Serena didn't sleep, nobody slept.

Hallie flopped back down against the mattress and pulled the blankets up over her head to shut out the light. Well, it was fine with her if her patient wanted to be a lazybones. She buried her face in her pillow and closed her eyes. She could certainly use an hour or two of extra sleep herself.

Yet, for all her exhaustion, Hallie couldn't fall asleep again. Her patient's hysterical behavior the night before had left her with an uneasy feeling. She had never known Serena to throw a tantrum without reason . . . as silly or slight as those reasons might be, and Serena had certainly never been shy about voicing her complaints.

Until last night. The woman had been positively taciturn when questioned about her discontent. And try as she might, Hallie had been unable to figure out what had provoked Serena's violent outburst.

Wide awake now, Hallie shoved the covers away from her face and squinted into the blinding morning light. She replayed the previous day's events over and over again in her mind, but to no avail. Aside from the disconcerting scene in the garden, the day had passed pleasantly enough. There had even been moments during the afternoon when Serena had appeared rational and had conversed in a coherent manner. To Hallie's satisfaction, her patient had been experiencing more and more such episodes of lucidity lately.

No. There was absolutely no explanation for Serena's hysteria. And as a doctor Hallie had learned to be wary of anything that couldn't be explained away by science or logic.

With that troubling thought in mind, she propped herself up on her elbows and listened for sounds of stirring on the other side of the connecting door.

There was only silence.

Hallie sighed. Perhaps she should check on Serena . . . just to make sure she was all right. Not that anything could possibly be wrong, she added to herself hastily, sliding from her bed.

After pulling a worn yellow-print wrapper over her

voluminous nightgown, she crept to the door. Carefully, she eased it open, a frown creasing her forehead as the hinges made a low squeal of protest. The last thing she wanted was to disturb her patient's slumber.

As covertly as a child intent on catching Santa stuffing her stocking on Christmas Eve, she slipped through the door. Only a faint shaft of pale morning light spilled around the edges of the drapes, forcing her to blink several times to adjust her eyes to the semidarkness of the room.

After several moments her gaze found the bed, and she cautiously tiptoed toward her patient. As she came to a stop next to the bed, she narrowed her eyes slightly, trying to make out the woman's tiny form beneath the enormous mound of blankets.

Not a skein of hair nor an inch of frilly gown spilled from the warm-looking cocoon. But that didn't surprise Hallie, for the night had been cold and Serena so hated the damp chill of the San Francisco fog that it had become her habit to sleep tightly curled beneath her covers. Hallie paused to draw a deep breath. Then she carefully lifted the edge of the blankets.

The bed was empty.

"Serena?" Hallie whispered, ripping back the blankets to confirm her fears. The woman was truly gone.

She called Serena again, this time more insistently, as she went to check the necessary room.

No one was there.

Growing breathless with alarm, her heart drumming with hectic percussion, she tried the bedroom door.

It was still locked, just like it had been the night before. Her hand flew to her throat, searching for the narrow length of red ribbon that held the key to the lock; desperately hoping, but not really expecting to find it still in place.

It was gone.

Double damn! Serena had somehow managed to steal the key while her keeper slept and had escaped, slyly locking the door behind her. The jailer was now the prisoner.

With fear blossoming into a full-blown case of panic, Hallie hurled herself against the door in a frenzy, shouting for help. Over and over again she struck, flesh against wood, until the pain from the repeated impact began to fade into numbness. The din in the small room was deafening, and she prayed the noise would be loud enough to bring somebody with the liberating key.

Just when Hallie was sure she would collapse from exhaustion, she heard a rattling at the lock.

"Lawdy! Ain't neva heard such a ruckus in all my born days!" It was Mammy Celine braced in the hall, staring at Hallie with round shoe-button eyes.

Hallie grasped the woman's arm with urgency. "Celine! Have you seen Serena!"

"Ain't seen no one, 'cepts you." She frowned fiercely as the meaning of Hallie's words sank in. "You be tellin' me Miz Parrish be lost?"

"Not lost. I'm sure she hasn't gone far."

Celine nodded. "Miz Parrish nivver leaves the house 'fore she drunk her mornin' chocolate. I 'member when—"

But Hallie didn't stop to listen. She was already halfway down the hall, her bare feet flapping against the wooden floor as she ran toward the stairs.

"Celine!" she shouted over her shoulder. "You search the house. I'll look outside." She didn't wait for a reply but ran through the maze of hallways, bounding down the back stairs and out the servants' door. She stopped just outside, panting. Clutching at the stitch in her side, she caught her breath in ragged heaves, remaining motionless until the burning in her lungs had subsided.

Still struggling for air, Hallie resumed her search. Calling Serena's name, she anxiously scanned the lawn. But her only reply was the whisper of the eucalyptus trees as they awakened to the caress of an early-morning breeze.

"Serena!" With a sickening rush of horror wrenching at her belly, an awful possibility entered Hallie's mind: what if Serena had somehow managed to escape the grounds and was now wandering the streets in her filmy nightclothes? Hallie shuddered convulsively. The consequences would be unthinkable.

"Serena!" she screamed, skirting the wall-like hedges of the rose garden. In her haste, she slipped on the dewy grass and tumbled heavily to the ground. She quickly bounded to her feet, barely noticing the dampness soaking her robe or the grass stains marring her white gown. As she entered beneath the flowering arch of the garden, she stopped short, sobbing her relief.

"Oh, Jake!" she expelled, overjoyed to see the figure crouching in front of the same bower where she had sat with Davinia. Except for a slight tensing of his broad shoulders, he didn't move at the sound of her voice.

"Jake?" She paused for a moment, staring at the oddness of his rough apparel. His ragged trousers were tucked into tall, badly scuffed boots, and his ancient seaman's sweater looked as if it had seen one voyage too many.

"Jake?" she repeated, her brow furrowing with concern when he didn't look up or respond to her anxious query. Hallie moved closer until she stood a few feet behind him. It was then that she saw Serena's prone figure.

As a sharp cry issued from her lips, Jake's hands flinched away from where they had been resting at his wife's throat and dropped limply to his sides.

Hallie fell to her knees next to him, staring numbly at the figure sprawled in front of them. With her nightgown half torn from her body, Serena lay at an oddly twisted angle, her pallid limbs obscenely exposed. Like blood on ivory, a tattered scarlet glove covered her outstretched left hand, its faux diamond buttons sparkling with obscene gaiety in the early-morning sun.

The picture was made all the more macabre by the doll, whose face had been brutally shattered and whose body now lay in a grotesquely broken position that mimicked that of her owner.

With violently trembling hands, Hallie pushed aside the spun-silver cascade of hair that concealed Serena's face. She could only stare in horror at what had been hidden by the silken curtain. With a sob, she tore her gaze away. But even when she closed her eyes the tragic scene remained vivid, for in those few brief seconds, it had been indelibly etched in her mind.

Try as she might, Hallie couldn't escape the wide blue eyes as they stared sightlessly at the early-morning beauty of the roses; nor could she shut out the pearl-like skin that had once inspired a hundred toasts across two continents but was now stained an angry, mottled purple; or the mouth that should have been laughing with joy but was drawn back as if in a silent plea, a stream of spittle trailing unchecked from one corner.

But what haunted Hallie most was the memory of Jake's hands flexed against his estranged wife's viciously bruised throat; for like a damning witness, those strong palms and fingers presented irrefutable proof of his guilt. And as tears slowly rained down her cheeks, she knew in her grief-stricken heart that she could no longer deny the truth.

She, Hallie Gardiner, loved Jake Parrish, and, God help them both, he had just murdered his wife.

Chapter 9

"You think I killed her, don't you?"

So absolutely emotionless were his words that Hallie abruptly ceased her examination of Serena's lifeless figure to gape at Jake in bewilderment.

Dear Lord! How could the man ask the question so calmly when he knew she'd seen him with his hands on his wife's throat?

Jake waited for her reply, returning her stare as impassively as if he had just inquired whether she took milk or sugar in her tea.

"What am I supposed to believe?" she finally asked, wanting to look away yet unwilling to abandon her search for a trace of humanity in his glacial features.

But his face remained unreadable, and his narrowed eyes betrayed nothing as he grated, "What, indeed? You come upon me kneeling in the garden with my hands on my wife's neck, and she happens to be dead. Strangled, to be exact. It doesn't take much imagination to know what's running through your head." His mouth twisted coldly. "Or could it be that you're one of those rare creatures: a woman with an open mind?"

"I don't know what to think . . . or feel," was Hallie's simple yet honest reply. Her head was prompting her to run for the police as fast as her feet could carry her, screaming *Murderer!* as she fled. But her heart beat with a hope for his innocence that was so strong it begged her to remain by his side and learn the truth.

And for the first time in her life, Hallie Gardiner's heart ruled her head.

"Jake?" She reached out to grasp his arm lightly. "Did you kill her?" She could feel his muscles tense beneath her hand, but she felt no fear at the evidence of his superior strength. There was a heavy silence as his eyes bored into hers.

"No."

And as Hallie penetrated the smoky depths of that stark gaze, all her doubts melted away. Without uttering a single word, he conveyed his feelings with an eloquence that moved her almost to tears. Mutely, he confessed his anguish for failing the woman he had once so desperately loved; tearlessly, he wept for the life he had wanted to share but couldn't; and tragically, he mourned the death of all his youthful dreams, now buried forever and marked only with single-word epitaphs: Love, Hope, and Promise.

Hallie drew in a sobbing breath and nodded.

"You believe me?" His tone was blandly curious, yet every line of his face seemed to beg her to trust in him.

"Yes," she replied in a broken whisper.

Jake stared hypnotically into her golden eyes as he reached out and lightly stroked the delicate line of her collarbone. Grimly he probed those tawny depths, searching for a betraying shadow of fear that would give lie to her avowed faith in him. With slow deliberation, he traced the base of her throat, his strong hands growing gentle as they lingered over the area where her pulse throbbed with warm vitality.

And though his compelling gaze dared her to flinch from his touch, Hallie returned his stare calmly. In acknowledgment to his challenge, she arched her head back and presented him with the vulnerable length of her neck. He hesitated for a moment, and then one corner of his mouth curled up in a half-smile at her display of trust.

"Good," he murmured, sliding his fingers up from her throat to push an errant curl off her cheek. "I'm glad you believe me."

"Does it matter?"

"Yes."

Jake seemed about to speak again, but then shook his head as if reconsidering his words, and released her with a sigh. Turning to his wife's prone figure, he gently arranged the remnant of her shredded garments over her naked limbs. He paused to run his fingers over the bare, bruised length of her arm, stopping to lift her fisted hand

and study the torn, broken nails. Very carefully, he pried open the clenched fingers.

"What is it?" Hallie asked, staring at the object in Serena's hand. It was a slightly misshapen, dark brown object that looked for all the world like a rotten pea.

Jake lifted it to his nose and sniffed. Then he let out a snort of disgust. "Raw opium." He examined the narcotic for a moment before handing it to Hallie.

She turned the tiny ball over in her palm curiously. In her practice Hallie had often dissolved fine brown opium granules in alcohol to formulate simple tinctures. She knew it to be useful in the treatment of myriad ailments, ranging from simple coughs to chronic diarrhea. But never had she seen it in its pure, crude form.

"Not much of a bargain when it costs you your life," Jake murmured, taking the drug from Hallie's hand and jamming it deep into his pocket. Then he glanced back down at Serena's distorted face, this time forcing himself to really look at her.

He wanted to remember something wonderful; how she had once smiled up him, or the way she had sucked on her lower lip as she plotted her amorous assaults on his willing body. Anything to shut out the horror of what she had become, and the senseless brutality of her death.

But all the gentle memories eluded him, leaving only the bitter ones. One by one, those tormenting scenes burned into his brain, searing images that festered like the wounds of a dying man.

Then, somewhere at the edge of his mind, he heard the joyful music of Serena's laughter. The demons of the past shrieked their protests at the jubilant assault as they were forced to retreat and were, at last, banished back into the private hell of Jake's soul. But before he could fill his heart with the warmth of the laughter it, too, faded, leaving him wretchedly empty.

As Jake shook his head to clear his thoughts, his gaze was captured by the glint of the early-morning sun on Serena's hair. The sun-kissed mane pooled beneath her head to form a shining halo, the length of it floating across the grass like the streak from a fallen star.

His hands hovered over it for a moment and then, with a tortured groan, he buried his fingers in the tangled softness. Closing his eyes, he caressed a thick curl, painfully trying to memorize the smooth texture.

It was the familiarity of that motion which served to spring the floodgate of his mind.

Out spilled a torrent of memories that forcefully recalled happier times—times when he had awakened in the darkness of the night to find himself caught in the gossamer web of that hair, times he had tucked Serena securely between his thighs to brush the moonlit tresses, smiling as she whispered her bright dreams for their future together.

As each picture flashed by, he bade it a sad farewell. What wrenched him most was the knowledge that he was saying his final good-bye to the love he had once thought to cherish forever yet had lost so long ago.

Hallie gently squeezed his shoulder, trying to tell him in her own mute way that she understood his inner conflict and the raw pain of his emotions. Not that he had in any way revealed his feelings.

He hadn't. His face remained stonily impassive.

Yet she recognized his rigid, almost cold expression, for it was the same one she had seen reflected in the mirror the day she had learned of her mother's death.

Her mother—poor, sweet, plain Georgianna; the only person in the world who had ever cared about Hallie. Together, she and Hallie had battled the loneliness forced upon them by the tyrannical Ambrose Gardiner and had withstood his cruelty only through the support of each other's love.

Hallie clenched her fists at the thought of her father. She hated the man, and though Marius DeYoung had preached a sermon just last Sunday on the sin of hate, Hallie thought that somehow God understood her feelings. Surely he knew how impossible it was for her to love the man who had robbed her of her home, her inheritance, and everything else that had been her life?

Her heart twisted with sympathy as she scrutinized Jake's beautifully hewn profile. Yes, she understood all too well what lay beneath that carefully composed facade.

Jake let the tendril of Serena's hair float to the ground, glancing up as he felt Hallie move near. With her face softened by compassion and her eyes warm with tenderness, she had been transformed into a being of unearthly splendor. She glowed with the rare kind of beauty that transcended the superficiality of flesh, one that came from a generosity of spirit and a goodness of heart, mirroring the true essence of the woman within.

For a long moment, they were held captive by the unspoken emotions reflected in each other's eyes. When she abruptly pulled him into her embrace, crooning to him as if he were a wounded child, he tensed slightly with surprise, and then surrendered against the warmth of her breast.

Gently she cradled him, laying her cheek against the sable softness of his hair. She rocked back and forth, lightly stroking his back, whispering words of comfort as much for her own sake as for his. When she ran out of words, she simply held him. And they seemed frozen in time as they silently shared their grief.

At last Jake eased himself out of Hallie's embrace and studied her tearstained face. Softly he grazed his knuckles across her cheek, wiping away the runnels of sorrow. When they were instantly replaced with fresh droplets, he smiled tenderly and folded her in his arms. Large, gasping sobs were torn from her chest as she clung to his broad shoulders, weeping into his time-softened sweater.

"Did you care for her so much, little Mission Lady?" he whispered, lightly kneading her heaving back.

Hallie nodded as she relaxed beneath his soothing ministrations; soon her violent sobs were reduced to sighing hiccups. "I often thought—*hiccup*—had I known Serena before—well, you know—before, that we might have—*hiccup*—been friends. Sometimes, during her lucid moments, we laughed together and discussed all those things women find so—*hiccup*—interesting. I've never had a close friend. It made me realize how wonderful it could be."

Jake looked down at her with surprise. Hallie had always seemed like such a busy and contented little soul. Never in a million years would he have suspected her loneliness. Impulsively he gave her a quick hug. "Serena was very fond of you in her own way, and I suspect you two would have become as thick as thieves had circumstances been different. I know she would have been honored to be your friend. Anyone would."

With a soft hiccup, Hallie shook her head. "I've never been very good at making friends."

"Mission Lady, there's nothing I'd like more than to be counted as your friend."

"Truly?" Hallie searched his face anxiously, half fearing that he was jesting, yet desperately wanting to believe his words.

Jake felt his heart skip a beat at the unguarded need in her expression. He smiled his tender reassurance. "Truly."

Her answering smile was so eager, so filled with gratitude, that he couldn't stop himself from tightening his arms around her protectively. What kind of a life had this poor creature led, that it took so little to please her? Irrationally, he found himself growing angry at the world that had deprived her of such basic pleasures as friendship. Well, he would be her friend—the best of friends—and make damn sure she never forgot it.

"Jake?" Hallie rested her chin against his chest to peer into his face, her eyes troubled.

"Yes, friend?"

Her lips twitched at his teasing tone, but her expression remained serious as she asked, "Who do you think killed Serena?"

"I don't know. I've turned that question over and over again in my head."

"I can't imagine who would want to kill a frail, confused woman like Serena. Or why, for that matter."

Jake stared unseeing into the distance and then shrugged. "I'm sure that in the course of her addiction, she came in contact with any number of unsavory characters. I think it's safe to assume that whoever killed her had something to do with the opium. As for why?" He paused for a moment before answering her second question. "What could be more dangerous than being at the mercy of a madwoman? I imagine someone was afraid she would inadvertently reveal his identity. However, I—"

"Dear God! Serena!"

Hallie and Jake jerked apart at the sound of the soul-shattering wail to gape up at Cyrus King, who was standing just over their shoulders. So involved were they in their conversation that they hadn't noticed his approach.

"My baby. My sweet, darling baby." Dropping to his knees, Cyrus pulled his daughter's lifeless body into his arms.

As he hugged Serena to his chest, her head lolled back at a peculiar angle and a trickle of dark liquid oozed from her mouth to stain her chin. As he rocked her, her head bobbed limply from side to side, looking grotesquely as if she were keeping time to the endless tempo of Death's lonely dirge. Futilely, Cyrus whispered against her hair, lightly patting her back, much like he had done when she was eight years old and had been ill with scarlet fever. As he crooned, his tears rained in a steady stream, the dampness falling in large droplets onto Serena's face and continuing its course down her cheeks, almost as if she wept with him. "My poor, poor baby. Serena."

Hallie was overcome with a rush of pity. That a father could so love his daughter was an alien idea to her, and her tears were as much for what she had never known as for the tragedy unfolding before her. Sobbing, she moved forward, feeling compelled to offer her sympathy. But Jake gripped her shoulder to stop her, shaking his head in warning.

It was Jake who finally placed his hand on Cyrus's twitching shoulder. "King—"

"Damn you to hell, Parrish!" Cyrus jerked his head back to glare at his son-in-law. "Have you no decency at all, making love to your whore over the barely cold body of my daughter?" He swung his enraged gaze to Hallie. "How does it feel, knowing your lover is a murderer?" He smiled malevolently as she flinched from his words. "They hang murderers, you know. Ever see a man hung before?"

Hallie let out a strangled sob and refused to meet Cyrus's glittering, tear-reddened gaze. When she didn't answer, he made a sound under his breath that made her think of a snake moving through dry underbrush. Then he chuckled horribly.

"Enough, King!" Jake roared, feeling the impulse to throttle the man for further adding to Hallie's distress.

But Cyrus disregarded the warning in Jake's tone. As he laid Serena's body on the grass, pausing to caress the bruises at her throat, he taunted, "No? Ah, well, it's quite a sight. Sometimes the poor bastards lose control and spill their seed when their necks snap." He cocked his head to one side, studying Hallie's ashen face with satisfaction. "I wonder, will you cry when you see that happen to your lover? Will you lie cold in the night, aching for his touch? Will you wish you were dead, because he is no longer beside you?"

Jake grabbed the front of Cyrus's shirt, hauling him close until they were face to face. Nauseatingly, Jake could smell the stench of stale, garlic-laced sweat and cheap gin emanating from the other man. But he ignored the rank odors and pressed his face nearer as he commanded, "That's enough, King! This is between you and me! Do you understand? *You and me!*"

Cyrus shook himself free from Jake's grip, his eyes narrowing with suspicion as he glanced at Hallie. Moving back a few feet, well out of Jake's reach, he scoffed, "Really? How do I know that in her eagerness for your paltry lovemaking she didn't help you carry out your vile plot?"

"You know damn well that she had nothing to do with this," growled Jake, balling his fists in a threatening fashion.

Cyrus was unfazed by the menace in his son-in-law's voice.

Narrowing his eyes at the man, Jake hissed, "What I want to know is, what are you doing here, and at this time of the morning? Must I remind you that I could have you arrested for trespassing?"

Cyrus threw Jake a look of unadulterated hate. "I've been watching the house for months now . . . plotting to take my baby from you once and for all." His lips contorted into a sneer. "It would have been an easy piece of work. I've learned that your houseboy unlocks the back door at six-thirty every morning and that the day servants don't start arriving until seven. I've also discovered that the hallways are quite deserted until that time. I intended to sneak through the back door and whisk Serena away before anyone noticed."

Jake snorted. "It's entirely possible that she wouldn't have recognized you, given her mental state. Just what did you intend to do if she cried out in surprise at your unorthodox appearance, and roused either myself or Dr. Gardiner?"

Cyrus chuckled. "Oh, I would have dealt with the two of you." He pulled aside his coat and whipped out a finely wrought pistol. Steadily, he trained it at Jake's head. "Handy little item, a gun. Useful in persuading even the most stubborn of bastards to see things my way."

"And if I hadn't been in the frame of mind to be *persuaded,* you would have just shot me?"

"With pleasure. Perhaps I should kill you now and save everyone a lot of trouble. I doubt anyone will object to a father serving justice to the man who killed his daughter."

He shook his head, an evil smile twisting his lips. "No. It would hardly be justice enough to let you die so easily." Cyrus lowered the gun until it was pointed squarely at Jake's belly. "While a shot in the head assures a quick death, a gut full of lead makes for a slow, excruciating, *entertaining* one. I want to watch you suffer, Parrish, to see you writhe at my feet in agony as you beg me to finish you off. Even your little doctor friend won't be able to save you once your bowels are blasted full of holes."

Hallie gasped with horror at Cyrus's threats. *Dear Lord! The man was serious! She couldn't just stand by while he murdered Jake in cold blood. If anything were to happen to Jake— No! The thought was simply too terrible to contemplate.* Hallie made a move toward the men, desperate to be near Jake, but he warned her back with a shake of his head.

"And what gives you the right to dispense justice?" Jake stared at Cyrus intently for a moment before he continued, "Isn't it Judge Dorner's job to see me hung? Or do you want to shoot me now and dangle in my place when you're found guilty of killing an innocent man? I'd consider carefully, King. Do you really think you can get away with shooting a man of my stature and have no one bother to investigate the matter?"

Cyrus's finger twitched on the trigger as he struggled with his conflicting emotions. There was nothing he wanted more at that moment than to see the bullets tear into Jake Parrish's body, to see the terror in his foe's eyes as he watched his blood spurt from the mortal wound.

Cyrus glanced down at Serena's contorted features.

Yes, it would be worth the risk of hanging for the satisfaction of knowing he had avenged all the wrongs his daughter had suffered at the bastard's hands. Resolutely Cyrus King's hand tightened on the gun.

Jake Parrish was a dead man.

"Mr. Jake! Mr. Jake! Police come!" Hop Yung came tearing around the hedge at breakneck speed, and before he could halt his helter-skelter flight, he plowed into the rigid obstacle of Cyrus King's back.

There was a deafening report from the gun as Cyrus and Hop Yung tumbled to the grass in a wildly flailing heap. Hallie screamed in horror as she saw the bullet explode into Jake's torso. She cried his name over and over again as he collapsed to the ground, his face a vivid mask of agony.

In moments, the tiny rose garden was overrun with a small contingent of uniformed policeman, all of whom seemed to be talking at once.

"Jake! Oh, dear God! Jake!" Hallie shrieked, rudely pushing at the officers who had surrounded his now still form. "For the love of God, let me through!"

She jabbed her elbow into a particularly solid specimen of humanity, eliciting a yowl of protest from the man, who glowered down at her with indignation.

"I'm a doctor," she shouted. "Move out of the way and let me through!" She gave him another shove.

The men looked at each other uncomfortably. Most of them had never heard of a woman doctor. At last, the one who appeared to be in charge nodded his consent; as if by magic, the wall of bodies parted.

Ignoring them all, Hallie knelt at Jake's side. He lay doubled over in pain, convulsively clutching at his midsection. She wanted to cry with despair as she noted the flow of blood soaking his sweater and staining his hands.

"Jake?" she whispered, gently stroking his pale cheek.

To her everlasting relief, his eyes fluttered open and he gave her a lopsided smile.

"Don't worry, Jake, I'll take care of you. You'll be fine."

He reached up to grasp her hand, smearing a crimson ribbon of his blood across her trembling fingers. "I'm not worried, Mission Lady. You're here, aren't you?"

Chapter 10

"Hallie?"

Hallie paused in her task of cutting away Jake's blood-soaked sweater to meet his pained gaze with her compassionate one. "I thought you'd fainted," she murmured.

"No such luck," Jake replied, lifting his head from the pillow to look down at his side. His already pale face blanched several shades whiter as he stared at the ugly wound, and with a groan, he fell back again. He lay breathing raggedly for a few moments before choking out, "Just how bad is it?"

"I don't think it's as awful as it looks."

"It feels awful."

"I know," she crooned, setting aside the scissors. Gently, so as not to cause him further pain, Hallie peeled away the remnants of the sweater, exposing a chest and torso rippling with strongly sculpted muscles. Frowning, she pushed at the waistband of his trousers, trying to assess the full extent of his injury.

It was a nasty one, no doubt about it. A large piece of flesh had been blown away when the bullet had passed through his side, leaving a good-sized hole. Thankfully, the bleeding had begun to slow.

Hallie wrung out a cloth in a basin of clean water and dabbed at the wound, once again tugging at his waistband. She would definitely need to remove Jake's trousers in order to treat his wound properly. Too bad Hop hadn't thought to do it when he'd slipped off his employer's boots.

"Jesus!" Jake bellowed, flinching violently beneath her hand. "That hurts!"

"I'm sorry." Hallie paused in her ministrations to stroke his chest, anxiously watching his contorted face.

When he closed his eyes with a shuddering sigh and began to relax beneath her touch, she returned to the problem of his trousers.

Oh, double damn! she cursed silently, a crease marring her forehead. She'd sent Hop to the infirmary to fetch chloroform, so she could rule out help from that quarter. Hallie peered down at Jake's still form as she mulled over her remaining options.

There were the policemen waiting to question Jake in regard to Serena's murder. Perhaps she could have one of them come in and undress him for her.

She shook her head as she resumed cleaning his side. No, that would never do. Those men had already made several slighting remarks about her abilities as a doctor; to ask them for help would simply confirm their unflattering suspicions.

And the undertaker who had arrived to tend Serena—well, he was definitely out of the question. Just the thought of letting him touch Jake seemed like a bad omen. Hallie couldn't suppress a shudder at the idea.

So what was she to do?

But she already knew the answer to her dilemma: if she was ever going to prove her mettle as a doctor, she'd have to stop these missish posturings over the idea of treating a nude man.

Hallie tossed aside the bloody cloth, groaning inwardly. Why did her first male patient have to be someone as virile as Jake Parrish? Why did it have to *be* Jake?

Fighting back her growing trepidation, Hallie stood up and began to remove her surgical instruments from her medical bag. With her back to Jake, she said as casually as if she'd said it a thousand times before, "Jake, I'm going to need to remove your trousers." She held her breath, tensely waiting for his reply.

It seemed like a decade before he answered, "Fine."

She let out her breath in a hiss of relief. Good. He seemed cooperative enough. After arranging the instruments in a basin, Hallie went to the fireplace to retrieve the kettle Celine had put to boil earlier. She poured the steaming water over her instruments. That task completed, she turned back to Jake with a no-nonsense expression on her face, ready to resolve the trouser issue.

But when she saw that his eyes were closed and his breathing even, almost as if he slept, her features softened.

He reminded her of a prince from some mythical kingdom as he lay amid the ornate splendor of his curious bed. Done in an Oriental style, the bed was a large, impressive piece of furniture, wonderfully fashioned out of black-and-gold-lacquered mahogany. The headboard was an intricate puzzle of intertwining woodwork topped with a canopy which was carved to resemble the exotically curving shape of an ancient pagoda. Four fancifully rendered dragons served as bedposts, standing in silent vigil over their sleeping master. With their fiercely bared fangs and smoothly carved scales, they looked poised to spring on anyone foolish enough to disturb his slumbers. The bed was an object of rare, undeniable beauty—just like the man resting upon it.

Hallie gave one of the dragons a pat before sitting on the edge of the bed beside Jake. Laying her fingers against his cheek, she murmured, "Jake?"

He opened his eyes.

"I'm going to undress you now." She was pleased to hear how steady her voice sounded.

He nodded once and then his eyes fluttered closed again.

Hallie heaved a sigh of relief. Perhaps this wasn't going to be as difficult as she'd imagined. Willing her hands to be steady, she began to unbutton his trousers. She was uncomfortably aware of the warm, hard flesh of his belly beneath her fingers and the way the crisp line of dark hair dipped below his navel, branding a path that led to his most secret regions. She felt herself growing flustered at the idea of exposing that area of his body and suddenly her hands became clumsy.

After what seemed like an hour, the fastenings fell loose. Gingerly, Hallie rolled down the right side of his waistband, fully exposing the hideous wound. Frowning at a raw flap of skin, she picked up a fresh cloth and wiped the blood away. The loose piece of skin would have to be cut away.

As she carefully lifted the jagged flesh to clean deeper, a descriptive oath exploded from Jake's lips, and she was forced to drop the cloth to brace his hips when he jumped at the sudden pain.

"I'm sorry," she whispered. "I need to clean your injury so I can examine it. I don't think the bullet penetrated any of your organs, but I'll need to probe to ascertain that."

"Pleasant thought," he grumbled beneath his breath.

Hallie released her hold on his hips and slipped her hands into his spasmodically clenching ones. She gave them a reassuring squeeze. "I know it hurts, Jake. And I'm trying to be as gentle as I can. Hop should be back with the chloroform soon. You can sleep through the worse of it. I can't say you—"

"No," he cut her off shortly.

"What do you mean, no?"

He removed his hands from hers, to grip at her forearms. "I mean no chloroform."

"The bullet appears to have gone cleanly through your side," she began, pointedly ignoring the mulish set of his jaw. "But it drove fragments of your clothing deep into the wound. I'm going to have to remove them and most probably I'll have to cut into your flesh to get to the deeper ones. The pain will be far too severe for you to endure. And of course I'm going to need to stitch you up afterwards."

"No."

"Jake, be reasonable. Why should you—"

He let out an impatient snort. "Just bind it tightly and leave it alone."

"Fine!" Hallie let out a snort that perfectly mimicked his. "Just imagine how wonderful it's going to feel in a few days when I have to probe into your swollen, *festering* wound." He looked positively nauseated by the idea.

Good, she thought. *A few more words to drive the point home, and the stubborn man will be eager to sleep through the whole procedure.*

Hallie nodded for emphasis. "Make no mistake about it, it will fester. That is, if you don't bleed to death first." She felt his hands tighten on her arms, but continued ruthlessly, "In case you haven't figured it out yet, every time you bend or move, you're going to tear that laceration open again. Of course, in a few days, you'll be half out of your mind with fever from the infection and so weak from the loss of blood that you won't be able to put up much of a fight. So you see, any way you look at it, I'll be probing and stitching. The only questions are when and how much you choose to suffer."

Jake dropped his hands from her arms with a groan and pressed his palms hard against his eyes. He lay still for several moments, considering her words.

God! He was all too familiar with the horrors of such infections. Vividly he remembered the waves of pain as the army surgeons probed the inflamed flesh of his thigh, pain intensified a hundred times by the madness of his fever. And the suturing. His gorge rose at the memory of the needle tearing through the edges of his wound, each stitch stinging far worse than the one before.

Jake Parrish remembered, and he was afraid.

"Please, Jake," Hallie implored, smoothing back his hair. "Let me give you the chloroform. I can't bear the thought of hurting you like that."

He dropped his hands to his sides and gave her a brittle smile. "And I'm not sure I can bear to be hurt." But he knew she was right. He needed to be properly tended, and as much as he hated to admit it, there was no choice in the matter. Perhaps the surgery wouldn't be quite so terrible when performed by someone as gentle as Hallie Gardiner. He prayed he was right.

Sighing heavily, he said, "All right. You win. Do what you must . . . but no chloroform."

"But why? It would make it so much easier—for both of us."

"They gave me chloroform in the army hospital—once. I almost died." He dug his fingers into the mattress beneath him. "All I remember is waking up wretchedly sick and having the doctors hem and haw something about chloroform sickness. From that day on, no matter how painful the treatments, they couldn't risk using it on me again."

Compassion surged through Hallie with a force that made her want to weep. Her poor Jake! She knew she couldn't even begin to imagine how much he must have suffered. And knowing that, how could she bear to put him through another painful ordeal? Yet what choice did she have? She stole a glance down at his face. There was another way.

"I can give you an injection of morphine," she whispered, looking everywhere but in his eyes. "It will take the edge off the pain."

"God, no!"

Hallie reached down and clasped his hand in hers, her expression pleading. "Please. It's the only way."

"No." He shuddered convulsively. "I know how easily the drug can entrap a man. And have you forgotten what it did to Serena?"

"This is different. Just one injection to help you through. I promise it won't harm you." When he stubbornly shook his head, she pointed out, "You're hardly the kind of man to fall victim to a vice like morphine."

"Damn it, Hallie! I *was* one of those men! How do you think I endured the pain and horror after I was wounded? How do you think I survived?" Jake's eyes bored into Hallie's, half daring her to recoil with the disgust he was sure she was feeling, half pleading with her to understand the anguish that had driven him to such degradation.

Hallie met his stark gaze squarely, aching for him, knowing what his confession had cost him. "Those days are over," she stated, gently cupping his cheek in her hand. "What's important now is that I care for your wound." There was a silent plea in her eyes, begging him to forgive her for what she was about to do to him. "I'll work as quickly and gently as possible. I promise."

Jake swallowed hard, terrified of his coming ordeal, yet touched by the expression of tender concern on Hallie's face. Pressing his cheek against her palm, he murmured, "I trust you. And I promise to lie as still as a statue while you probe to your heart's content." And he meant it. He did trust Hallie, and for her, he could bear anything.

She smiled, pleased by his faith in her skills.

"I also promise not to holler more than, ah, three times, while you sew me up."

Hallie's smile broadened at that. "Jake," she whispered, grasping at the waistband of his trousers. "Do you realize how truly wonderful you are?"

He chuckled feebly. "Wonderful, you say? And you haven't even seen me without my britches yet."

She turned the color of a well-boiled lobster at his words, a shade of red he found remarkably charming at that moment. *When had Hallie Gardiner become such a beauty?* he wondered.

"You're a wicked man, Jake," she chided. And then, without further prompting, she slipped his trousers down his hips.

Flames of embarrassment burned across Hallie's cheeks as a thatch of dark curls sprang into view. When she realized where she was staring, she quickly averted her gaze, mortified. Refocusing her gaze in the vicinity of his knees, she gave the form-fitting garment another yank. To her relief, it glided the rest of the way down his hips, stopping at what she judged to be about mid-thigh level. Not that she actually looked up to verify the location.

Why did the man have to have such long legs?

Groaning inwardly, she tugged at the trousers with all her might. This time they slid the rest of the way down his legs, and with a sigh of relief she eased the garment over his feet.

"Bravo, Mission Lady." Jake actually managed to laugh at her tortured expression. "Done without so much as a peek." Then he let out a moan of sheer agony and doubled over onto his undamaged side, gasping as pain ripped through him at the sudden movement from his laughter.

Hallie jumped. "Jake?" Leaning close, she unconsciously stroked the silky curve of his bare hip, desperate to soothe him. She waited until the tension had eased from his body before coaxing him onto his back in a more comfortable position. Tenderly, she tucked the pillow beneath his head, pausing to pat his cheek. It was only then that she really looked at him.

Oh, Lord! Hallie thought, unable to stop herself from admiring his naked splendor. *He's beautiful everywhere!*

And he was. He was a masterpiece of sleekly carved muscles. His body was perfect in its symmetry, every inch covered by satiny skin the color of sun-warmed honey. Powerful arms united with impossibly broad shoulders, and his sculpted chest tapered to a belly tightly rippling with sharp definition. And those legs, so long and sinewy with strongly corded thighs, were more wonderful than anything she could have imagined.

Hallie frowned as her gaze traced the thick, vicious-looking scar twisting up his left thigh. Curiously, she followed its undulating path, pausing to stare at the inner curve where the tissue had healed into a star-shaped depression. When she looked up to ask him about it, a squeak of surprise escaped her lips. For there, nestled in a thatch of inky curls, was his manhood.

Her breath caught in her throat as she stared at it, mesmerized. It certainly didn't bear any resemblance to those tiny, thimblelike affairs she had seen on baby boys. Nor was it like the wrinkled-up scrape of flesh between the legs on that dissection cadaver.

"Making one of your famous *intimate examinations,* Doctor?" Jake drawled.

Hectic color infused Hallie's cheeks as she realized just how immodestly she had been staring at his most personal parts. At that moment she would have sacrificed anything to have melted into the ground like a snowman during a spring thaw. Turning an even deeper shade of red, she grabbed a towel from the bedside table and quickly draped it over his loins.

As she made to rise, Jake caught her arm, stopping her. "Hallie, look at me," he commanded softly.

Miserably, she did. His expression wasn't angry, or even mocking, as she had expected. It was almost tender.

"It's all right if you want to treat me to your *intimate examinations.* I like it. You're even welcome to touch the part you seemed to find so fascinating a moment ago." His voice faded into softness until it caressed her senses.

Swallowing hard, she forced herself to look away from his warm gaze and mumbled, "That part of you looked healthy enough to me. Unless it's paining you, I don't think it will be necessary to examine it closer."

"Believe me, Mission Lady, there are times when it aches. Badly." Jake grinned as Hallie turned away in embarrassed confusion and began to wash her hands.

Over and over again she scrubbed, cleansing her hands with the strong lye soap until her skin glowed a fiery red. Then she removed her instruments from the now cooling water and arranged them on a clean towel. She paused to study him for a moment, a frown creasing her forehead.

"It would be best if you were to lie stretched out on your left side. Do you think you can hold still in that position?"

He nodded his assent. "Whatever you think is best."

She helped him ease onto his side, nearly groaning when the towel slipped off and he lay exposed again. With great aplomb, she repositioned the cloth.

After firmly wedging one pillow at the small of his back and another against his belly to steady him, Hallie reached for a wickedly sharp-looking probe and a long, narrow pair of forceps. She could see the fear in his eyes as he stared at the instruments in her hands.

"You tell me when you're ready for me to begin," she whispered, giving him a reassuring smile.

Shuddering violently, he pulled his pillow against his chest and braced himself. "Just do it."

And Jake Parrish proved himself to be a man of his word. As she eased the probe into the core of his wound, he gasped softly and buried his face in the pillow but made no other sound. Hallie could feel his muscles twitch convulsively every time she moved to explore deeper, and she could hear his breath growing ragged as she inserted the forceps to remove the scraps of clothing. When she was forced to use her scalpel to cut away the powder-charred flap of flesh, he arched his head back with a strangled sob, one tear escaping from the corner of his eye as he stared at her in agonized shock. Yet he never cried out.

"There." Hallie pressed a clean cloth against the wound to stanch the bleeding. "I think I got it all." Closing her eyes, she caught a deep, sobbing breath, thankful that she was almost done with the awful task. Hurting Jake was the hardest thing she'd ever done in her life.

After dropping her instruments back into the bowl of water, Hallie knelt beside the bed to stroke Jake's sweat-dampened hair. Though his face was still hidden in the pillow, his trembling had begun to still.

"Darling—" The endearment slipped out before she

could stop it, but at that moment she was so overcome with tenderness that she didn't care.

When Jake raised his head to look at her, Hallie saw that his eyes were rimmed with red, and she could see the dampness streaking the linen where his face had rested.

"My poor, brave Jake," she whispered, softly pressing her lips to his colorless cheek. Her heart sickened with remorse when she tasted the salt from his tears, and she hated herself for having caused them to fall.

Jake slowly turned his head until his mouth was almost touching hers. *Darling.* How long had it been since anyone had called him that? Or said the word with such genuine emotion? *It sounded wonderful—Hallie Gardiner was wonderful.*

As the sweet warmth of her breath fanned across his face, Jake lowered his gaze to stare at the trembling fullness of her lips. Then he tipped his face nearer and kissed her.

Before Hallie could react, or do more than just stare at him in dazed wonder, Jake sighed and sank back against his pillow.

"What else needs to be done?" he asked quietly.

Hallie stared at his handsome face, groping for an answer. "Uh—" she watched his lips tug into a slight smile at her confusion and found herself mesmerized by their provocative shape. How wonderful their texture had felt against hers.

"You were going to turn me into one of your needlework masterpieces if I remember correctly," he prompted.

One little kiss and you're acting like a blushing schoolgirl, she scolded herself. *Get your mind off Jake Parrish's lips and back on his wound, where it belongs.*

Somehow she managed to quip, "Impatient man! Eager to be my sewing canvas, are you?" And his answering grimace was enough to break the sensual spell of his kiss completely.

Jake watched as Hallie lifted a small black case from her bag and then, after a moment's deliberation, produced a bottle of dark liquid. When she removed a thick, curved needle from its box and began to thread it with a length of ligature, he turned his head away. He lay tensely, waiting for the part of his ordeal he had been most dreading. He could feel the bed sag beneath Hallie's weight as she sat beside him and a soft splash as she uncorked the bottle. When he felt her lay a cool hand on his rib cage, he braced himself for the inevitable.

And the howl that exploded from his lips was deafening in its volume.

"Jesus Christ, Hallie!" he spat through gritted teeth, tossing his head back to fix her with a resentful glare. "What the hell is that stuff? It burns!"

"Tincture of iodine. I saw it used while I was studying in England. The findings were impressive, with hardly any infections resulting in those wounds treated like this." She furrowed her forehead and peered at his injury thoughtfully. "Of course, this is the first time I've had a chance to try it for myself."

"Oh, great!" he groaned. "Not only am I your embroidery sampler—I'm your scientific experiment as well."

Hallie laughed at the indignant look on his face. "Ah, well, just think of it as doing your part toward the glorious advancement of medical science."

Replying with one of his snorts, Jake plopped his head to his pillow and lay in long-suffering silence while she finished treating the area.

As she recorked the bottle and reached for the needle, Hallie heard him murmur, "One."

She paused, needle hovering over the laceration, to glance down at him. "What?"

"One," he repeated, meeting her gaze seriously. "I've only hollered once. I have two more left on account." He stared at the needle poised in her hand. "I intend to use them both."

And he did. Loudly. But only twice, as promised.

Hallie sloshed her hands through the soapy water in the basin, one by one, removing her now clean surgical instruments. As she slowly dried each one, the indistinct murmur of Jake's voice caressed her ears, tempting her, for the fifteenth time in the last quarter hour, to glance at him. Just looking at him gave her a surge of pleasure.

So what if he was far too pale, or if his face was tight

with strain? He was still the most magnificent man she'd ever seen. Even lying propped up on a mound of pillows, clad only in a burgundy velvet dressing gown, Jake Parrish managed to look commanding.

Hallie stared as he took another sip of the "No Mean-Head, No-Pain" potion Hop had mulishly insisted he needed, and she smiled at his grimace. God only knew what was in the nasty concoction. Or in the poultice Celine had insisted that Hallie apply to Jake's side. Hallie had said as much to Jake when the pair had appeared at his bedside, arguing loudly between themselves. But he merely smiled at the bickering servants, listening seriously as each presented the superior virtues of his or her particular medicine.

At one point the debate between the duo became so heated that it looked as if it might come to fisticuffs. Like wise King Solomon, Jake settled the dispute, diplomatically agreeing to try both remedies. It was obvious to Hallie that the servants cared a great deal for their employer, and in that she was in complete accord.

Suddenly Jake smiled at her over the rim of his cup. Hallie looked away quickly, flustered at being caught staring. Lord! This was getting ridiculous. It seemed as if watching Jake Parrish had become quite a preoccupation with her of late.

So, she was staring again, was she? thought Jake, as Hallie glanced away, her color deepening to a darker shade of red. Her face seemed to have become permanently stained with crimson, one blush deepening into the next before the previous one had had a chance to fade. What was she thinking that made her look so uncomfortable?

Was she, perhaps, remembering the way she had bathed him earlier? That particular thought flamed Jake hotter than the fire blazing in Hallie Gardiner's cheeks. He'd thoroughly enjoyed the feel of her rough little hands as she sponged his torso clean of all traces of blood. Especially the part where she pushed aside the towel to cleanse low on his belly.

Pointedly, she had tried to ignore the concealing cloth, pretending not to see the bulge of his arousal. Yet, for all her nonchalance, Jake had caught her casting furtive glances at his cloaked hardness, her interest obvious. If only the blood had splattered a bit lower—

"Mr. Parrish?" Mr. Folsom, the incongruously cheerful-looking undertaker, peered into his client's face. He'd seen corpses with better color.

"Excuse me?" Jake turned his attention back to the rosy-cheeked man next to him, who was studying him with a professional interest that made Jake want to laugh. He might look to be on his deathbed, but parts of him were definitely stirring in a lively manner.

Mr. Folsom inclined his head courteously and cleared his throat. "We were discussing the casket. Might I suggest one of our new airtight metallic burial cases? I have a lovely model covered with the finest French silk and trimmed with fringe. It has a new, improved sealing flange, which, of course, makes it quite airtight. Always an important consideration."

"Very important, I'm sure." Jake swallowed the last of Hop's nasty concoction and set the cup aside. "Is it your best?"

The man nodded vigorously, sending a lock of his thick gray hair tumbling over his forehead. "Oh, it's quite the most fashionable and expensive unit we carry," he replied, his smile broadening. "Of course, if you want the optional white satin lining, it will cost an additional twenty-one dollars."

"We'll take the satin. I want only the best for my wife." Jake had promised Serena the best, and it was a vow he intended to keep, even now. "Are there any more arrangements to be made?"

The undertaker mulled over his list for a moment and then shook his head. "No." He smiled kindly as the ill-looking young man yawned. "You've made very fine choices, Mr. Parrish. This is going to be the grandest funeral San Francisco has ever seen. Such a touching tribute to your wife! I can tell you loved her a great deal."

Jake stared into Mr. Folsom's face, suddenly shamed by the man's expression of genuine compassion. Shouldn't he be feeling grief, or at least some subtle shading of that emotion? Shouldn't he be feeling something besides an eagerness to dispense with the distasteful business at hand?

After a moment's hesitation, Mr. Folsom squeezed Jake Parrish's arm in a soothing manner. Poor Mr. Parrish looked absolutely bereaved, lying there with that lost look on his face. "With your permission, sir, I'll attend to Mrs. Parrish now. I promise to give her my utmost attention."

"Of course. One of the servants will show you to the parlor where my wife is to be laid out. We will be receiving callers this evening."

The undertaker nodded and then shook Jake's proffered hand. "Everything will be ready."

"Thank you." Jake leaned his head back into his pillows, closing his eyes as he heard the door click behind the man.

"Jake?"

"I'm all right." He didn't need to open his eyes to know Hallie was standing over him, her face a study of concern. "Just tired. Would you let the police in now?"

"Are you sure you're up to it?" She laid her hand on his forehead. It was slightly warm, but that was to be expected after all he had been through. Gently, she moved her fingers down to touch his cheek, letting them linger longer than necessary. She loved the feel of his skin, especially the smooth contours of his face. Hallie looked at his still features and frowned. What would happen if he couldn't prove his innocence? How could she bear it if he were to be locked away where she couldn't see—or touch—him? What if they really did hang him?

"Jake, I'm afraid for you. What if the police think you're guilty?"

Jake turned his head and kissed her palm. "Do you trust me?"

"You know I do."

"Then ask them to come in now."

Hallie obeyed, but she allowed only the officer in charge to enter the room. The rest of the policemen grumbled among themselves at being left out of the investigation, though no one actually voiced any objections.

"Officer Dewey Rigney, sir." The man moved to Jake's side, removing his cap courteously.

Jake took the officer's proffered hand and shook it

firmly. "Thank you for coming." He nodded him to the chair that Mr. Folsom had recently vacated, waiting patiently until he was settled. "I believe you wanted to question me?"

"Yes. Just a—*ur*—formality, mind you." Officer Rigney was a beefy, rather rough-looking man with a spiky shock of brown hair that had been lopped off unfashionably short. He removed a small pad of paper from his pocket and then a stub of a pencil, frowning severely as he peered at the worn-down lead.

Feeling protective, Hallie moved to stand next to Jake, her arms crossed and her legs firmly planted. *Just let this Rigney person try to bully my patient,* she thought belligerently. *I'll set him straight quick enough.*

But after giving her a dismissive glance, the man simply ignored her presence. "Mr. Parrish, I've heard that you and your wife were somewhat—*ur*—estranged. Is that true?"

Jake nodded.

"*Ur*—yes. Her father, Cyrus King, mentioned that your behavior was less than warm toward his daughter and that you had, on occasion, expressed—*ur*—hostility toward his own person. Is that true?"

"It most certainly is not true!" exclaimed Hallie, cutting off any retort Jake might have made. "As Mrs. Parrish's companion and personal physician, I can attest to the fact that Mr. Parrish treated his wife with the utmost consideration. As for Cyrus King—" Hallie snorted. Out of the corner of her eye she saw Jake grin at the noise. "The man has forced his way into this house on numerous occasions, physically attacking his son-in-law. And poor Mr. Parrish! Still so weak from the grievous injuries he suffered while fighting to preserve his country's unity."

Jake and Officer Rigney stared at Hallie in amazement, the policeman with his mouth wide open and Jake with his eyebrow cocked in amusement. She was the picture of an outraged ragamuffin, with tendrils of hair straggling from her tight braid and dirty feet peeking out from beneath the hem of her bloodstained wrapper. So frantic had she been when Jake was shot that she hadn't thought to get dressed.

Dewey Rigney came to his senses and snapped his

mouth shut. Tactfully glancing away from Hallie's improperly clad state, he deferred to the man before him. "Is this—*ur*—true, Mr. Parrish?"

Jake shrugged with a yawn.

"Of course it's true." Hallie saw Jake's eyes cross and then close. With a jerk of his head, he opened them again to regard her groggily. *Lord! Whatever had Hop Yung given him?*

The officer cleared his throat. "*Ur*—yes. Of course." He made a note on his tablet, stopping once to wet the pencil lead with his tongue, and then returned his attention to the man dozing on the bed. "Now, sir, if you could just tell me what happened?"

"He was taking his daughter for an early-morning walk in the garden when he found his wife dead. You see, Officer Rigney, the poor baby had had a restless night, and Mr. Parrish thought the fresh air would do her good. Jake Parrish happens to be a doting father." Hallie cast Jake a warning glance at the sound of his snort. He was sitting cockeyed, regarding her with a dim-witted sort of interest.

"What do you have to say, Mr. Parrish?" asked Officer Rigney, giving Hallie a severe stare that was meant to silence her.

It didn't work. "He has nothing to say. He's in a state of shock, poor man. You would be, too, if you'd been shot by a maniac and then had to endure agonizing surgery without the benefit of chloroform."

The policeman paled visibly at her words, "*Ur*—I hadn't realized—"

"Obviously." Hallie narrowed her eyes at the now squirming policeman. "Tell me, Officer Rigney, do you have children?"

"Five."

"Then as a father you can understand how distressing it is for a man to have a sickly child. Why, Mr. Parrish walked the floor with the poor darling all night long, refusing to let anyone relieve him of his duty. And now the babe is motherless."

Such a dramatic little liar! thought Jake, yawning. Why she practically had that hard-boiled policeman in tears as she continued spinning her yarns about his sickly daughter and his own devotion to the virtues of fatherhood. He would have to remind his Mission Lady that lying was a sin. He yawned again and could feel his eyes rolling. Damn it! Things were just getting entertaining and here he was, barely able to keep awake.

"Is this true, Mr. Parrish?" Officer Rigney looked at Jake Parrish with a respect that had absolutely nothing to do with the immense size of his monthly donations to the policemen's fund.

"Sure."

"Good." The man scratched at his notes once more and then frowned. "*Ur*—excuse me, sir. But how did Mr. Tyler happen to be with you when you found your wife? When he summoned us, he mentioned that he could vouch for your—*ur*—innocence."

"Mr. Tyler?" Hallie gave Jake an accusatory stare. So Seth had been with Jake, and it appeared that he had been the one to send for the police. That was why he was downstairs pacing a hole in the parlor carpet. Oh, Lord! Why hadn't Jake told her about Seth Tyler's part in all of this?

Jake fixed his bleary green eyes on Officer Rigney for a moment, and Hallie held her breath. God only knew what he would say, given his besotted state.

"Seth Tyler *loves* children," he finally replied, closing his eyes and rubbing at them wearily. "You see, Mr. Tyler is my business partner and it is customary for us to meet early in the morning to plan our day's agenda. It's not unusual for Seth to accompany my daughter and me for a walk. The babe is rather taken with him, like all the ladies, though she's only two months old."

"Good. Very good!" The man smartly snapped his tablet closed and stuffed it back into his pocket. "I don't see any reason to pursue this—*ur*—interview any further. Your word and that of Mr. Tyler are enough for me." With that, he rose to his feet. "*Ur*—about Cyrus King. Would you like to press charges?"

Jake heaved a weary sigh. "No. Just hold him overnight. That should give him enough time to come to his senses."

"As you wish." The officer shook Jake's hand politely. "I'll leave you to your rest now, sir. Sorry to have to question you. It's—*ur*—standard procedure, you see."

"I see. Thank you, Officer Rigney. You will keep me informed on any findings regarding this matter?"

"Of course." After nodding his head in Hallie's direction, the man left. There was the sound of heavy booted feet echoing down the hallway, and then silence.

Hallie glared down at Jake's drowsy face. "You had an alibi?"

"Yes. Seth and I competed in a rowing contest this morning. Against Judge Dorner and Police Chief Devlin, no less. Hell of an alibi, wouldn't you agree?" Jake grinned like a half-crocked idiot. "Oh. We won the race."

"Why didn't you tell me?"

"You didn't ask. Besides, I was hardly in any condition to mention it while you were probing at my wound."

She let out a snort of exasperation. Those snorts were becoming quite a habit with her these days. "You could have stopped me before I'd become so entrenched in my lies."

"True." He yawned and poked at the poultice on his side. The damn thing hurt. "But I didn't want you to stop."

"Enjoyed making a Mission Lady lie, did you?" Hallie gently lifted his hand away from his wound and folded it in her warm clasp. "I know it hurts, Jake. But it will feel worse if you keep prodding it."

"Fine. I won't prod. But I also won't apologize for making you lie. I've stood up for others all my life, and I've always tried to help those who needed me. But this is the first time anyone has ever done it for me. And with such flair, I might add." He yawned and then closed his eyes. His last words were barely audible. "It was wonderful. You were wonderful."

"Jake?"

His only response was a soft snore.

With loving hands, Hallie tucked the blankets around his shoulders and smoothed the hair off his face. She watched him for a few moments, filling her heart with every detail of his handsome face. He looked almost childlike as he slept, with his long eyelashes resting in inky crescents on his cheeks and his lips slightly parted. Trembling, she traced the beautiful shape of his mouth with her thumb. When he didn't stir, she bent down and gently kissed him, savoring the feel of his lips against hers.

"I love you, Jake," she whispered fervently. "I love you."

And when she finally tiptoed from the room, Jake Parrish smiled.

Chapter 11

Jake awoke with a start as a burning log gave a sharp crackle and then tumbled within the glowing confines of the fireplace.

Gunshot. He panicked for a moment, fighting through the last vestiges of the sleep misting his mind. *Guns and fire. Terror. Pain.*

Jesus! He was suffocating from the smoke-blackened air, air thick with gunpowder from the reports of a thousand rifles. The screams of men as they lay dying among the heaps of human carnage deafened him. It was like a scene from Dante's *Inferno* when the fiery canopy of tree branches collapsed, igniting the bed of dry grass upon which they lay. As the flames fed on the tortured bodies of the fallen soldiers, the smell of burning flesh permeated Jake's nostrils, and he felt himself choke on his own vomit.

He had to run . . . had to get away. Jake tried to take a step forward, but as if he were a fly trapped on flypaper, his feet stuck firmly to the ground. His legs felt like forged iron, stiff and impossibly heavy, and his arms hung paralyzed at his sides. Death was everywhere, stalking him. Yet he couldn't escape.

Jake sobbed as he felt the leather of his favorite chair give pliantly beneath his hands. *Only a dream.* He had been dreaming of Virginia again. *Hellish inferno.* The Wilderness.

Shivering violently, he ground his fists hard against his eyes, desperately trying to chase the lingering apparitions from his mind. *Would these nightmares never cease?*

Nightmares? *But the pictures always seemed so real!* And such was their power that they often haunted him well into the daylight hours, their dark memory casting a pall of shadow and a midnight chill over the cheerful warmth of the morning sun.

Go away, damn it! he commanded the visions. *Leave me in peace.* Mercifully, they obeyed.

Yet he felt no peace.

Tipping his head back against his chair, Jake at last lowered his hands and stared into the fire. He wondered vaguely, without any real interest, who had lit it. Whoever it was must have crept into the room as quietly as the falling night, for he couldn't remember being disturbed from his slumbers. Of course, he always slept deeply when he was in the gut-wrenching clutches of one of his nightmares.

There was a soft knock, followed by a low creaking as the door eased open.

"Jake?"

He glanced across the library to see Hallie framed in the doorway, her slender figure silhouetted in the light from the gas lamps flickering in the hallway. As she paused to steady the heavily laden tray in her hands, Jake could see she was gnawing at her bottom lip. Even in the dimness of the room and at a distance, he could read the anxiety on her face.

Remaining politely by the door, Hallie waited for some signal or gesture of encouragement from Jake. When it didn't come, she slowly advanced toward him. Like a blind person she moved in a cautiously halting shuffle as she tried to accustom her eyes to the darkness. She could see Jake's slightly averted profile outlined against the glow of the fire, and when he didn't turn at her approach, she wondered if he slept.

Jake listened to the crisp whispers of Hallie's silk skirts as she closed the gap between them. He knew she had reached his side when the soft hissing was abruptly silenced.

"Is it over?" he asked quietly, not looking up from the fire.

"Yes. The last of the guests have left."

"Good."

"Everyone said it was a wonderful funeral."

Jake let out a harsh bark of laughter and stared up at her incredulously. "Wonderful? Somehow, I fail to see anything wonderful about death, or anything even remotely related to the event."

"They're your friends, Jake. They meant well." Hallie fidgeted with the tray, feeling increasingly uncomfortable beneath his brooding stare. She hadn't expected him to be in a pleasant mood, and he wasn't.

"Friends? Hell! I didn't even recognize half the people here today," he exclaimed with disgust. "Most were gossipmongers and curiosity seekers, I suspect. After all, there's nothing people love more than to see the mighty fall." His mouth twisted ironically. "The others? Acquaintances, at best. Only a handful can be counted as real friends. Of course, there were those who came for the free food."

"Of which you need to eat." Hallie held out the tray for his inspection. When he didn't even glance at the food, she coaxed, "Celine said these are all your favorite dishes. Look, she even baked you one of her special rhubarb pies." She moved the tray beneath Jake's nose temptingly, sending the delicious scents wafting in all directions.

But he merely sighed and returned his gaze to the fire.

Hallie frowned as she studied his face in the dim light. Lord! The man looked dreadful. His eyes were like darkly shadowed pools in the pallor of his face, the smoky green orbs providing the only hint of color on an otherwise white canvas. And though Jake's clothing was immaculate, as always, the unrelieved black of the mourning suit served only to further emphasize his unhealthy appearance. Every now and then he would tremble violently, and when he shifted in his chair, a spasm of pain exploded across his features.

But what disturbed Hallie most was the weariness that sat heavily on every line of his face. It wasn't the kind of weariness that came simply from lack of sleep or from a hard day's work. It was the soul-sickening kind, the kind that came from utter defeat. It was an expression usually reserved for those who had been crushed and beaten by life—a life which Jake Parrish, at thirty-three, had only just begun to sample.

Hallie set the tray on the tea table next to his chair, grimacing with distaste as she pushed the almost empty whiskey decanter as far from him as possible. Even at this distance she could smell the overpowering scent of liquor that clung to him. Though Hallie suspected he'd been drinking heavily since the night before, she couldn't find it in her heart to condemn him for his indulgence. Not after all he'd been through.

Only hours after being wounded, Jake had insisted on dressing and greeting the hordes of mourners himself. Stubbornly, he had ignored Hallie's pleas that he rest, wincing as she bound his midsection tightly. By the time Hop Yung arrived to help him dress, Jake was shaking with weakness and Hallie was certain he was on the verge of collapse.

Yet, as each of the callers had expressed condolences, Jake had risen politely, never once revealing the agony she knew him to be suffering. Like the devoted husband, he remained by the side of his wife's casket, nodding somberly as everyone commented on how lovely Serena looked. When the last of the visitors departed, Jake disappeared into his library, not reemerging until the following morning.

It was nothing short of miraculous that he'd been able to endure the long funeral service and had made the tedious trek to the cemetery afterward. More amazing yet was the fact that he wasn't now in bed delirious with fever from his exertions.

Kneeling in front of him with her hands clasped in a manner reminiscent of a sinner praying for forgiveness, Hallie murmured, "You're going to make yourself ill if you don't rest. Why don't I have Hop help you to bed?"

"I'm all right."

"Half-drunk, maybe," she snapped as he reached for the whiskey and poured himself a healthy measure. "But not all right. Look at yourself! You're shaking so badly, I doubt you could walk even if the house was on fire. You need to put something in your stomach besides liquor, and you should be in bed with a hot brick at your feet."

He merely snorted and drained the entire contents of his glass in one gulp.

"Jake, I understand how much it hurts to lose someone you love." Hallie gently pried the empty tumbler from his hand and set it aside. Clasping both his trembling hands in her steady ones, she said, "After my mother died, I found it helped to talk about the pain. You can talk to me if you want."

Jake stared at her through narrowed eyes for a moment before growling, "Fine. Then let's talk about how your jabbering is making my head throb. Or would you rather hear about my side? It feels as if someone is stabbing it with a red-hot poker. Ah, yes. And my leg does rather ache, now that you mention it. There. We've discussed my pain. Are you happy now?"

"You know that's not what I meant." Hallie dropped his hand and sat back on her heels, sighing with exasperation. He really was a difficult man!

"Sorry to disappoint you, Mission Lady. But those are the only pains I'm feeling at this moment. What did you expect? Tearful confessions from the grieving widower?"

"I expected you to feel something." How could he sit there looking so remote? Had she been wrong in thinking Jake Parrish a good man? Was she as foolish as her mother had been, becoming enamored of a handsome face and endowing its owner with all kinds of noble attributes that in reality didn't exist? The uneasy thought made Hallie's heart give a sudden flip-flop.

Looking away from his rigid features, she choked out, "I realize things weren't right between you and Serena, but by your own admission you loved her once. I thought you might still have cared a little bit. I thought you might even have found it in your heart to mourn her."

In a lightning-quick motion, Jake shot forward and roughly grasped Hallie's shoulders. Muttering a foul oath at the burning sensation that lanced through his side, he hauled her close until their faces were only inches apart.

"Damn it, Hallie! Do you think I would have endured the company of that pack of vultures today if I didn't care?" His hands trembled badly as they tightened on her flesh. "Do you?"

She shook her head mutely. The expression in his eyes was as frigid and mercurial as a storm-swept sea. With a shudder, she looked away, frightened by the intensity of that gaze.

"Look at me, damn it!" Jake seized Hallie's chin and jerked her face toward his, ignoring her struggles to escape. "You think I'm a cold, heartless bastard, don't you? Ah, well, perhaps you're right. But before you condemn me in that self-righteous little mind of yours, hear this: I left my bed to play the grieving husband, not because I care what society thinks of me but because it was the last thing I could do to honor Serena's memory."

He smiled grimly as Hallie stilled in the punishing bonds of his grasp. "Oh, and don't think I haven't mourned, either," he ground out. "I have—deeper than you'll ever know. You see, Mission Lady, because of her all-consuming hatred of me and her subsequent alienation, Serena has been dead to me for years. Given her feelings, what choice did I have but to learn to live with the loss of the woman I loved? And I accepted that loss long ago. So don't expect tears now, for I have none left to shed!"

Jake released Hallie abruptly, his face twisted with bitterness. Rubbing at her abused shoulders, she watched, without comment, as he poured another drink and tossed it down his throat. Then, with a growl that seemed to give voice to his raw emotions, he hurled his glass forcefully against the marble surface of the fireplace, and as the tinkle of shattered glass echoed in the silence of the room, he buried his face in his hands. He sat like that for a long moment, his shoulders shaking convulsively.

"Jake?" Hallie whispered, wondering if he was weeping. "I'm sorry. I-I didn't understand." When he lifted his head to meet her gaze, his face was filled with such terrible bleakness that her heart ached for him.

"And you still don't. How could you, a spinster, ever understand what it's like to lose someone with whom you've been intimate?" Jake's lips tightened into a harsh line.

"Oh, I'm not talking merely about the carnal intimacies," he continued in a raspy voice, "although those in themselves are nothing short of miraculous when shared with someone you love. No, I'm talking about the freedom to share your innermost thoughts, no matter how silly or frivolous they might sound, and know that the other person will understand exactly what you mean. It's having someone to whom you can express your fears, pain, and disappointments and know you'll still be loved despite your failings. It's caring for someone more than you care for yourself and knowing she feels the same. When you lose all that, it's like losing a piece of your soul."

He was right. She didn't fully understood the nature of his grief, though she could see it in every line of his face and hear it in the emotional texture of his words. Hallie slipped her hands into his to give them a reassuring squeeze. But Jake's fingers didn't close around hers, and there was no answering pressure. He simply stared at her impassively for a moment before firmly disengaging himself.

Letting her arms drop to her sides, Hallie whispered, "I want to understand, Jake. I want to know, so I can help you."

"Why?"

"Because I care about you."

"Why?" He punctuated the word with a snort of incredulity.

For the tenth time in as many minutes, Hallie reminded herself of the hell Jake had endured in the past twenty-four hours. As a doctor, she knew from experience that people often expressed pain and grief with anger.

Thus excusing Jake's ill temper, she patiently explained, "We're friends, remember? I may not have had much experience with friendship, but I do know that friends care about their friends."

"Fine. Then be a friend and find me another glass so I can finish the rest of this whiskey."

"As your doctor, I'll have to say no. The last thing you need is more liquor. What you need is sleep."

He eyed her derisively. "Why do you think I need the whiskey, Doc? Perhaps if I get drunk enough, I'll be able to sleep."

"And make yourself violently ill in the process." Hallie frowned as a tremor shook his body. "Lord! Look at the way you're shaking—and your face looks all flushed. Definite signs of fever, in my professional opinion."

She reached up to feel his forehead, but he jerked his face away with an impatient growl.

"Damn it, Hallie! Will you stop poking at me? I'm a grown man, and the last thing I need, or want, is a nursemaid." He glared at her in a manner that would have silenced a more fainthearted soul.

But timid Hallie wasn't. "Oh, I can see what a wonderful job you're doing of taking care of yourself. Why, a few more days of such tender care, and we'll be sending for Mr. Folsom to prepare his next customer—you!"

Jake chuckled humorlessly at that. "Tell him I prefer a nice wooden coffin. None of this silk-covered metallic burial case nonsense for me."

Her patience snapped. "Damn it, Jake! This isn't funny. Perhaps if you weren't such a mule-headed creature, you might see that I'm trying to help you."

"Fine!" he snorted. "Then help by leaving me alone."

"Fine!" Hallie snorted back, rising to her feet. "I'll go. It will serve you right if you end up confined to your bed babbling with delirium like a lunatic." She gave him an assessing look. "Come to think of it, there are several rather unusual treatments for fever I've wanted to try. Of course, they're a bit on the unpleasant side, but quite effective, I'm told."

She shrugged dismissively. "When the need arises, you may contact me at the Mission House. I was going to offer to examine your wound before I left, but, God knows, I certainly wouldn't want to be accused of poking at you again. So with Your Highness's most gracious leave, I'll finish my packing and leave for the mission this evening."

"By all means, Dr. Gardiner. And you can tell Hop to have the carriage brought around. We can't have one of San Francisco's few do-gooders braving the evils of the streets after dark."

Hallie sketched a mock curtsy as if deferring to some imperial deity. "Your wish is my command, Your Royal Arrogance."

"Oh, and never fear, Mission Lady," he said in a condescending manner that made Hallie long to kick him, "I'll have the bank set up a fund for your infirmary first thing in the morning. You've sure as hell earned it."

"I sure as hell have. A big one, let me remind you." With her nose firmly in the air, Hallie turned to leave. "Oh!" She lightly slapped her forehead as she remembered her forgotten question. "Would you like me to send a woman from the mission to help with the baby?

She's doing much better, but still requires constant attention. The wet nurse is exhausted from the effort. I could recommend several women who would be grateful for the job."

"I don't care. Do what you think best."

Hallie felt her spine stiffen at his callous attitude. With a stamp of her foot, she spun around to face him. Bracing her hands on her hips, she snapped, "Obviously you don't care! That poor baby was born six weeks ago, and you haven't even named her yet."

"I thought you and Serena would concoct something."

"Serena wasn't even aware of the baby's existence half the time, and she was hardly in any condition to think of a name. You would have known that had you bothered to ask after your daughter more often."

Jake shrugged indifferently. "You can have the honor then. Call her whatever you like." Then he closed his eyes and tipped his head back against his chair, satisfied that the matter was settled.

But it was far from settled in Hallie's mind. She stared at Jake's composed face, her anger growing fiercer as the minutes ticked away. Finally she erupted. "How can you be so heartless? Are you so unforgiving of Serena's wrongs that you would take it out on your own child? Will she spend her life bearing the brunt of your bitterness? That baby has your blood running in her veins as well as her mother's, you know. By virtue of that very fact, she's got a last name and like it or not, that name is Parrish. Don't you think it's about time you acted like a real father? The poor little thing is motherless, surely you don't intend to treat her as if she's fatherless, as well!"

"She's not mine to name," Jake muttered, cracking his eyes open to look at her through narrowed slits.

"Don't be ridiculous. As her father—"

"You're not listening to me, damn it! She's not mine. I'm not her father." His eyes flew open, and he fixed Hallie with a glowering stare. *She wanted answers? Fine. She'd get them—and regret the asking.* "I left San Francisco in '62 and didn't return until January of this year. The baby was born the twenty-first of August. Surely you can count, Dr. Gardiner?"

"Well, the baby was very small at birth. I thought it

was due to Serena's poor condition, but I suppose it could be that she was born too early."

"Early or not, she isn't mine." Jake saw Hallie's mouth open as if to protest, but he cut her off with a commanding wave of his hand. "It would be impossible. You see, Dr. Gardiner, I haven't had relations with my wife in years. She couldn't bear my touch—or anything else about me for that matter. And though I may be a bit of a bastard at times, I've never forced a woman."

Seizing the cane resting against his chair, Jake struggled to his feet, cursing beneath his breath at his weakened state. As he began to waver dangerously, Hallie rushed forward and slipped a supporting arm around him. But he rudely pushed her away and braced himself against the mantel.

"Of course, once she discovered herself pregnant, my darling Serena had a change of heart and tried to seduce me. She was good too, the way she fondled and coaxed me while whispering all sorts of carnal suggestions into my ear."

Hallie forced a note of calmness into her voice as she interjected, "I don't think you should be telling me all this. You're overwrought and don't know what you're saying. Perhaps it would be best if I left now." And though she had managed to sound composed, she could feel the color rising in her face at the blatant nature of his confession.

As she turned to go, Jake dropped his cane and grabbed her arm. Roughly, he brought her reeling against his chest. "I know exactly what I'm saying. You begged to understand, my friend, and I'm simply obliging that request. I expect you to listen to every last word of what I have to say." He crushed her closer until he could feel the frantic beating of her heart.

"Yes, Serena teased me in ways that would have done the most skilled of whores proud. Yet, despite her impressive efforts, I couldn't rise for her. God knows I tried. I thought if I could make love to her, it might help break some of the barriers between us. But when I tasted the foulness of the opium in her mouth and smelled the way that sickening odor mixed with her usual fragrance of roses, I couldn't get aroused. She hated me for that. I hated myself, too."

"Jake, please don't—"

"Just listen, damn it!" he snarled, commanding her silence with his wrathful gaze. "I'm not blind. I've seen the way you look at me. But before you get any more of your silly, romantic notions about me, I think you should know the truth: I'm unable to father a child."

Hallie stared at him, dumbstruck. "I don't see how that can be true. I've seen you naked and witnessed your—uh—response. I'll admit I'm no expert in such things, but that part of you seemed vigorous enough."

"You really are naive, Dr. Gardiner. Even with all your medical expertise and education." His brow raised with sardonic amusement and he chuckled dryly. "However, you are correct about my so-called vigor in that area. The failure to produce a child didn't come from a lack of lovemaking, but from Serena's failure to conceive. In my arrogance, I simply assumed she was barren. Of course, since I loved her so, I convinced myself it didn't matter. You can imagine my shock when I found her pregnant by another man. The humiliation I felt at discovering that another man had succeeded where I had failed was almost more than I could bear. You see, my dear, I was at last forced to face the shameful truth: I am only half a man."

Jake released Hallie abruptly, not able to bear her expression of pity a moment longer. With some difficulty, he eased himself around to gaze into the fire. He welcomed the shadows that shrouded his face, for they obscured his features from Hallie's probing gaze and he didn't want her to see how much his confession had pained him.

Jake had expected Hallie to flee as soon as she found herself free. But, as usual, she did the unexpected, remaining close by his side. He heard a rustle from her skirts and then felt the familiar shape of his cane as she slipped it into his hand. He gave a sharp nod of acknowledgment.

"Jake." Hallie stopped to clear her throat uncomfortably several times. Lord! Not only had she just treated her first naked man, but here she was discussing problems of a sexual nature with him as well. She'd certainly come a long way in the last two days. "It's not uncommon for a man not to be able to father children. I've heard the male doctors discuss the subject when they thought I wasn't listening. And though I can't claim to have any answers or cures for your affliction, it doesn't change the fact that I still think of you as the most masculine man I've ever met. Besides, I've seen instances where children were born to men who had long since given up hope. Perhaps someday that will happen to you."

"Are you finished with your uplifting little lecture, Dr. Gardiner?"

"Yes."

"Good. Then please go and leave me alone."

Hallie clutched Jake's arm, beseeching him, "Why won't you let me help you?"

"Because I don't need your help." He roughly shook off her hands.

"You need help worse than anyone I've ever met. You're just too stubborn to admit it!"

"Damn it, Hallie." Jake twisted his head around to fix her with a look of such vehemence that Hallie gasped and took a step backward. "When, and if, I want your advice, I'll ask for it. Until such time, I want you to get out and stop prying into my personal affairs." He practically shouted the last words.

"Jake, please—"

"Out!"

Hallie threw up her hands in a motion of surrender. "All right! Fine! Wallow in your self-pity alone. See if I care. I'll be out of your house within the hour, and I promise I won't disturb your sulking to say good-bye." She marched out of the room, slamming the door with resounding finality.

Jake stood poised for several moments before turning to stare at his beloved library. All the warmth seemed to have fled the room along with Hallie. Not that he was surprised. He sighed and hobbled back to his chair. Groaning loudly at the pain that wracked every muscle and nerve in his body, he settled into the well-worn seat.

Yes. In the past weeks, Hallie had become his beacon of hope, guiding him through the terrible despair that plagued his life and showing him a joy he'd thought lost forever. She'd taught him how to smile again and how to laugh. She'd taken that which was mundane in everyday life and, somehow, made it seem special. She'd become the reason he looked forward to the beginning of every day.

A lonely ache blossomed in Jake's chest. Hallie was leaving now. He had driven her away.

But it's all for the best, he told himself fiercely. *She's in love with me.* That fact was irrefutable.

Yet she deserved so much more than he could ever give her. Hallie should have a man who could offer her a love that was untainted by bitterness and distrust. Someone who would never fail or disappoint her. A husband who wasn't a cripple, and one who could give her the children he knew she craved.

It's all for the best.

For the first time that day, Jake felt real sorrow and he wept.

Chapter 12

So he's back, thought Hallie, watching as Jake leaned forward to whisper into Arabella Dunlap's ear. Arabella was considered to be the prettiest girl in town, and from the way Jake was hovering over her, it seemed he agreed. Apparently his three-month absence from San Francisco had made certain hearts grow fonder, for the Widow Dunlap appeared to be equally charmed by the dashing Mr. Parrish.

As Arabella twined her arms around Jake's neck and pulled his face close to hers, something uncomfortably akin to jealousy flooded Hallie's heart. Arabella, with her darkly exotic beauty, and Jake, looking more handsome than ever, made a striking couple. Hallie hadn't missed the way several passersby had paused to cast admiring glances at the pair, though, of course, the twosome were far too involved in each other to notice.

Jake and Arabella remained pressed close, engaged in what appeared to be an intimate discussion, until Jake shouted with laughter and nodded. Squealing with delight, Arabella stood on her tiptoes and pressed a kiss to his lips.

The woman was beaming at him as if he'd just promised to slay a dragon for her, observed Hallie, irrationally annoyed by Arabella's simpering. Fighting her urge to kick the perfect couple in their well-groomed backsides, she tried to look away. After all, what that Parrish man did was none of her affair.

Yet try as she might, Hallie couldn't seem to stop herself from staring longingly at Jake . . . or from wishing all sorts of horrible fates to befall Arabella.

Unaware that they were the objects of such close scrutiny, Jake tucked Arabella's hand into the crook of his arm and escorted her to a trim barouche waiting at the curb. As he handed the beautiful widow into her carriage, Jake caught sight of Hallie and waved.

Hallie groaned inwardly. She was cursed—definitely cursed! What other explanation could there be for the way she was continually finding herself in these awkward positions? Embarrassed at being caught spying, she sheepishly waved back and then fled, as sedately as possible, down the street.

Fool! she scolded herself, halting her flight only long enough to shift her cumbersome medical bag from one hand to the other. *Of course someone with Jake Parrish's looks and money would want someone like Arabella Dunlap. Did you really think he'd be interested in a plain, carrot-headed, bluestocking such as yourself?* The obvious answer to that question made her heart give a painful lurch.

By the time Hallie rounded the corner of Montgomery Street, her bag had become impossibly heavy, and she paused to set it down in front of a fashionable millinery shop. With a dejected little sigh, she turned to stare, without really seeing, into the plate-glass window.

It was the glitter of gold that finally drew her attention to the festive display before her. *Gold paper snowflakes.* Hallie felt a stab of nostalgia at the cheerful sight. When she was five years old, her mother had taught her how to make paper snowflakes like the ones in the window. And though her childish efforts had been rumpled and misshapen, her mother had exclaimed over them, calling them perfect. From that time on, the creation of foil snowflakes became a joyful yearly tradition.

Hallie stifled a sob. Here it was almost Christmas, and she'd never felt so alone in her life. If she hadn't been standing amidst a bustling crowd, she probably would have burst into tears.

Just when she'd convinced herself that she was the most desolate creature on earth, Hallie felt someone come up behind her. She didn't need to turn to know who it was, for she could sense the sweet familiarity of his presence. They stood like that for a long while, neither speaking nor moving.

"I like the green one," he finally said, breaking the awkward silence.

"Excuse me?" Hallie turned to glance up at Jake as

he moved to her side. He looked wonderful. His face was more tan than she remembered, and, for a change, he looked well rested.

Jake pointed to a frilly hat liberally bedecked with ribbons and feathers. "The hat. I like it."

Hallie made a show of studying his hunter green coat and then glanced back at the hat in question. "It would go perfectly with your jacket," she teased. Actually, the bonnet in question was a softer shade of green, a color that reminded her of his eyes. Those particular thoughts, however, she refrained from voicing.

Jake grinned at her jest. "I've missed you, Mission Lady," he murmured, taking her hands in his.

Though they both wore gloves, Hallie could have sworn she felt the warmth of his touch, even through two layers of kidskin. As she stared up into his handsome face, she suddenly wished that their hands were bare, craving the feel of the smooth texture of his skin as he caressed her palms.

"I never properly thanked you for everything you did for Serena . . . and me. I acted like an ungrateful bastard the night of the funeral. You didn't deserve to be treated in such a callous manner and I'm truly sorry."

Hallie smiled gently at his pleading expression. He looked uncertain, almost as if he half expected her to reject his apology. Giving his hand a reassuring squeeze, she said, "It's not necessary to apologize. You were tired and in pain. I understood."

"Are you sure? You took off quicker than General Lee being chased by Lincoln's ghost when you caught sight of me just now. I could have sworn you were avoiding me."

"That's ridiculous. I'd forgotten to do something at the infirmary and was in a hurry to get back."

"I may have been away for several weeks, but I do recall that the infirmary is that way." Chuckling, Jake pointed in the opposite direction. To his delight, her face pinked in a fetching manner.

Just then, a gust of salt-tinged wind whistled down the street, forcing the holiday shoppers to clutch at their hats. Fiery tendrils of hair danced over Hallie's forehead, and Jake found himself unable to resist the temptation to capture an errant ringlet and tuck it beneath her bonnet. His fingers lingered on her curls for a moment, before sliding lower to trace the curve of her jaw.

Staring intently into her eyes, he whispered, "I don't think I could bear having you angry with me. Forgive me?"

The intimacy of his gesture and the seductive huskiness of his voice caught her off guard. It was several seconds before she could answer,

"I'll forgive you, but only if you apologize for running off before I had a chance to reexamine your wound. I came to check on you two days after the funeral, and Celine told me you'd gone to Panama City on business. I've been plagued with all sorts of horrible visions of you succumbing to infection, or tearing your sutures and bleeding to death."

"Poor Mission Lady," he crooned, stroking her cheek. "I apologize for causing you such horrible thoughts, though I'm pleased you cared enough to have them. You'll be happy to know that your tincture of iodine experiment was a complete success. The wound healed perfectly. The ship's doctor, who removed my sutures, said it was some of the neatest stitching he'd ever seen. Of course, he did seem a bit taken aback when I informed him that it was the handiwork of a beautiful lady doctor."

Beautiful. Jake had called her beautiful. It was Hallie's turn to feel pleased. She couldn't stop herself from grinning like a miner who had struck a million-dollar bonanza. Indeed, Jake's compliment was far more precious to her than all the gold in the world.

Jake couldn't help smiling back at the radiance of her face. "It seems I've been forgiven. The question is, do you forgive me enough to help me with my terrible dilemma?"

"What dilemma?"

"Well, you see, there's this young lady with whom I've very recently formed an attachment, and I need help in selecting a Christmas gift for her."

Suddenly Hallie's pleasure in the moment faded away. *Arabella,* she thought, feeling as if the wind had been punched out of her. He had to be talking about Arabella. Pain flickered through her as she pictured Arabella cradled in Jake's strong arms, and she quickly lowered her lashes to hide her hurt. *Jake loved Arabella.*

Swallowing her choking despair, Hallie murmured, "Perhaps Penelope would be better suited for that task. I'm not familiar with what is considered to be a proper gift for a gentleman to present a lady."

"Penelope hasn't returned from New York yet. Besides, this particular lady is special, and I think you would be better suited for the purpose."

"I suppose I could try."

Jake cocked an eyebrow in Hallie's direction at the listlessness of her reply. All the joyous light had fled from her face, and she looked about as pleased as if she'd just swallowed a spoonful of castor oil. Strange. Most women enjoyed helping him spend his money. But then, Hallie Gardiner wasn't like any other woman he'd ever met.

Tossing her a baffled look, he hoisted her bag in one hand and presented her with his opposite arm. "The shop I had in mind is just around the corner."

With a sigh, Hallie tucked her hand in the curve of his elbow, trying hard to ignore the steely bulge of muscles beneath his sleeve. As she adjusted her energetic stride to his slower one, she commented, "Arabella is very beautiful."

"Yes."

"I imagine that she's the kind of woman every man dreams of marrying."

He grunted.

"Too bad about her husband," she persisted. "I heard he died on their wedding night. Of course, he was ninety-two years old."

"Poor old devil."

"He left her a wealthy woman."

"Good for her."

Hallie cocked her head to one side and, from beneath her lashes, stole a glance at Jake's face. He didn't look any too enthralled with their conversation. Amused maybe, but hardly like a man who was discussing the love of his life.

Repressing the urge to ask point-blank if he was, indeed, enamored of the beauteous Arabella, Hallie pointed out, "Her mother comes from royalty, you know."

"Fascinating."

The exasperating man actually chuckled. Barely able to conceal her frustration, Hallie decided to try a more direct approach. "Are you and Arabella—" Then she stopped abruptly, gaping at Jake in astonished delight. "Jake Parrish! You're walking without your cane!"

"I'm having a good day." He shrugged nonchalantly, though he was secretly pleased by her reaction. He stopped to nod at a shop just ahead. "I think we'll find the perfect gift in there. That is, if you're finished with your glowing report on Arabella's virtues." He almost laughed aloud when she flushed an intense shade of scarlet. Good. It served the minx right for assuming that he'd been taken in by Arabella's questionable charms.

As Jake opened the shop door for Hallie, she paused to glance around, perplexed. "Just how old is your lady friend?"

"Quite elderly. She'll be four months old tomorrow." Setting Hallie's medical bag on a counter, he peeled off his gloves and stuffed them into his pocket. "She also has a tendency to drool."

When he looked up again, Hallie was staring at him with such luminous eyes that he couldn't help but stare back. Her face was awash with happiness, and she seemed to glow as brightly as a candle on a Christmas tree. Even when she turned away to examine a magnificent toy puppet theater, he remained transfixed. Jake shook his head and chuckled at himself. Damn. He was behaving like a besotted youth.

It was a magical shop, and Hallie was instantly caught up in its enchantment. The shelves were filled with playthings of every imaginable type—and some that defied description completely. Happy people were everywhere. One couple beamed as their young son jumped up and down pointing at a toy ship, while a father with two daughters listened indulgently as the girls squealed in wonder at the sight of an automaton monkey playing a musical fiddle.

Hallie smiled at Jake as he stopped to finger the silk dress on a fine French fashion doll. When he glanced at her in a questioning manner, she shook her head.

"A doll like that will win your lady's heart in a few years' time, but she's much too young to appreciate it now. However, this," Hallie picked up a stuffed mohair elephant and danced it in front of his eyes, "would be perfect."

Jake took the toy and studied it closer. "Someday I'll take her to the circus and show her a real one," he mused, lightly stroking the little elephant's raised trunk. "She's mine now, and I want her to be happy."

"How can she help but be happy? She's got you for a father."

Jake chuckled at her words. "Had a change of heart, have you?"

"As have you, apparently. Did you finally choose a name?"

"Ariel."

"Pretty, but unusual."

"The first time I held her, I remember thinking that she weighed no more than a sprite."

Hallie looked at him oddly.

He nodded, his expression serious. "When I was ten, my tutor forced me to read all of Shakespeare's plays. I hated most of them, especially the romantic ones. However, I loved *The Tempest*. I was taken with the sprites."

Hallie burst out laughing. "Fanciful man! You named her for Shakespeare's sprite!"

Grinning, Jake looked down and considered the little elephant in his hands. He could imagine the fairylike Ariel clutching the toy in her chubby arms as she cooed and sucked on one of its floppy ears. Hallie was right. It was perfect. He looked up to tell her so, but the words died in his throat.

Jake Parrish was captivated.

Hallie glanced over her shoulder in time to see Jake duck behind the whimsically painted puppet theater. Mystified at what had so completely captured his attention, she followed. Did the man have a predilection for puppets or was it the carved Noah's ark on the shelf behind the theater that had him so enraptured? It wasn't until she saw him kneeling on the floor, his face flushed with excitement like an awestruck child, that she understood.

It was a train. Perfect in every miniature detail, it ran

by clockwork on a shiny track, occasionally emitting an off-key whistle. The polished brass locomotive pulled a string of colorfully painted cars, and there were even tiny passengers at some of the windows.

Carefully restraining her billowing skirts so as not to upset the little railroad, Hallie crouched beside him. "A train? I would have thought you to be more interested in the toy ships."

"I own plenty of real ones, and I get to play with them every day." He glanced up, his face utterly serious. "You're looking at the future. Railroads. Someday you'll be able to go from New York to California in less than two weeks' travel time. It's a dream I believe in, and I've invested heavily in it."

"Less than two weeks, you say?" Hallie exclaimed, bending forward to study the model closer. "How wonderful!"

"Yes. Wonderful," Jake agreed, shifting his gaze from Hallie's spellbound face to stare up at the beribboned greenery festooning the shelf full of dolls and puppets behind her. Then he grinned.

With a roguish expression, he leaned close to Hallie, whispering, "Merry Christmas, Mission Lady."

When she looked up to return his felicitation, she found his face only scant inches from her own. His eyes were glowing with a warmth that captured her heart, and when he smiled, she felt as if the rest of the world had melted away.

"Merry Christmas," Jake repeated, sweeping her into his embrace.

So firm and persuasive were his arms as he crushed her close, that her whole being was filled with the desire to savor his masculine strength. She became breathless with pleasure as their eyes met. His appeal was even more stunningly potent than she had remembered, his musky scent more sweetly intoxicating.

Holding her captive with the mesmerizing green fire of his gaze, Jake lifted his hand and gently traced the shape of her mouth. When he lingered to caress the tender skin lining her lower lip, her senses reeled in spiraling rapture.

Like a spirited filly gentling beneath a stallion's powerful command, Hallie trembled once and then surrendered to the hypnotic persuasion of his touch. With a sigh, she closed her eyes and relaxed, letting the soft curves of her body mold to the hard contours of his.

Jake liked the way Hallie felt in his arms, half lying in his lap with her full breasts crushed against his chest. Their bodies fit together like perfectly matched pieces of a jigsaw puzzle.

Tightening his arm around her in a fierce hug, he tipped her face up to his, murmuring, "Mistletoe." Then his mouth claimed hers with exquisite slowness.

Never in her most wishful dreams had Hallie imagined that his kiss could taste so sweet. Her lips tingled as he gently moved his mouth against hers, and when he caught her lower lip between his teeth, she shuddered with pleasure. Sensuously, he teased her, alternately nipping and sucking on the sensitive flesh until she twined her arms around his neck to invite him deeper.

Jake's loins tightened at the eagerness of her response. Almost savage now in his need to explore the dark delights of her mouth, he boldly parted her lips with his tongue. With deep, delving thrusts he probed the heated mystery, groaning with pleasure as she pliantly welcomed him. Currents of desire telegraphed throughout his body at the tentative reply of her tongue against his, and he felt himself harden with rampant need.

As his lips grew demanding, so did his arousal and even through the heavy layers of her skirts, Hallie could feel its insistent prod. She knew she should escape his embrace, knew she should ignore the way his kisses sent bolts of pleasure streaking through her body. But she didn't have the power to deny his kisses any more than she had the power to deny her love for him.

When Jake at last pulled his lips away, they could only stare at each other in emotion-filled silence—she breathless with desire, he panting heavily with need, and both too stunned by their passion to speak.

"Sir? Madame? Is there some way in which I can be of assistance?" The clerk smiled courteously. He had come in search of a dragon puppet but had discovered the couple embracing behind the theater instead.

Jake felt Hallie start at the man's interruption, and he jerked uncomfortably as her hip rubbed against his engorged sex. Catching his breath sharply, he tightened his arms to still her movement. Damn! Another motion like that and he would lose control completely.

Without loosening his hold or taking his eyes off Hallie's prettily flushed face, Jake tossed the stuffed elephant up to the clerk. "We'll take this."

The toy hit the clerk squarely in the chest. The man, used to dealing with errant children who were intent on wreaking havoc to his shop, caught it before it tumbled to the ground. With great aplomb, he inquired, "Will this be all, sir?"

"We'll take anything else you think would be appropriate for a four-month-old baby." Stifling a groan as Hallie squirmed against him again, Jake paused to hiss into her ear, "Unless you want me to disgrace myself right here and now, I'd suggest you sit still." He pressed his arousal against her hip in warning. With her eyes wide, she nodded and became as still as a statue.

Giving Hallie a crooked smile, Jake returned his attention to the clerk. The man was tactfully staring at the toy elephant and Jake had to clear his throat several times to get his attention. "And the train. We'll take the train." Pressing his face close to Hallie's, he inquired, "Anything for you, Mission Lady? That box of chemical experiments over there, or perhaps a magic lantern?"

Hallie giggled and shook her head.

Sighing with disappointment, Jake waved the man away.

As the man bustled off to select the appropriate items, Jake pulled Hallie's rakishly askew bonnet straight and asked, "What is it you desire for Christmas, Mission Lady?"

You, she thought wantonly. But she suppressed her urge and replied, "Snow. It hardly seems like Christmas without it."

"I agree. I have yet to get used to San Francisco's mild climate myself."

"And you, Jake. What would you ask of Santa Claus?"

He thought for a moment. "A clue. One that would lead to Serena's murderer. I've turned her death over and over again in my mind. Nothing makes sense."

"I know. I can't seem to make sense of it either."

They fell silent, each captured in private thoughts, as

Jake struggled to his feet. It was with great care that he managed to brace himself on his stiff left leg. As he reached down to assist Hallie, she peered skeptically at the greenery above his shoulder.

"Why, you wicked man! That's not mistletoe at all. It's plain, ordinary holly."

Jake looked up and squinted in an exaggerated manner. "Really? It looked like mistletoe to me." He cocked his head to one side. "You know, Mission Lady, I think you're right."

Then he swept her into his strong embrace and kissed her again.

When he finally released her, she sputtered, "Why did you do that?"

"Since that wasn't mistletoe, I had to take the kiss back. It was a mistletoe kiss, you see." Chuckling, he turned to make his way to the counter.

While Jake paid for his purchases and gave instructions for their delivery, Hallie wandered to the front of the shop, stopping to examine the gaily decorated door. When Jake at last joined her, her forgotten medical bag in tow, she threw her arms around his neck with a force that almost knocked him off balance and soundly kissed him.

Grinning with stunned delight, he asked, "And what did I do to warrant such a wonderful treat?"

Hallie grinned back and pointed above his head. "You stood in the right place. That, Mr. Parrish, is mistletoe!"

"Cissy, I need you to hold still while I examine your throat," pleaded Hallie, pushing aside the sobbing girl's hair to expose the damaged skin at her throat.

At Hallie's touch, Cissy whimpered like a wounded puppy and shrank back against her pillows, staring at her would-be savior with blatant distrust.

Hallie sighed. She really couldn't blame the girl for being wary. Not only had the poor creature been beaten within an inch of her life, she'd had to endure the pain of having her lacerated scalp stitched and her broken ribs bound. She'd behaved quite bravely up until now.

Giving Cissy her most reassuring smile, Hallie promised, "I'm not going to hurt you. I just want to take care of your neck. But I can't unless you cooperate."

"Ya behave y'self and do as the doc says," scolded an older woman standing on the opposite side of the bed. The woman, dressed in a black mourning ensemble complete with a widow's veil, tapped her foot impatiently and glared at the cringing figure in the bed.

Fat tears coursed down Cissy's cheeks as she obeyed, leaving tracks of black kohl trailing through the layers of powder and rouge. With the shadow from her lids smudged like bruises around her eyes, and her blood-red lip paste smeared across her chin, she had the look of a boxer who had lost one fight too many. Yet, beneath all the heavy paint, Hallie could see that she was pretty. Young, too. Pathetically so.

"How old are you, dear?" Hallie inquired, bending down to examine the girl's neck.

"Fifteen last month."

Fifteen and already a seasoned prostitute. The thought made Hallie want to weep. She'd seen many such creatures at the infirmary back home. Riddled with syphilis and broken by life, they were considered old by the age of twenty-five. While many of her fellow doctors refused to treat the women, Hallie reached out to them with compassion. She had cared when others had turned a blind eye, shown mercy while most had condemned, and done her best to give the desperate beings comfort in their otherwise dismal lives. Most important, she had never judged them.

Hallie drew in a sharp breath when she saw the full extent of Cissy's injury. *Lord! Someone had tried to strangle the poor girl!*

Like an ominous pendant of black, yellow, and purple, livid bruises ringed the slender throat. The marks darkened brutally over the now pounding pulse point and fanned up the sides of her neck in perfect fingerlike impressions.

"She gonna live, Doc?" inquired the older woman as she lifted her black veil and frowned at the discolored flesh.

Hallie nodded. "I stitched the cut on her head and splinted her right wrist. The wrist doesn't appear to be broken, though it is badly sprained. Unfortunately, Cissy wasn't quite so lucky with her ribs. It appears that two of them were fractured. She's badly bruised and has had a nasty shock. However, she should be fully recovered in several weeks' time."

"Several weeks? There's gonna be an awful lot of disappointed fellas in San Francisco. Cissy's the most popular gal in the house. Real talented, if ya take my meanin'."

Hallie did take her meaning, and it was only with the greatest of effort that she managed not to blush. To look at Coralie LaFlume, with her severely coiffed gray hair and demure black gown, one would never have guessed her to be the madame of San Francisco's most notorious brothel. Why, she looked about as wicked as a grandmother at a church social. Yet there was something in the way she looked at a person, her gray eyes shrewdly assessing, that left little doubt as to the sharpness of the mind beneath the amiable exterior. And those eyes were now as hard as nails as she stared at Hallie.

"Jist think of the bundle we'll lose!" she exclaimed. "Ya sure Cissy needs several weeks? After all, she works on her back, if ya take my meanin'."

"Uh, yes. I understand Cissy's—um—duties. However, the ribs will take a while to heal and she shouldn't be jostled around—if you take *my* meaning." Seeing Coralie and Cissy's faces fall with disappointment, Hallie suggested, "Perhaps, when she feels up to it, Cissy could work at one of the gaming tables downstairs. That shouldn't do her any harm—provided she sits."

Coralie brightened perceptibly at that notion. Carelessly twisting a corner of her veil, she mused, "Smart idea, Doc. The fellas'll see Cissy dealin' the cards and they'll get real itchy. 'Specially when they learn they cain't have her. Why, after a few weeks of teasin', they'll be willin' ta pay twice her usual price."

Cissy smiled and nodded in agreement. The girl actually seemed taken by the idea.

As she rubbed her hands together in anticipation, the madame chuckled. "Ya know, Doc, if ya ever get tired of pokin' around that musty old Mission House and want a real excitin' time, why, ya come talk ta Coralie LaFlume. Sure could be usin' a smart gal like ya 'round here."

"I'll keep that in mind." Hallie held a measure of laudanum to Cissy's lips, smiling as the girl obediently drained the cup. As she tucked the blankets around her patient's shoulders, she asked, "Who did this to you, dear?"

"Ain't never seen his face."

Hallie let out a snort of disbelief. "How could you—"

"Strange man, that 'un," cut in Coralie, sitting on the edge of the bed and patting Cissy's golden curls in an affectionate manner. "Ain't none of us seen him. Never comes himself. Sends some nasty-tempered China fella to fetch the gals."

"But surely someone has seen his face? I mean considering the intimate nature of your business."

"Nah. He always keeps his face covered." Coralie shook her head in a perplexed manner. "Most fellas like some kissin'. But not this 'un. He likes it quick and with his clothes on. Why, he won't even let a gal touch his—well, ya know—unless she's wearin' special gloves. Red silk ones with fancy diamond buttons."

That caught Hallie's attention. "Red silk, you say?"

Coralie nodded. "With fancy buttons."

"And your girls don't object?"

"The fella pays real good." With a sly grin, Coralie added, " 'Course, he has ta, considerin' his special tastes."

"Special tastes?"

"Yep. Likes to be switched, if ya take my meanin'."

Hallie certainly did, and it sickened her. Looking up from the bandage she was rolling, she exclaimed, "How can you encourage your girls to do business with such an awful man?"

"Been harmless enough in the past." The madame shrugged in a matter-of-fact manner. " 'Sides, the gals all like him. Says he talks real cultured-like. Got the manners of a high-flutin' gentleman, too. Pearl got his clothes half off once, says he's got a fine-lookin' body, 'cept for a nasty scar."

"Scar? Where?" Hallie's attention was fully arrested now. She shoved the last of her equipment in her bag and frowned as she waited for Coralie to reply.

The woman mulled over the question for a moment before shaking her head. "Don't recall Pearl mentionin' where. Jist said it was all red and twisted-lookin'."

"Could I talk to Pearl?"

"Pearl run off a few weeks back. Ain't seen hide nor hair of her since. Treated the gal like a daughter, and she jist takes off without a word."

"Would there be anyone else who could tell me about the man?"

Coralie's eyes narrowed at the urgency in Hallie's voice. "Ya seem awful interested in the fella. Care ta tell me why?"

"A friend of mine was murdered a couple of months ago, and the murderer left marks on her throat similar to those on Cissy. She was also wearing a glove like those you described." Hallie's voice rose in desperation. "There might be a connection. You say he's always been harmless enough in the past. Why would he attack Cissy now?"

There was a muffled sob from the bed. "He couldn't git hard. So he started hittin' me and talkin' all crude. Claimed it was my fault. Made me git on my knees and beg."

Serena's words echoed through Hallie's mind. *I hate it most when he's crude. He can't take his pleasure unless I cry and beg. He blames me if his man's part can't—*

"When it stayed all shrunk up, he got crazy." Cissy's tone verged on hysteria. "He grabbed my neck and started squeezin' 'til I couldn't breathe no more. Don't remember much else." She buried her face in the pillow, her shoulders heaving violently as she wept.

"Yep," finished Coralie, taking the girl in her arms and stroking her back with maternal expertise. "We found poor Cissy layin' half dead on our doorstep."

"Have you contacted the police?"

Coralie laughed raucously at that. "The police don't care about what happens to a whore."

"Well, I do," announced Hallie. "And I'll be back the day after tomorrow to check on Cissy. You can send for me at the mission if she gets any worse."

Coralie looked positively stunned by Hallie's words. "Really? Ya don't mind bein' seen at a whorehouse, Doc?"

"I'm here, aren't I?"

"Yep. But, I mean, them men doctors made it clear they ain't interested in tendin' a pack of whores. Don't approve of our business, if ya take my meanin'." Coralie's mouth twisted cynically. " 'Course, the old hypocrites ain't above usin' our services."

Hallie reached out and gave the madame's shoulder a warm squeeze. "I'll be glad to help your girls in any way I can. Sick people are the same no matter who they are or what they do. It's not my place to judge."

Coralie's eyes were bright with gratitude. "You won't be sorry. I promise. We'll pay you real handsome-like, and if anyone says anythin' bad about you, I'll have my doorman rough 'em up good." She slammed her right fist into her left palm to illustrate her point.

Hallie laughed. "I doubt the roughing-up part will be necessary. However, if you wish to make a donation to the Mission Infirmary, we'll be more than glad to accept it. I do have one request, though."

"Jist ask, Doc."

"If you hear anything else about the strange man, or find any clues as to his identity, will you let me know?"

As Hallie left the brothel, she paused on the front steps to admire the bold artistry of the rising sun. Glorious shades of pink and gold streaked the sky as dawn broke over the city. She should have been exhausted; she should have wanted nothing more than to crawl into her hard little bed and sleep the morning away. But her excitement over what she had learned from Coralie and Cissy overruled her tired body's commands.

Carefully avoiding the glass from a shattered liquor bottle, Hallie descended the stairs. She kicked a gaudy slipper out of her path and then stopped to pick up an abandoned piece of mistletoe. Staring at the crushed greenery, she pictured Jake's beautiful face, and her lips burned at the memory of his kisses.

It was December 24 and she was in love.

"Ho, ho, ho, Jake Parrish," Hallie laughed into the cold morning breeze. "You're about to get your Christmas wish."

Chapter 13

The face in the mirror looked decidedly worse for wear.

Damn! That Seth Tyler had a nasty left hook.

With a grimace, Jake prodded the bruise marring the right side of his jaw. It was ugly and it hurt. Still, it was minor compared to the damage he had suffered at Seth's hands during the past few months.

Giving his reflection a lopsided grin, Jake noted with satisfaction that neither eye had been blackened. The days of his crushing defeats were definitely over, as were Seth's easy victories in the boxing ring. He'd even be willing to bet that his friend was sporting a few colorful marks himself this morning.

Of course, knowing Seth Tyler as well as he did, Jake had no doubts at all that the man had turned his battered appearance to his own roguish advantage. He was probably lying in the arms of one of his admirers at this very moment, groaning in an exaggerated manner, while the doting young lady held cold compresses to his face. Seth so enjoyed the tender ministrations of his women that he always made sure he received at least one bruise, just so he could play the wounded hero. He claimed that nothing made a woman grow all soft and loving quicker than a man in need of tending.

When Jake thought about the way Hallie had cared for him after he had been shot, he was inclined to agree. In fact, her tender attention was *all* he'd thought about during his recent voyage to Panama City.

Plagued with pain and fatigue, he had lain in his luxurious cabin desperately wishing for his Mission Lady's gentle touch. He had wanted so badly to feel her calloused little hand against his cheek as she checked him for fever and to see her forehead crease with concentration as she carefully tended his injured side. Why, he would have even welcomed her poking at the sore wound, just to have her near.

Jake had known upon leaving San Francisco, that he would miss his little doctor friend; he just hadn't realized how much. Restlessly he had tossed and turned in his spacious bed, calling himself every kind of a fool for thinking he could run away from his growing feelings for her. Every waking moment had been filled with thoughts of Hallie, and when he slept, she had haunted his dreams. By the time he had reached Aspinwall, he'd finally faced the truth: he needed his Mission Lady.

Still thinking of Hallie, Jake bent closer to the mirror and took an inventory of his injuries. Perhaps he could use some of the good doctor's loving care now? Aside from the swollen jaw, there was a small cut beneath one bloodshot eye, and another at the corner of his mouth. The dark stubble shadowing his cheeks didn't do a hell of a lot to improve his appearance either. And his head . . .

Jake groaned and rubbed at his temples. Damn! It felt like someone was hammering a staccato inside his brain. At this point he couldn't be quite sure if the throbbing was due to the pounding he had taken from Seth in the ring or if it was a legacy from the bottle of fine brandy they had consumed afterward. Come to think of it, the only thing he was sure of in regard to last evening was that Seth had been the victor of their contest. But if his memory served him correctly, it had been a close match. Next time he intended to win.

In the days before the war, Jake's athletic prowess, coupled with his unblemished record of victory in the ring, had made him a legendary force at the Olympic Club. No one, including Seth, had stood a chance against his raw strength and catlike agility. So formidable an opponent was he that the other members of the club were forced to acknowledge his physical superiority and consequently ceased their jests regarding his too pretty face. Jake was fiercely proud of his hard-won reputation.

But that was before the battle that robbed him of his athletic ability, leaving him a maimed left leg as a tragic souvenir.

Jake smiled bitterly at his reflection. He had heard

over and over again how lucky he was to have his leg. On good days, when he merely walked with an ungainly limp, he was inclined to agree. But on bad ones, such as today, when he was virtually lame and the improperly healed wound ached unbearably, he seriously questioned his good fortune.

As he tightly grasped the edge of his ebony dressing table for support, his mood grew foul in the extreme. God, he dreaded these bad days. It wasn't the pain that made them so awful, it was the debilitating weakness. He hated feeling so helpless and frustrated.

Wavering unsteadily, Jake decided it was going to be an especially bad day, and he was damn well going to make sure everyone else shared in his misery.

"Hop Yung!" he bellowed. "Get your worthless hide in here—now!"

Where was that Chinaman when you wanted him? He was always underfoot until you needed him and then . . .

"Hop! Where the hell are you? Just wait until I get my hands—"

Jake was startled into speechlessness as he lurched around in a fit of fury and almost knocked Hop Yung over. The houseboy was standing behind his employer holding out a robe, his expression bland.

A shadow of annoyance crossed Jake's face as he felt his leg give out and he was forced to steady himself against the dressing table again.

"Where have you been?" he demanded through clenched teeth, skewering the servant with a rancorous stare.

Hop looked back at him with suppressed amusement, making Jake suddenly aware of what a ridiculous picture he made, standing there stark naked and scowling with menace at a Chinaman half his size.

With a snort of irritation, he shrugged the emerald-green-and-black-striped dressing gown over his shoulders and belted it at his waist. Running his hand through his sweat-dampened hair in a gesture of ill-tempered agitation, Jake scowled at the now grinning houseboy.

"Why didn't you come when I called? And where the hell is my coffee? Damn it, Hop! You know I like my coffee first thing in the morning. And wipe that simple-minded grin off your face. I ought to replace you with an Irishman. I had one come around looking for a job just yesterday. *He* showed me proper respect. You could afford to take a lesson or two from that man!"

"Hop best houseboy. Irish houseboy no good. Got meaner head than Mister Jake. You chop-chop-kill each other!" Hop made slashing motions into the air to demonstrate his point. Smirking wickedly, he waited for his employer's outraged response.

The scenario was a familiar one, having been played out countless times over the years. Hop, used to his employer's tirades, had been threatened with the hated Irishman many times before, and the threat now failed to have any real impact. Still, mean-head or no, the little man couldn't imagine working for anyone else. Since that day eight years ago, when Jake Parrish had saved him from being lynched for a crime of which he was innocent, Hop had discovered his rescuer to be a man of fairness and good judgment—despite his tendency to rant and rave. And Hop Yung had vowed to be loyal to Mr. Jake until his dying day.

"Meaner head, Hop? I'll show you meaner head if you don't get my coffee now," Jake threatened, though his mood was starting to lighten a bit at Hop's saucy behavior.

Hop rolled his eyes mournfully and shook his head in mock despair. With an offended air, he gestured behind his employer. "Mister Jake get mean-head, no reason. Coffee on table. Hop best houseboy."

And sure enough, the table by the vaulted window was neatly laid out with coffee, toast points, and the morning edition of the *Golden Era.*

After accepting his cane from Hop with a curt nod, Jake limped over to the table and eased himself into a high-backed chair. The effort sent a pain radiating through his damaged leg. With a sigh, he rubbed at his thigh until the discomfort had been reduced to a dull throb. *It was a bad day indeed,* he thought, closing his eyes and leaning his head back in a resigned manner.

When he heard Hop Yung laying out his shaving implements, Jake opened his eyes and stared at the man. " 'Mean-head'? What the hell kind of language is that? Is that what they taught you at the mission school?" He paused to pour himself a cup of coffee. "You're going to have to remind me to have a word with Reverend DeYoung. I would hate to think that all the money he's managed to swindle out of me on behalf of that school has been wasted on teachers who teach phrases like 'mean-head'."

Jake sat back in his chair and took a sip from his cup. He immediately released a loud oath as the hot liquid burned his mouth. Slamming the delicate Limoges cup back on the table, he returned his gaze to the busy houseboy.

"Hot-tempered, Hop."

The little man threw his employer a questioning look.

"Hot-tempered, foul-mannered, nasty-dispositioned, moody bastard. Take your pick. They're all correct terms for mean-headed."

Hop smiled in mischievous understanding. "Mr. Jake foul-mannered bastard. O.K. Hop no forget. Mr. Jake foul-tempered, nasty bastard. Is Mr. Jake pleased with Hop?" He braced his hands on his hips and peered at the man by the window expectantly.

" 'Pleased' is hardly the word I'd use for being described as a foul-tempered, nasty bastard. However, I see you're quick to grasp the concept, and it does please me to know that I don't have a half-witted houseboy. So, fine. End of lesson."

While Hop went to prepare his bath, Jake scanned the newspaper idly. Today, however, the *Golden Era* failed to hold his interest, and he felt himself growing impatient. He drummed his fingers on the table in bored agitation, wondering what was keeping the houseboy.

When Hop finally returned, Jake opened his mouth to vent his displeasure. But before he could say a word, the little man announced, "Lady to see Mr. Jake. Say it urgent."

A sardonic smile wreathed Jake's lips as he raised his brow in mock wonder. "Urgent? Then by all means send the lady up."

Hop looked horrified as he rushed to correct his employer. "No! Not that kind of lady. Kind Mr. Jake sees with clothes on. Lady from mission."

"Appetizing thought," groaned Jake, grimacing with distaste. It had to be Lavinia Donahue. Not only was the venerable Mrs. Donahue the most prune-faced of the mission crows, she also had the indisputable distinction of being the town's biggest gossip. She had threatened to pay him a visit this morning. She was probably going to try and shove that pasty-faced daughter of hers down his throat. He groaned again. "Tell her I'm indisposed—tell her anything. But for God's sake, get rid of her! My head aches enough without some self-righteous harpy yammering at me!"

"Hop try. She no go. Say it 'portant. Stubborn lady." Hop wrung his hands in visible distress.

"Fine!" Jake snorted. "If she wants to wait, then let her wait. You may finish preparing my bath now. And Hop? Make sure the water's hot. I'm in the mood for a good, long soak."

Whatever could be keeping Jake? Hallie wondered, shifting uncomfortably on the overstuffed blue-and-white-patterned loveseat. It had been well over an hour and a half since Hop Yung had ushered her into the formal parlor, and she was beginning to wonder if the rude little man had alerted his employer of her presence at all.

Hallie sighed with frustration. Wouldn't it be just like the houseboy to conveniently forget about her? After all, he hadn't looked exactly pleased to see her. She knew she hadn't been in the man's good graces since the morning Jake had been shot and she had refused to let him treat the wound with some suspicious-looking powder. Undoubtedly she was now paying the price for pricking his ego.

Just when Hallie had decided she'd waited long enough and was about to conduct a search of her own, the door flew open. There stood Jake Parrish. Clad in a dark gray morning suit that emphasized the magnificence of his build, he looked every inch the man they called the Young Midas. His cheeks had a slight blush, as if freshly shaven, and his still damp hair was neatly brushed off his face. She also noticed, with a surge of compassion, that he appeared to be leaning heavily upon his cane. His handsome face was set in lines of brooding ill-humor . . . until he caught sight of her.

Then he smiled. It was a beautiful, genuine smile, the kind that made the dimple crease his lean cheek and never failed to send Hallie's heart turning cartwheels in her chest. Suddenly she felt all her agitation over being kept waiting melt away, and she smiled back.

As Jake limped toward her, flinching with every step, Hallie had to battle her urge to rush to his side and assist him as if he were an invalid. Such treatment, she knew, would be shameful in his eyes. For though she had heard him joke about his clumsy state on several occasions, there had been a dark edge of bitterness shadowing his lighthearted words. And when he had smiled in acknowledgment of the laughter drawn by his quips, she'd seen the bleakness that had momentarily flared in the otherwise indifferent gleam of his eyes.

It was during such a moment that Hallie had silently vowed never to add to his humiliation by treating him as a cripple, or as anything less than what he was: a man of incredible strength and capabilities.

By sheer force of will she managed to continue smiling, ignoring the way his expression of obvious pain made her ache with sympathy. When he stumbled at the edge of the carpet and had to struggle to retain his balance, she pretended to be preoccupied with the removal of her bonnet.

Jake uttered a curse beneath his breath. Another move like that and he would find himself face down on the floor. He shot Hallie a furtive glance as he steadied himself. He had expected to find her staring at him, her face awash with pity. But she seemed completely oblivious to his plight as she busily fussed with her hat. *Good.* At least he'd been spared the indignity of having her witness his near tumble.

Resolutely bracing himself against his cane, Jake mentally measured the distance between them. With a little luck, he might make it to one of the chairs without disgracing himself. Lady Luck was smiling on him, and when he finally came to a stop in front of Hallie, he warmly clasped her hand in his. "I'm sorry to have kept you waiting. I thought you were Lavinia Donahue, and I was hoping if I stalled long enough she would leave." He lifted her palm to his lips and gave it a lingering kiss, his eyes never wavering from hers. "You, however, I'm glad to see."

A shiver of delight raced through Hallie at the feel of

Jake's firm lips against her flesh. The seductive tenderness in his gaze made her feel breathless and flushed all over. When she spoke, her voice sounded strangely husky. "I had to see you, Jake. I have some important news."

"News?" He sighed with exaggerated disappointment as he eased himself into the chair opposite hers. "And here I was hoping that you had come with the express purpose of luring me under the mistletoe again." He stretched his damaged leg stiffly in front of him, carefully suppressing a groan as a stabbing sensation knifed through the limb.

Hallie could feel her face burning with embarrassed pleasure at his provocative remark. No man had ever paid her such flattering attention before, and she had no idea how to respond. Especially to a man who was eyeing her with such blatant interest.

In a choked tone she managed to croak, "Do you always greet ladies in such an outrageous manner?"

"Only those who have experienced my mistletoe kiss."

"Oh? And have there been many?"

"Just one," he whispered, casting her a meaningful glance through his lashes.

Lord! What now? Hallie wondered, her mind scrambling for a response. What could she say to a man who was so obviously a master at the art of flirtation? To her despair, she drew a blank. If the devil had appeared at that very moment, offering a dazzling retort in return for her soul, Hallie undoubtedly would have found herself condemned to eternal damnation.

Jake smiled wickedly, thoroughly charmed by her obvious confusion. "You know, Mission Lady, I have a particularly fine piece of mistletoe hanging in the family parlor. *Genuine* mistletoe, mind you. Want to try it out?"

"You're shameless, Mr. Parrish."

"Only where you're concerned." Though he kept his tone light, Jake wanted nothing more than to crush her body against his and plunder the heated velvet of her mouth with his tongue. Just the thought of Hallie Gardiner in his arms sent a slash of heat cutting through his loins.

Hallie stared back at him for several seconds, the

smoldering heat in his gaze making her feel as boneless as a jellyfish she'd once seen floating in the surf. Heaven help her! She wanted to lie beneath the mistletoe and let Jake take all sorts of improper advantages of her body. She yearned to tangle her fingers in his thick hair as she tasted the sweetness of his kisses. A now familiar tightness twisted in her belly, and she squirmed uncomfortably with a need she didn't quite understand.

Firmly ignoring her wanton urges, Hallie drew her gaze away from his and fumbled with her reticule. Removing a crumpled scrap of paper, she extended it to Jake, saying in a slightly breathless voice, "Merry Christmas, Mr. Parrish."

Jake read the hastily scribbled address and then crooked an eyebrow at her in question. "Are you suggesting that I invite one of Madame LaFlume's girls to join me beneath the mistletoe?"

"No-no. O-of course not!" she stammered, feeling a sudden stab of jealousy at the thought of Jake kissing one of Coralie's delectable tarts. "I just—" She stopped in midsentence, gaping at Jake incredulously. "And just how is it that you recognize Madame LaFlume's address?"

"Every man over the age of sixteen and under the age of one hundred knows about Madame LaFlume. And as you know from your *intimate examination* of my body, I'm most definitely a man."

Hallie blushed hotly. He most certainly was.

"Not that Madame LaFlume's establishment holds any particular charms for me, mind you."

"Really? I took you for a man with a—uh—lusty nature."

"Only where a certain little Mission Lady is concerned."

His gaze was soft as it captured hers, the color of his eyes reminding Hallie of new spring grass misted by the morning dew. She stared into his beautiful face in stunned disbelief. What possible interest, save friendship perhaps, could a magnificent man such as Jake Parrish have in a drab little wren like herself? With his looks and money, he could have any woman he wanted. He couldn't seriously want her? Could he?

She felt her breath catch in her throat as she ruthlessly discarded the romantic notion. Of course he didn't want her. She was a fool even to have imagined such a thing. The man was simply an unprincipled rake who enjoyed toying with her emotions.

As Jake leaned forward and clasped her trembling hands in his steady ones, she murmured, "Please don't tease me, Jake. I haven't any experience with such talk, and it makes me uncomfortable."

"Who's teasing, Mission Lady?" he replied in a solemn tone. When she didn't respond, he studied her bowed head for a second, puzzled by her sudden coolness. Could it be true, then? Was she really so inexperienced with men that she found his remarks disconcerting?

No. Jake didn't buy that story for a second. How could a woman as lovely and vital as Hallie Gardiner have managed to reach the age of twenty-six without ever once experiencing the attentions of a suitor? The very idea was ludicrous.

He looked down at Hallie's hands cradled in his and absently stroked one of her calloused palms with his thumb. But if it weren't true, then what could have prompted her to imply such a thing?

He shivered as a sudden chill gripped his soul, and he could have sworn that he heard Serena's ghost whispering the awful truth in his ear: his Mission Lady had become so repulsed by his crippled leg and his confessed inability to sire children that she could no longer bear his touch. That very real possibility hurt him far more than he cared to admit. Cursing beneath his breath, Jake let Hallie's hands drop to her lap.

"I believe you had some news to impart, Dr. Gardiner?" he asked in a harsh voice.

Hallie glanced up at him, shocked by his brusque tone. His face had taken on a wooden expression, and his gaze, as it met hers, was unreadable. Troubled by his abrupt mood change, she bit her lower lip and looked away. "Of course." And she proceeded to recount her encounter at Madame LaFlume's house, avoiding Jake's stony gaze as she spoke.

She can't even stand to look at me, he thought bitterly, watching as Hallie's eyes landed everywhere except on his face. Yet could he really have been so wrong about her response to his kisses? Had he misinterpreted the warmth he saw flaring in her eyes every time she looked at him? All at once he felt an overwhelming need to grasp her face in his hands and force her to look into his eyes while he demanded that she confess her feelings for him. But was he really brave enough to hear the truth? Somehow that thought frightened him more than the prospect of facing a hundred stitches.

As Hallie finished her story, she glanced at Jake's face and waited for his response. His eyes narrowed as he seemed to consider her words.

Then he gave a snort of disbelief. "And you think that Serena was in some way involved with that perverted creature?"

"The bruises on Cissy's neck were identical to those on your wife—and there is the matter of the scarlet gloves," she pointed out, not caring for the way he was looking at her. He was staring down his nose at her like she was a particularly witless court jester and he was some royal deity who was about to have her beheaded for telling a bad joke.

Hallie chewed her lower lip as she debated whether or not she should mention Serena's words the day Ariel was born. It might serve to convince him of her theory, or at the very least wipe that infuriatingly superior expression off his face.

But did she dare? Hallie studied his coldly arrogant face for a moment. Though Jake had always been gentle with his wife in her presence, she had no way of knowing what kind of private relationship the couple had shared. Perhaps—?

No! She firmly pushed the picture of Jake as an abusive husband from her mind. Of course he hadn't mistreated Serena. Surely she would have seen evidence of such behavior had it been true. Wouldn't she?

"Well, Mission Lady? Is that the extent of your clue?" he prompted in a bored tone

She stared down at her lap and fidgeted restlessly with her reticule. "Not quite."

"Then pray tell."

"On the day Ariel was born, Serena mentioned a man who couldn't get—um—aroused unless she begged and cried. She claimed he hit her. She seemed terribly frightened of him."

When her revelation was greeted by silence, Hallie stole a timid glance at Jake in an attempt to gauge his reaction. She could see the tension in every line of his face, and as their eyes met, the implacability of his expression unnerved her.

In a voice as sharp as the report from a pistol, he asked, "And you believe Serena was speaking of her lover?"

She nodded once.

Cocking his head to one side, Jake proceeded to study her in a way that made Hallie feel as though he were reading her thoughts. At his next utterance, she was sure of it.

"Tell me, Dr. Gardiner—and please be truthful—isn't there some niggling doubt eating at your brain that makes you wonder whether or not I'm that man? After all, by my own confession, you know that I was unable to perform my manly duty with Serena. And you've heard me curse, so you know I can be quite crude."

Hallie shook her head and looked away. "I never thought—"

He cut her off before she could finish choking out her denial. "Of course you've thought, Mission Lady. And a great deal, I would imagine. Why else would you have been so reluctant to inform me of Serena's words?"

Jake watched as Hallie recoiled from his words. Damn her! Not only did she view him as an impotent cripple, she seemed to think him capable of unspeakable perversion as well. The thought sent a shaft of pain lancing through his heart and darkened his mood to a more ominous shade of black. So be it then. If she chose to think of him as a dissolute miscreant, then, by God, he'd oblige her by acting like one.

With lascivious thoroughness, Jake let his gaze sweep the length of Hallie's body. Boldly focusing his stare on the outline of her breasts, he said, "There are a thousand kinds of passion, Dr. Gardiner. Some of them very—well, unusual. Surely even you understand that?"

When she regarded him in silence, a frown creasing her forehead, he snorted his derision. "Of course not! What would a starchy old maid like you know about such things?"

The suddenness of Jake's verbal attack caught Hallie

off guard. Staring back at him in shock, she could only sputter with indignation.

But he pointedly ignored her pique as he purred, "Shall I tell you all the different ways a man and a woman can seek their carnal pleasure?"

Quickly finding her tongue, she snapped back, "No, you shall not!" Snatching up her bonnet and reticule in hands trembling with anger, she began to rise. "And if you think I'm going to sit here and endure your rudeness, well, then you'd better have Dr. Barnes examine your head. Your brains have obviously been addled from taking one blow too many in the boxing ring. I can't imagine what else could have prompted you to behave like such a boor."

As Hallie lifted her nose in the air in a contemptuous manner, she was stunned to feel Jake's hands clamp around her arms. With head-spinning speed she was hauled forward, and before she could let out even a squawk of protest, she found herself kneeling between his legs.

"Not interested in hearing what I have to say, Mission Lady?" he drawled, leaning forward to press his face close to hers. "Ah, well. Perhaps you would rather be shown instead."

Angered as much by his condescending tone as by his suggestion, Hallie struggled to free herself. "You can save your filthy little lessons for Coralie's girls," she hissed, trying to lunge out of his grasp. "For twenty dollars, I'm sure they would be more than happy to play the eager pupil."

He tightened his grip and pulled her nearer. Twisting his lips into a caricature of a smile, he murmured, "True. But I prefer my students completely untrained. There's nothing more tedious than breaking a woman of undesirable habits . . . especially when those habits diminish my pleasure."

"I'm going to diminish more than your pleasure if you don't let me loose this instant!" she retorted, clumsily butting her head against the unyielding surface of his belly.

To her frustration, he simply laughed. Bending close to her ear, he whispered, "Lesson number one . . ." Slowly he traced the delicate inner shell with his tongue, pausing now and again to tease her delicate lobe with his teeth.

A tremor ran down Hallie's spine as she felt the warmth of his breath tickling against her ear. The heat of his mouth stirred her senses, and as a rush of excitement spiraled through her body, she forced herself to become rigid in an attempt to combat the unwelcome sensations.

Resolutely jerking her head away from his seductively probing tongue, she snapped, "Damn you, Mr. Parrish! Save your carnal lessons for someone who's interested!" When she tried to move from his disturbing proximity, he clamped the steely shackles of his legs around her body and she found herself helplessly imprisoned.

Ignoring the burst of pain exploding through his thigh, Jake tightened his viselike grip until she grew still. "Not interested, little Mission Lady?" he purred, lightly blazing a trail of kisses from her ear to where her curls lay in a subdued coil at the base of her neck.

A shuddering sigh escaped through Hallie's gritted teeth.

He chuckled at her response. "Not interested?" he repeated. "Your response to my kisses just now told a far different tale." To demonstrate, he bent down and playfully nipped at her neck. As a tremor ran through her body, he lightly admonished, "Even I know that the Bible says it's a sin to lie."

"Not nearly as big a sin as lust, carnality, and depravity," she growled, twisting her neck away from his marauding lips to fix him with a resentful glare.

"And not nearly as pleasurable either." Lifting one hand from Hallie's arm, Jake threaded his fingers through her hair and one by one, drew the pins from the tight chignon.

At the gentleness of his touch, Hallie experienced another unwilling surge of something that felt dangerously close to desire.

Feeling her quiver beneath his hands, Jake nodded. "Good. It appears that you understand the rudimentary stages of lust. Perhaps you're ready for lesson number two . . . to experiment with something more . . . daring."

Fiercely Hallie battled the heated languor that was stealing through her limbs. Jake's power of seduction might be strong, but he was about to find out that her power of resistance was stronger.

Like brave David facing the mighty Goliath, she squared her shoulders and spat, "You randy bastard! How dare—" But his lips claiming hers effectively silenced her protests.

Hungrily he ravished her mouth with his tongue, his strong arms crushing her body nearer until she was cradled in the sensitive junction between his thighs. As she squirmed in a futile attempt to escape his grasp, Jake could feel the weight of her breasts pressing against his manhood and he groaned aloud at the fierce torment that immediately inflamed his loins. Damn! His revenge was rapidly turning into a double-edged sword, and it appeared that he was the one straddling the sharper side.

To Hallie, the power of his kiss was more disturbingly persuasive than she could ever have imagined. It wasn't the sweet, coaxing kiss of her childhood fantasies, nor was it anything like the tender one they had exchanged beneath the mistletoe. No. It was the hard, demanding kiss of a passionate man—a man whose naked desires seared her with their white-hot intensity, a strong man whose thinly reined control frightened even as it drew her. And despite her anger, she was finding her edge every bit as sharp as he was finding his.

No! she scolded herself sternly. *You will not give Jake Parrish satisfaction by becoming one of his easy conquests. You're going to gather what few wits you have left and show him that his kisses have absolutely no effect on you.*

Yet, as his mouth brutally demanded a response from hers, she gasped aloud, and the raw heat of his kisses forced her reluctant mind to succumb to her body's treasonous will. As an aching need blossomed in her belly, Hallie returned his kiss with reckless abandon. Something stirred deep inside, and she felt herself seething with a dark sensuality that was utterly foreign to her narrow scope of experience. With a soft moan, she involuntarily arched her body against the bulge of his arousal.

Jake let out a strangled sob as he felt himself harden completely. Abruptly, he drew back from the intoxicating ambrosia of her lips. Everlasting hell! He had meant for his kisses to punish the uppity little Mission lady, but he was the one who was suffering.

Cursing himself for a lecherous fool, Jake violently thrust his hips and ground the evidence of his desire against the soft swell of her breasts. She uttered a low moan and moved against him in a way that further inflamed his lust.

Desperate with need now, Jake slid from the chair in one fluid motion, his body sparking with erotic friction as it moved against hers. He dropped to his knees in front of her, thigh to thigh, with Hallie's face pressed against his chest.

Uttering a hoarse cry, he ensnared her in the steely trap of his embrace and buried his face in the warm hollow of her throat. He could feel her pulse racing in perfect harmony with his and was maddened by the urgency he felt as her body melted against his.

Gently Jake eased Hallie's unresisting form back until she lay sprawled upon the soft blue and white Aubusson carpet. As he straddled her hips, his gaze raked her body and he felt his breath catch in his throat at the wanton image she presented.

With her hair tumbling in an autumn profusion around her face and her lips bruised and swollen from his kisses, Hallie Gardiner was every inch the beautiful temptress who haunted his dreams. Slowly Jake let out his breath. "Dear God! Do you know what you do to me, sweet Mission Lady?"

Hallie could only nod, far too caught up in her own maelstrom of need to deny the knowledge of his. Yes. She knew exactly how he felt. Just as she knew that she should struggle to control her body's turbulent response to the dark flame of his touch, knew she should push him away and run from the swollen evidence of his lust, knew she should feel shame at being so easily caught in his enticing web.

Yet, as he covered her now yielding body with his conquering one, she could do nothing but surrender to the onslaught of her own desires.

With trembling fingers, Jake fumbled at the buttons on Hallie's shapeless gray morning gown. To his frustration, his urgency made him clumsy, and he was unable to release more than three of the stubborn fastenings.

In a fit of impatience, he gave the bodice a rending tug that sent the buttons scattering in all directions. Then, with a growl of victory, he flung the ugly garment aside to reveal a chemise that was surprisingly sheer.

He had expected to find one of those thick flannel affairs favored by elderly women. But this dainty, scarlet-edged confection was so transparent, he could clearly see the coral ripeness of her nipples through the fabric. Just the sight of those thinly veiled peaks made Jake's groin tighten viciously and with an intensity that made him painfully aware that he hadn't had a woman in over three years.

Embarrassed and frightened by the fervor of Jake's gaze, Hallie made a move to cover her breasts. Before she could do more than grasp the edges of her bodice, Jake caught hold of her hands and pushed them away.

"Don't hide your breasts from me," he whispered, gently outlining one rosy crest with his fingertip. "They're beautiful. *You're* beautiful." He caught his breath sharply, only to release it the next instant with a groan as her nipples hardened beneath his touch.

Hallie sobbed as the heat from his hand branded her through the filmy fabric. God forgive her! She wanted to feel his hands on her bare flesh with an intensity that made her ache. Unable to control herself any longer, she moaned and arched her back, crushing her breast impatiently against his palm.

The effect on Jake was electric. With a tormented sob, he ruthlessly ripped Hallie's delicate chemise until she lay naked to her waist. Then he plunged his face deep into the valley of her cleavage, his body twitching violently as he fought to suppress his quickly approaching climax.

Damn it! he cursed to himself. Unless he wanted to humiliate himself by spilling his seed like an inexperienced youth, he had better get away from Hallie Gardiner—and quickly! Never in his life had he needed, or wanted, a woman so badly.

But Hallie picked that very moment to grasp him in her embrace and undulate in a sensuously unbridled rhythm against him. As her pelvis rubbed insistently against the raw fire of his sex, he lost control.

Savagely he ground his manhood against her belly,

sobbing with equal parts shame and pleasure as his trousers became stained with the evidence of his release. As the hot tide of his passion ebbed, Jake jerked once and then lay motionless.

As he lay with his head pillowed on Hallie's breasts, he suddenly felt like weeping; never in his life had he felt so embarrassed or so unfulfilled. Aside from the obvious physical sensations of Hallie's body against his, he had received no more pleasure from his climax than if he had sought relief from his own hand.

"Jake?" When he didn't reply, Hallie gently grasped his chin and tipped his face up to her. Every plane of his face revealed a bleakness that she didn't understand. He looked as if his best friend had just suffered a fatal accident. Stroking his cheek tenderly, she asked, "Is something wrong?"

He cocked a wry half-smile at the naivete of her inquiry. The woman had tormented him until he'd lost control, and she didn't even realize it. With a harsh laugh, he replied, "It appears that you were the teacher and I was the pupil in our little experiment."

At her uncomprehending expression, he rose to his knees, exposing his soiled trousers.

Her eyes widened for a moment. "You should have told me you needed to relieve yourself. I would have waited while you visited the necessary room."

To which he laughed uproariously. Lifting one black brow in mock humor, he replied, "The kind of relief I needed—and got, I might add—had nothing to do with the kind found in the necessary room."

"Oh, Lord!" Hallie exclaimed, and then she flushed a shade that gave new meaning to the word "red" as understanding dawned. So stunned was she by his revelation that she continued to lie motionless beneath him, half naked and in a pose that could only have been described as wanton.

Which is exactly how Lavinia Donahue later described it to her sanctimonious cronies at the Ladies' Mission Society. For no sooner had Hallie's exclamation left her lips than the parlor door flew open and Hop Yung announced the woman.

Bossy to a fault, Lavinia pushed the flabbergasted

Hop Yung aside and swept into the room with her homely daughter in tow.

She stopped in her tracks at the sight of Jake straddling Hallie, and her heavy jowls shook with affronted dignity as she took in the ravaged disarray of both parties on the floor.

In a protective gesture, Jake drew the speechless Hallie up against his chest, shielding her face and breasts from the prying eyes of the intruders. Fixing Lavinia with his most quelling stare, Jake snapped, "What do you want, Mrs. Donahue?"

Lavinia's mouth worked soundlessly for several seconds. Why, the man didn't even have the good grace to look ashamed of his scandalous behavior. Imagine, cavorting with that hussy, Dr. Gardiner, in broad daylight, and on the parlor floor, no less. The man was a regular cretin! As for that loose woman in his arms, well, she would see that the Jezebel was ruined. Why, she would drive the little tart right out of town!

"Get out, Lavinia," Jake growled, tightening his hold on Hallie's now sobbing form. He wanted nothing more than to toss the interfering old bat out on her backside and to kiss his sweet Mission Lady's tears away. But to move would have meant further exposing their scandalous state, which, for Hallie's sake, he couldn't do.

Lavinia's mouth opened and closed rapidly, like an overwrought blowfish, as she tried to think of a properly scathing remark. All she could manage to blurt was, "Well! I never!"

To which Jake replied with a humorless bark of laughter, "Of course you have, Lavinia." He let his gaze rest suggestively on her daughter, Edith. "Well, at least once."

Chapter 14

Life just keeps on getting better" Hallie mumbled sarcastically as a fat raindrop pelted her on the head. She rolled her eyes toward the heavens above and heaved a long-suffering sigh. *Oh, great!* It looked as if they were in for a storm, and if those quickly gathering clouds were an accurate indicator, there was no way she would make it back to the Mission House before it broke.

As if to confirm her fears, a silvery flash of lightning streaked across the sky, followed closely by an ominous clap of thunder. Hallie started nervously. Lord! There was nothing she hated more than thunder!

Except the wind. And those cold gusts were tearing at her unbound hair with the violence of a scalping Indian. With a snort of exasperation, she paused in midstride for what seemed like the hundredth time and shoved the tangle of curls out of her face. As she tucked a particularly stubborn ringlet behind her ear, Hallie caught sight of her reflection in a shop window. If she hadn't felt so utterly miserable, she probably would have laughed.

With her hair snaking in fiery tangles around her face and her eyes red from crying, she bore an uncanny resemblance to the illustration of Medusa in her book of mythology. *Hardly the type of woman to incite uncontrollable lust in a man,* she thought bitterly as she turned away.

Yet that was exactly what had happened less than an hour ago. Hallie cringed inwardly at the shameful memory. She had behaved just like the wanton creature Lavinia Donahue had accused her of being, falling easily under the spell of Jake Parrish's enchanting kisses. And to think that she had let the man fondle her in such an intimate fashion . . .

Hallie shivered and wrapped her arms around herself as the wind cut through the thin wool of her gown. She'd been so mortified by her passionate display that she had fled Jake's house without stopping to retrieve her reticule or bonnet from the floor. Nor had she attempted to collect her coat, something she was now regretting.

"Oh, double damn," she swore beneath her breath as another booming report of thunder rocked her senses. Fine kettle of fish she was in now!

Of course, it would be her own fault if she got soaked to the skin, caught a nasty cold which developed into pneumonia, and died a miserable death. A sob caught in her throat at the tragic thought. What would Jake do when he heard the news? Would he be moved enough to shed a tear or two over her untimely demise?

The very notion made her imagination soar to melodramatic heights. In her mind, Hallie pictured a tender scene where a brokenhearted Jake Parrish wept while she weakly uttered her last—albeit brave—words. He would cradle her in his arms and beg her to live, to stay with him always. And then, through the power of love, they would defeat death together.

She released a sigh at her fanciful musings. She had definitely read one dime novel too many. Knowing Jake, he would probably feel bad about her death, rather as if his favorite dog had been run over by a carriage. Yet she seriously doubted that he would mourn overly much.

With a cynical grate of laughter that made several passersby stare, Hallie admitted to herself that the thought of death did hold a certain morbid charm at that moment. After all, if she were dead, she wouldn't have to face Lavinia's nasty accusations.

She shivered again, but in a way that had nothing to do with the cold. Her life in San Francisco was ruined. Lavinia had been very clear on that particular point. Of course, when Jake had mentioned something about calling due the notes he held against Mr. Donahue's bank, the woman had fallen silent.

After having the intruders shown to the door by a rudely smirking Hop Yung, Jake had cradled Hallie in his arms and assured her that he would take care of everything. He'd told her not to worry. He'd even apologized, and profusely at that. Yet he hadn't told her he loved her or cared about her; nor had he given any indication that he felt anything beyond regret over their passionate episode. To him, it had obviously been nothing more than a casual flirtation gone wrong.

To her, it had been a confirmation of her most heartbreaking fears: he had merely been toying with her emotions.

Too humiliated and hurt to look at him, she had struggled until she was free from the restraint of his arms. Then she had fled. Because of his bad leg, he had been unable to stand, much less pursue her, and he'd had to content himself with shouting after her. His language had become quite colorful by the time she'd slammed the door behind her.

Now, walking along the drafty streets without a coat, without the funds to hire a public hack, and still several miles from the Mission House, Hallie cursed her foolhardy flight. Surely she could have paused just long enough to collect her belongings? That would have been the prudent thing to do. But prudence wasn't her strong suit these days, especially where Jake Parrish was concerned.

"Hey, girlie! How's about a bit o' fun?"

A rough-looking young man dressed like a dock worker was half leaning against a door above which was written something in Chinese. He eyed Hallie with less than wholesome interest. Subtly lengthening her stride, she made a show of ignoring him.

Not easily deterred, the man vaulted over the porch railing and scampered after her.

"What's yer hurry, darlin'?" he drawled as he fell into step with his prey and let his hungry gaze rove over her body. Looked as if she'd had a busy morning, what with her hair tumbling down and her bodice half undone. Her lips had that swollen, bruised look too, as if she'd been kissed real passionate like. He licked his own lips in anticipation.

"Was about to git myself a yeller gal." He jerked his head toward the building against which he'd been lounging. "But seein' as yer here, well, always been right partial to the taste of strawberry tarts. Strawberry tart! Ya get it?"

He buckled over, guffawing at his own wit. When he finally recovered, he found himself alone. "Now where'd she go?" he mumbled, looking up and down the street. No little redheaded darlin' anywhere in sight. He glanced back at the *House of Golden Virtue,* his favorite brothel, and then down the street at the *Dusty Gulch,* his favorite waterin' hole.

Hell, it was barely noon. Too early to get stinkin' drunk, but the Chinese whores had suddenly lost their appeal. With a shrug, he headed toward the saloon.

It wasn't until Hallie slipped into a narrow alley that she finally dared to pause for breath. Lord! Not only had she behaved like a loose woman with Jake, she was now being mistaken for one on the streets.

She peered out of her hiding place, anxiously scanning the passersby for familiar faces. With a sinking feeling, Hallie noted that the streets were becoming crowded now, and she shrank back into the shadows as she recognized two men who were elders of Ascension Tabernacle.

She groaned out loud. Since it was the day before Christmas, every good Samaritan in town would be out on some sort of mission of mercy. Like angels cut from their heavenly bonds, they would indulge in a head-spinning frenzy of spreading cheer, feeding the hungry, and, of course, saving every vagrant soul within miles.

Which meant that Hallie couldn't risk being seen on the streets in her current state of disarray. She glanced into the passage behind her. Perhaps if she kept to the alleys . . .

Another drop of rain made up her mind for her, and she slipped back into the foreboding gloom of the alleys. So be it, then. Somehow she would find her way through the maze of Chinatown's alleys.

She walked for several blocks, shivering violently as the wind whistled through the narrow passages between the buildings. With the wind came an awful stink of rotting debris.

By the time she reached the end of the alley, the smell had become so overwhelming that she was forced to take her breaths in quick, choking gasps. It wasn't until she heard a slosh beneath her boots and skidded on something slippery that she peered into the shadows at her feet. What she saw made her gorge rise sharply.

There before her was a large pile of putrid fish heads lying amidst what appeared to be fish entrails. The stench was appalling.

It was too much for Hallie. She decided then and there that she would rather risk the scandal of being seen in her current disheveled state than brave more such slimy horrors in the alleys. Having come to that decision, she veered sharply to her left in the direction of the street, lifting her skirts high as she carefully sidestepped the malodorous mess.

The wind came racing around the corner like an overeager sweetheart and engulfed Hallie in its chilly embrace as she paused at a break between the buildings. Leaning back against the uneven surface of a shingled wall, she took several gulping breaths of the clean, crisp air. Just as her stomach began to right itself and she'd steeled herself to reenter the street, a small body hurled itself into her with a force that knocked her on her backside.

Hallie could only stare in dazed wonder at the Chinese girl sprawled across her lap. *What in the world?*

With a moan, the girl clutched at her belly and rose unsteadily to her feet. Still doubled over, she took several stumbling steps forward before uttering a piercing cry and collapsing to her knees.

"Did you hurt yourself?" Hallie asked, moving to the spot where the girl lay huddled. When she received no answer, she laid her hand on the girl's shoulder and gave her a gentle shake. "I'm a doctor. Perhaps I can help you."

"She's going to need a doctor, and quite badly, when I'm finished with her," replied a beautifully modulated voice.

A dark shadow fell across Hallie as a man loomed into the opening. He was a tall man, richly dressed, and, from what she could see of his face, not unattractive. Ignoring Hallie, he sauntered over to the now whimpering Chinese girl.

"Thought you could escape, did you?" he inquired, jerking the girl to her feet with one hand. "It was stupid of you to run. I paid dearly for the privilege of your company, and I intend to take my pleasure with, or without, your cooperation."

With that, he pulled the limp form closer an gave her a vicious slap across the face. The girl let out a strangled scream laced with equal parts terror and pain; he smiled with satisfaction, pleased by the sound.

"That's better." Laughing triumphantly, he lifted his palm to administer another blow, but before he could land the strike, a pair of restraining hands clamped onto his arm. Infuriated by the interruption, he let out a string of foul curses and flung the Chinese girl hard against the wall. Then he rounded on his opposition.

He felt the blood rush to his face as he glared down at the unkempt, red-haired spitfire clutching at his elbow. She seemed unafraid of his fury, and he could have sworn he read a challenge in those glowing gold tiger eyes.

That very lack of fear enraged him beyond reason. When Nick Connelly frowned like he was doing now, people—especially women—were supposed to dissolve into an intimidated mass of quivering flesh. Obviously this particular female was in need of a lesson in the meaning of his scowl.

With lightning speed, he shook his arm free from her grasp, breaking her hold as easily as if he had been bound by chains of paper. Emitting a feral growl, he brutally backhanded the little busybody across the side of her head. She reeled from the blow.

"I'll teach you to interfere!" Nick hissed, catching the other side of her head with another loud *whack*. He chuckled as the impact sent her flying backward.

Pain burst through Hallie's head as the man's fist made bruising contact with the area just above her ear, and as she was thrown up against a brick wall, it jolted down her spine. Stunned, she slid silently to the ground. Then everything blurred before her eyes.

It was the revolting sensation of fish entrails beneath her hands that snapped her back to the frightening reality of her plight.

"Just who the hell are you? And what gives you the right to stick your nose into my business?" Nick ground out as he hovered over the figure on the ground.

But Hallie was gagging uncontrollably and was unable to answer. She heaved drily for several seconds before being seized by her cascading hair and hauled to her feet.

"Answer me!" he growled, punctuating his words by banging her head against the wall.

Struggling to escape the man's hold, Hallie managed to gasp, "I'm from the Mission Infirmary! I'm Dr. Hallie Gardiner."

"An angel of mercy from the mission," Nick purred, abruptly ceasing his battering and pulling her close to study her features. There was fear in her eyes now, and tears slid unchecked down her pale cheeks.

How he hated these so-called good women. He hated the way they avoided him, hated the way they crossed the street when they saw him coming, acting as if to pass him meant to risk some terrible contamination. And all because he'd roughed up a couple of the girls who were under the protection of the Mission House.

Hell. Once a whore, always a whore, he'd figured, though that high and mighty Davinia Loomis had made it very clear that she disagreed. When she'd publicly called him to task for his deeds, she'd effectively ensured that he would be snubbed by every decent woman in the city.

From that point on, he had dreamt of wreaking vengeance on the sanctimonious goody-goodys at the mission. Now that his chance was at hand, he intended to make the most of it.

"Well, Dr. Hallie Gardiner," he began in a falsely cordial tone, "it seems as if my companion is no longer in any condition to fulfill her duties." He nodded at the motionless figure of the Chinese girl. "A fact that sorely disappoints me. I'm not a man who copes well with disappointment."

Nick coiled the length of Hallie's hair around his hand and wrenched her head back cruelly. Lightly tracing the deep valley between her breasts with one well-manicured finger, he mused, "I know you wouldn't want me to be disappointed, would you, Doctor?"

Hallie shrank from his intimately probing fingers, too stunned from the blows to her head to do much else. As he pressed against her, trapping her between his body and the rough surface of the wall, she could smell the cloying scent of his cologne.

"Mr. Connelly," she pleaded, feebly attempting to push him away. "I don't—"

In one savage motion, he ripped open the tattered remains of her bodice and watched hungrily as her breasts were exposed. He groaned with pleasure. They were perfect. All round and white, with nipples like ripe cherries. Nick couldn't resist the temptation to swoop down and sink his teeth deep into one creamy globe.

Shrieking with pain and outrage, Hallie lunged forward, throwing all of her weight against him. The surprise of her counterattack knocked him backward a few inches, freeing Hallie's hands, which had been pinned between their bodies.

Blindly she clawed at his face. Nick Connelly howled like a wounded coyote as her nails found their mark, and he released his hold on her hair to grab at his lacerated face. As he drew back to stare at the blood on his hands, Hallie took her opportunity to escape and darted toward the street.

But she had seriously underestimated Connelly's recuperative powers. She was shocked by the impact of his body as he hurled himself at her back. Tumbling to the hard-packed ground with Nick on top of her, she heard him shout, "I'll teach you to cut Nick Connelly! I'll make you sorry the notion ever entered your mind!"

Tangling his hands in her hair, he gave it a scalp-rending yank that made her scream in agony. "Shut up," he hissed and jerked her head up to deliver a glancing blow across her cheek.

Hallie sobbed as she felt the sickening sensation of blood welling her mouth, though the rest of her face was numb from the impact of his assault. This had to be a nightmare! How could something so awful be happening to her? But another slap reassured her that it was no dream.

Nick groaned aloud as the sight of his victim's humbled state heated his lust to a fever pitch. With her cheeks red from his repeated strikes and blood seeping from the corner of her mouth, she was too exciting to resist. Damn it! And he had looked forward to making her suffer for a good, long time. Yet, as he stared down at the lady doctor lying helplessly beneath him, her face a tear-streaked mask of terror, he was filled with an aching need to take her now—and quickly. Right here in the filth of the alley.

Panting with desire, he wrestled Hallie onto her back, easily pinning her fists to the ground above her head with one sizable hand.

Straddling her hips, he hissed, "I'm going to enjoy hearing you scream while I force you to take this—" He ground the swollen evidence of his need against her belly.

Hallie willed herself to go limp as Nick Connelly twisted slightly to draw her soiled skirts up her legs. She didn't dare move or make a sound, for fear that he would beat her completely senseless. As he ran his hand up the length of her thigh, stopping to claw impatiently at her sheer batiste pantalettes, a desperate idea blossomed in her muddled brain.

Cursing, Nick bent down to loosen the waistband of her drawers, widely straddling her legs. Hope gave Hallie courage, and with all the strength she could muster from her abused body, she brought her knee up and slammed it into the sensitive juncture between his legs.

He released an agonized scream. Stunned by the intensity of the pain, he clutched at the damaged area and then crumpled to the ground beside Hallie, where he lay in a whimpering heap.

Shivering uncontrollably, Hallie forced herself to rise to her knees. She glanced over at the Chinese girl, who hadn't moved or made a sound since Nick had thrown her against the wall. She had to get help! But as she tried to gain her feet, she was overcome by a fierce queasiness that doubled her over, making her retch miserably. By the time her stomach was empty, her head was reeling crazily and she buried her face in her hands in an attempt to regain her equilibrium.

Hallie remained in that position until a groaning threat from Nick pierced her agony-filled haze. Staggering like a sailor with three pints of rotgut down his gullet, she wove in an unsteady gait toward the end of the alley. Clutching at her head, she was about to step out into the safety of the open street when she fell against the unyielding wall of a solidly built body. As her arms were grabbed in an iron grip, her mind shrieked in panic, *Oh, Lord! What now?*

With a choked sob, Hallie forced her eyes to focus on the bright buttons of the man's dark uniform. Rolling her head back, she stared rather stupidly into the scowling face of a policeman. Relief penetrated her disoriented mind, and with a sigh, she collapsed against the man's chest.

"How often have I warned you doxies to stay off the streets?" he lectured, giving her a shake that made her stumble. "I won't have you accosting decent folks, do you hear? And just look at you! Drunk as an Injun! Why, I have half a mind to—"

But the officer's tirade was cut short by a moan that escalated into a gasping sob.

"What's that?" bellowed the policeman, staring suspiciously into the shadowed darkness of the alley.

Roughly dragging Hallie behind him, the officer stalked over to the whimpering figure on the ground. Squinting down at the prostrate man, he expelled, "Jeez! It's my man, Nick Connelly!"

Nick sobbed mournfully, "Not much of a man anymore, Tully. The whore kicked me in my privates." He rubbed at the damaged area, moaning with renewed drama. "Hired her and her Chink friend for a little fun. Paid them generously, too. They lured me into the alley, promising me a real good time, and then they tried to rob me. Seems as if a man can't take his pleasure these days without risking his life!"

"That's a lie!" shrieked Hallie, shaking an accusing fist at Nick Connelly. "I'm certainly no prostitute! This filthy excuse for a man tried to rape me."

Officer Tully eyed Hallie dubiously for a moment, his gaze taking in her disheveled appearance. Then he snorted his disbelief. "Seems to me that only a whore would know where to kick a man to do the most damage. Jeez!" He shuddered in sympathy.

"What do you intend to do about this, Tully?" Nick's face was the very picture of wounded innocence as he looked up at the officer. "Surely you can't let her continue robbing and emasculating decent men?"

"I kicked him because he would have raped me!" Hallie shouted in frustrated rage. "He was beating that girl over there." She gestured desperately at the still form lying several yards away. "And when I tried to stop him, he turned on me. Then he tried to rape me! Can't you see he's lying?"

"I've known Nicholas Connelly since the strike in '49. Worked the North Fork together. You get to know a man pretty well after sixteen years. Never known Nick to fib, and I can't imagine he'd have a reason to start now. Isn't that right, Nick?"

A grunt of affirmation seemed to satisfy the policeman.

"He lied because he's guilty of assaulting two innocent women!" she hissed, narrowing her eyes at Nick in a menacing fashion.

The man released a strangled cry and curled his body into a protective ball.

"Enough!" roared Officer Tully, frowning at the exchange. "It's high time I made an example out of one of you whores. You're starting to get way too bold for my liking." He roughly seized Hallie's arm and began pulling her toward the street. "Let's just see how impertinent you feel after enjoying a few days of hospitality—courtesy of the Broadway Street jail!"

"Damn heathen Chinee!" snarled the young policeman running his hand over his head to smooth the few remaining strands of blond hair. "Knows how to kick up a ruckus—that much's for sure." Spitting on the floor, he tossed a look of undisguised contempt at the screeching girl huddled on the cot.

"If you don't shut up, and quick-like, I'll give you something to holler about!" he threatened, advancing forward a step.

But the girl was oblivious to the man's presence, lost in her own private hell, and she emitted another series of shrieks while clawing convulsively at the rough woolen blanket.

As swiftly as a striking serpent, the officer grabbed the girl's shoulder and gave her a bone-jarring shake while barking something in Chinese.

"No! Don't!" gasped Hallie. But as she made to spring from the cot where she sat braced against the wall, she was overcome with a dizziness that made her sink back with a groan.

The man paused his yapping tirade long enough to glower at Hallie through narrowed eyes, then turned his attention back to the young girl squirming in his grasp.

Giving his prisoner another jerk, he continued his diatribe, punctuating his words at intervals by jabbing his thumb in Hallie's direction. The Chinese girl lifted her head high enough to fix the flame-haired woman with a horrified stare and then, giving a strangled moan, shrank tightly against the cot.

Whatever the officer had said had the desired effect, and the girl, struck silent now, curled into a tight fetal position, her face a twisted mask of tearful despair. Giving his prisoner a final warning look, the man jabbered one last barrage in Chinese and then shoved her away, expectorating a foamy stream of spittle for good measure. Then he turned to leave.

As he brushed past Hallie, she made a desperate grab for his arm.

"Wait!" she exclaimed, latching on to his elbow. "You can't just leave her here!"

The officer impatiently shook his arm free from Hallie's grip, not even bothering to look down. "Can't I?" he asked in a taunting voice as he sauntered toward the barred door. "Just watch me."

"No! Please." Hallie's voice had taken on an urgent quality that made the man stop in his tracks. "Can't you see that this woman has been badly beaten and is in need of medical care?"

The policeman let his gaze travel between the two women for a moment as he seemed to consider her words. Then he shrugged and pushed open the cell door.

"Are you stupid or just blind?" Hallie was relieved to see the man pause at her berating tone. Though his expression didn't bode well, she forced herself to brazen it out.

"This woman should have been taken to a hospital, not to this hellhole."

The man leaned against the door, stroking at his luxuriant side-whiskers, and stared at Hallie smugly. "Oh? And what hospital do you suggest?" he drawled. "Can't think of any Chinee hospital offhand."

Hallie returned his gaze coolly. "Surely you're not suggesting that this woman would be denied medical care simply because she happens to be Chinese?"

"I'm not suggesting anything. I'm telling you. There's not a white hospital or doctor in this town who would tend a Chinee."

"Then you're wrong." Their eyes remained in silent combat for several tense moments before she broke the spell with a superior-sounding snort, "I happen to be a doctor at the Mission Infirmary, and I would suggest you release me this instant so I can see to this girl's care."

"Right. A female doctor." He snickered as skeptically as if she had just announced that she was running for the presidency of the United States. "Well, *Doctor,* what *I* suggest is that you stop your whining and tend to your patient." With that, he slipped out the door and gave it a decisive slam shut.

"Please." Hallie rose to her still wobbly legs and staggered the short distance to the door. As she wrapped her hands around the bars for support, the officer looked up from his grappling with the jammed door lock and frowned. Forcing herself to look contrite, Hallie pleaded, "Please, Officer—?"

"Brady," he supplied, banging on the problematic lock.

"—Brady," she echoed with an ingratiating smile. "I really do need to get this woman back to the infirmary. As you can see, I don't have the proper equipment here to help her. If you could just open this door and let me—"

"You're not going anywhere—" he interjected, grunting with satisfaction as the lock clicked into place, "—either of you. At least not without Judge Dorner's say-so."

"Then, for God's sake, get the judge."

With a pleased smile, Officer Brady removed the key and tested the door by giving it a pull. It held securely. As he reattached the key to the heavy ring hanging from his belt, he replied, "You can see the judge day after tomorrow. He left distinct orders that he was not to be disturbed today. Seems he's having a big Christmas Eve party tonight. And, tomorrow being Christmas Day, well, wouldn't want to disturb the judge on account of a couple of antsy whores."

"But the girl—"

"Judge doesn't give a damn about a Chinee whore—or a white one, for that matter."

"But—"

"No buts about it. You'll see the judge day after tomorrow." Jerking his head decisively, Brady spun on his heel and headed down the corridor.

"Wait!" Hallie shrieked, loudly enough to make him turn and scowl in her direction. "Can you at least ask her what's wrong?"

He spat on the floor. "Do I look Chinee to you?"

"But I heard you speak Chinese, and the girl seemed to understand what you said."

"Oh. Well, I know a few words here and there. Enough to get my point across."

He winked at Hallie in an infuriating manner that made her long to shout a few select words of her own.

"And just what point did you get across?" Hallie ground out, hating herself for asking, yet curious about what had struck such terror into the girl's face.

"Why, I simply told her that if she didn't stop yapping, I'd turn her over to you. Nothing scares a Chinee whore more'n the thought of being sent to the mission."

"Why?" But Hallie's question hung in the air unanswered, for the policeman was halfway down the hall, whistling a rousing rendition of "We Wish You a Merry Christmas" as he went.

In the hours that followed, Hallie had no time to reflect upon the man's strange words. The afternoon had crept by unnoticed, and the fuchsia glow of the setting sun now failed to draw even a quick sigh of appreciation from either woman. Somewhere deep in the bowels of the jail, someone sang snatches of a Christmas carol, but even that didn't get any more than a passing grimace from Hallie.

Bending over the still Chinese girl, Hallie groped for the pulse at her neck. Nothing. With a surge of panic, she moved her fingers lower, holding her breath apprehensively. Relief flooded over her like an incoming tide as she discerned a weak, irregular beat, and she let out her breath in a ragged gust.

The young woman had lost a great deal of blood over the course of the endless afternoon, hemorrhaging in a torrent that had quickly saturated her loose-fitting trousers. Hallie looked down at the blanket now stained an ugly, rusty red and, with a hopeless sob, resumed massaging the girl's belly.

In those early hours following the exchange with Officer Brady, the girl had refused Hallie's assistance. So taken aback had Hallie been by the hostile suspicion reflected in those beautiful eyes that she had simply watched helplessly as the girl rocked back and forth on her cot, crooning something to herself in a singsong voice.

But sometime in the blur of the afternoon she had at last turned to Hallie, her eyes brimming with mute appeal. As she moved to the girl's side, Hallie gave silent thanks for the experience gained during her stint as Sanitary Visitor to the Philadelphia tenements. As frustrating and painful as it had been at times, it taught her to reach beyond the barrier of language and to give comfort simply as one human being to another. After all, weren't pain and illness a universal plight?

Cautiously, Hallie turned her palm up and offered her open hand to the girl in a gesture of wordless friendship. It was at that moment that a pain chose to lock the girl in its cruel grasp, and she seized Hallie's outstretched hand with desperate brutality.

Thus the first seeds of trust were planted. Hand motions and sounds replaced words, for Hallie knew no Chinese, and the few words of English uttered by the girl gave little doubt as to her station in life. Through patience, Hallie was able to learn that the girl's name was Tuberose, but little else.

As the twilight faded, so did the fragile communication between the women. Tuberose's breathing was now little more than a shallow whisper; her heartbeat a faint sigh. And the truth was almost more than Hallie could bear: Tuberose was dying and there was nothing she could do.

"Damn it!" Hallie swore, rubbing at the tears of frustration that stung her eyes. "Where has that worthless warden gone?" After Brady had delivered a dismal repast of thin soup and water, of which neither woman had partaken, no one had bothered to check on them.

"Damn! Damn! Damn!" Hallie sobbed, driving her

fist against the brick wall with knuckle-splitting force. As pain flamed through her abused hand, she was filled with a desperation that made something deep inside of her snap. Snatching up the tin soup bowl, Hattie emptied the unpalatable contents into the relief bucket and then stalked over to the door.

Taking a long, ragged breath, she struck the bowl across the bars with all her strength. Over and over again she banged, shattering the calm with the chaotic din of metal against metal. She could feel the impact of the blows radiate up her arm, and her shoulder joint soon ached from the impact.

"Get your sorry, godforsaken hide in here now!" She screamed above the deafening clatter. She was startled into dropping the bowl when a clear voice, projecting calmly above the noise, answered her.

"I certainly hope he hasn't forsaken it. I have a feeling my hide's going to need his protection if—HELL AND DAMNATION!" Davinia ejected as she came face to face with the prisoner.

"Davinia, thank God!" Hallie exclaimed, reaching through the bars to clutch at her friend's arm.

Frowning with concern, Davinia gently touched Hallie's bruised cheek. "What happened?"

"The whore kicked Nicholas Connelly in his man parts and then tried to rob him. They say he's ruined for life," replied Officer Brady, who had been following Davinia, with Marius DeYoung close at his heels.

"Good for her!" cheered Davinia, moving her hand from Hallie's cheek to give her friend a congratulatory pat on the back. "I'm sure the lecher deserved a good swift kick. Would have done it myself, had the opportunity presented itself. But a whore and a thief? Really, Brady! Even you know better than to believe that durn Connelly creature." She stared at the policeman in her most quelling manner for a moment before snapping, "Well? Are you going to stand there gaping like a day-old market fish, or are you going to unlock this door? You've obviously made a mistake."

Brady glanced nervously from Davinia Loomis's imperious scowl to the lady doctor's angrily flushed cheeks. "Can't. Not until she sees the judge."

"Day after tomorrow," supplied Hallie miserably.

"Why, that's absurd!" interjected Marius, joining Hallie and Davinia in their glaring match with the policeman. "Surely allowances can be made? I can personally vouch for this woman's character, and let me assure you, it's beyond reproach."

"Rules is rules," Brady quoted. "And I always follow them to the letter. She's not going anywhere."

"But the girl," Hallie motioned desperately at the figure on the cot, "is dying. Please, at least release her. She can't harm anyone."

"Rules is rules."

"Hell and damnation!" shouted Davinia again, throwing her hands up in the air in disgust. "Marius?" She pulled the preacher aside, and they conferred in an inaudible whisper for several minutes. Giving a vigorous nod, Marius spun on his heels and left.

With that bit of business completed to her apparent satisfaction, Davinia rounded on the policeman. "Well, Brady, if you won't release the doctor, you can at least let me into the cell to see if I can lend her some assistance with her patient. I speak Chinese, you know."

Brady shook his head. "This woman is violent. After what she did to Nick—" His words faded away, and he paled at the thought.

"Well, since I don't possess the anatomy in question, I should be safe enough." She smiled cunningly. "Of course, if you're afraid to open the door—"

The man straightened to his full, lanky height, his face the picture of wounded dignity. "Officer Brady, afraid? Of a mere female? Ha!" he exclaimed. "Just trying to protect you, ma'am. However, if you insist on consorting with the prisoners, well, then, all right. Just don't say you weren't warned."

"Hush now, dear," Davinia crooned, tightening her embrace around Hallie and patting her friend's heaving back. "You did what you could."

"Hallie gave a choked sob and shook her head against Davinia's shoulder. "B-b-but it's all so c-cruel! I-I can't imagine anyone f-forcibly performing an a-abortion on a young girl and e-expecting her to service men that s-same day!"

At least two hours had passed since Davinia had entered the cell. Rousing Tuberose from her deathly stupor, Davinia had been able to extract bits and pieces of the girl's horrifying story.

It seemed that the young prostitute had found herself pregnant, and when the Chinese woman who ran the squalid crib establishment where she was enslaved had found out, she'd had the girl held down while she performed an abortion with a buttonhook. Nick Connelly had shown up several hours later, bellowing for his favorite whore, Tuberose. When the girl had objected, the madame had beaten her into submission and then turned her over for further abuse at Nick's hands. He had already forced himself on her several times before Hallie had come upon her.

Staring down at the outline of the girl's corpse shrouded in the bloodstained blanket, Hallie sniffled. "She was so afraid of me. I only wanted to help her, but s-she wouldn't—"

"I know," Davinia whispered, stroking Hallie's hair.

"B-but w-why?"

"It's a terrible situation. The brothel keepers tell their prostitutes lurid tales about mission ladies. One of the more effective stories is that we like to boil little Chinese girls and eat them for dinner. Rumor has it that we like them crispy. Of course, we scratch out their eyes and pull out their nails before we toss them into the stew pot."

Hallie pulled away from Davinia to stare at her in disbelief. "Those women can't possibly believe such nonsense."

"But they do. Why, it seems that we also like to end our cannibalistic feast with a demure glass of brandy mixed with the blood of Chinese prostitutes." Davinia removed her spectacles and rubbed them on the hem of her gown. She frowned as she peered at a particularly stubborn smudge. "Of course, once I get my hands on the poor dears, they come around quickly enough."

"But what of those who don't? There are so many of them."

With a sigh, Davinia balanced her glasses on the bridge of her nose. "Many die. The others spend their days in wretched squalor. We do what we can, but—"

"—but it's never enough," finished Hallie, dry-eyed

Chapter 15

Jake Parrish! And long overdue, I might add," scolded Davinia as she sprang to her feet and stalked over to the barred door, where he stood scowling at them.

Jake forced his gaze away from where Hallie sat concealed in the shadows and met Davinia's irate glare coolly.

"Charmed to see you, too, Davinia," he drawled, tipping his top hat in a mock salute. "But long overdue? I received your message exactly—" he pulled out his musical pocket watch and snapped it open with a flourish, "—forty-two minutes ago. Therefore, I feel safe in considering myself prompt in answering your rather unusual summons."

Hallie jerked her head up in sudden recognition as the lilting melody from the timepiece drifted across the small space of the cell. *"Invitation to the Dance,"* she thought, feeling almost sad when Jake closed the watch cover and the charming waltz ceased. She shook her head with a sigh. Since the first day she had met Jake and he had opened that watch, she'd struggled to place the tune. Strange that after all these months of trying, she should remember now.

"You know exactly what I mean by 'prompt'," Davinia lectured, shaking her finger at Jake as if he were a naughty toddler from her Sunday morning Bible class. "Why, the poor dear has been in this stink-hole for hours now, and the way I see it, this whole unfortunate incident is all your fault. I was shocked to hear of your ungentlemanly behavior."

Jake shot a questioning glance in Hallie's direction, wondering just how much she had told Davinia about their amorous encounter. But the infuriating woman was pointedly ignoring him, studying the writing on the walls as intently as if it contained the answers to the meaning of life. With a snort of frustration, he looked away.

He'd been a fool to think that she would want his help. Here he had come charging to the jail like a lovesick knight bent on rescuing his lady fair, and the lady didn't seem any too eager to be rescued. At least not by him.

That thought made his mood growl foul in the extreme. Skewering Davinia with his glare, he snapped, "How the hell do you figure this is my fault?"

"Lavinia paid me a visit this afternoon. She had quite a bit to say about the morals of our new doctor. Seems she dropped by your house for a neighborly visit this morning and walked in on you and Hallie at a rather—shall we say—inopportune moment."

Jake made an impatient sound. "So?"

"So—if it hadn't been for what I'm sure was her unwilling ravishment at your hands, Hallie would never have been wandering the streets in such a disreputable state."

"Unwilling ravishment?" Jake murmured, signaling Officer Brady with a brusque hand motion. "Interesting point of view."

Hallie cringed inwardly at his subtle reference to her wanton behavior. He was right, of course. She hadn't been at all unwilling. She retreated deeper into the shadows. Lord! Hadn't she been humiliated enough for one day? The last thing she wanted was to have Jake here, seeing her at her lowest point. She would never be able to look him in the eye again. Not if she lived to be a hundred years old.

Nodding curtly to the officer, Jake commanded, "You can unlock this door now."

"Well, sir—" The policeman's prominent Adam's apple bobbed up and down as he shot the mighty Mr. Parrish an anxious look.

"Open it."

"But—"

"Am I not making myself clear, Officer Brady?" Jake arched his brow in question and stared down at the man in a manner that never failed to intimidate even the most stalwart of individuals.

Unnerved by the cold intensity of that green gaze,

Brady found his Adam's apple giving a lurch that almost choked him. Rumor had it that it wasn't prudent to cross Jake Parrish.

The officer glanced at the two women in the cell and then back at the powerfully built man in front of him. With a shrug, he fumbled for his keys. Mr. Parrish looked perfectly capable of handling the redheaded she-devil. Besides, the man had always been more than generous when it came to contributing to the various policemen's funds, a fact which went a long way toward making up Brady's mind.

Hallie watched the exchange silently, her face veiled by the heavy curtain of her hair. *Isn't it just like that nasty toad, Brady, to grovel all over His Royal Highness? And isn't the air in the cell getting a bit close?* she thought, feeling suddenly breathless as Jake moved into the room, resplendently dressed in formal evening wear, complete with a long black cape. His commanding presence seemed to make the already small space shrink to claustrophobic proportions.

Davinia, however, was unperturbed by Jake's proximity. Glaring up at him, her hands firmly braced on her hips, she demanded, "Just what do you intend to do about this fiasco, Mr. Parrish?"

"I need to know the nature of the fiasco before I can do anything about it." Bracing himself securely on his cane, he leaned toward Hallie and demanded, "Exactly what happened, Dr. Gardiner?"

Tightly reining her desire to demonstrate exactly what had brought her to this impasse, Hallie calmly raised her eyes and with a nonchalant shrug, replied, "Why some poor innocent beat me up and tried to rape me. Being the reprehensible wretch that I am, I defended myself. Surely, Mr. Parrish, you can see what a heinous criminal I've become and how deserving I am of my imprisonment."

Jake closed the narrow space between them in several long, uneven strides. With his free hand, he grasped Hallie's upper arm and pulled her to her feet. As her battered face was touched by the light, he drew in a sharp breath. "And did he succeed?"

With a short, bitter laugh, Hallie replied, "To beat me? As you can see, at that he was most effective. But at rape?" She was unable to stop the single tear that escaped from the corner of her eye. "At that he was no more successful than you."

Jake flinched at the accusing note in her voice. Is that really how she viewed what had happened in the parlor? Attempted rape? He could have sworn that, before the Donahue women had barged in upon their tryst, Hallie had been just as inflamed by passion as he. Had he been wrong about the willingness with which she had melted into his embrace and about the eagerness with which she had returned his kisses? Could it be that he had been so long without a woman that he could no longer differentiate between one who was willing and one who was not?

Frowning, Jake raised his hand and gently smoothed away her tear with his thumb, his touch growing light as he traced the livid bruise on her cheek.

"What I had in mind, Mission Lady, was an act of love, not violence," he whispered. "I guess I went about it all wrong. I promise never to force my attentions on you again. Forgive me?"

Hallie released a ragged sigh. Slowly, she reached up to the hand that was cupping her cheek and laid her palm against it, lacing her fingers through his. Then she nodded.

"Hallie," he groaned.

There was such yearning in his voice, such a note of pain, that Hallie glanced up at his face in wonder. As their gazes touched, the tenderness in his eyes was enough to crack the fragile dam that held her emotions in check. With a strangled sob, she allowed the torrent to flow forth. She would have fallen weakly to her knees had Jake not caught her and crushed her against the reassuring warmth of his chest.

Heartrending sobs racked her body as he held her, her tears falling as freely as the rain that splattered against the window. When she felt Jake's hand move down her back in long, soothing strokes, Hallie buried her face in his shirt, not caring that she was making a mess of the immaculate linen. Unbidden, she reached up to clasp his wide shoulders, desperately seeking comfort from his closeness.

In silence, Jake held her, mentally cursing himself for

being an inadequate fool. Damn it to hell! Why did he always fail those for whom he cared the most? First he had failed Serena, and now Hallie. Both had found nothing but disappointment with him, found him not worthy of their love, found him lacking as a man.

Jake's arm tightened around Hallie in a fierce hug. Worst of all, he had failed to protect them. When he thought of that bastard hurting Hallie and touching her like that—

With a groan, he buried his face in Hallie's tangled hair. He would find the man who was responsible for abusing her in such a manner and make sure he never touched her again. He would make sure no one ever harmed her again, even if it meant defending her with his life. Anything. If only she would give him the chance to prove himself.

Sucking in a deep, shuddering breath, he pleaded, "Trust me, Hallie. Please let me be the one to keep you safe."

But his pleas, which were little more than a longing sigh, were lost in the wrenching sounds of her distress and faded in the air, unanswered.

Gradually the storm of Hallie's tears abated until all that remained was the persistent rhythm of her hiccuping. Dropping a kiss on top of her head, Jake reluctantly released her and slipped his handkerchief into her hand.

Hallie gave him a tremulous smile of thanks before pressing the soft linen square to her nose and blowing. Everything was going to be all right now. Jake was here. She found a dry corner of the handkerchief and mopped away the remainder of her tears, absentmindedly noting the monogrammed initials JVP. *V*? She sighed and gave her nose one final wipe. JVP—her wonderful Jake. She was safe now. Jake was here.

Hiccuping more softly now, she looked up to thank him properly. But his attention had turned to signaling Officer Brady, who had been watching the exchange nervously.

As the man came scrambling into the cell, Jake inquired through clenched teeth, "What exactly are the charges against the lady?"

Oblivious to Jake's thinly concealed wrath, Brady answered, "Why, she's a thief and a whore. And besides that, she's dangerous!"

Hallie groaned to herself. *Here it comes again.*

Jake's eyes narrowed with fury at the slur to Hallie's character. Forcibly containing his urge to wrap his hands around the jailer's neck and wring an apology out of him, he barked, "Who leveled the charges?"

"Nick Connelly." Brady jerked his head in Hallie's direction. "She kicked the poor man square in his privy parts."

Hallie let out a squeak of outrage. But before she could protest further, Jake interjected, "Square in his privy parts, you say?"

Was that a note of satisfaction she heard in his voice? Hallie glanced up at Jake in wonder, only to find him staring down at her, his face awash with tenderness.

Wrapping his arm protectively around her waist, he bent close to her ear and whispered, "Good for you, Mission Lady. I hope you kicked the bastard good and hard."

She moved closer to his side and nodded.

Brady, who had missed the whole exchange, bobbed his head vigorously. "Word has it," he continued, his voice taking on a tone of confidentiality, "that Nick is real bad off. The doctors say he'll be ruined for life—if he lives at all!"

"Tragic." Jake winked at Hallie. "It seems we have a desperate character on our hands. I had no idea my fiancée had such an unfortunate temper."

"Fiancée!" chorused Davinia and Brady, while Hallie merely stared at him, her eyes bulging and her mouth gaping.

Jake cupped Hallie's chin in his hand and casually snapped her jaw shut. "Why, yes. I can't imagine why Miss—or more correctly, Dr.—Gardiner, didn't mention the happy news. You should have seen Judge Dorner's face this afternoon when I told him the glad tidings. He was so looking forward to meeting my bride-to-be at his party this evening." He frowned slightly. "I can't imagine what he's going to say when I tell him that the bride is unable to attend because his officers have locked her up."

Brady paled visibly. "I had no way of knowing that she was to marry you. But you see, she did kick Nick—"

"I know where she kicked him," Jake ground out irritably. "I've been kicked there a few times myself, and unless my betrothed has legs like a mule, which I assume she doesn't," he contemplated Hallie in a dubious manner until she stamped on his foot, forcing him to finish in a pained tone, "I seriously doubt that Nick is either half dead or ruined for life."

"But Nick said she was—"

"A whore?" Jake snarled, his expression turning menacing. "Were you about to refer to my future wife as a whore, Brady?"

Brady made a choking sound and gestured helplessly. "Well—"

Jake cut him off with a sharp slashing motion. "I would be careful where I cast aspersions if I were you. I find I'm growing touchy when it comes to the subject of Dr. Gardiner and very impatient with this whole episode. Now, I'd suggest you release the doctor into my custody."

"But I can't just let her go," whined Brady. "She has to see the judge."

"Fine. Then I'll have Judge Dorner brought here."

Brady sputtered at that suggestion. "B-b-but—"

"The judge was most anxious to meet my—oh, yes, he referred to her as the 'luckiest little woman in San Francisco.' " Jake flinched as Hallie responded to his "luckiest little woman" remark with a sharp pinch to his arm. Quickly composing himself, he proceeded to beam down at her as if he were indeed the proud husband-to-be.

Davinia Loomis, who had stood quiet witness during the exchange, made an exasperated noise. "Hell and damnation, Brady! Stop being such a durned idiot. We all know this woman is no whore, just as we all know what a goat Nick Connelly can be."

Brady chewed his lip indecisively. "But—"

"But, nothing!" Davinia scolded. "Think, man. Do you really want to have to tell Judge Dorner that you've mistakenly arrested Jake Parrish's fiancée?"

Brady's Adam's apple bobbed convulsively at that thought, and he turned an alarming shade of purple.

"Well, seeing as Mr. Parrish is such a good friend of Judge Dorner, I'll release her. But only if he promises not to let her out of his sight until after she's been to court."

Jake let his gaze caress Hallie's face. "You have my word on it. I promise to be most attentive to Dr. Gardiner."

"As for the matter with Nick Connelly—"

"Leave Nick Connelly to me," Jake snapped. "I'll make sure he receives proper compensation for his part in this matter."

Davinia chortled at the threat in Jake's voice. "Compensation in the form of a fist in the face, I'd wager." She chuckled and bent over to whisper into Hallie's ear. "I'd hate to be in Nick Connelly's shoes when Jake catches up with him. I have the very unchristian notion that he'll get exactly what he deserves!"

Hallie leaned forward to look out the window as Jake's carriage came to a clattering stop. The Mission House at last. Never had the old frame building looked quite as welcoming as it did at that moment. The curtains had yet to be drawn for the evening, and the warm glow from the gaslights was spilling through the windowpanes, infusing the raindrops beading the glass with a diamondlike brilliance. Visible to passersby was the charming tableau of several mission workers bedecking a Christmas tree with gaily colored ornaments.

"Home," Davinia boomed, breaking the awkward silence which had prevailed for most of the ride from the jail. "Don't know how we can ever thank you enough, my boy. You went way beyond your Christian call of duty to pay for the burial of that Chinese girl." She leaned forward to pat Jake's cheek with motherly approval.

"You know I'm always glad to help in any way possible. All you have to do is ask "

"Proves my point, eh, Hallie? Always said there was more to Jake Parrish than just that sinfully handsome face and that nice backside."

"Davinia!" Hallie gasped, genuinely shocked by Davinia's reference to Jake's buttocks, while Jake collapsed against his seat in a paroxysm of laughter.

"It's nothing but the gospel truth," insisted Davinia, giving Jake a naughty wink. He emitted a loud whoop of hilarity in response. Training her gaze on Hallie, she frowned. "Never could abide folks who hem and haw about things that are common knowledge, and it's common knowledge that Jake Parish has a fine backside. The ladies at the mission have been known to discuss the subject in great detail from time to time. I seem to remember you partaking in that particular discussion as well, Hallie."

Hallie shrank deeper into the engulfing folds of Jake's heavy cloak, which was draped around her shoulders, and prayed, *Please, God, let the ground open up and swallow me now . . .*

Though the ground remained firmly closed beneath her feet, God seemed to be in a magnanimous mood and she was saved the humiliation of having to respond by the driver, who picked that particular moment to open the door.

Clasping Jake's hand and giving it an energetic pump, Davinia said, "Well, thanks again and Merry Christmas. You can be sure I'll include you in my prayers tonight. A man's soul can never have too many prayers said on its behalf, you know."

Jake chuckled as Davinia ducked through the door. "Make sure you include my backside in your prayers too. It seems to be one of my few admirable traits these days. And Merry Christmas to you, too."

Hallie fumbled to remove Jake's cape while Davinia was assisted out of the carriage by the driver. Avoiding Jake's eyes, Hallie murmured, "Thank you. You've been extremely kind." Folding the fine woolen garment in half, she extended it to him and made to rise. "I'll meet you at the courthouse day after tomorrow. Nine o'clock sharp."

"No, you won't." He gently pushed her back against the seat. "You're in my custody, remember? You'll be staying at my house until after you've seen Judge Dorner."

"You can't be serious!" she gasped. "I have patients to attend, and then there's the mission's Christmas celebration in the morning. I promised to play carols on the pianoforte."

"I didn't know you played."

" 'Play' isn't exactly what I'd call what she does to the instrument. But she's all we've got," Davinia chimed in, poking her head back in the carriage. "What's this about Hallie staying at your house?"

"She's in my custody until day after tomorrow. As her custodian, I've decided that she needs food, a bath, and a good night's sleep, the last of which I doubt she'll get here."

Davinia considered his words for a moment and then shrugged. "You're probably right. Undoubtedly someone will send for her in the middle of the night, and she'll go flitting off to their rescue. Besides, we wouldn't want to break the law, would we?"

"I can't—" Hallie began as Davinia pulled her head out of the carriage to confer with the driver.

But Jake cut her off, "You can and you will. As your *legal* guardian, I insist that you put that cape on before you catch pneumonia." He studied her raptly for a moment. "Not that the view isn't breathtaking, mind you."

She let her gaze follow his and was aghast to discover the source of his scrutiny. Her torn bodice was gaping wide open to reveal a shocking expanse of her breasts. Tossing the cape across her exposed flesh, she sputtered, "Will you stop ogling me like some kind of—of—*callow schoolboy*! If you were any kind of gentleman at all, you would've tactfully averted your eyes."

A slow, knowing smile painted itself across Jake's lips. With a throaty laugh that sent shivers down Hallie's spine, he mused, "But I'm neither a schoolboy nor, in this situation, a gentleman. I'm simply a man who enjoys the pleasure of looking at a beautiful woman. Especially one who's offering so much to see."

With a gasp of outrage, Hallie clutched the cape tighter.

Davinia thrust her head back into the carriage. "Make sure you bring Hallie by in the morning so she can hack her way through those Christmas carols."

"I wouldn't dream of missing it." He laughed, signaling for the driver to close the door. "It should prove to be an entertaining experience."

The horses had picked up their pace, their hooves

drumming steadily on the deserted streets, before either of the occupants of the carriage spoke again.

"So you like my backside, do you?" Jake inquired soberly.

Hallie rolled her eyes to the heavens. Wasn't it just like Jake Parrish to pursue such an improper topic of conversation? And what could she say? It wouldn't do any good to lie. Davinia had already made sure he knew that she had noticed his posterior. What could she do but admit, "I-It's very nice."

"Is that from a doctor's, or a woman's, point of view?"

She sighed with exasperation. She'd answered his question. Why couldn't he just let the subject drop? Adopting her most professional manner, spine stiff and tone brisk, she replied, "As a doctor, my primary interest in your backside would stem from the necessity to take your temperature or to give you an enema. Unless you're prone to boils in that area, which, of course, would necessitate lancing. Seeing as you aren't feverish, in need of an enema, or, I assume, plagued by boils, what do you think?"

"I think I'm pleased that there's something about me that you find attractive. It's a relief to know that you don't find me completely repulsive."

Hallie was stunned by his words and even more so by the bitterness with which they were uttered. Repulsive? Lord! Didn't the man realize that she was infatuated with every last wonderful inch of him? She shook her head, perplexed. "What in the world would make you think I find you repulsive?"

"I may be many things, but stupid isn't one of them. You made your feelings quite clear this morning. I'm worldly enough to know when a woman doesn't want me." There. He'd finally said it. And it made him feel as sick as if someone had just kicked him in the stomach.

"N-Not want you?" Hallie was dumbfounded. How could he think such a thing? Especially after the way she had responded to his caresses that morning. Didn't he know that there was nothing in the world she wanted more than to be in his arms? She distractedly pleated the fabric of his cape between her fingers. Perhaps he was teasing her again?

But as she glanced at his face, which was clearly illuminated by the carriage lantern, the naked vulnerability of his expression and the terrible longing in his eyes drove home the truth. He wanted her. Beautiful Jake Parrish wanted plain Hallie Gardiner. Impossible, but true.

"Jake, I—" The words died in her throat. How many nights had she lain sleepless, tormented by the picture of his handsome face, wishing for a moment such as this? And when she had at last fallen into an uneasy sleep, how many times had she dreamt the hopeless dream in which he desired her as much as she desired him? In truth, there hadn't been a day—or a night—since they had met when he hadn't occupied her thoughts, and now that her dreams had turned into reality, she found herself as tongue-tied as a debutante at her coming-out ball.

With a sigh, Jake turned his face until it was hidden in the shadows. It was so like Hallie to be kind in her rejection.

"It's all right," he finally said, trying to spare her the embarrassment of expressing her objections, and himself the pain of hearing them. "I understand. I can't blame you for not wanting to be saddled with a foul-tempered cripple. A woman like you deserves a whole man. One who can offer you a love untainted by a bitter past, and a houseful of children to love, which we both know I can't give you."

The quiet dignity of his voice lacerated her. Didn't he realize that all she wanted was him? Finding her voice at last, she choked, "Jake—"

"No. You don't have to say anything. Just remember that I'd be honored to remain your friend and to—"

Before he could finish the sentence, Hallie hurled herself across the narrow space separating them and threw her arms around his neck, knocking his top hat to the floor. Without further ado, she ground her lips fiercely against his.

"I love you, you foolish man," she declared between kisses. "And I want you more than I can say."

With a groan, Jake grasped her around her waist and hauled her onto his lap. "Not nearly as much as I want you, sweet Mission Lady." And as their gazes met in the flickering lantern light, he found his salvation in the loving tenderness of her eyes.

Never in his life had he felt so alive as he did at that moment, for deep in the barren wasteland of his heart, Hallie Gardiner had planted seeds of hope, and her love, like the warm summer sun, had coaxed it to spring forth and bloom. Once again, after months of merely existing for the moment, he dared to dream of a happy future.

"I love you," Hallie repeated, reaching up to cradle his face in her trembling palm. It was all too wonderful to believe. He really was *her* Jake. Hers to love, treasure, and touch. Hers to kiss whenever she felt the urge . . . which was now.

As if he had read her thoughts, Jake's mouth smothered hers with a savage intensity that made her quiver. But this time she felt no guilt or shame at her desire, and she burrowed her hands into the ebony silk of his hair, boldly urging him on.

With reckless abandon, she returned his kiss, instinctively parting her lips to the heated demand of his questing tongue. And as the kiss deepened, she hungrily answered his seductive beckoning, letting her eager response match his with a passion that stunned her senses. If what she felt was sinful, then she would gladly burn in the fires of hell forever.

It wasn't until Jake had eased Hallie back onto the yielding surface of the seat, his body covering hers, that he finally drew his lips away. He couldn't help grinning like the proverbial idiot when she made a moue of disappointment. There was such unexpected fire in his prim little Mission Lady—he reveled in the joy of kindling it.

Propping himself up on one elbow, he let his gaze move from Hallie's prettily flushed face down to where her breasts lay partially exposed in the tattered remnants of her gown. Rising softly with each breath, those globes were as succulent as perfectly ripened peaches, the delicate ivory of the skin blushing to dusky apricot where one nipple peeked out from the mound of fabric. His reaction to the sight of that tender peak was swift and violent.

He moaned. His manhood was rapidly becoming the bane of his existence. Ever since he'd met Hallie Gardiner, that particular region of his body had been chronically inflamed. Perhaps he should submit to one of her famous ice treatments. Or try dosing himself with some saltpeter.

He shifted his hips uncomfortably, trying to ease the now tight fit of his trousers. Damn thing ached. Worse yet, it was like a stick of dynamite—and Hallie was like a lit match. All it took was one touch from her and it exploded. Not a comforting thought, considering his dismal performance that morning.

Mustering every ounce of control he had left, which admittedly wasn't much, Jake forced himself to pull away from the temptation of Hallie's bewitching body.

God! That act alone should be enough to qualify me for sainthood, he thought, staring down at her longingly. Lying there in half-clothed splendor, her eyes luring him with sensual promise, Hallie Gardiner was enough to tempt the pope right out of his vestments.

Which was almost more than a man in Jake's sexually deprived state could bear. His hands trembling with desire, Jake hastily covered the tantalizing sight of Hallie's breasts with his cloak and tugged her into a sitting position.

"Jake?" she whispered, hurt by the abruptness with which he had pulled away. Had her inexperience been so obvious and her kisses so woefully lacking, that he found her efforts unpleasant? After all, he was the only man she had ever kissed. Well, the only man she'd ever kissed like *that,* at any rate. And a man like Jake was bound to have had plenty of experience in such matters.

Bowing her head to hide her distress, she murmured, "I'm sorry if I did something wrong."

"Wrong, Mission Lady?" He chuckled, wrapping his arms around her midsection and drawing her close until her back rested against his chest. "You did everything too right. In another few minutes, you would have had me making a mess of my trousers again, and I had a hard enough time explaining the stain from this morning to Hop Yung."

She felt her cheeks grow warm at the intimacy of his conversation. It was all so improper—and new—this talk of messed trousers. She flushed again.

After dropping a kiss on the top of her head, Jake rested his cheek on her shoulder. Gently nuzzling her neck, he murmured, "Don't you know what you do to a man, sweetheart? Surely you've had admirers before?"

"No."

His head jerked up in disbelief. "You're teasing me."

"Of course not." Gesturing at her face and body, she retorted, "Just look at me!"

"I am." The warm timbre of his voice left little doubt as to the meaning of his words.

"Then if you don't see why, I'd suggest you look into getting some spectacles."

"Nothing's wrong with my vision, Mission Lady. It's you who needs glasses if you can't see the reflection in your own mirror." He cupped her chin in his palm and frowned. "What makes you think you're not beautiful?"

She gave a brittle laugh. "I look like my mother. Everyone in Philadelphia said so. My father always said he'd never seen a more whey-faced pair than my mother and me."

"Then your father is either a blind fool or a bastard who deserves to be on the receiving end of a discharging pistol."

Hallie shrugged and tried to turn her head away.

But Jake tightened his grip on her chin, forcing her to look at him. "You've never told me much about your family."

She sighed. "There's not much to tell. I'm an only child. My mother died of yellow fever last year, and my father still lives in Philadelphia."

"What kind of a man is your father, letting you come all the way to San Francisco with no friends or money?"

Hallie jerked her chin out of his hand and looked away. "Well, of the two types you mentioned, he isn't of the blind fool variety. He was glad to be rid of me." Though she tried to keep her voice neutral, Hallie couldn't stop a note of grief from shrouding her words. "You see, my mother contracted the fever during a heat wave in the summer of '64. Many of our friends and neighbors came down with it. I was fresh out of medical school, and I honestly believed I could save them all. I—I thought I could play God."

As if defeated by some inner battle, she sagged back against Jake's chest. Hearing the raw anguish in her voice, Jake hugged her close with one arm while stroking her hair with his other hand.

Hallie closed her eyes and let his nearness soothe her for a moment before continuing, "It was awful . . . so many people died. And then I contracted the disease. I was told my mother died alone." She let out a jagged sob. "That's the worst part. I should have been there. Nobody should have to die alone."

It hurt to remember her mother's death. So much so that this was the first time she had spoken of it to anyone. Yet, lying here in Jake's arms, with his heart beating strongly beneath her cheek, she found the strength to speak of her pain. Somehow she knew he would understand exactly how she felt.

Jake's arm tightened around Hallie. "Your mother must have been a remarkable woman to have a daughter like you," he remarked quietly.

"She was." Hallie sniffed, groping in her pocket for the handkerchief Jake had given her. "Not only was she a popular hostess in society, she was an astute business woman. Why, if—" she paused to blow her nose. "—it hadn't have been for her good sense, my father would have bankrupted the Sinclair Mines and foundries years ago."

"Sinclair?" Jake tipped his head down to study her profile. "Then your mother was Georgianna Gardiner? I'm surprised that I didn't see the resemblance right away."

Hallie sniffled loudly with surprise. "You knew my mother?"

"I met her once. It was ten years ago, right after I'd lost both my parents in a fire. I was young and frightened, finding myself suddenly responsible for the vast Parrish empire, as well as for Penelope's upbringing. I'd gone to Philadelphia to contract for iron to use in the new line of steamships my father had planned to build. Everyone knows that Sinclair iron is the finest in the country, so your mother was the first person I contacted. When she heard of my parents' deaths, she took me under her wing and fussed over me like a mother hen. Rather like you have the tendency to do."

With a noise that was halfway between a chuckle and

a sob, Hallie retorted, "That's because she was as much of a fool for a pretty face as I."

"She did call me pretty," Jake teased roguishly, pleased to see Hallie smile at last. "Then she invited me to dinner and proceeded to brag about her wonderful daughter. Her eyes positively glowed when she spoke of you. Rather like yours do when you're discussing probing a wound."

"Or stitching," she snickered back, then laughed when he gave a groan of mock pain.

"They didn't glow quite *that* much," he chuckled. "Anyway, as she spoke, I remember envying your father. I found myself wishing that she wasn't a married woman so I could court her. She was everything a man could want: intelligent, sensitive, kind . . . and beautiful. So it seems that your father was right in one respect: you are like your incredible mother."

Hallie pivoted in Jake's embrace until she faced him. Twining her arms around his neck, she pulled his face close. "You know something, Mr. Parrish? I really do love you."

He suddenly choked. "Good God, Hallie! You smell worse than the wharf on a hot day. What is that smell?"

Her? Stink? Hallie was stunned. She was about to inform him that there was nothing wrong with the way she smelled and point out his rudeness at suggesting such a thing, when she remembered falling into the pile of rotten fish entrails. Looking down at herself, she saw that the repulsively stained section of her hem had twisted up to her waist. She sniffed and then frowned. After inhaling the foul scent all day, she must have become inured to it.

Struggling to pull herself out of his embrace, she grumbled, "You try getting knocked into a pile of rotten fish guts and being deprived of washing facilities. Then let's see how sweet you smell." Watching as Jake took several gulping breaths of air, she mumbled beneath her breath, "Of course he's sensitive to smells. Bet the man doesn't even sweat."

Jake tightened his grip on Hallie's waist, drawing her near again. "I seem to remember sweating quite profusely this morning. Or have you already forgotten our encounter in the parlor?"

"Of course not," she groaned. "Neither, I imagine, has Lavinia Donahue or, by this time, the rest of San Francisco."

"The wagging tongues will stop soon enough when Davinia leaks the rumor that you're my fiancée. She's almost as bad as that sister of hers when it comes to a piece of juicy gossip."

"Sister?"

"Lavinia. Not that either woman makes any claim to the relationship. Bad blood."

Hallie shook her head. "Can't say I blame Davinia." Then she slanted Jake an uneasy look. "But Jake, what are people going to say when we tell them that we're not getting married?"

"Why would we tell them that?"

Her heart missed a beat. "You can't mean that you really want to marry me?"

He shrugged and gave her a lazy smile. She couldn't resist caressing his dimple. If only it were true. How she would love to marry him and see his smile every day for the rest of her life!

Giving her lower lip a quick bite, she ventured, "I can't imagine why you would want to marry me. You don't have to, you know."

"I know I don't, sweet Mission Lady," he purred, bending close and giving her full lower lip a nibble of his own. "But it just so happens that I like a woman who can make me sweat."

Chapter 16

Boom! An angry clap of thunder rumbled through the night, vibrating the Parrish house to its very foundations.

Hallie clutched at the satin coverlet uneasily. It wasn't that she was afraid of storms; she'd conquered that particular fear when she was nine years old. No, she wasn't precisely *afraid,* she was . . .

She flinched as the wind pounded against her windows with a force that made the glass rattle in their frames. Startled. Yes, that was it. She had been startled out of her sound sleep by all the hellish commotion.

Tell yourself that enough times, and you might start to believe it, taunted a voice from somewhere deep within the recesses of her mind.

I do believe it! But her fragile inner argument crumbled as lightning flashed through the windows and illuminated the room with an eerie blue glow.

"Oh, Lord!" she gasped. Had she seen something moving in the corner just now? She squinted into the gloom but could see nothing through the mask of darkness.

In the space of a heartbeat, the lightning was followed by a violent crack of thunder. Hallie jumped what felt like a mile into the air and, with a whimper, clapped her hands over her ears. In the stillness of the mansion the noise amplified and then resonated through the cavernous hallways.

It's the sound of the gates of hell bursting open!

Hallie shrank deeper into the soft mattress. It was on nights like this that her father's tale came back to haunt her.

She had been five at the time, and if she lived to be a hundred and one, she would never forget the fierceness of the storm that night. The wind had torn at the roof and the windows, shrieking its fury at earsplitting volume. Wild streaks of lightning bolted across the pitch black midnight sky, and the thunder—oh, Lord!—the thunder had rumbled so loudly that she'd been certain the world was coming to an end.

Terrified by nature's violence, she had run sobbing from room to room, frantically searching for her mother. But it was to no avail. Her mother was nowhere to be found.

Finally, in an act of desperation, she burst into her father's study, a room which she had been strictly forbidden to enter. There she found her father alone, sitting in the semidarkness, surrounded by his astounding collection of antiquities and relics. With a tenderness he had never shown his only child, he was cradling a large wooden crucifix in his arms, an artifact which Hallie later learned was a rare prize from the Spanish Inquisition.

Just the sight of his daughter, barefooted and clad in a thick flannel nightgown, was enough to make Ambrose's handsome face contort with distaste. Eloquently his glare conveyed his wrath, silently vowing punishment for her unwelcome intrusion into his domain.

When he opened his mouth to vent his rage, there was another peal of thunder, a particularly bombastic one, and Hallie clapped her hands over her ears, crying out in alarm.

Her father smiled then, in a twisted caricature of goodwill that intimidated her far more than his scowl ever could. Beckoning her nearer, he whispered, Do you hear them?

Even in the dimness of the room and from a distance, Hallie saw the peculiar light glowing in his amber-colored eyes. His strange expression frightened her, and for a moment she was sorely tempted to run away. But she knew better than to disobey him. It was with trepidation that she crept nearer, daring to stop only when he motioned for her to do so.

As she stood trembling before him, he trapped her

panicked gaze with his malevolent one and hissed again, Do you hear them?

Hallie swallowed hard and forced herself to listen to the storm outside. I hear wind and thunder, *she finally ventured.* And rain. N-nothing more.

Ambrose shook his head, his upper lip curled into a snarl. It's the fury of the devil's disciples you're hearing. Ungodly creatures who ride the wings of the storm and prey on the souls of the unwary. Especially those of foolish children.

There was a crash of thunder then, one that sounded as if the earth was being torn asunder. Hallie whimpered aloud in terror.

Ambrose laughed, feeding off her fear. Gently caressing the crucifix, he growled, Do you know what that sound is?

Hallie bit her lip to keep from crying out again and shook her head.

It's the sound of the gates of hell bursting open!

As if in response to his words, the wind clawed at the study windows like hobgoblins intent on mischief.

Pray, Hallie Gardiner! *he keened, thrusting the crucifix just inches from her face.* Pray hard and well this night, lest one of the demons whose name we daren't speak sets its evil sights on you.

Hallie stared at the crudely wrought crucifix. There was a nightmarish quality about the carved face of the corpus Christ which frightened her almost as much as her father's macabre tale.

Mesmerized by the sheer grotesqueness of the thing, she was unable to tear her gaze away from the sight of those pupilless eyes cast beseechingly toward the heavens and the horror of that mouth distorted in a scream of eternal agony. Most gruesome of all were the rivulets of painted blood flowing from beneath the crown of thorns, made all the more livid by their vermilion contrast against the otherwise plain wood surface.

Pray before your soul is lost forever . . .

Hallie sank deeper into the protective cocoon of her blankets. Suddenly the years seemed to roll away, and she felt five years old again. Shuddering, she peered into the shadows.

Gargoyles. With wings like bats and eyes glowing blood-red . . . Hurtling out of the darkness to suck out her soul. She could almost feel the pain as the monsters grasped her in their razor-sharp claws . . .

Stop it this instant, Hallie! Such nonsense! There's no such thing as monsters, she scolded herself. Then a flash of lightning blazed across the sky, followed by a deafening peal of thunder. With a gasp, she ducked her head beneath the blankets. *Not afraid.* Well, maybe she was feeling just the tiniest bit *anxious* after all.

Think about something else. Anything. Something comforting. Something that makes you feel safe.

Jake. She would think of Jake. Being held by Jake made her feel safer than if she had been sheltered by a whole army of guardian angels, and the sound of his whispers as he urged her to sleep was more comforting than any heavenly lullaby.

Hallie poked her head out from under the covers and glanced sharply toward the hearth. Exactly when had Jake left her side? When she'd drifted off to sleep, the fire was blazing cheerfully in the hearth and Jake was perched on the chair next to the bed.

But now the flames were little more than a pile of gleaming embers . . . and the chair was empty. She sighed with longing. She would gladly trade her new thermometers, all twelve of them, just to feel the reassuring warmth of Jake's nearness. He had made her feel a way she'd never felt before. Special. Cherished. *Loved.*

When they had arrived from the jail that evening, he'd taken charge of everything, barking orders which had sent the servants scurrying to do his bidding.. When it appeared that all was being done to his satisfaction, Jake personally escorted her up to a luxurious suite of rooms and turned her over to Celine's kindly ministrations.

From that point on, she was waited on hand and foot. She had felt like a princess, relaxing in a tub of hot water while a servant brushed the tangles from her freshly washed hair. Scrubbed clean within an inch of her life and smelling of lavender, with her damp hair neatly braided, she was slipped into what looked to be one of Jake's nightshirts.

Just as she was being tucked into bed with hot bricks warming her feet, Jake had reappeared. He watched for a moment while Celine prepared to cleanse Hallie's battered face; then he took the cloth from the woman's hand and dismissed her with a nod.

Sitting on the edge of the bed, he tended her himself. His hands were gentle as he soothed her bruises with cool water, his handsome face filled with such tenderness that it made Hallie breathless just to remember it. As he had treated each injury, he paused to give it a soft kiss before turning his attention to the next one. His kisses were more soothing than any balm in Hallie's black bag. And though his brand of doctoring was alien to anything found in the pages of a medical journal, she had felt much restored when he had finished.

Shortly thereafter, Celine returned, bearing a tray of savory-smelling food. Hallie squealed in protest and Celine chuckled with amusement when Jake tucked the napkin around Hallie's neck and insisted on feeding her as if she were no older than Ariel. With a sigh of surrender, Hallie relaxed against her pillows, obediently eating whatever he put in her mouth. She had no idea what she'd eaten, so preoccupied had she been with Jake's coaxing smiles.

When Celine had at last removed the tray, Jake settled in the chair close to the bed and sat stroking her hair and urging her to sleep in a low, hypnotic voice. Almost immediately, she complied. She probably would've slept the whole night through had it not been for the thunder. Speaking of which . . .

Hallie clapped her hands over her ears to shut out the fiendish roar. It didn't work. Lord! This was the worst squall she'd seen in years! She could remember huddling in her crib during such a storm, her terrified screams drowned out by the thunder. She had been three at the time, little more than a baby.

Like Ariel.

Ariel! Hallie bolted to a sitting position. Was Ariel terrified, too? Did she lie sobbing in her crib, her cries unheard above the noise, with no one there to soothe her? The thought of the poor babe alone in her nursery was too much for Hallie to bear.

Snatching up the dressing gown Jake had left at the

foot of the bed, she bounded out from the security of her blankets. For a moment she imagined, as she had when she was a child, that there was a monster under the bed waiting to grab her ankle and pull her into its lair.

Then she laughed. What was it about a storm that made her feel like a five-year-old again? As she slipped her arms into Jake's robe, the same one she had wrapped him in on the day he was shot, she could smell traces of his clean, masculine scent lingering in the velvet folds. The familiarity of the fragrance was reassuring, giving her the much-needed courage to brave the darkened corridors.

Which she did with an aplomb that made her want to give herself a pat on the back. When she finally reached the nursery, Hallie found the door slightly ajar and heard not the screams of a frantic child but the soothing sounds of a murmuring voice. Sighing her relief, she eased the door open and peeked in.

Sitting in a rocking chair close to the fireplace, with his left leg propped up on a low stool, was Jake. And lying contentedly in his arms was Ariel.

"So you see, Sprite, the angels have a particular fondness for bowling." Jake paused to point out the window where a bolt of lightning was cutting across the midnight sky. "See that streak of silver light? That's the trail left by the angel's ball as it rolls across the sky. He's trying to knock down that line of stars just over the horizon." He shifted Ariel to show her the stars, but she was far more interested in staring at the colorfully patterned silk of his dressing gown.

Then there was the inevitable roll of thunder, and Hallie, caught up in Jake's fanciful story, let out a cry of surprise. His head jerked up at the sound.

When he saw Hallie standing in the doorway, nervously balling up a section of her robe in her hand, he smiled. She who had fearlessly attacked Cyrus King with a parasol and who had kicked Nick Connelly in his private parts was apparently afraid of storms. He found his Mission Lady's childish foible thoroughly endearing, just as he did everything else about her. If his arms hadn't been occupied at that moment, he would have wrapped her in his embrace and promised to protect her from storm monsters.

Still smiling, he beckoned to her.

Hallie practically flew to his side. As she knelt on the rug at his feet, he reached down and gave her shoulder a reassuring squeeze. He could feel her trembling beneath his hand.

Gently he cupped her chin in his palm and lifted her face so that her features were lit by the warm glow of the fire. Staring hypnotically into her frightened eyes, he continued his tale.

"Two points for the angel," he whispered, nodding at the storm outside yet never once letting his gaze stray from hers. "Don't you know that thunder is the sound of an angel's ball striking the stars?"

"And the rain?" Hallie asked, leaning forward to rest against his knee, basking in the sanctuary of his presence. "What causes the rain?"

Jake chuckled and let his hand drop from her face. "It's tears, sweet Mission Lady. Angels are notoriously poor losers."

Ariel's only response to that bit of whimsy was a yawn. Emitting a little squeak, she burrowed deeper against Jake's chest, where she lay sucking on her chubby fist and staring at Hallie with drowsy eyes.

"She looks like Serena," Hallie commented, tearing her gaze from Jake's tip-tilted green eyes to study the baby in his arms. From her wide blue eyes and the silvery down crowning her head to the dainty toes peeking out from a fold of the pink silk quilt, Ariel was the very picture of her beautiful mother.

Jake stared down at the bundle in his arms. "Thank God for small favors," he whispered, more to himself than to Hallie.

Yes. Thank God, Hallie repeated to herself. She could only imagine how awful it would have been for Jake if the baby had resembled her unknown father. Awful to have spent his days scanning the faces of friends and strangers, wondering, looking for some minute similarity. Awful to have looked into the child's unfamiliar face and be painfully reminded that some unknown man had given Serena what he couldn't.

Propping her elbows up on the arm of the chair, Hallie noted the way Jake caressed Ariel's cheek with his thumb. She smiled at his apparent fondness for the child.

Ariel nuzzled against his hand like a newborn kitten seeking milk at its mother's breast. She gave another yawn, and her eyes fluttered shut.

"Was she frightened by the storm?"

"Not as much as some people I know," Jake teased, reaching over to give Hallie's thick braid a tweak.

Hallie grinned sheepishly. "I was worried that the noise had disturbed Ariel. I thought she might need soothing."

"Perhaps it was *you* who needed *her* soothing," he replied in a semi-serious tone. "Holding her does have a calming effect. Sleep doesn't come easily to me these days, and I've found that it helps to discuss whatever is on my mind with her. Ariel is an excellent listener."

"She's only four months old."

"She's also the only female I know with whom I can get a word in edgewise."

"Then you're spending too much time with the wrong kind of women."

Jake reached down and lightly traced the shape of her mouth with his fingertip. "That's because the right one spends her time avoiding me."

Hallie nipped at his finger playfully. "You're welcome to discuss anything you like with me. I promise to be as attentive as Ariel."

"Anything?" he asked, raising one eyebrow suggestively.

"Within reason, you wicked man!"

"Pity." He sighed theatrically. Giving the sleeping Ariel a wink of mock conspiracy, he murmured, "Remind me to tell you about my intentions toward a certain Mission Lady, Sprite."

"You're a rogue, Jake Parrish!" Hallie giggled. "Still, despite your naughty ways, I'm glad you've taken an interest in the baby. I was worried you would never accept her."

It was Jake's turn to look sheepish. "I did behave like a bastard, didn't I?"

"I distinctly remember pointing that out."

"Yes. You did." He chuckled.

"What made you change your mind?"

A tender smile curved his lips. "Do you remember how restless she was the night after Serena's funeral?"

Hallie nodded. Ariel had howled incessantly that evening, much to the despair of the wet nurse and the nanny. Hallie had examined the poor babe but had been unable to find anything wrong with her. It was puzzling.

"I understood exactly how she felt." He sighed. "I, too, was feeling out of sorts. I was exhausted, my wound hurt, and there was nothing I wanted more than to sleep, which, of course, was out of the question considering the racket she was making."

Jake raised his eyes and caught Hallie's compassionate gaze with his hungry one. No. That wasn't quite true. What he'd wanted more than sleep was to curl up in Hallie Gardiner's arms. And it hadn't been just the noise that kept him awake, it had also been the void he'd felt after she left for the Mission House.

He glanced down at the bundle in his arms, unconsciously toying with the lace edge of the blanket framing Ariel's face. "The screams went on for hours. Finally, out of sheer desperation, I ordered the baby brought to my bedchamber. I didn't know exactly what I was going to do, I only knew I'd go mad if she didn't quiet. I remember looking into her little red face and thinking that she looked as lost as I felt. She seemed so helpless that I suddenly had an overwhelming urge to comfort her. I didn't know what to do—I'd never held an infant before, so I simply laid her against my chest, her heart against mine, and stroked her back. Like magic, she calmed."

Jake smiled with fond remembrance. "I thought of you when her sobs faded and she began to make little hiccuping noises. Anyway, before I knew it, we had both fallen asleep. It was the soundest I'd slept in months. It comforted me to feel someone else near, to feel another heart beating next to mine."

Hallie could picture Jake asleep with the fairylike Ariel curled up on his powerful chest. The thought made her ache to wrap him in her embrace and to press her own heart against his. What a lonely man he was. And how she loved him!

"I imagine she sensed that something was wrong," Hallie murmured. "You made her feel safe. Any woman would feel safe sleeping in your arms."

"But there's only one woman I'm interested in having

sleeping there," he purred, his gaze raking her body provocatively.

Did he know how he tempted her when he looked at her like that? Hallie blushed and looked away. Lord! How she longed to say yes to his seductive invitation—to fall sleep with the feel of his naked skin warming hers, to wake up next to him and to let his smile be her dawning light.

Embarrassed by her own desires, Hallie turned her attention back to Ariel. "She's fast asleep now. Would you like me to put her into her cradle for you?"

He nodded. "My leg is usually strong enough to allow me to stand unaided. But tonight, well . . . I'm glad you're here." It was a statement of fact, and for once there was no bitterness in his voice as he referred to his handicap.

"I'm glad too," she whispered, taking Ariel from his arms. A smile tugged at Hallie's lips as she tucked the blankets around the diminutive form. Wasn't it just like Jake to purchase something as beautiful—and impractical—as a pink silk coverlet for an infant? Obviously little Ariel was on her way to becoming thoroughly spoiled.

When Hallie at last turned from the cradle, her heart was wrenched by the sight of Jake struggling to rise to his feet. His face was drawn in lines of frustration, and she noticed that the motion of the rocking chair was doing nothing to aid his efforts.

Wordlessly, she held out her hands to him.

He grew very still as he sat poised at the edge of the chair, staring at her open palms. Slowly, he let his gaze travel from her hands to her face. She nodded her encouragement.

After a moment's hesitation, he slipped his hands into hers and let her help him to his feet. It was the first time he had willingly let anyone aid him in such a manner, for to do so was to acknowledge defeat to his shameful weakness. He let out his breath slowly. It wasn't nearly as hard as he had imagined.

As Hallie slipped her arms around his waist and held him while he positioned his cane, Jake decided that he liked her assistance a great deal. He liked the way her hands felt clasped against the small of his back. He liked the way her unbound breasts grazed his silk-clad chest, and most of all he liked the way she met his gaze without a trace of pity. The only thing he read in the tawny depths of her eyes was love.

Steady now, he leaned forward to drop a quick kiss on her lips. "Thank you," he whispered before stepping away.

In companionable silence, they made their way down the corridors. The storm had eased until all that remained was the gentle tapping of the rain against the windows. Somewhere in the house, a clock struck midnight. It was Christmas Day.

Grinning, Hallie paused to wish Jake a Merry Christmas. But when she saw his expression, the gay felicitation died in her throat. Every line, every feature of his face was rigidly controlled—too controlled. She'd seen that look too often not to recognize it. It was the face of a man who was suffering, of a man who had become so accustomed to hiding his pain that even in an unguarded moment such as this, he kept his discomfort well masked.

"Jake." She grasped his arm to halt him. "Let me help you."

One corner of his mouth curled up. "I know I'm moving slower than a snail over hot tar, but I'm perfectly capable of escorting you back to your room." Looping his free arm around her shoulders, he teased, "Besides, someone has to protect you from all the ghosts and goblins brought on by the storm."

"Of course you're capable," she declared, snuggling close to his side and wrapping her arm around his taut waist. "I don't doubt you could walk me all the way to Timbuktu—and back—if you wanted to. What I was referring to was your pain."

"I'm fine."

"Liar."

He shrugged. "All right, so this damp cold makes my leg a bit stiff."

"And it aches?" she prodded gently.

"Like the devil," he admitted with a sigh.

She stared down at the lattice print of the hall carpet. "In Europe they use massage and hot poultices to relieve such pain."

"Indeed?"

"Yes." She stole a glance up at his face. He was staring down at her, his expression unreadable. Clearing her throat nervously, she suggested, "I could do it for you if you'd like."

He continued to stare at her for a moment, before shifting his gaze down to his hand clutching the gold top of his cane. Now there was a dangerous idea. Did she realize what her hands caressing his naked thigh would do to him?

He chuckled softly. "Do you really think that would be a wise idea?"

"I wouldn't suggest it if I didn't think it would help. I promise you that when I'm finished with the treatment, you won't spare your leg another thought."

"Oh, I don't doubt that for a minute. At least the part about sparing my leg a thought." He wondered vaguely if anyone had ever died from unrelieved lust. If not, he was sure to make the medical annals as the first. That is, if he was thickheaded enough to submit to Hallie Gardiner's ministrations, which he wasn't.

"If you'll just let me get you settled in your bed, I can run down to the kitchen to get what I need. Let's see now, a—"

Jake's groan cut her off. "No." *Never! Well, at least not until hell froze over.*

"Please, Jake," she pleaded, tightening her arm around his waist and pulling him to a stop. "Let me do this for you. You've done so much for me today. I want to do something to repay you."

"Hallie . . ." he began, glancing down into her face. She was gnawing on her lower lip, her soft eyes entreating him. Damn. How could he possibly say no to that beseeching expression? Administering this treatment obviously meant a great deal to her.

He groaned again. Lord give him strength! It looked like hell was about to freeze over.

Chapter 17

Within half an hour, Hallie had stoked the waning fire in Jake's bedchamber, set a kettle of water to boil, and laid out the makings for a linseed poultice on a small table.

Jake, who had adamantly refused to lie in bed for the treatment, was relaxing in a chair in front of the hearth with his leg propped up on an ottoman.

"No wonder your leg aches," Hallie scolded as she knelt between his knees and uncorked a small brown bottle. "It's freezing in here. On nights like this, you need to make sure the servants set a proper fire, and you'd probably be more comfortable if you had Hop put some hot bricks around your leg."

"Fine," Jake mumbled, closing his eyes and swallowing hard as Hallie began to pull up his dressing gown to expose his disfigured limb. Did the woman realize he was naked underneath? he wondered. Not that he was worried about his modesty being compromised, mind you. It was just that he was becoming aroused by Hallie's touch, and he found his lack of control embarrassing.

Every muscle in his body tensed as she pushed the hem to the uppermost region of his thigh. *A few inches more . . .*

Then he released a quick breath of relief. She had stopped just short of the articulation where his thigh joined his groin and had let the excess fabric drape modestly between his legs. With that mound of silk shielding him, perhaps she wouldn't notice the way his hardened flesh was beginning to protrude.

Gently, Hallie prodded the length of the ugly scar. *No wonder it pains him so,* she thought, her heart swelling with sympathy. He'd obviously been badly hurt, and whoever had tended to the injury had been less than skilled. The damage was extensive, leaving an ugly red scar that was about two inches wide and ran from several inches above his knee to just below the apex of his groin. She felt him flinch as her fingers found the hard protuberance where the torn muscles had healed over the crookedly knit bone.

"I'm sorry, Jake," she whispered, more out of compassion for what he must have suffered at the hands of the army surgeons than for any discomfort he'd felt during her examination.

Not looking down at her, Jake buried his cheek against the velvet of the wing-backed chair and nodded tersely. She hadn't hurt him, though his throat was too constricted from his sudden panic to tell her so. Christ! He'd forgotten how much he hated having the maimed area touched. Even now, after all these months, he associated being touched there with being subjected to more pain.

His gut tightened, for he half expected to feel the agony of a scalpel cutting through his flesh. Then his gorge rose with terrible swiftness. *The probe. They would dig deeply into the wound, scraping metal against bone, unmindful of his tortured screams.* A groan escaped his lips.

Hallie watched the sweat bead up on Jake's ashen face. Lord! It must hurt even worse than she'd first imagined. Pouring a generous amount of Celine's liniment into her palm to warm it, she crooned, "Try and relax, darling. It'll feel better in a little while."

She spread the oily liquid over the limb and began her manipulations, keeping her touch light at first. As Hallie gradually increased the pressure, she could feel Jake's tense muscles begin to loosen beneath her palm. And though he didn't make a sound or open his eyes while she worked, his face began to lose its strained expression.

It feels wonderful, he thought, surrendering to the soothing sensation of Hallie's now deeply kneading motions. Whatever she'd used on his leg had turned warm beneath the friction of her hands, and the heat penetrated all the way to the bone, easing the chronic ache.

It was the first time since he'd been wounded that his leg had actually felt good.

Neither spoke for a long while, he caught up in the pleasure of being free from pain, she scrutinizing the twisted configuration of the injury. Just as Jake felt the last of his tension ease away, Hallie's movements abruptly ceased and he felt her fingertips graze an area in his inner thigh.

"Gunshot," he supplied, looking down at where she was tracing a star-shaped scar. "Fortunately, the Reb who shot me wasn't armed with rifled musket."

Jake sighed and leaned back, relaxing again as she resumed her massage. "He was probably some poor farm boy toting his daddy's shotgun. I would have lost the leg for sure if I'd taken a minié ball. At least that's what the surgeons said. As it was, the bone was badly broken, and they wanted to amputate it at the thigh and be done with it."

Hallie stared up at him in horror. "They would have amputated your leg without trying to save it?"

"When you have thousands of wounded and comparatively few doctors, there is often no choice. You do whatever is quickest and most likely to save the patient's life." He opened his eyes and forced himself to study his maimed limb.

He'd always avoided looking at it, hating the nightmarish memories that the scar brought back. And aside from Seth, who had been with him through his ordeal, he'd never discussed his wound with anyone. It was too hard to remember.

But looking at his thigh now, cradled between Hallie's hands, it didn't seem nearly as disturbing as it once had, and he felt an odd need to tell her about it. If anyone would understand what he'd been through, Hallie would.

"I was afraid," he confessed in a hoarse voice, watching her hands move fluidly over his ugly war memento. "I remember lying in the dark alone. It was cold . . . raining . . . I was terrified that no one would find me. Almost as afraid as I was of what would happen when they did."

His hands tightened on the arms of the chair at the horror of his remembrance. "I would have died undiscovered on the battlefield if Seth hadn't been so relentless in his search for me. It was a good thing I was moaning, or he probably wouldn't have found me lying among the piles of dead soldiers."

Hallie wanted to weep at the thought of her beloved Jake lying on the cold ground, hurt and alone. What she wouldn't give to have been there to comfort him, to have been able to spare him the nightmare of such memories, to have saved him from being mutilated in such a tragic fashion.

As she fought to suppress her sob at the horror of his story, her hands tightened on his thigh. She felt him flinch at the sudden pressure. Shooting him an apologetic look, she quickly resumed her gently kneading manipulations.

"You're lucky to have a friend like Seth," she murmured.

Jake gave her a gentle smile and nodded. "Yes. He even insisted on staying with me while the surgeons did their work. It was he who convinced them not to do the amputation. I was told that he persuaded them to remove the bullet and set my leg by holding them at gunpoint. He paid for that bit of insubordination by being assigned the duty of burying all the amputated limbs that had piled up outside the medical tents."

Hallie let her fingertips trace the jagged path of the scar. "It must have been a terrible wound."

"It got worse with the surgeons' efforts." He reached down and after a moment's hesitation touched his thigh. Pointing to a wide puckered area, he explained, "That's where the bone came through the skin. They cut me from here—" his hand mapped out an area encompassing several inches above and below the puckered scar. "—to here to probe for the bullet and remove the bone fragments."

He swallowed hard as a shudder rippled through his body. Unable to keep from trembling now, he ran his finger over the entire perimeter of the long scar. "A few weeks later, they cut me from here to here to remove the infected tissue and to probe for the fragments they had forgotten the first time." He fell silent for a moment, stroking the area reflectively.

"How awful for you!" she blurted out, hating the

thought of her Jake being subjected to such savagery. "No wonder you think of doctors as a pack of butchers."

With some difficulty, he admitted, "It was awful. They were afraid to give me chloroform, because of what had happened the first time, so they tied me down and operated without it. Even with morphine, it hurt so badly I wanted to die."

Jake squeezed his eyes shut for a moment. He'd hated being tied and helpless. He could almost feel the rough hemp ropes cutting into his wrists and ankles as his body arched uncontrollably at the agonizing brutality of the procedure.

"Jake?" Hallie pulled his hand away from the scar and clasped it in hers. He clung to her with bone-crushing desperation. His face was as pale as ashes, and he looked as if he was about to be sick. "You don't have to tell me about it if it's too painful."

He opened his eyes to focus on Hallie's upturned face. The tenderness of her expression and the loving warmth of her eyes chased away his dark musings.

"No," he whispered, squeezing her hand gratefully. "I want to tell you."

She nodded, understanding his need to talk. Perhaps, if he could release the festering memories from his sickened soul, he could begin to truly heal. Only then would he be whole again.

"Were you all right?" she asked. "I mean, after they'd cut out the infection?"

"I wouldn't call how I felt 'all right.' I thought I had died and gone to hell."

"No wonder. You'd been through hell." She kissed the hand clasped in hers. "What I meant was, was the infection gone? I've heard there's only limited success in doing such operations."

"No it wasn't. That's when they suggested amputation again. At that point I almost agreed, I was so miserable."

"Whatever did you do?"

"Celine happened to be working at the hospital, cleaning the floors and changing the bed linens. Sometimes she would help bathe the soldiers, myself included." He shrugged. "You get to know someone pretty well when they wipe your bare bottom for you. For some reason she took a liking to me."

Hallie smiled a little at that. "I guess Celine is no more immune to your handsome looks than the rest of us poor females."

For the first time since he had begun his story, Jake laughed. Wrapping her braid around his hand and giving it a tug, he teased, "You're a saucy baggage, Dr. Gardiner. Perhaps Celine developed an infatuation for my backside—rather like a certain Mission Lady I know."

He chuckled again at her embarrassed squawk. "Whatever it was, she used to make me special treats and coax me to eat them, even when I was at my worst. It was her care that saved my leg . . . and probably my life. Never underestimate those nasty unguents and poultices of hers. They work."

Hallie nodded, making a mental note to ask Celine what she'd used to cure such an infection.

"But do you know what was worse than anything else?"

She shook her head.

"The loneliness. Seth eventually had to move on with the army, and though he did manage to check up on me from time to time, I didn't see much of him. There were other patients to talk to, of course, but only Seth could make me laugh."

"How long were you in the hospital?"

"Six months. I was confined to my bed most of the time, although toward the end I was able to get around on crutches. Since I couldn't do much else, I wrote volumes of letters to Penelope and Serena. Penelope was a lively correspondent, but Serena . . ."

He drew a ragged breath, remembering the pain of waiting for a letter that never arrived. "How I longed for a kind word from her."

The desolation of his words wrenched Hallie's heart. With a sob, she threw her head back and met his anguished gaze, exclaiming, "If you'd been mine, I would have fought the whole Rebel army just to get to your side. I never could have borne it, knowing that you were alone and suffering."

Grasping her face between his hands and staring into her eyes, brilliant with emotion, Jake murmured, "I believe you, Mission Lady. And God help any Rebel who would have tried to stop you." Then he swooped down and crushed his lips against hers in a needful, urgent kiss. As his lips claimed hers, Hallie's head fell back and she welcomed his kiss with an ardor that made him moan.

How she loved him! She loved the feel of his mouth moving against hers, drawing her lower lip into his mouth, sensuously sucking and nipping in turn. She loved how the masculinity of his scent stirred her senses, making her quiver out of control. He was like a heady drug, and she craved him as desperately as an addict craved opium.

With reckless abandon, she deepened the kiss, hungry to taste every intoxicating inch of his mouth. She could hear him moan again as his tongue, so wet, hot, and insistent burned against hers. And as if in answer to his primal call, a searing ache exploded low in her belly. Gasping with a need she didn't understand, yet desperately wanted to fulfill, Hallie pressed her quivering body into the junction between his legs.

Jake gasped with erotic torment as she undulated against his thinly veiled heat. Dear God! She was like a fever in his blood, fueling his desires until he burned with a heat that he knew could be cooled only by dipping into her soothing flesh.

With a sob, he crushed her face closer to his. Her lips were ripe with a provocative invitation which his body begged to accept, and the passion with which she met his kiss inflamed him until his need to possess her was almost unbearable.

Unmindful of anything but the way his kisses made the secret places in her body tingle, Hallie let her hand slide up the length of his thigh. So lost was she in their unbridled passion that she didn't notice when her fingertips grazed the dark thatch of curls beneath the pooling silk of his robe.

Groaning now with savage desire, Jake grasped Hallie's buttocks and pulled her nearer. She jerked as a jolt of excitement raced through her body. Unbidden, her hand slipped the rest of the distance until she was intimately cupping his engorged sex.

Fire streaked through Jake's loins at the sudden contact, and his head snapped back as if he had been burned. Panting harshly, he could only stare at her, stunned.

With a small cry she jerked her hand away, struggling to escape from between his legs. Never in her life had she been so mortified.

"Sweetheart. Look at me," Jake ordered, catching her shoulders in an immobilizing grip.

She shook her head with a sob and continued to try to squirm from his grasp. She wanted to die. Die! But since she knew that was bound not to happen, she would have to settle for running away and hiding like the coward she was. What he must think of her, fondling him like one of Coralie's girls!

Jake tightened his hold on her shoulders and drew her near. Bending close to her ear, he whispered, "It's all right. You're welcome to touch me there any time you want. I like it."

She grew still at his words. *He liked it.* Turning her head ever so slightly, she stole a glance at his face. His lips were curled in a tender smile and his eyes were darkened with . . . what? No man had ever looked at her in quite that way before. It made her tingle all the way down to her toes.

Shyly, she cleared her throat. "I-I've never touched a man's—uh—you know—before."

"And aside from peeking at mine, I doubt if you've ever really looked at one either."

Turning as scarlet as a field of poppies, she shook her head.

"Then it seems as if your education in anatomy has been sadly neglected. Perhaps you would like to make an *intimate examination* of mine?"

She gulped and stared down at the bulge beneath his dressing gown. She *was* curious.

Cupping her chin in his palm, Jake forced her to look into his eyes. "All you have to do is to say yes, Hallie. Then I'll sit here quietly while you conduct your research." At least he hoped he'd have enough control to sit still. He was beginning to seriously question his sanity at making such a suggestion.

Hallie chewed her lip indecisively for a moment, staring into his smoldering green eyes.

He nodded his encouragement.

"Yes," she sighed, almost inaudibly.

Chapter 18

With his gaze holding hers captive, Jake reached down and loosenend the tie at his waist. As he leaned back in the chair, the silk robe slithered open. He smiled and nodded again.

Slowly Hallie let her gaze drop from Jake's face to the broad expanse of his bare chest. Over the months since she'd seen him nude, she had often found herself daydreaming about the magnificence of his physique. That is, before she gave herself a mental slap and accused her mind of liberally embellishing the memory. After all, no man could be that perfect. Could he?

Jake could. She sighed inwardly. And it seemed that she wasn't losing her wits after all. He as just as she remembered, with skin like tawny satin, impossibly fine and smooth. Just looking at him made her fingertips tingle to explore its texture. Hesitantly Hallie raised her hand, and then paused to meet his gaze again, seeking permission to touch.

Jake nodded his consent. Drawing a deep breath, he closed his eyes and tipped his head back against the chair. Waiting. *He was crazy, definitely crazy, to willingly submit to such torture.*

With trembling hands, Hallie lightly traced the shape of Jake's strongly sculpted muscles. He felt every bit as good as he looked, silk over granite with a sprinkling of dark hair that tickled her fingertips.

Experimentally, she caressed his flat nipple. She could feel him quiver as it hardened beneath her hand. The ache coiling in her belly tightened as she remembered how wonderful it had felt when he stroked her own sensitive nipple, and she wondered if her touch there made him feel the same way. When she looked up to ask him, she saw him watching her through narrowed eyes, his provocative lips slightly parted as if in a silent moan.

Somehow he managed to nod at her questioning look. *She was driving him insane, touching him like that.* He clamped his teeth hard into the flesh of his inner cheek and tried to think of his plans to expand his shipping operation in Panama City. *The cost of transferring building materials between . . .*

But it didn't work, and he gasped uncontrollably as she teased his other nipple. Damn! All he could think of was wrestling his fiery temptress down to the rug and plunging deep into her woman's flesh until he found his long-denied release.

He's so well formed, Hallie thought, completely unaware of Jake's insistent hunger. She let her fingertips trail from his chest down to his tapering waist, her pulse surging at his masculine splendor. Every muscle was as carefully defined as if it had been molded by the hands of a great artist. Why, he was even more magnificent than the sculptures she had seen in Europe, and she had been told that they represented perfection of the male form.

She stopped to push his dressing gown away from his side and bent close to examine where he had been shot. He shifted slightly to allow her a better view. The wound had healed well, though the scar was still dark pink from its relative newness. Impulsively, she pressed tender kisses across its length. It was a shame that his beautiful torso had been marred. It was almost as bad as the defacing of a rare work of art, which was how Hallie viewed his breathtaking looks.

Jake groaned at the feel of Hallie's lips, warm and soft, against his side. *He was going to die—explode—with wanting her!* It was terrible, the throbbing ache in his groin. He couldn't remember ever being so painfully aroused. He squirmed with discomfort as he felt her hands trace over the curve of his hips. And when she abruptly changed directions to move inward toward the source of his yearning, he almost howled with need.

Hallie could only stare at his sex straining hard against the naked contours of his belly. Amazing. She rested her hands on either side of him, her fingers splayed low on his groin, taking care not to touch his swollen length. His whole body seemed to convulse at her contact.

Biting her lip, she looked up at his face and was stunned to see it twisted into a mask of raw suffering. "Jake?" she whispered, suddenly concerned. The man looked to be in agony.

He opened his eyes enough to stare at her through slits and somehow managed to grunt. She had leaned so close to him that he could feel the warmth of her breath caressing his manhood. God! Now he understood the true meaning of the word "torment."

She frowned. "Are you in pain?"

"Good God, yes!" And the ache was increasing a hundredfold with every passing second. Her hands were scant inches from him now, and moving closer. An agonized sob escaped his lips.

"Poor darling. Did you have fish for dinner? There has been an outbreak of illness from bad fish—"

He cut her off with another groan. "I didn't have fish."

She continued to stare at him, unconsciously teasing his black curls with one fingertip. When she felt him jump beneath her touch and heard him stifle an oath, understanding crashed through her mind.

After clearing her throat several times, she asked, "Are your—uh—male parts troubling you?"

He made a choking noise and nodded.

Lord! He must be very sore indeed. His face was flushed a deep red, and his breath was coming in great, heaving rasps. She stared down at his inflamed flesh. Was that why he'd been so eager to have her examine him? Had he been too ashamed to tell her about it, thus preferring to show her?

Studying him closely, she scolded, "I realize it's embarrassing to discuss afflictions of your male parts, but you really should have mentioned it before it became so painful." She could see a muscle spasm in his jaw as he tried unsuccessfully to clamp back a moan. *Poor, poor man! He really is suffering!*

If Jake hadn't been so consumed by the engulfing fires of his lust, he would have laughed. For all her education and experience, Hallie Gardiner was still an innocent. She honestly believed he was suffering from some frightful medical condition. Undoubtedly, she was about to offer some sort of treatment.

He grinned inwardly at that. *Come to think of it, I could use some of her tender care down there.* Screwing his eyes shut, Jake uttered a pathetic moan and graced her with a look of abject misery.

It worked like a charm.

"Jake, darling. I know it hurts, but I'll need to examine you closer if I'm to find the problem."

He groaned weakly in response.

"Poor darling," she cooed in a soothing manner, moving her fingers closer to the source of his distress. "If I promise to be gentle, do you think you can bear having it touched?"

He made a sound halfway between a moan and a chuckle. "Probably not. But go ahead anyway."

"How long have you had this problem?" she asked, carefully encircling his shaft with her fingers to pull it away from his belly. Lightly she prodded it, noting the way the pulse thundered down its length. She heard him sob and saw the muscles tighten in his belly as she applied pressure, but aside from that he held very still. *He was such a brave man!*

Jake inhaled through his teeth. "It's been in this condition since I met you," he muttered breathlessly. *No lie there.*

Nodding, Hallie moved her hand upward to run her finger over the silky red tip. This time he let out a yelp and his hips heaved violently.

"Sorry," she murmured, caressing his inner thigh in an attempt to calm him. He jerked away from her hand, groaning.

Utterly perplexed now, she inquired, "Did you injure yourself, perhaps? I've read that it's not uncommon for men to sustain damage in that area from riding accidents."

He pretended to consider the question for a moment. Shaking his head negatively, he sighed, "No."

She tilted her head to one side, her brow creased in concentration. "There are several other male problems I've read about. Perhaps—" Suddenly a look of shock settled over her features. "Jake Parrish! You haven't been indulging in relations with Coralie's girls, have you?"

"I haven't indulged in relations with anyone since before the war," he replied, stifling his grin at her self-righteous expression. "I can safely assure you that I'm free from those kinds of diseases."

For some reason, Hallie found herself absurdly pleased by his answer. Smiling inwardly, she quickly finished her examination. After gently poking his masculine sac and feeling his belly, she admitted, "I can't figure out what's wrong with you. Aside from your pain, you seem normal enough, at least according to everything I've read. Of course, since I've never treated a man's private parts before, I'm no authority on their afflictions."

She glanced up at his face apologetically, expecting to be met with a look of bleak despair. Instead, he was staring down at her with one corner of his mouth curled in a half-smile. How typical of her brave Jake to smile during such an ordeal!

Hallie gave him a reassuring smile of her own. "Don't worry, darling. I know a male doctor who's qualified to treat such problems. I'll have him look at you first thing in the morning. Until then, I could rub you with some of Celine's numbing salve. Or if you prefer, I could make you an ice pack."

Jake couldn't stop himself from chuckling at her suggestion. "The last thing I want is to have a male doctor poking at me down there, and I hardly think salve or an ice pack is necessary." He raised his one eyebrow sardonically as he guided her hand back to his hardness. "Look closely, Dr. Gardiner. It's true I'm afflicted ... with a plain, ordinary case of lust."

Gasping, Hallie tried to pull her hand away. But Jake was too fast, catching her wrist and forcing her palm to remain against him.

"Don't you know that men harden when they become aroused?" he asked, cupping his other hand beneath her chin and forcing her to look at him.

She gave him an indignant look. "I'm not completely ignorant about the workings of the male body. And I understand about your—uh—turgid state. But from what

I've read, arousal is supposed to be pleasurable for a man, not painful."

Jake lightly traced the shape of her lower lip with his thumb. "When a man is denied sexual release for long periods of time, such as I've been, his arousal begins to hurt. And being intimately handled by a beautiful woman only makes the condition worse. Damned unbearable, actually."

She flushed scarlet at that. Lord! It was all so wickedly improper, the sensual nature of their discussion.

Yet, kneeling between his legs, mesmerized by the scintillating hunger of his gaze, she didn't care. Heaven help her! She liked touching him intimately, liked the way it made the longing build up inside her. If this was sinful and made her fallen woman, then let her fall.

Emboldened by her thoughts, Hallie brazenly caressed his rigid length with her thumb. His back arched wildly and he released her wrist with a growl. The uncontrolled violence of his reaction made Hallie feel powerful . . . and desirable.

Placing her hands demurely on his thighs, yet never once letting her eyes stray from his impressive display, she whispered, "Are all men so, well, large?" He looked enormous.

Jake's mouth twisted into a roguish smile. "Of course not," he teased. "I happen to be generously endowed. A veritable giant among men."

Her jaw dropped and her eyes bulged as she stared at the part in question. "Yes. I—I see."

For a moment he considered letting her believe his manly boast. But she looked so serious, studying him like he was some sort of rare specimen, that he relented. Chuckling at her charming gullibility, Jake confessed, "I'm just teasing, Mission Lady. Though I don't make a habit of studying other men, I'd guess I'm fairly average in that department."

"Wretched man!" Hallie squealed, reaching up to tickle his bare ribs playfully.

Jake laughed and made a grab for her hands, but she was too fast for him. "Ask any man about his endowments," he managed between guffaws. "And he's bound to exaggerate a bit."

"You men are insufferable liars! Every last one of

you! You deserve to suffer with your lust." Giggling, she resumed her attack on his ribs. He shrieked and doubled over, thrashing about in an attempt to evade her ruthlessly tickling hands.

Practically howling with laughter now, Jake lunged forward out of the chair and wrestled Hallie to the carpet. Growling with mock ferociousness, he rolled her onto her back. She grabbed for him again, but he easily captured both her hands in his and pinned them to her sides.

Straddling her wildly thrashing hips, he chuckled, "Lust is a highly contagious disease. Why, I hear it's reaching epidemic proportions, infecting both men *and* women. Come to think of it, you do look a bit flushed, Dr. Gardiner. Could it be that you're coming down with a case of it yourself?"

He grew suddenly serious as he stared at her. The way she was lying beneath him, smiling up at him with maddening boldness, was enough to make him moan with need. His Mission Lady, swathed from head to toe in layers of concealing fabric with her hair scraped back in a tight braid, was more seductive than a naked French courtesan. She ignited his blood, and his desire to possess her was becoming more ravenous with every passing second.

Moving his face close to hers until he could inhale the sweetness of her breath, Jake purred, "Perhaps I should conduct an *intimate examination* to find out if you've been infected."

As he covered her lips with his in a sweeping kiss, he could taste the hunger in her. She was exquisite in her response, sucking his tongue into her mouth and twining it with her own. With a moan, he felt his restraint begin to lapse as her hands slipped from his now loosened grasp and snaked beneath his open robe, stroking the length of his bare back.

In one fluid motion, Jake tore himself away from the enchantment of her lips and balanced himself on one elbow. She looked so beautiful, lying there in voluptuous submission. The velvet robe had fallen open and he could see the soft curves of her body through the thin linen of the nightshirt. His pulse drummed in his ears as his gaze skimmed from the dark circles crowning her breasts down to the barely veiled mound of her auburn curls.

"Tell me, Dr. Gardiner," he whispered hoarsely, "do you have a fever deep in your loins? Does your body ache to be touched? Teased?" He tipped his face close to hers. "Caressed?"

Hallie whimpered as the sizzling heat from his gaze made her body burn in its darkest, most secret recesses. He was the fever that simmered in her blood, and with just a look he made her ache where no decent woman should ache. How she longed to feel his hands worshiping her flesh, touching her like a man revering the woman he loved.

Something deep and primitive quickened in her belly at the thought of Jake's fingertips exploring her so tenderly. Oh! To feel the warmth of his skin as he covered her body with his . . .

Unable to stop herself, Hallie reached up and eased the silk dressing gown from his shoulders. He let it slide down his powerful arms before sitting back on his heels to remove it.

He was glorious in his nakedness—all sleek muscles and sun-kissed skin, his face heart-stopping in its perfection. She was entranced by his masculine beauty. Mesmerized by his potent appeal. And shamelessly, she wanted to kiss every wonderful inch of him. She let out a strangled gasp. *May God have mercy on my soul!* The longer she looked, the hotter her primal fire grew.

With a groan, Jake swept Hallie into his arms and buried his face in the hollow of her neck. He held her close for a moment, simply enjoying the feel of her in his arms.

"Poor Mission Lady," he murmured, lifting his face to nuzzle her ear lightly. "It seems as if you've indeed been infected with lust. Of course, I'll need to examine you much closer to be certain. Touch you."

Hallie arched her body against his with a moan, maddened as much by his words as by the warmth of his breath tickling against the delicate skin of her ear.

"Shall I remove your gown and study you closer?" he asked, drawing her lobe into his mouth and sucking on it. "Shall I explore you until I find the source of your ache?"

"Yes," she panted, feeling as if she would die if he didn't touch her.

Leisurely, he branded her with wet kisses, letting his lips slide from her ear down the side of her neck. Playfully nipping and sucking on her throat in turns, he began to release the buttons.

"Please, Jake," she sobbed, barely able to endure the exquisite feel of his mouth as he moved lower to kiss each newly exposed area of her skin.

"Patience is a virtue, Mission Lady." He chuckled, pushing the linen aside to expose her full breasts. With tantalizing slowness, he traced the shape of one soft mound with his tongue, pausing to tease her sensitive nipple. It turned hard beneath his lips and she whimpered in response. As he moved to her other nipple, he felt her hands slide around his hips to massage his buttocks. His carnal response was immediate, and it was his turn to whimper.

With hands made clumsy by desire, Jake reached down to grasp the hem of the nightshirt. In one quick motion, he pulled it up over her hips. She shifted to help him, lifting her arms to let him slide it up her torso and, finally over her head. Impatiently he tossed the voluminous garment aside. Then he rose to his knees to stare down at her.

She was truly beautiful, his sultry enchantress. In the glow of the firelight, her skin shimmered with all the luster of a rare pink pearl, and as he released her hair from its confining braid, it pooled around her head like a halo crowning a Renaissance Madonna.

Hungrily, he let his gaze drop lower, his breath catching in his throat as he admired her unclothed splendor. He'd always suspected that her unflattering gowns hid a fine shape, but he'd never dreamed that she would be quite this breathtaking.

In awe, he let his palms shape the fullness of her breasts and caress the narrowness of her waist. For all her fine-boned slenderness, she was deliciously curved in all the right places. He paused to tease the shadowed indentation of her navel. She shuddered, softly moaning his name. That sound, halfway between a plea and a demand, made his body roar for its release.

Jake sucked in a labored breath. How she ravished

his senses! It took every last ounce of his self-control not to thrust himself into her and promptly spill his seed. And considering the way she was squirming beneath his touch, her pliant body begging for fulfillment, he doubted that she would stop him. But she was a virgin and to use her in such a manner could sour her to the act of lovemaking forever. To do so would be unforgivable, for she had more fire, more natural sensuality, than any woman he had ever known.

"Do you burn deep and low, sweet Hallie?" he murmured, bending down to lick her navel. With his tongue, he traced the silken contours of her stomach until he came to the triangle of curls at the junction of her thighs.

"Jake!" she gasped, as he parted her legs. "What are you doing?"

"Intimately examining you, of course." And as his fingers parted her passion-slick flesh, he felt her tense at the intimacy of his invasion.

"J-Jake," she moaned, involuntarily thrusting against his hand. Though she knew she should be mortified by her shamelessness, she was powerless to deny the desperate urgency burning in the part beneath his touch.

Gently he explored her until he found the hardened bud of her desire. "You're very swollen, Mission Lady," he murmured, lightly stroking the sensitive area.

"No!" she whimpered as she felt an embarrassing rush of moisture drench the pulsating source of her desire. She moaned and buried her cheek against the silken pillow of her hair. With every touch, her body was sucked deeper and deeper into the vortex of new sensations until she was lost to the insistent demand of her body's need. "I—I . . ."

"Ache?" *He* certainly did. In fact, he was perilously close to losing himself then and there. Jake let his tortured groan echo hers. Beneath that prim exterior, he had guessed his Mission Lady to be capable of great passion. He just hadn't realized the depth of her hunger, nor had he expected the volatility of his body's answering response.

Trailing warm, wet kisses up her inner thigh, he whispered, "Shall I soothe you? Shall I show you how a man doctors a woman in this condition?"

Hallie's hips thrust in wordless reply. *Yes,* her body

begged. In answer to her mute appeal, she felt his lips replace his stroking fingers, and as his tongue probed the scalding fire of her womanhood, she was taken to heaven and back.

Waves of pleasure washed through her, drowning her in the ecstasy of her release. She arched up again and again, crying out as she was swept away by surge after intense surge of glorious sensation.

When the fury of her passion was at last spent, Hallie could only lie in weak, trembling awe, stunned by the power of her release.

Jake groaned as he felt the spasm of her climax pulsate against his lips. Dear God! She was sweet in her rapture! Her moans of pleasure vibrated through his body, and like a youth in eager anticipation of his first sexual experience, he could feel his manhood harden until it was throbbing against his belly.

Breathless with desire, he rose to cover her body with the long line of his. Balancing his weight on his elbows, Jake stared down into her passion-softened features.

"Do you know how you make me ache?" His voice was hoarse.

Stroking his rigid length, she sighed, "Then let me soothe you, darling. Show me how a woman doctors the man she loves."

He moaned, his whole body jerking at her touch. With a strangled noise, he pulled her hand away from his inflamed flesh.

Parting her knees with his leg, he whispered, "Open for me, sweet Hallie." And like a blooming rosebud, unfurling its petals, she parted her thighs. Reaching down, he let his fingers slide inside her. He felt another rush of warm moisture and his control splintered further at the evidence of her desire.

Panting now, he positioned himself between her legs. "Sweetheart," he murmured, pressing his face against hers. "I'll be as gentle as I can, but there's still going to be pain."

"I know." Her voice sounded breathless as her hips rose up to meet his straining hardness.

Fighting to contain his eagerness, Jake gently eased himself inside her. As he became sheathed in Hallie's warmth, he could feel her muscles contract in protest to the unfamiliarity of his invasion. With great effort, he forced himself to remain still until he felt her begin to relax around him.

The feel of her, so moist and welcoming, was almost more than Jake could bear. Catching his breath sharply, he shifted his hips to resume his penetration. At his slight motion, Hallie's supple flesh tightened around him in an erotic embrace, and he struggled desperately to regain the last fraction of his restraint.

Gasping with pleasure, Hallie arched beneath him, urging him deeper. It felt wonderful, having Jake inside her, stretching her so intimately. Never in a thousand years would she have guessed that it would be like this. She wanted to feel every last wonderful inch of him moving inside her.

Drawing a deep breath to steady himself, Jake complied, pushing himself deeper until he came to the fragile barrier of her maidenhood. Claiming her softly parted lips with his in a tender kiss, he made one hard thrust that easily tore the delicate membrane. Then he plunged his full length into her, stifling her sharp cry of pain with his mouth.

"I'm sorry," he murmured, gathering her into his arms and pressing soft kisses all over her face. "Relax. The pain will be gone soon." And he forced himself to remain still while she adjusted herself to his size.

Hallie squirmed uncomfortably, desperately trying to ease her pain. It hurt. She felt as if she had been torn in half and now that he was fully inside her, his manhood felt as enormous as it looked.

Burying her face against his throat, she mumbled, "You lied."

He stared down at the top of her bright head in wonder, momentarily forgetting how he was about to explode with need. "How did I lie?"

"You really are abnormally large. Otherwise I wouldn't hurt like this." She gave her pelvis a tentative undulation. It was beginning to feel better, although he still felt awfully big.

Jake sucked his breath between his teeth at her sensual movement. He was close to the edge—too damn close. His body screamed with protest as he fought to deny it its quickly approaching climax. If only she would stop moving like that.

With desperate appeal, he groaned, "Hallie. Please . . . don't." He wanted her first time to be special, perfect. He wanted her to find her woman's pleasure with him buried deep inside her and to feel her throbbing around him as they found their release together. *Damnation. If she would only lie still for a moment.*

Yes. Now the ache was beginning to subside. Hallie tested his length. It felt good. She arched again. Very good. There was just the slightest pain now, but it was quickly becoming replaced by the pleasure mounting deep inside of her unmentionable places.

"Now, Jake," she pleaded, reaching around him to grasp his tightly flexed buttocks, rubbing herself against him with wild abandon.

It was too much. With a hoarse scream that would have roused the house had the walls not been so thick, Jake thrust once and promptly spilled himself. Tears rolled down his cheeks at the exquisite violence of his long-denied climax. His body convulsed uncontrollably, heaving, as his senses exploded with an ecstasy that was far more intense than anything he had ever experienced.

Again and again his body jerked, unconsciously driving himself deeper and deeper into Hallie's eagerly embracing depths. So possessed was he by the turbulence of his release that he barely heard her shriek of rapture as she joined him in paradise.

Then his body spasmed one final time, and he collapsed on top of her, his face drenched with his tears.

"Hold me," he pleaded, his voice raw with emotion. "Please. Just hold me." And as she hugged him fiercely, he buried his face between her breasts, sobbing. They lay like that for a long while, she holding him tenderly and he clinging to her as if she was his salvation.

When he at last lay still, his breathing even, Hallie lightly kissed the back of his neck. "Are you all right?"

He raised his head to stare into her face. "Are you?"

She nodded with a tender smile. "Never better."

"Thank God," he sighed, rolling off of her to sit up. He sat very still, his cheek resting on his bent knees and his arms wrapped around his legs.

Hallie moved to snuggle up behind him. With her legs

around his hips and her arms around his chest, she molded her front to his back, propping her chin on his shoulder. She tickled his stomach lightly, trying to make him smile. Nothing. She tried again, this time more insistently. He didn't move a muscle.

"Did I do something terrible?" she finally asked.

"Good God! No!" He turned his head to meet her troubled gaze. "You were magnificent. Amazing. It was I who was terrible."

"I don't understand." Suddenly a dawning light flared in her eyes. "If you're feeling bad because you took my virginity, don't. You didn't take it. I gave it to you. I love you."

Jake shuddered and hid his face against his knees. Never in his life had he felt so inadequate—or unworthy. What had happened to him over the years? He had once been considered quite the lover, never failing to bring his partner the ultimate pleasure before finding his own. But now he was a pathetic shadow of his former self, either spilling his seed prematurely or unable to perform at all.

Drawing a ragged breath, Jake propped his chin on his knees and stared into the fire. "Your first time should have been wonderful. Memorable. It should have been with someone tender and patient. Not with some fool who spills himself after one thrust."

Hallie was stunned by his words. "But it *was* wonderful," she declared honestly. "And I couldn't imagine doing it with anyone more tender or patient than you were."

He raised his head and stared at her. She looked so earnest. He shook his head with a sigh. "That's because you don't know any better. A man should be able to give a woman pleasure from his body."

"But you did."

"Not from any conscious effort on my part," he ground out bitterly. "In time you'll want a man who can perform his duty properly." And in time she would probably grow to hate him because he couldn't function like a real man.

"That man is you."

He raised one eyebrow in question.

She nodded vigorously. "You see, Mr. Parrish, as your doctor, I have a theory about your so-called problem."

"Indeed?"

"Yes. By your own confession, you've deprived yourself of sexual release for an unhealthy period of time. I read an article in one of my medical journals on the subject of sexual abstinence in men. It supposedly affects a man very badly. It makes him likely to lose control at the slightest provocation. Even in his sleep. Were you aware of that?"

Jake chuckled at the seriousness of her expression. "I've been known to soil a few sheets recently. Especially when I've been dreaming of you."

"My point exactly." She nodded with satisfaction. "It seems to me that you've had enough provocation tonight to make any man lose himself. If the article was correct, you should be better able to control yourself next time."

"Perhaps." He shrugged one shoulder. She could be right. But what if she wasn't? It was an awful thought.

Her hand snaked lower until she found his now flaccid sex. Almost immediately he began to rouse.

"There's one way to see if the theory is correct," she whispered, teasing his earlobe with her teeth. He hardened in her palm. "It's called research, Mr. Parrish. Care to be my subject?"

With a growl, he surged his arousal against her hand. "Willingly, Dr. Gardiner. I place my manhood in your very capable care."

And through thorough research, Dr. Hallie Gardiner proved her theory correct.

Chapter 19

Jake couldn't remember the last time he'd been this furious.

Damn that Hallie Gardiner! he cursed silently for the hundredth time that morning. She'd given him a taste of paradise last night, and like a starving man fed an exquisite feast, he'd been left hungering for more. Far more.

Damn her to hell! How dare she steal away like that? But dare she had. When Jake had awakened that morning, fully aroused and eager to resume the previous night's activities, he'd found himself alone in his big bed. It hadn't improved his mood any to discover that Hallie had fled the house at dawn.

Tightening his jaw with determination, Jake urged his horse on. The blood bay gave a whinny of protest before picking up the pace and sending the barouche flying at head-spinning speed.

Jake eyed the animal sourly. *Blasted beast's hide is the same color of copper as Hallie's hair.* Then he let out a humorless grate of laughter. *Yes. But unlike his willful Mission Lady, this particular redhead has the good sense to do as she was told.* And so would Miss Gardiner when he finally got his hands on her.

Scowling fiercely, Jake rounded the corner with a neck-breaking recklessness that almost upset the carriage. The light vehicle careened dangerously on two wheels for a moment before miraculously righting itself again.

Had it been his lovemaking that had put her off? he wondered, going over every pleasurable detail in his mind.

After his poor start he'd done well enough, making love to her two more times. Hell. If her screams of ecstasy were an accurate indicator, the prim Miss Gardiner had enjoyed herself every bit as much as he had. And though his intimacy-starved body could have loved her a few more times, he could tell that she was getting sore. So when she curled up next to him, her head cradled on his chest, he contented himself with the simple joy of holding her close. After all, there would be plenty of opportunities in the future to take care of his own carnal needs.

Or so he had assumed.

Jake's head snapped up as the morning stillness was shattered by the sound of wildly clanging bells, and he instantly became alert to his surroundings.

Fire? Pulling his horse to a halt, he scanned the horizon, narrowing his eyes against the sun's glare. Insidious billows of smoke made great black smudges against the pure azure of the rain-washed sky and hung in the air like an ominous pall.

Fire . . . at the edge of Chinatown, Jake thought, mentally gauging the distance to the darkly rising cloud. A tendril of uneasiness snaked down his spine. The Mission House was located down there. It stood in an old section of the city where the buildings were flimsily constructed of cheap wood and where the living conditions could only be described as overcrowded. If not quickly contained, a fire in that area would spread from building to building quicker than a message through telegraph wires.

Making a loud clicking sound between his teeth, Jake gave the reins a smart slap and the horse lurched forward to resume its brisk trot. Of course, just because the fire was near Chinatown didn't necessarily mean that the Mission House was in danger. Damned unlikely, actually. Nonetheless, he found himself urging his horse to pick up its pace.

As he turned down Sacramento Street, Jake could see orange flames shooting high into the sky and his eyes began to water from the heavy smoke. All down the street were lines of fire engines, each one manned by a group of burly men intent on pumping water from a hydrant almost two blocks away. The thick rubber hoses, which were linked together to form a water line that ran from engine to pumping engine, lay writhing against the cobblestones like furious black snakes.

Unable to drive any further, Jake reined in his horse

and jumped from the carriage. Grabbing a loitering youth by the shoulder, he shouted, "Where's the fire?"

"Someone dynamited the Mission House. Blew those nosy Mission Ladies to kingdom come. *Ka-boom*!" The boy flailed his arms in the air to illustrate his point. But before he could further embellish his tale, his audience of one had taken off down the street toward the raging inferno.

Putting all good manners aside, Jake pushed his way through the crowd. With every step, he could feel his panic rising closer and closer to the surface of his tightly controlled calm, threatening to crack the strained facade at any moment. Never had he been so afraid . . . not even when he'd faced his own death. And losing Hallie now would kill him in ways that would make him pray to die. Without her love, his life would once again become a meaningless blur of minutes, days, months, and years—time to be filled but never savored, his only companion loneliness.

Damn it! No! Hadn't he lost enough already? Surely God wouldn't be so cruel as to snatch away the only piece of heaven he'd found on this earth?

None too sure of God's mercy, Jake frantically elbowed aside another onlooker. As he pushed his way through the last of the human barricades, the Mission House came into full view.

The upper floors were engulfed in flames, as was the north side, which was where the infirmary was located. Shards of glass from broken windows glittered like teardrops among the sooty rubble on the sidewalks, and the smoke, thick and black like flowing oil, poured from the empty frames. The whole second floor was a wall of incendiary orange from which drifted cinders that fell like scalding rain. And even at this distance Jake could feel the shimmer from the heat.

Like a sleepwalker he stepped into the nightmarish scene, mindless except for one thought: he had to find Hallie.

Panicked Chinese girls ran back and forth, babbling to the Mission House workers who sought to calm them. On the south side of the house, a red-uniformed fireman stood on a ladder, pulling a young girl out of a flaming second-story window. Volunteers holding tangled lengths of hose were shooting torrents of water into the blaze, shouting orders at one another in an attempt to be heard above the roar. And it seemed as if hundreds of women swarmed in the streets, but none of them was Hallie.

Terrified, Jake shoved his way through the crowd. Over and over again he shouted her name, desperately scanning the throng for a glimpse of her bright hair. He stopped to ask several of the workers if they had seen her, but they either stared at him, too stunned to reply, or merely shook their heads no.

As he elbowed deeper into the melee, Jake heard someone call his name. Hope surged in his heart as he whipped around, and then it died as quickly as it had been born. It was Davinia Loomis who was hurrying toward him.

The normally neat-as-a-pin mission directress looked as unkempt as an unmade bed. Her hair was falling about her face in sweat-soaked straggles, and her gown, once a festive red, was streaked with soot.

"Where's Hallie?" Jake shouted, rushing to meet her halfway.

Davinia shook her head, wincing as he grasped her arms in a bruising grip. "I thought she was with you."

"Then she didn't come back here?" His hope was reborn.

"I don't know. I've been out since dawn making my calls."

Jake let his hands fall to his sides with a grunt of disappointment.

Davinia scratched at her head, mystified. "You say she went flitting off? Odd. It's not a bit like Hallie to behave so irresponsibly. Perhaps—" Then her brows drew together in a fierce scowl. "Jake Parrish! What did you do to the poor girl now?"

Jake shook his head impatiently. "Later. Now, who would know if she came back here?"

"We could ask Marius. He's been here all morning." Davinia straightened her bent spectacles to study the faces around her. As a very thin Chinese girl flew past, she hollered, "Mary!"

The girl came to an abrupt halt, staring fearfully at the scowling man by Missy Loomy's side.

"Have you seen Reverend DeYoung?"

The girl shook her head.

"It's all right, dear," Davinia coaxed. "This is Mr. Parrish. He's looking for Dr. Gardiner. Have you seen her?"

Jake forced a smile to his face as he nodded at the girl.

"Docta tell Mary light parlor. Docta—she go to big hole. Get songbook." Mary bobbed her head, pleased by her English recital.

"Big hole?" Jake looked to Davinia for an explanation.

"The cellar."

Wanting to scream with frustration, yet not wanting to scare the girl, Jake asked, "When was the last time you saw Dr. Gardiner? Have you seen her since she went down to the cellar?"

The girl cocked her head to one side and looked at Davinia, puzzled. Patiently, Davinia repeated the question in Chinese. Shaking her head in response, the girl chattered something back. Davinia's face turned ashen at her reply.

"Hell and damnation! Hallie never returned from the cellar!"

Desperation, raw and powerful, infused every fiber of Jake's being. The thought of his Mission Lady trapped in the cellar, alone and possibly hurt, was devastating. He had vowed to keep Hallie safe, to protect her . . . always. And even if he died trying, it was a promise he intended to keep.

Grabbing hold of Davinia's arms again, he growled, "The cellar. Where is it?"

"It's too dangerous. Let me get the firemen."

Punctuating each word with a sharp shake, Jake hissed, "Just-answer-the-damn-question!"

Davinia hesitated for a moment before replying, "Through a door beneath—ouch! my arm!—the stairs in the entry hall. Wait!"

But having gained the information he needed, Jake was already halfway across the lawn. As he disappeared through the open front door and was swallowed up by a seething bank of smoke, Davinia whispered, "Please, God. Go with him."

Heedless of anything except his need to find Hallie, Jake hurled himself through the door. As he pushed himself into the hallway, he was met with a suffocating wall of smoke that rendered the close space as dark as a moonless midnight. The heat was almost paralyzing in its intensity, and as he drew in a gasping breath, the air seemed to scorch his throat all the way down to his lungs.

With his throat burning painfully and his eyes tearing from the smoke, Jake began to grope his way along the wall beneath the stairs. Like a blind man memorizing the planes of a loved one's face, his fingertips explored every nook and cranny. Nothing.

Hacking for air, he dropped to his hands and knees and crawled beneath the nebulous black cloud, which hovered a couple of feet above the floor. To his everlasting relief, he found the wood planking cool. The fire hadn't yet reached the cellar below.

But not for long, he cautioned himself. Above his head, Jake could hear the crackle of timber as the ceiling caught fire. Through the smoke, he could see the flames beginning to drip down the walls. From across the narrow corridor came the ominous groaning of the doors as they bent outward, threatening to explode from the pressure building up within the rooms.

Panic slugged him deep in his belly. Any minute now those doors would be blown apart and the corridor would become a raging holocaust from which he would be unable to escape. It would be over.

Dizzy from smoke inhalation, his lungs screaming for oxygen, Jake ran his palms along the wall. Somewhere upstairs he could hear an explosion of glass. Time was running out.

Then his fingers caught onto a ridge and he felt the outline of the door frame. From behind the opposite wall, he could hear a sound like a scream of a twister, growing louder and louder with every passing second. Frantically, Jake fumbled for the knob. If he didn't find the damn thing soon, that shriek would be the last sound he'd ever hear. It would be his death knell.

His guardian angel must have been sitting on his shoulder, for as soon as the morbid thought had entered his mind, Jake's hand clamped around a bulbous shape. With a hoarse shout of victory, he tore the door open.

Just as he lurched to his feet, the opposing doors burst

outward into the corridor. In a roar of deafening noise, the rooms behind him lit up and the explosive pressure pitched him forward down the stairs.

Down he tumbled, his body slamming helplessly against the walls, striking every step with agonizing brutality. It seemed as if he was falling in slow motion, as if it was taking forever to reach the bottom. Finally, after falling what seemed like a mile, he landed on the hard cellar floor with a loud *thump*!

Wincing with pain at every movement, Jake rolled onto his back and tested his limbs for injuries. Though nothing seemed to be broken, he could feel blood oozing from a cut on his temple.

"Hallie?" he whispered, struggling to rise to his knees. But his throat was too swollen from the smoke to produce much more than a croak, and his voice was barely audible, even to himself.

When he tried to suck in a deep breath to clear his throat, tears of pain sprang to his eyes. His airways felt as if they were blocked by red-hot chunks of coal, and he was unable to do much more than just gasp. The tiny trickle of air that he did manage to inhale made his lungs burn as if they were being seared with a branding iron.

Dizzy from a lack of oxygen and impossibly sore from his fall, Jake staggered to his feet. It was through sheer force of will that he remained standing. Clutching a barrel for support, he stared about the room, momentarily disoriented.

Though the filthy window high on the wall was designed to let in the sunshine, the thick smoke outside obscured the light, dimming it to a feeble haze. Gradually, however, his eyes began to adjust to the darkness and he was able to make out the details of his surroundings.

It was a small space, overcrowded with a jumble of boxes, crates, and discarded furniture. Jake glanced toward the cellar door nervously. The flames from the corridor were already licking at the top steps. All it would take would be for one spark to come shooting down the stairs, and the whole area would burst into an inescapable pit of fire. They would be trapped.

"Hallie," Jake rasped, his effort making him double over in a paroxysm of coughing.

No reply. Jake felt momentarily relieved. When he'd tumbled down the stairs he'd made enough noise to alert a deaf man, and knowing Hallie, he was sure she would have rushed to his side to give aid. Obviously she wasn't in the cellar.

While every last bit of common sense told him that he should get out, to save himself while he had a chance, there was still a niggling doubt the back of his mind. *What if Hallie had met with an accident and was unable to answer him?*

The picture of Hallie lying helpless while the fire raged around her was enough to send Jake searching behind the piles of boxes and barrels.

God! If only he didn't feel so weak and dizzy. Jake tried to suck in a breath, but the effort made him gag as blistering pain seared through his chest. *If only it didn't hurt so badly to breathe.* He heard himself moan.

Or had he? No. The sound was coming from the far corner.

"Sweetheart?" he choked out, falling to his knees and crawling toward the sound. Every movement was as difficult as swimming against the current of a rapidly flowing river.

There was another moan, this one louder.

"Hallie?" His voice was so faint that he doubted if she could hear it.

Miraculously, she did. He heard her sob, "Over here!"

Her voice appeared to be coming from behind an enormous barrel to his right. As Jake knelt before it, a soft rustling confirmed his suspicions. It appeared that the barrel had fallen during the explosion and was now wedged between two towering piles of crates. The only way to get to Hallie was to move it.

Wrapping his arms halfway around the heavy container, Jake gave it a tug. From the other side, he could hear Hallie thumping against it as if she was trying to help. That made him smile. *No vapors or hysterics for his Mission Lady. She was quite a trooper.*

A dead trooper if he didn't get her out quickly. The fire was almost to the bottom of the stairs, and it was only a matter of minutes before the whole cellar would become a deadly inferno.

Summoning every last bit of his flagging strength, Jake

gave the barrel a mighty yank that sent it tumbling over onto its side—and him onto his back.

With a sob, Hallie pulled herself out of her prison. The last thing she remembered was bending down to pick up a stack of Christmas hymnals. Then, in a flash of pain, everything had gone dark. Shaking her head in confusion, she crawled over to check on the filthy man who was lying motionless on the floor.

His face was covered with a mask of soot and blood, and his eyelids were so swollen that only the slightest sliver of color was visible. Yet she didn't need to see that fragment of green to recognize Jake's beloved face.

"J-Jake?" she sobbed, not really daring to believe it was him, yet desperately wishing it to be true.

"In the battered flesh," he croaked, rolling over onto his belly and forcing himself to rise to his knees.

Sobbing his name, she threw herself into his arms.

And as Jake held her close, relief such as he had never known before flooded through him. His Hallie was alive.

But not for long, he reminded himself, staring over the top of her head at the advancing flames. Smoke was quickly gathering in the tight space and the fire was consuming the last two steps at a voracious pace. The heat was getting unbearable.

Jake's arms tightened around Hallie's shivering form as he shifted his gaze to the window above. The only way out was through that window. Yet he'd seen enough fires during the war to know that opening the window would bring the air-starved fire flashing down into the cellar. But what were his options?

Unwillingly, he had to admit that there were none. Planting a kiss on Hallie lips, he murmured, "Stay here, sweetheart."

"No. I want to go with you."

"I'll be right back," he wheezed, seizing an old piece of canvas from a tattered chair. "After all the trouble I've gone through to find you, do you think I'd let you come to any harm?"

She smiled wanly at that. "Of course not. It's you I'm worried about."

"I'm not going to let anything happen to myself either, Mission Lady." His voice broke with every other word, he was so hoarse. "I'm looking forward too much to punishing you for running out on me this morning." Without giving her a chance to reply, he draped her from head to toe in the cloth.

Crawling nearer to the window, yet remaining as far out of the fire's path as possible, Jake picked up the first solid item he could find. It was a white alabaster angel with one broken wing. And if Jake's aim was true, it would be their salvation.

As he raised the graven messenger high above his head, he whispered, "Fly home, angel," and threw it at the window with all his might. As he heard the glass shatter, he dove to the floor and rolled to the far side of the cellar.

In a fraction of a second, the hungry fire flashed toward the new source of oxygen, catching everything in its path. Flames shot everywhere before settling to consume the litter of discards strewn across the floor.

Forcing his abused body to move, Jake pulled himself over to Hallie, peeking out from beneath the canvas. With a sob, she tossed aside the cover and hurled herself into his arms.

Holding her close, Jake rasped, "We need to crawl to the window. Can you manage?"

She nodded. And together they crawled the short distance, carefully winding their way through the pillars of flaming debris. Above their heads they could see the ceiling beginning to buckle, threatening to collapse at any moment.

As they reached the window, Jake seized Hallie and began to ease them both to their feet, none too sure if either of them was capable of standing. To his everlasting relief, they were.

"I'm going to lift you up to the window and you're going to crawl through," he commanded, praying that he still had strength enough to lift her.

"But what about you?" She clung to his broad shoulders, unwilling to let him go. "I won't leave you alone."

Reaching up to the window and sweeping away the shards of broken glass with his sleeve, he asked, "Do you love me?"

"More than anything!"

"Good," he murmured, drawing her into his embrace

and pressing his lips against hers in a swift, desperate kiss. "Then do as I say."

With that, he stooped down and yanked her skirts up to her waist. Wrapping his arms around her thighs, he somehow managed to lift her to the window. When she hesitated, he screamed, "Go!" And to his relief she obeyed, pulling herself to safety.

As Hallie disappeared through the window, Jake could feel the heat from the fire searing across his back. The blistering intensity of the flames was enough to bring tears to his eyes, and the smoke was so thick that he felt as if he was suffocating in a mire of black Mississippi mud.

Everything was growing dim now, his vision was fading. But Jake didn't need to see the flames to know that they were almost upon him. Time had run out.

Above the roar of the fire, he could hear Hallie screaming his name; he could tell that she was crying. But all that mattered was that she was safe. He hadn't failed her.

"Jake! Here!" Hallie shrieked, trying to reach him through the window. He raised his hand up to hers, and for a brief moment, their fingers touched. Then she was pulled away by strong arms.

Her last glimpse was of Jake surrounded by flames with his arms outstretched toward the window, reaching for her. His face was stark with emotion, and as the ceiling began to collapse into the cellar, she thought she heard him say, "I love you."

It was as if he'd been saying good-bye.

Chapter 20

Jake's still down there!" Hallie screamed, struggling against the fireman's arms. She tried to pull free, to run back to the cellar window, but the man merely tightened his hold on her waist.

"Look." He crushed his squirming burden against his chest in an immobilizing grasp. "The chief is doing everything in his power to save Mr. Parrish. The last thing he needs is some hysterical female getting in his way."

"I am *not* hysterical!" Hallie planted her feet on the ground and stubbornly refused to budge. "And I will *not* leave Mr. Parrish until I've had a chance to give him aid."

"You'll give aid when and if it's needed. Until then, you'll wait safely in the street with everyone else." With that, the frustrated fireman bent forward and tossed her over his shoulder.

"Put me down!" she shrieked, kicking her legs impotently. As he hoisted her into the air, Hallie's crinoline skirt flew up over her backside, and as she tried to push it down, her hair came tumbling from its pins.

"Please," she begged, shoving the blinding curtain from her eyes. "Let me go to him." Then her voice broke and she could only whisper, "Can't you see that I love him?"

But the man turned a deaf ear to her pleas and walked through the gate, trudging toward the front of the house.

Frantically, she jabbed her knee into the fireman's ribs. She had to get to Jake. Irrationally, she believed that nothing terrible could happen to him as long as she was by his side.

Grunting at the pain in his ribs, the fireman pinned his charge's legs to his chest, effectively stilling her struggles.

Keep him safe, Lord, Hallie prayed. *Please, I'll do anything. I'll even promise never to indulge in the pleasures of the flesh again. Unless, of course, I'm married. Anything. Just let him be all right. And please—* She paused in her plea with God long enough to cuff the fireman across the back of the head. She managed only to knock the man's helmet askew and to bruise her hand. *Please make this lumbering oaf put me down!*

As if in answer to her prayer, Hallie saw Davinia rushing toward her.

"Hallie! Thank the Almighty Lord!" Davinia would have recognized her friend's mop of curly red hair anywhere—even trailing down a fireman's back. Following close behind the man, she peered anxiously into Hallie's tear-streaked face."You aren't hurt, are you, dear?"

"No." Hallie beat her fists against her captor's back. "But Jake is, and he's still trapped in the cellar." She punctuated her speech by giving the man a smart punch to the kidneys.

With a yelp of pain, he dumped her into the sooty street.

"Hell and damnation!" Davinia rounded on the beleaguered fireman shrieking like a maniac. "Durned fool! Don't just stand there gaping like a hooked fish. Get Mr. Parrish out this instant." She gave the man a shove. "Go!"

Massaging his lower back and glaring at the women, the man snapped, "Chief Killian and his men are doing everything they can to get the gentleman out." He reached up and yanked his helmet straight. "I'll go see if I can give them a hand—if," he paused to pass a look of admonishment from one woman to the other, "if you two ladies promise to stay put."

"Just go, man." When he didn't move, Davinia stamped her foot impatiently. "All right, then. We promise."

After giving the women one final look of warning, the fireman hurried back to the cellar. When Hallie tried to follow him, Davinia caught her arm.

"No. He's right. It's too dangerous."

Hallie wrenched herself from Davinia's hold. "I don't care. Jake needs me."

"He needs you alive and unhurt."

Shaking her head mutely, Hallie turned to face the inferno that had once been the Mission House. Before her horrified eyes, the flaming structure shuddered once, and then crumbled into the cellar. As it collapsed, it emitted a chillingly human-sounding scream that joined with Hallie's own in a duet of heartrending anguish. Like fireflies swarming on a hot summer's night, the sparks from the blaze scattered into the smoke-blackened sky, darting here and there before settling back into the now silent pile of smoldering timbers.

Stunned, Hallie sank to her knees. Over and over again she cried Jake's name. Then she too fell silent. It was finished.

Raw pain rushed over her. *Her Jake was gone, buried beneath a ton of charred debris.* Never again would she hear the warm timbre of his voice as he called her his sweet Mission Lady; never again would she see the dimple crease his taut cheek as he smiled down at her with gentle humor, and, most wrenching of all, never again would she know the security she had known lying wrapped in the safe cocoon of his arms, comforted by the reassuring strength of his heart beating against hers.

Never again would she know a love such as she had known with Jake Parrish.

Dear Lord! Help me! Hallie doubled over clutching at her belly. *I hurt so bad!* Her agony was unbearable, her sorrow paralyzing.

She felt herself being pulled into Davinia's embrace and through the red mist of her pain, she heard the woman speak. Slowly Hallie raised her head to stare into her friend's face. She, too, was crying.

Wordlessly they clung together, sharing their grief. One woman mourning the loss of a cherished friend, and the other, the death of the man who was her heart's blood.

With a sob, Hallie closed her eyes and buried her face against Davinia's shoulder. In the despair-filled darkness of her mind rose the ghost of Jake as he'd looked when she had left his bed.

He had been so beautiful, lying there in the dim morning light. Like a peaceful child, he'd slept, lying on his side with his face cradled against one fisted hand. Even if she lived to be a hundred, Hallie would never forget the way his long lashes had curled in dark crescents against his cheeks and how his lips had been twisted into a smile, as if he were dreaming a particularly naughty dream.

Sometime during the night he'd thrown off the blankets and now was lying there in all his naked splendor. Possessed by an overwhelming ache to touch him, she'd let her fingertips gently explore the muscular planes of his torso. She loved the way he'd groaned in his sleep and become aroused by her caress.

And at that moment, she'd wanted nothing more than to stimulate him until he was awakened by the urgency of his need. She'd longed to take him deep inside her and ride him until they met on the wild crest of their mutual pleasure.

But she'd been too much of a coward to follow her heart's desire, too embarrassed by the memory of her own unbridled wantonness to face her lover in the morning light. So she had simply kissed his cheek good-bye, savoring the feel of his stubbly beard against the passion-ravished flesh of her lips.

Hallie let out a strangled cry. *What she hadn't known was that she'd been saying good-bye forever.*

"Hush now, dear," whispered Davinia, soothingly patting her friend's shoulders. "We don't know for sure that they didn't get him out. He might be all right."

Hiccuping violently, Hallie raised her head and gazed into Davinia's face. The woman's expression was woefully unconvincing.

"Ma'am?"

Both woman spun their heads around with whiplash speed. It was the burly fireman who had carried Hallie away from the fire.

"Jake? Is he . . ." Hallie choked before she could finish her question, frightened of his reply.

"He's alive. But, well—" The man looked down at the helmet in his hands and fidgeted nervously at the emblem.

"Where is he?" Hallie sprang to her feet, fear gripping

her heart. It was obvious by the way the fireman refused to look at her that something was terribly wrong. "Take me to him."

Nodding, the man took her arm and escorted her around the wreckage of the Mission House.

As they entered the back yard, Hallie saw a handful of firemen standing around a figure on a blanket. Even from a distance, she recognized the long, elegant lines of Jake's body. Crying his name, she picked up her skirts and ran to him. The brief seconds it took to reach him seemed like forever.

"Jake, darling," Hallie whispered as she knelt by his side. Even without examining him, she could see that he was badly injured. His breathing was little more than a fast, shallow wheezing, and as he exhaled, he choked on the thick black mucus that was bubbling from his nose and mouth. His face was too covered with soot and the blood from the gash on his forehead to tell how badly he'd been burned, but Hallie could see that his eyes were swollen shut. He appeared to be unconscious.

Using a soft corner of her petticoat, she gently wiped the suffocating secretions from his nostrils and lips. She was glad he couldn't see her, for she was unable to stop the tears from coursing down her cheeks.

Fighting the panic welling up inside her, Hallie laid her fingertips against Jake's neck and felt his pulse. It was racing at an alarming speed. Not a good sign. She'd treated only one other patient in this condition before, a child who had been trapped in a factory fire. It had been when she was a student back in Philadelphia.

Respiratory burns, her instructor had told her. Usually fatal. And in that case, they had been. Hallie could only pray that Jake would be luckier.

"Chief Killian, ma'am. At your service," offered a middle-aged man who came forward and knelt next to Hallie. "He took in an awful lot of smoke. He was unconscious by the time we got him out, but we were able to get to him before the fire touched him. His burns shouldn't be too severe."

"Is there anything we can do to help?" It was Hallie's burly rescuer. "Anything for Mr. Parrish."

There was a murmur of assent through the quickly

gathering crowd. It appeared that Jake was very popular among the group.

"We need to get him home where he can be properly tended," she replied with more confidence than she felt. "He also needs to be propped up. It might help to ease his breathing a bit."

Nodding gravely, Chief Killian barked orders to his men. One man went to get a stretcher, the other to secure a wagon. Everyone seemed eager to help.

Two of the firemen carefully raised Jake's head and shoulders onto Hallie's lap so she could keep his airways swabbed clear. As she sat holding the unconscious Jake, alternately whispering unheard words of love into his ear and wiping away the mucus, Hallie braced herself for the biggest battle of her life.

Her opponent would be death, and the prize they both coveted was Jake's life.

Suffocating . . . dark . . . cold. Jake struggled to see through the roiling black mist. It was everywhere. Endless shadows surrounded him, closing in, smothering him. He tried to breathe, to fill his oxygen-deprived lungs, but he couldn't. There was no air. Just fog. Murderously thick, wet fog that slithered deep into his airways. Blocking them . . . choking him. Making his lungs ache and his throat burn.

He would die if he didn't escape. Desperately he searched for a beacon, for some feeble light to guide him out of the oppressive gloom. To take him where the air flowed free; to someplace warm.

Warm? A sob escaped his lips as pictures, vivid and terrifying, flashed through his mind. Awful memories of heat, smoke . . . and Hallie. *Fire.* He remembered fire. *Hallie . . . sweet Hallie. Safe? Yes.* But he'd been trapped . . . it'd been hot. *Scorching. Hurt.*

Then why was he so damn cold? Why was he shivering so uncontrollably, convulsing with the chill?

Strange. It was as cold as the grave.

Grave? Panic, more visceral and hideous than anything he'd ever experienced before, paralyzed him. He opened his mouth to scream. Nothing. Silence.

As silent as death.

Had they thought he was dead? Had they buried him

alive? Or was this death: a great void with no heaven or hell? Eternal darkness?

Jake tried to scream again. This time he heard a low, hoarse cry. His cry. He wasn't dead.

They'd buried him alive.

Frantically, he struck out, desperate to beat against the confining coffin lid. *Had to get out. To the air . . . the light. Escape.*

But his fists simply flailed in empty, *airless* space.

Where the hell was he?

Terrified, he flung his arms out to his sides, searching for something solid. Something familiar. Anything.

Still nothing.

Disorientation made him violent. Ignoring the way every move made his body scream with pain and left him breathless to the point of suffocation, Jake thrashed about wildly. *He had to get out . . . before he died.*

There was something wrapped around his naked body.

Tangled . . . in something cold . . . damp. His shroud?

He let out a horrified sob and clawed at the fabric. It twisted around his hips. Repulsed, he tried to hurl himself as far from the foul thing as possible.

Then he felt a steely grip clamp around his shoulders, restraining him. He arched his back, trying to escape.

"Jake! It's all right, darling."

Darling? Had he heard Hallie's voice? Or had it all been a cruel trick of his imagination?

"H-Hallie?" he whispered, frantically groping in the dark, looking for her. *Please, God, let her be there.*

"Hush, darling. I'm here."

Jake felt something cool and rough against his cheek. *Hallie. Yes. He'd know the feel of that calloused palm anywhere.* Relief took the fight out of him, and he let his body fall limp.

Everything would be all right now. Hallie was here.

With a sigh, Seth released his hold on Jake's shoulders. *Christ!* he thought as he watched Hallie peel the urine-soaked sheets from his friend's hips. *Even during that terrible crisis period after he'd been wounded, Jake had never lost control like that.* It frightened Seth more than he cared to admit.

Feeling as if he would go crazy if he didn't do something to help his friend, he asked, "Is there something I can do?"

"Light," Jake rasped in reply. For though he could feel Hallie touching him, he wanted to see her face.

Hallie exchanged a worried look with Seth. What could she tell Jake? That his eyes were swollen shut from the heat and smoke and that she couldn't promise that his vision would be restored even after the swelling was gone? She had cleaned his eyes the best she could, but his eyelids were so badly swollen that she couldn't open them enough to determine if there was damage. Only time would tell.

"Light . . . n-now." His voice came out in a soft gurgle. Then he choked as something thick and wet clogged his throat. Painfully, he surrendered to a paroxysm of coughing.

Hallie carefully eased Jake's head into her lap, where she held him until his hacking stopped. He sounded as if his chest was being ripped apart, and by the tears seeping from the corners of his eyes, she could tell that it felt as bad as it sounded. As Hallie swabbed the dark mucus from his nose and mouth, she was horrified to see that it was tinged with blood.

"Light."

Swallowing hard, she tried to inject a note of encouragement into her voice. "Your eyes are swollen shut . . . from the heat and smoke. You'll be fine in a few days." She prayed that she was right.

Jake lay silently absorbing the meaning of her words—and the false note of cheerfulness in her tone. Had he heard her breath catch as well?

Strange. When you're blind, every subtle shading of the voice reveals the truth behind the words. He felt his guts twist with dread.

Blind. Was that why Hallie had sounded so distressed? Was she groping for a gentle way to tell him the truth? A sob escaped Jake's lips. The very thought of living the rest of his life in such helplessness was devastating.

"Your eyes will be fine. I promise." And if God couldn't forgive her that lie, then so be it. Hallie could read the fear in every tense line of Jake's body, and there was nothing she wouldn't say or do to reassure him.

"Will you trust me, darling?" she whispered, gently stroking his heaving chest.

He nodded once and calmed beneath her touch.

"Good. You also inhaled a lot of heat and smoke, and your air passages are swollen. That's why it's so hard to breathe." She paused while he succumbed to another fit of coughing.

"Your lungs are badly irritated from the smoke, and they're full of secretions. I know it hurts, but you need to try to cough up all the mucus. Can you do that for me?"

"Try."

"Good." She could only hope he had the strength to do it.

In the long hours since they'd arrived at the house, Hallie had had a chance to fully examine Jake. His body was as badly bruised as if he had been severely beaten, and the forearm he'd used to clear the glass from the window frame was deeply gashed.

Gently she touched his bandaged left arm. Thanks to Seth Tyler, she had been able to stitch his worst wounds properly.

Hallie smiled gratefully at Seth, who was kneeling next to Jake recounting a naughty story involving a prostitute and a donkey. When this was all over, she intended to find out exactly where the man had found a medical kit to replace her burned one. After all, it *was* Christmas night.

"Hallie?"

"I'm here, darling," she crooned, seeing Jake groping the air around him, searching for her. Tenderly, she took his hand in hers and cupped his cheek with her other palm. Like a kitten to its mother's belly, he nuzzled against her.

At least Chief Killian had been right about the burns, she thought, staring at his beloved features. Jake's face was in no worse condition than if he had received a very bad sunburn. It probably hurt, but barring infection, there should be no scars.

She watched as Jake tried to smile at the punch line of Seth's story. Dear God! How she loved him! He was such a strong, brave man. It broke her heart to see him so vulnerable.

Hallie felt tears prick her eyelids. If only she could help him, make him better. But, of course, there wasn't much she could do. Except pray.

And put dry sheets on the bed. Which she did with Seth's assistance. When the bed was made and Jake comfortably propped against a mound of pillows with a cooling compress on his eyes, she set about bathing him.

As she gently washed his male parts, Hallie was amazed at how at ease she felt handling him so intimately. Strange to think that even as recently as two days ago, she thought of touching him down there as an embarrassing ordeal. Now it seemed perfectly natural. Jake obviously agreed, for after tensing briefly at the feel of the wet cloth, he relaxed and lay still beneath her ministrations.

"Like it . . . touch . . . there," Jake wheezed. And she did. Not that he was any more capable of getting an erection at the moment than he was of flying to the moon. Still, he liked the fact that she cared enough to tend to him so personally. Especially when she could have just as easily summoned Celine to do it. The intimacy of her actions made him feel secure in her love.

He heard her chuckle as she swaddled what felt like a thick cloth between his legs and secured one end over his manhood.

"You're a rogue, Jake Parrish," she teased, giving her handiwork a final pat. As she pulled the warm covers up over his nakedness, she added, "I don't doubt that you'll revert to your old ways soon enough and accuse me of poking at you."

"Never—" but Jake was overcome by an agonizing attack of coughing before he was able to finish his sentence. God, it hurt! He was sure he'd die if he didn't catch his breath.

Then he felt Hallie slip her hand in his, and he clung to it with the desperation of a drowning man. Her touch gave him strength; it comforted him.

"I love you," he heard her murmur, and he felt her press a kiss to his forehead. When his coughing finally ceased, Jake lay limp and trembling, fighting for his breath.

Hallie was terrified. He sounded worse, much worse.

The rattling in his chest scared her, and he was getting weaker.

Struggling to keep the panic out of her voice, she whispered, "Try and sleep now. It's past midnight. You need to rest."

"Stay?" he gasped. The effort almost choked him.

Hallie squeezed the hand in hers. "Forever," she vowed.

If only she could promise him a lifetime first.

Chapter 21

By the following morning, it became apparent that Jake's injuries were as bad as Hallie had originally feared. His condition had deteriorated during the night, and by noon his fever had begun to rise at an alarming rate.

Every breath he drew sent him into paroxysms of coughing, doubling him over to clutch painfully at his midsection, gasping for the air he was unable to inhale. And like those of a stallion brutally run to ground, his nostrils and lips became flecked with a dark, bloody foam.

"Try to breathe slowly, darling," Hallie coaxed, as Jake began to thrash wildly about on the bed, making frantic choking sounds. Tenderly, she stroked his chest and, to her relief, he eventually calmed beneath her hand.

He was so helpless in his blindness, so terrified of being left alone. All through the night, he had clung desperately to her hand, growing panicked if she broke contact even for a moment.

Never in her brief medical career had Hallie felt such frustration as she did now, watching the man she loved struggle for his life.

Insidiously the fever snaked into Jake's brain, coiling around his consciousness and squeezing out his last vestiges of lucidity. With the delirium came violence.

Baring his teeth in a growl, he struck out at the shadowy assailants lurking in the corners of his febrile mind, cursing in a manner colorful enough to bring a blush even to the worldly Seth Tyler's cheeks.

At one point, as he engaged in a frenzied battle with the demons of his twilight state, Jake threw himself off the bed and reopened the cut on his forehead. It took six burly male servants to restrain him while Hallie tended to the wound. It was then that Seth and Hallie reluctantly agreed that the only way to keep Jake from doing himself further harm was to tie him to the bed.

Jake panicked at being bound, reacting like a man terrified of something more awful than death itself. With his body twisting and turning in furious protest, he struggled to free himself from his bindings. When he at last collapsed against the mattress, fighting for breath, his trembling was so intense that the whole bed shook.

Tied spread-eagled to the bed, naked save for the towel between his legs, Jake lay in utter vulnerability. Hallie tried to soothe him by gently stroking his cheek and chest, but he cringed from her hand, moaning in a way that broke her heart. His reaction was that of a man who had been badly treated in the past and expected more such abuse. And she could only sit by his bed, bleeding inside for the torment he was suffering.

It was when she had to tend to his personal needs that his violence escalated to a frightening peak. Screaming hoarsely, Jake wrenched against his bindings so forcefully that dark welts rose on his wrists. His back arched wildly as he tried to escape, and tears rolled from beneath the bandages swathing his eyes.

"It's all right, darling," Hallie cried, appalled by his obvious terror. She stroked his hip in an attempt to calm him, but her caress seemed only to madden him further.

Seth, who had been snatching a few moments of rest, was awakened by Jake's cries and rushed to his friend's side. Understanding dawned as he accurately sized up the situation.

"I think he's damaged inside," Hallie exclaimed, glancing up at the tousled man standing by her side. "I was changing the cloth between his legs, and he acted as if I was hurting him."

Seth shifted his gaze from his friend's flailing form to Hallie's troubled face. "In his mind, he probably thinks he's being hurt."

"I don't understand."

"Sweetheart . . ." Seth paused for a moment, trying to think of the best way to proceed. Jake was a proud man, and he wasn't sure if his friend would want him to tell Hallie how he had suffered at the army surgeons' hands.

He stared down at the man writhing on the bed. Yet how else was he to explain Jake's reaction?

Seth let out a long sigh. "I don't know what Jake has told you about his leg, if anything, but—"

"He told me how you refused to let the doctors amputate it," she interjected quietly. "That was very brave of you."

Seth smiled bitterly at her praise. "There were times when I wondered if I had been foolish in insisting that they try to save the leg. The wound festered . . . horribly so. In my worst nightmare, I never could have imagined a man living in such a condition."

Uncomfortably he shifted his gaze from Hallie's to stare down at the toes of his boots. "I can only imagine how terrifying the ordeal must have been for Jake. And the pain he suffered . . ."

His voice caught as he remembered his friend's agony. "Because I refused to let them take the leg, he was subjected to a series of brutal operations and treatments. They wouldn't give him any chloroform, since he almost died the first time they used it, so they tied him down and did the procedures without it. There were a couple of times when they didn't have any morphine to give him to take the edge off his torment. A lesser man would have died from the shock."

Hallie stared down at where Jake lay muttering and jerking about on the bed. "My poor love," she crooned, wanting to cry for what he'd suffered. "No wonder he thinks that doctors are butchers and charlatans."

"Can't say as I blame him," Seth replied with a grimace. "Do you know what he said was the worst part?"

Hallie shook her head mutely.

Seth reached down and touched the rope that bound Jake's right wrist to the headboard. "Being tied. It frightened him to be lying there helpless and at their mercy."

"He must have been terribly weak. Surely they could have held him instead?"

"They did try, but the pain from their handiwork maddened him to uncontrollable violence." Seth let his hand drop from the rope. "Even as weak as he was from being wounded, Jake was still too strong to be restrained by the orderlies."

It was with new understanding that Hallie turned back to the man she loved. As she finished cleansing him, she took care to touch his leg as little as possible. And though he cried out, shrinking convulsively from the probing of the damp towel, he eventually calmed to the familiar sound of her voice.

The remaining afternoon hours melted away, and as dusk deepened into night, Jake fell into a deathlike stupor. By midnight, his breathing was little more than a harsh, strangled wheeze, and his lips had taken on a bluish tinge that Hallie recognized all too well. Jake was suffocating.

Hallie's heart gave a painful thud. If she didn't do something to help him breathe, he would die. With dread coiling in her stomach, she went to awaken Seth, who was dozing on a pallet near Jake's bed.

"Seth." She gave him a frantic shake.

His years in the army had made Seth a light sleeper, and almost immediately he was awake. Pushing his tangled mane of hair out of his eyes, he stared into Hallie's face. The urgency of her expression made his gut twist with fear. "Jake? He isn't—"

"No!' ' Hallie interjected, not wanting to hear him say the ominous word. She could feel death's presence hovering near, and superstitiously she thought that to say the word would bring the dark creature swooping down to take Jake.

Giving her head a sharp shake, she repeated, "No. But he will be if we don't help him. I-I need—" Then her voice faltered.

"Hallie?" Seth reached up and grasped her arm. "What do you need? Just say it, and I'll make sure you have it."

She swallowed hard. "I have to c-cut into his throat . . . to help him b-breathe. I need you to assist me."

Seth turned the color of putty at her proposal. "Is there no other way?" He'd seen the bloody procedure done during the war, and he was all too aware of the possible consequences.

"I wish there was."

Without comment, Seth rose from the cot and followed Hallie to Jake's bed. One look at his friend told him that Hallie was right: there was no other choice.

Watching as Hallie quickly laid out her surgical instruments, he asked, "Do you have everything you need?"

"You're going to have to tell me where you found this case sometime." Hallie pulled out a peculiar-looking contraption with long rubber tubes, and after rummaging about for a moment, she produced a strangely shaped silver tube. With a satisfied smile she added, "And to answer your question, yes, I've got everything I need. The kit is amazingly complete."

"Good. Then I guess Dr. Barnes wasn't lying."

Hallie almost dropped her retractors. "Dr. *Barnes*?"

Seth chuckled at Hallie's reaction. "The venerable Dr. Barnes is as inept at cards as he is at medicine, and I simply decided to call due his gambling debt. The man assured me that this is the finest case in all of San Francisco."

Hallie paused in her preparations to give his arm a fond squeeze. "You're a wonderful man, Seth. And I promise to find some way to repay you for the case."

"You've already more than repaid me with everything you've done for Jake."

"Jake's lucky to have a friend like you."

"And even more lucky to be loved by a woman like you." He winked roguishly. "Why, if Jake wasn't my best friend, I'd charm you right away from him."

"And if I wasn't so in love with him, I'd probably be swooning at your feet." Hallie winked back, and then turned her attention to measuring out a liberal portion of morphine into a syringe. She knew how Jake would object to being given the drug if he were rational; yet in this too she had no choice. She needed to keep him calm during the surgery and since he was beyond reason, she could think of no other way.

"Forgive me, my love," she murmured under her breath as she gave him the injection.

Jake fought against Seth's hold at the initial pain of the needle, but he soon began to relax as the drug took its effect. When he lay completely sedated, Hallie began her grisly task.

She could feel Seth's eyes on her face as she shaved Jake's throat clean of its blue-black stubble. She knew he was mutely pleading for reassurance, but she had none to give.

"You'll need to hold his head still while I work," she said, finally breaking her silence. And when all was ready, Hallie picked up her scalpel.

With trembling hands, she let the blade hover over the tender skin at the base of Jake's throat. He looked so helpless lying there, awaiting what might well prove to be the fatal cut. Hallie hesitated for a moment and then lowered the knife.

"I can't," she choked out. "I'm afraid."

Seth released Jake's head and pulled Hallie into his embrace. Stroking her heaving back, he murmured, "Of course you can do it. I have faith in you. And so does Jake. Why, you have no idea how many hours he's spent bragging about your wondrous medical skills. Bored every friend he has with the topic."

"He didn't!"

"Cross my heart," Seth vowed solemnly. "He even went so far as to say that he would trust you with his life. We all know what a glowing recommendation that is, coming from Jake, considering his low opinion of the medical profession."

"Did he really say that?" Hallie sniffled and met Seth's gaze, her eyes flaring with gratitude at his vote of confidence.

"I already said honest Injun, didn't I?" He rummaged in his pocket and produced a handkerchief. Typically Seth, it was a vivid shade of orange. "He claims that there's nothing you can't do, as far as doctoring goes. You wouldn't want to make him into a liar, would you?"

After Hallie had wiped her eyes and blown her nose, he picked up the scalpel and slipped it into her hand. "For Jake's sake, prove him right."

Hallie stared at the knife in her hand and then back up into Seth's face. He winked at her. Jake trusted her. That in itself was enough to give her much-needed courage.

And this time when she pressed the blade to Jake's throat, her hand was steady. Working quickly yet cautiously, she made the necessary incisions. Jake seemed oblivious to the pain, and for that she was eternally grateful. Aside from a violent bout of coughing when she inserted the curved silver tube through the incision and down his trachea, he remained senseless.

After securing the tube in his throat, she began the painstaking job of suctioning out his airways. It was a repulsive task, one that made Seth turn away retching, but Hallie was beyond all disgust in her quest to save Jake's life.

"There," she whispered, giving the tube in his neck a final swabbing. "He'll be all right for a little while, but we'll have to watch him carefully. He'll need to be suctioned at regular intervals, and we have to make sure he doesn't disturb the tube."

Seth grimaced at the odd hand pump. "For how long?"

"If all goes well, not for more than a day or so. By then, the swelling in his air passages should be down and the secretions about gone. I can remove the tube then." She saw Seth shudder with aversion as he glanced at the pump again.

She knew what it cost him when he offered, "If you'll show me how it's done, I'll help with the pumping."

The man's obvious devotion to his friend deeply touched Hallie. Giving his hand a grateful squeeze, she whispered, "As I've said before, Jake's lucky to have a friend like you."

Seth returned her squeeze. "I'm the lucky one. I'd still be a gutter rat if it wasn't for Jake. That is, if I wasn't dead from drink and hard living."

Hallie laughed at that. Gutter rat? Seth Tyler? Why, there wasn't a more courtly or elegantly mannered man in all of San Francisco. Expect for Jake, of course. And she mentioned as much.

"You should have seen me ten years ago." He chuckled. "I didn't have two cents to rub together, and I smelled so bad that the ladies would cross the street when they saw me coming."

"Now I know you're teasing me!" But when Hallie glanced up at his face, she saw that his expression was wholly serious. Leaning forward to soothe Jake's cracked lips with a piece of ice, she asked, "How did you meet Jake?"

"It was in '57. I'd been working a silver claim at Mount Davidson and came across what I thought might be a substantial vein." He smiled ruefully. "Well, not having the funds to mine the claim, I applied to every bank in Virginia City for a loan. Of course they turned me down. So I came back to San Francisco in search of backing."

He paused to study the man on the bed. "I'll never forget the first time I saw Jake. He looked like a young prince. I was at the bank, begging for a loan, when he walked in. Everyone snapped to attention, falling all over themselves to accommodate him, and I was roughly shown to the door. After all, my lowly presence might have offended the mighty Mr. Parrish. I remember shouting my proposal as I tumbled into the street."

Seth sighed. "How I hated the exalted Jake Parrish at that moment. Hated him for his money and position, hated him for the power he wielded. So you can imagine my surprise when he stepped into the street and offered his hand to help me up."

"He did that?"

"Yes. At first I refused to acknowledge his presence, bent on hating him. But then he told me that he'd overheard my proposal and might be interested in investing. Unmindful of the eyebrows being raised by passersby, he pulled me to my feet. Then he took me to a restaurant, where he fed me the first real meal I'd had in days. Best of all, he actually listened to me."

Hallie smiled at the thought of her elegantly dressed Jake sitting down to dine with a ragamuffin Seth. "He invested?"

"Better. He became my partner. And I worked hard to make sure he never regretted the association. The claim yielded over five million dollars in less than a year. He could easily have cheated me, since I couldn't read or write and was ignorant on the finer points of the law. But he didn't. Jake played square with me then, and he always has. When he discovered I couldn't read or write, he taught me himself. And when I told him that I wanted to be a gentleman, he helped me smooth out the rough edges. He made me what I am today."

How so very like Jake to bring out the best in a person, Hallie thought. Hadn't he done the same for her? Making her feel special after a lifetime of being told she was worthless? Taking a plain spinster and making her feel beautiful? Cherishing her?

And how had she repaid him? A sob caught in Hallie's throat. By almost getting him killed.

Jake began to stir restlessly, obviously not liking the tube in his throat. Gently, Seth lifted his friend's head and fluffed the pillows into a more comfortable position. He could feel the heat from Jake's fever beneath his palm.

"Do you know what mattered more than anything else?"

Hallie shook her head.

"That Jake had faith in me. He gave me the chance to prove myself. You see, even if I hadn't made my fortune from that mine, I would have been all right. He made me believe in myself."

All through the night and through the following day, Hallie worked over Jake. He was out of his head with fever, and though it broke her heart to do so, she was forced to keep him bound for fear that he would tear the tube out of his throat.

As Hallie sat by Jake's bed holding ice to his lips and letting the melted droplets wet his dry tongue, she despaired that his fever would ever break.

"Hallie." It was Seth, rising from the pallet. "You need to get some rest. Why don't you let me sit with Jake for a while?"

She *was* tired. Her eyes felt all scratchy from a lack of sleep, and every inch of her body ached with bone-crushing fatigue. Hallie pushed Jake's matted hair off his brow. He moved restlessly beneath her hand, his body twitching as uncontrollably as if he lay upon a bed of sharp stones. He was so terribly ill. What if he should take a turn for the worse while she slept? What if he died and she wasn't with him?

As if reading her thoughts, Seth reassured her, "I promise to wake you if there is any change." He pulled Hallie to her feet and pushed her toward the pallet he'd recently vacated. "Go."

"But—"

"Sleep. You're half sick yourself with worry and fatigue." He gave her another nudge. "I'll count to five. If you're not lying on that pallet by the time I finish, I'll carry you there myself. One . . ."

Of course he was right. She *did* need to rest. Maybe just for a few minutes . . .

"Two."

Hallie sighed. "Only for a half hour. Not a second longer."

"All right. Three." He smiled as Hallie settled for a nap. Good. Jake would never forgive him if he didn't watch over Hallie.

"Four and five. Pleasant dreams."

And she did have a pleasant dream. One where Jake was taking her in his arms, seducing her as much with his sultry gaze as with his caresses. Her heart contracted with longing. Oh! He looked so handsome! He was smiling in his special way that made the dimple crease in his cheek, setting the flames burning low in her belly. Just as his lips were about to claim hers, she was roughly shaken awake.

"For God's sake, Hallie! Wake up!"

Even through the murkiness of her sleep-fogged mind, Hallie could hear the panic in Seth's voice. As she forced her heavy lids open, she could feel her body being pulled into a sitting position.

"Hallie—"

She stared at the tears coursing down Seth's cheeks. "Jake?"

Wrapping her in his arms, he sobbed, "It's over."

Chapter 22

"No!" Hallie screamed, impotently beating her fists against Seth's chest. "You promised to wake me if he got worse." She pounded her fists against his chest again, this time more weakly. He didn't even flinch. "Why didn't you wake me, damn it? I didn't even get to say good-bye!"

Seth stared down into Hallie's sorrow-twisted face; her agony mirrored his own. "I-it happened so fast. One minute he was thrashing about with fever, and the next he was lying still. His skin felt clammy . . . cold. I couldn't find a pulse."

With a sob Hallie flung herself out of Seth's arms and rushed to the bed. The contest was over, and death had been victorious.

Jake looked so pale, so beautiful. Peaceful. Hallie felt as if her heart were being wrenched from her chest. Memories. They were all she had left of the man who was her life.

Whispering Jake's name as softly as a prayer, Hallie sank to her knees. With trembling hands, she picked up her stethoscope and fitted it to her ear. As she pressed the chest piece against his breast, his crisp hair tickled her fingertips, just the way it had when she'd caressed him early on Christmas morning.

Then her hand froze. Was she imagining things?

"Seth!" she shrieked, shifting the stethoscope slightly and listening again. Yes. She could make out a faint but steady heartbeat, and he was breathing softly. "Seth! Jake's not dead, his fever's broken!"

So exhausted was Jake from his illness that he didn't rouse until the following evening. Not even when Seth and Hallie removed the sweat-soaked sheets from the bed and wrapped him in blankets warmed by the fire.

"Darling?" Hallie whispered when Jake finally stirred. He was tugging weakly against his bindings, and she slipped her hand into his to still his struggles. "Can you hear me?"

He nodded once and tightened his fingers around her hand.

"I know you're uncomfortable, but I had to open your throat and insert a tube to help you breathe. We've kept you tied for your own protection. The tube is why you can't talk."

He yanked against the bindings again and jerked his head.

"I'll untie you, but only if you promise to hold still while I take care of your throat. Now that you're conscious, the tube will need to be removed, and if you're able to breathe normally, the wound will have to be stitched."

She paused to smile at the face he made at the word "stitch." Her Jake was definitely back to his right mind. "Do you promise?"

He hesitated for a moment and then nodded.

Quickly Seth and Hallie untied Jake. As Hallie pulled the coverings back over him, Jake clumsily reached up as if to touch the tube in his throat. She caught his hand, frightened that he might inadvertently hurt himself, and gently guided his fingers, letting him explore the area. In soothing tones, she explained what she needed to do.

"Would you like an injection of morphine? It's going to hurt when I remove the tube."

Jake shook his head fiercely. Then he patted the bandage covering his eyes.

"I put ointment in your eyes a couple of hours ago and they need to remain covered until tomorrow morning. They're still a bit red, but they'll be just fine." She hoped.

As Jake lay waiting for Hallie to tend to his throat, Seth entertained him with the current news. Above the sound of his friend's voice, Jake could hear the clank of metal against metal and the splash of water being poured into a bowl as Hallie washed her instruments.

What he wouldn't give to be able to see his Mission Lady at that moment. He wouldn't even mind watching her thread her needle, knowing that it was about to be used on himself.

When Hallie finally began working on him, Jake almost regretted his decision not to take the morphine. The procedure *was* terrible. Painfully he clutched at Seth's hand, choking wretchedly as the tube was pulled out of the raw wound. And when Hallie plugged the incision to make sure he could breathe by himself, he was positive he would suffocate.

Just when he was sure he would never be able to breathe again, Jake somehow managed to suck in a large gulp of air through his nose and mouth, quickly followed by another. And another.

Seth and Hallie exchanged relieved looks as Jake's breathing normalized. He was going to be all right.

Hallie leaned against the door frame with a blissful sigh as she let her senses drift on the sea of melodic tranquillity. The voice was exquisite. Heavenly. Like the voice of an angel raised in celestial exultation, every note was pure and sweet.

Dressed in a traveling suit of dusty rose, with her dark hair softly haloed in the late-afternoon sunlight, Penelope Parrish looked every bit as enchanting as an angel. *Especially,* Hallie noted, *with her face transfixed with love like that.* It was true, for Penelope's adoration for her older brother was glowingly apparent as she sang him a soothing lullaby.

Hallie let her gaze stray to the man in the bed. He was breathtakingly handsome. His neatly brushed hair gleamed from being freshly washed, and Hop Yung had shaved the thick stubble from his cheeks. And though Jake's eyes were closed, Hallie knew that he had only to open them to see her standing there.

As the last notes of the song faded away, Hallie clapped her hands softly, exclaiming, "You've got an amazing voice, Penelope. I had no idea you were so talented."

The girl's head jerked around. When she saw Hallie standing at the door, she nodded stiffly.

"Sweetheart?" Jake's voice was still as rough as coarse sandpaper, though it had gotten better over the last couple of days. His lips curved with pleasure as he drank in the sight of his Mission Lady. She was the most glorious woman he'd ever seen, despite the fact that she still wore the ugly gown she'd been wearing the day he had rescued her.

Selfishly, Jake thanked God for destroying Hallie's dowdy clothes and made a mental note to order her a new wardrobe. A flattering one that showed off her superb figure. One of beautiful fabrics . . . and whisper-thin undergarments. Jake's loins tightened at the thought of Hallie's full breasts veiled in a gossamer-sheer chemise and her long, slender legs encased in silk stockings with lacy garters.

As he felt a slash of heat knife through his belly, Jake chuckled. He was definitely on the mend to have his mind on such lustful matters. Warmly caressing Hallie with his gaze, he held out his hands.

"And how is my patient doing this afternoon?" she murmured, taking his hands in hers and sitting at the edge of the bed.

In a quicksilver motion, Jake pulled her on top of him, crushing her in his embrace. "Much better now, Doctor." With that, he soundly and thoroughly kissed her.

"Jake!" Hallie squealed, squirming out of his arms. "What your sister must think of me!" She cast Penelope an apologetic look.

The girl was staring at her through narrowed eyes, her expression perfectly imparting her less-than-flattering opinion. With a contemptuous snort, she looked away.

Hallie sighed. Penelope's visit to New York had certainly done nothing to sweeten her disposition.

Ignoring his sister's obvious disapproval, and her presence, Jake pulled Hallie back into his embrace and pressed a sucking kiss to her collarbone.

"Jake!" Hallie admonished, flushing beet-red at the impropriety of his action. "Behave yourself! You're much too ill for such exertions."

"Want to make an *intimate examination* and find out if I'm too ill?" he asked with a leer, raising one brow suggestively.

Penelope paled at her brother's suggestion. "You can't be serious, Jake!" she snapped, her scornful green gaze sweeping Hallie from the top of her simply coiffed head to the toes of her scuffed boots. "Obviously your fever has addled your brain. That being the case, I'll send Hop to fetch Dr. Barnes immediately. After all, Dr. Barnes is a real doctor, not some sort of . . . glorified midwife."

Hallie stiffened like a cat with its back up, outraged by Penelope's insulting assessment of her medical skills. As she opened her mouth to retort, determined to put the spoiled chit in her place, Jake said firmly:

"Without the courage and excellent medical skills of this so-called glorified midwife, I would have suffocated days ago. It is only because of her superb care that you're here carrying on like an ungrateful brat instead of at the cemetery watching the undertakers shovel dirt over my coffin."

Tightening his arms around Hallie's waist and staring into her face with unbridled admiration, he declared, "That being the case, I can think of no one more deserving of the title 'doctor' than Hallie Gardiner, nor is there any other doctor in the world to whom I would willingly entrust my life. I owe her far more than I can ever repay, and I'm proud to be in her debt."

Joy, fierce and sweet, expanded Hallie's heart. Jake's understandably poor opinion of the medical profession made his words of praise all the more meaningful. As for the way he was looking at her . . . never had anyone looked at her with such an expression of tender pride.

Penelope had the good grace to flush at Jake's words, though she still looked unconvinced of Hallie's competence. Fidgeting with the tasseled braid that trimmed the hem of her jacket, she muttered, "Be that as it may, it's still highly improper for a woman who isn't your wife or mother to be seeing you in a state of undress."

Jake grinned at his sister's prim response. "It may not be proper, but it's sure a hell of a lot more fun to disrobe in front of a beautiful woman than for the puffed-up Dr. Barnes. Besides," he paused to give Hallie a roguish wink, "seeing a nude man is hardly anything new to Dr. Gardiner. By her own admission, she has intimately examined hundreds of men."

Hallie groaned inwardly. Sick or not, the man deserved a swift kick in the backside for baiting her with her own rash lie.

"Hundreds?" Penelope gaped at Hallie with horrified

fascination. Her mouth opened sharply, as if to question the statistic, but then snapped shut again.

"Hundreds," Jake confirmed with a nod. "And unless you wish to witness such an examination yourself, I'd suggest you leave us now."

That threat was enough to make Penelope turn on her heel and stalk out of the room, but not before she cast one final look of disapproval toward Hallie.

As the door slammed shut, Hallie slipped out of Jake's arms and opened her bag with a sharp snap. "You, Mr. Parrish," she scolded, "are a wicked man."

When she came back to the bed carrying her thermometer, Jake seized her free hand and slipped it beneath the blankets. Crushing her palm against his arousal, he chuckled, "Want to see just how wicked I can be?"

Oh! How he tempted her! She wanted nothing more than to share in his wickedness and demonstrate just how much she loved him. But, of course, she couldn't. She had promised God that if he saved Jake, she would never indulge in such pleasurable activities again. Except with a husband. And since they weren't married . . .

Snatching her hand away from Jake's tantalizing hardness, she murmured, "I promised God that I wouldn't indulge in fleshly pleasures ever again."

As Jake's jaw dropped in amazement, Hallie seized the opportunity and slipped the thermometer between his lips. With a menacing frown, she snapped his jaw shut, effectively silencing his protests.

At that moment there was a quick rap at the door and Seth breezed into the room. He stopped in his tracks, staring at the thermometer between his friend's lips. With mock innocence he asked, "Say, Hallie. Does that thing work in that end of his body, too?"

Jake choked, and the thermometer would have fallen to the floor had Hallie's reflexes not been so good. "Seth! Stop teasing Jake this instant," she chided. "You know he's been terribly ill and is still too weak to defend himself." With that, she gave Jake's cheek a pat of encouragement and stuck the thermometer back in his mouth.

"Oh, I see. It works the same way." Seth's eyes brightened with interest. "Yes. You pat his cheek and slip it in."

"Seth!" Hallie shrieked, and when Jake made to spit out the thermometer again, she held it firmly in place. "It's all right, darling," she reassured him. "This is a different thermometer."

"Yes. A much smaller one," Seth supplied helpfully.

"Seth!" Hallie groaned, as Jake spit out the thermometer and glowered at her. "The other one wasn't any bigger."

"Oh? And what else did you do to me while I was helpless and at your mercy?"

"Saved your life, you ungrateful man!" she snapped back, trying to reinsert the thermometer. Stubbornly, Jake refused to open his mouth.

"Would you like me to hold him down while you get the other one?" Seth offered mischievously.

"If he doesn't cooperate, we just might have to do that."

"Oh, no," Jake purred, seizing her arm and pulling her close. "You're not prodding my backside or any other part of my anatomy until you tell me about this promise you made to God."

Hallie flushed scarlet and glanced over to where Seth was tactfully studying the papers in his hands. "Later. In private."

"Now. You can whisper the details into my ear." Her mouth was only inches from his, and it took all of Jake's self-control not to claim it with his. "Surely whispering isn't forbidden?"

Pressing her lips close to Jake's ear, she haltingly told him about her promise. He smelled good, like spicy shaving soap, and it was all she could do to keep her train of thought.

When Hallie had finished with her explanation, Jake threw back his head, laughing hoarsely. "Seth," he said, his voice raspy. "Fetch Judge Dorner and Reverend DeYoung now. Drag them here, if necessary. I want them here within the hour."

Seth stared at Jake as if he'd lost his mind.

"Go! I intend to marry my Mission Lady."

"Jake," Hallie whispered, as Seth scampered out the

door with a delighted whoop. "You don't have to do this, you know."

"I know. But if you'll have me, I'd very much *like* to marry you." He lightly traced the shape of her ear with his tongue, pleased with her trembling response. "Don't you know that you're everything to me, Miss Hallie Gardiner? That I don't want to be without you, even for a moment? Say you'll marry me, sweetheart."

Hallie wrinkled her forehead as if considering his proposal. "Only if you tell me what the 'V' stands for." She traced the monogram on his pillow case with her fingertip.

"Valentine," he mumbled, with a pained expression. "My mother was a sentimental woman."

"But your birthday is in November?"

"Nine months later—on the sixteenth," he replied with a meaningful smile.

"I don't understand . . . Oh!" She flushed a dull red as she grasped his meaning.

"Exactly. My parents knew how to celebrate Saint Valentine's day right. Care to spend it in the same manner, Dr. Gardiner? This year and every year?"

She threw her arms around him, drawing him close until his head rested against her breasts. "I want you so badly it makes me ache! Yes!"

"Not nearly as badly as you're making me ache." With a sigh, Jake burrowed his cheek against Hallie's pillowing softness, contentedly molding his body against hers. They fit together as perfectly as if they'd been made for each other.

"I certainly hope Seth hurries back," he muttered, his body throbbing at her closeness. "I'd hate for you to break your promise to God."

And on the first day of the year 1866, wearing her tattered old gown, Dr. Hallie Gardiner became Mrs. Jake Parrish. Though she hadn't walked down a rose-strewn aisle to the strains of Mendelssohn's "Wedding March" or worn a gown of fine Brussels lace, Hallie couldn't have asked for a more beautiful wedding. She was marrying the man of her heart, and that made it perfect.

Chapter 23

Hallie stood in the cool entry hall, stripping off her cocoa-colored kidskin gloves. She had just spent the afternoon inspecting the framing of the new Mission House and Mission Infirmary and was now preoccupied with making a mental list of the furnishings and supplies that would be needed once the buildings were complete.

True to Jake's generous nature, he had offered to rebuild the Mission House, as well as adding a separate, forty-bed hospital. He insisted that both buildings be built of only the finest materials and by the most skilled of craftsmen, and just thinking about the staggering cost was enough to make Hallie cringe. Thrifty by nature, she frequently tried to point out ways to save money, but he merely shrugged and ordered the sturdier flooring or the heavier roofing, claiming that the extra expense was a small price to pay to ensure Hallie's safety.

Hallie felt her heart swell with joy, as it always did when she thought of her wonderful husband. She was the luckiest woman in the world to be married to Jake Parrish. Unlike most men she knew, who would have keeled over of apoplexy at the mere idea of their wives practicing medicine, Jake was proud of her accomplishments and never failed to introduce her as his wife, *Dr.* Parrish. And though she was often called away from home on emergencies, sometimes at the expense of their evenings together, she had yet to hear him complain.

Feeling truly blessed, she laid her gloves on the foyer table and began to remove her fashionable pillbox hat. As she looked into the gilt-framed mirror before her, she grinned at the frivolous creation on her head.

The hat was as different from her burned-up bonnets as a butterfly was from a moth. Made of copper-colored crushed velvet and liberally trimmed with ribbons in shades of cocoa and gold, it was the most beautiful hat she had ever owned. She paused to caress the soft fabric before laying it on top of her gloves. The hat was a perfect example of Jake's exquisite taste, as was every item in her extensive new wardrobe.

When she had first seen the dazzling selection of gowns and feminine frippery he'd ordered, she had accused him of taking leave of his senses. It was positively sinful the way the man spoiled her. Speaking of sinful . . .

She had been speechless with equal parts shock and pleasure when he had unwrapped a daring array of gossamer undergarments; she had been overwhelmed with desire when he had then whispered temptingly into her ear, begging her to don her new unmentionables and treat him to an intimate examination.

Consequently, every time she felt the silken undergarments caressing her flesh beneath her clothing, she was reminded of the way Jake had loved her that afternoon. Not that she needed reminding, of course. For how could one forget a trip to paradise?

So blissful was Hallie in her new life that she had playfully renamed Parrish House "Eden," a change which had prompted Jake to suggest some sinfully wicked uses for apples. Unfortunately, like Eve in the biblical garden paradise, Hallie, too, was plagued with a serpent who sought to expel her from her heaven on earth.

That serpent was named Penelope.

Heaving a frustrated sigh, Hallie turned away from the mirror. After numerous sharp rebukes and stern lectures from Jake, Penelope no longer openly expressed her hostility toward her new sister-in-law. In fact, unless she was spoken to directly, she didn't speak at all. And in those instances when she was obligated to reply, she would likely as not answer in monosyllables. As for the girl's relationship with her brother, it had become cool almost to the point of alienation.

It was that change in relationship that concerned Hallie the most. Though Jake never discussed the troubling situation, she could tell that his sister's withdrawal hurt him.

Hallie bristled defensively at the thought of Penelope's spiteful behavior. Well, she'd be damned before she would allow the spoiled brat to cause Jake any more pain. He deserved his sister's love and respect, and she intended to see that he got it. That decision made, she squared her shoulders and tightened her lips into a determined line. There would be peace in the Parrish household. Now. Before it was too late and irreparable damage had been done to the Parrish siblings' relationship.

Steeling herself for what was bound to prove an unpleasant encounter, Hallie marched down the hall toward the music room. Penelope's great love in life was her music, and the girl spent most of her afternoons at the piano practicing her singing.

But this afternoon the music room was empty.

"Hop!" Hallie hollered, spying the houseboy at the far end of the hall.

Quick as a speeding cannonball, the little man was by her side. Sketching a deferential bow, he inquired, "Mis-see Par-rish need Hop?"

Hallie nodded. "Have you seen Penelope?"

The mere mention of Penelope's name was enough to make Hop assume an expression of long-suffering martyrdom. He grumbled something in Chinese, and rolled his eyes toward the heavens. "Mis-see Pen-lop in room. She say she sick." He made a derogatory noise. "Hop say she mean-headed only. Been mean-headed all week. She always mean-headed."

Though Hallie was too discreet to voice her thoughts, she secretly agreed that Penelope had been acting more "mean-headed" than usual. Why, the girl had done so much scowling during the past few days that she'd be lucky if her face wasn't permanently frozen into lines of discontent.

After thanking the houseboy, Hallie headed toward Penelope's room, formulating a plan of action as she went. If Penelope was truly ill, it wouldn't hurt to look in on her. If not, if the girl was indeed sulking, as Hop suspected, then they would have their long overdue talk. With that agenda in mind, Hallie knocked at her sister-in-law's bedroom door.

"What?" was the muffled response.

"Hop said you were feeling ill," Hallie half shouted through the door. "I thought I might be able to help."

There was a long silence before Penelope finally replied, "I'm fine. Go away and leave me alone." Even through two inches of solid wood the annoyance in the girl's voice was unmistakable.

Hallie smiled to herself. Aha! So Hop had been right. Penelope was indulging in one of her sulks again. That being the case . . .

"No. I won't go away. It's time we had a talk."

Hallie thought she detected the sound of a snort, but given the thickness of the door, she couldn't be certain. However, Penelope's next words were audible enough.

"I don't have anything to say to you . . . now or ever!"

"Well, I have plenty to say to you, and whether you like it or not, you're going to listen. You have five seconds to prepare yourself before I come in. One."

In a loud voice, Hallie announced each number. On the count of five, she pushed the door open.

Decorated in shades of pale blue and salmon pink, Penelope's bedroom was a young lady's dream come true. On the floor lay a rug loomed in a fanciful pattern of vines, flowers, and fruit. The walls were papered in blue, pink, and white stripes. Against one wall stood a mirrored armoire, its doors slightly ajar to reveal the girl's opulent wardrobe. Opposite the armoire was a marble-topped dressing table, the surface cluttered with perfume bottles and silver-handled brushes.

In the center of the room stood a mahogany canopied bed daintily carved in a rococo design and accented with gold leaf. Huddled into a ball beneath the embroidered brocade coverlet was Penelope. Hallie paused a few feet from the bed, taken aback by her sister-in-law's haggard appearance.

Half-hidden beneath her sweat-dampened tangle of ebony hair, the girl's face was pasty white and pinched with pain. Faint grayish-purple shadows ringed her glittering green eyes, and her lips, normally tinted a dusky pink and curled downward into a pout, were drawn into a tight, colorless line.

If this was Penelope's idea of "fine," Hallie thought, she would hate to see what the girl considered "ill." As to what was wrong? Hallie sighed inwardly and advanced toward the bed. The trick was going to be getting the patient to confide in her.

At Hallie's approach, the trembling figure on the bed shrank further beneath the coverlet. Fixing her unwelcome guest with a belligerent glower, she hissed, "What do you want?"

Assuming her most reassuring manner, Hallie replied, "You're obviously ill, and I'd like to help you if you'll let me."

Emitting a classic Parrish family snort, Penelope flopped over onto her side and presented her would-be savior with her back. Here she was, suffering from the worse case of monthly cramps she'd had in ages, and her brother's gold-digging wife insisted on playing nursemaid.

She groaned softly and flinched as a sudden pain radiated through her belly and down her thighs. Why couldn't this Dr. Gardiner person mind her own business and just leave her to suffer in peace? It wasn't as if the blasted woman really cared anything about her . . . or Jake. Curling back into a ball, she miserably pressed her thighs against her throbbing abdomen. Perhaps if she ignored the woman, she would give up her pretense of being a good Samaritan and go away.

But Hallie wasn't about to go anywhere. She hadn't missed Penelope's stifled moan, nor had she missed the way the girl had flinched with pain. Concerned, she sat on the edge of the bed and studied the tense form beneath the covers. After a moment's hesitation, she gently laid her hand on Penelope's shoulder. "If you're ill—"

"I told you, I'm fine!" Penelope snapped, jerking away from Hallie's touch. "I just want to be left alone."

Hallie almost smiled at the girl's response. How often had she heard Jake utter those very words? Stubbornness was definitely a Parrish family trait.

Using the same no-nonsense tone she had often used with Jake early in their acquaintance, she said, "As a doctor, I've taken an oath to help those in need. To leave you alone when you're obviously in need of care would be to break that oath. And since I never break my word, I guess I'll just have to stay by your side until you allow me to help you."

Penelope's only response was another snort.

This time Hallie did smile. The girl was a Parrish through and through. That being the case, it could be a long while before she finally unbent enough to accept help. With that possibility in mind, Hallie leaned back against the headboard and made herself comfortable.

The two women remained like that for a quarter of an hour: Penelope alternately feeling sorry for herself and wishing all sorts of hideous fates to befall Hallie, and Hallie grappling for the best way to break through Penelope's defensive wall.

It was Penelope who finally broke the deadlock of silence. Rolling over onto her stomach and propping her head up on her hands she glared at Hallie through the veil of her hair. "Why are you doing this?" she demanded in an accusatory tone.

Hallie let her serene gaze meet Penelope's hostile one. "I already told you why. It's because I'm a doctor, and it's a doctor's job to tend sick people."

"Is it also a doctor's job to force attention on people who don't want help?"

Hallie shrugged. "That depends."

"On what?"

"On the identity of the patient. If the patient refusing my aid is a complete stranger, then I'm obligated to honor her wishes and pray for the best. However, when the patient happens to be the sister of the man I love, well, then it's my duty to render aid . . . no matter how stubborn or unwilling that sister might be."

Penelope's beautiful green eyes narrowed with suspicion. "And when you decide that you no longer love Jake, will you still consider it your duty to tend me when I'm ill?" Restlessly she twisted a long strand of sable hair around her finger. "Or will you pretend that I no longer exist, like Serena did?"

Hallie stared down at Penelope, her eyes widening with sudden understanding. How could she have been so blind? Why hadn't she guessed that like Jake, Penelope too had been scarred by Serena's betrayal? Why hadn't she realized that the girl's wretched behavior was simply a ruse to hide her pain and fear?

Looking at her sister-in-law now, garbed in only a simple cotton nightgown, with her hair unbound, Hallie remembered something she often tended to forget: Penelope was little more than a child. She was only eighteen . . . barely out of the schoolroom. And yet, for all her youth, she had seen more tragedy than most people saw in a lifetime. No wonder the poor child was so unhappy and distrustful.

Suddenly overwhelmed with tenderness, Hallie sought to reassure the girl. Tilting her head to one side, her lips curved into a gentle smile, she replied, "I'll never stop loving Jake. He's more dear to me than life itself."

Penelope shifted her gaze from Hallie's face and stared at the sable-colored curl coiled around her index finger. "Serena claimed that she loved him, too. But she didn't . . . not really. If she had truly loved him, she never would have treated him so horribly."

Hallie shook her head. "I know it's hard to understand why—"

But before she could finish her explanation, Penelope cut her off. "It's her fault he went to war!" she accused wildly, her face contorting with sudden rage. "It's her fault he was wounded! She drove him away with her hatefulness."

Tears escaped the corners of Penelope's eyes, and her voice faded until it was little more than a pain-filled whisper. When she glanced back up at Hallie, her eyes were brilliant from emotion. "How she laughed when she got Seth's telegram informing her of Jake's injuries. She said she hoped he would die. I hated her then." With a soul-shattering sob, she began to weep in earnest.

Hallie's heart went out to the girl. She knew from her own wretched childhood experience how devastating it was to live in a household torn apart by marital strife. She knew how examples set in the home molded and influenced a child's perception of the world. Most important, she knew how those examples, good or bad, could affect the rest of a child's life.

After years of watching her father wound her mother with his vicious insults and adulterous affairs, she herself had grown into womanhood distrusting men. Apparently Serena's influence had been equally damaging to Penelope, instilling a distrust of other women.

Tentatively Hallie reached down and gently stroked the girl's violently heaving back. Though Penelope stiffened beneath her touch, she didn't pull away. It was a small concession, but a concession nonetheless.

As Hallie continued her soothing ministrations, she made a silent vow: through love and understanding Jake had proved to her that men could be trusted; she would use the same approach with Penelope and teach her that it was possible to trust another woman.

With that vow made, Hallie declared, "I'm not Serena, and I'd as soon kill myself as hurt Jake."

Penelope made a disdainful noise between her sobs and raised her tear-ravaged face from her hands to shoot a wary glance in Hallie's direction. "Why should I believe you?"

"I'm not asking you to believe my words, I'm asking you to judge my actions. I'm asking you to believe your own eyes and ears."

Penelope's only response to Hallie's plea was a loud sniffle.

Without taking her gaze from Penelope's face, Hallie reached into her pocket and pulled out a clean handkerchief. As she offered it to the girl, she asked, "Does your brother look miserable?"

Penelope eyed the lace-trimmed handkerchief thoughtfully. In truth, she couldn't remember ever seeing Jake look quite so relaxed and happy as he'd been since marrying Hallie. Not even during the honeymoon period following his marriage to Serena. Reluctantly she shook her head and took the proffered handkerchief.

"Have you ever heard me raise my voice to him or say or do anything hurtful?" Hallie quizzed.

Penelope blew her nose. The woman had a point. Even when the couple had one of their rare disagreements, Hallie never reviled her brother or wounded him with vicious recriminations. Nor did she snub him with stormy silence, like Serena always had. No, Hallie rationally stated her point and in turn listened to Jake's. Regardless of who won the dispute, the couple always ended up in each other's arms, nuzzling and cooing to each other like a pair of mating doves.

With that picture in mind, Penelope shook her head again.

"Nor will it ever happen," Hallie promised. "Please believe me when I say that I love and respect Jake. There is nothing I want more than to spend the rest of my life showing him how much I care. I know you were both hurt by Serena, but Jake has chosen to allow his heart to heal. If you'll let me, I would like to be your friend and help your heart do the same." Hallie held her breath, waiting for the girl's response.

"Serena promised to be my friend," Penelope whispered, catching her breath as her lower abdomen was seized by a particularly nasty cramp. "I loved her at first. She was so beautiful and full of life. She was everything I wanted to be. When she discovered my love for music, she took me to the theater to see all the latest musical plays. And when I told her that I intended to sing on the stage someday, she didn't laugh or look shocked."

Hallie smiled and took Penelope's hand in hers. "It's important to have someone with whom you can share your dreams. My mother always believed in my dream of being a doctor, even though the rest of our family and friends were scandalized by the notion. Without her love and support, I never would have had the courage to attend medical school."

"Serena used to make me believe that I could do anything . . . until she stopped loving Jake. Then she hated me too. I-I tried to make her like me again, but she pretended that I no longer existed." Penelope's voice wavered slightly. "It's all my fault everything went wrong. If I had been able to make her happy, she never would have needed the opium. I thought—" Then her voice broke and she was unable to continue.

Hallie gave the hand in hers a reassuring squeeze and cupped Penelope's cheek in her free hand. "What happened to Serena wasn't your fault. Serena was an unhappy woman who had a weakness for opium. I can't explain why such things happen, or why people behave as they do, but I do know that it's never anyone's fault."

Meeting Penelope's bleak gaze with her comforting one, she added, "As for her hating you? I know for a fact that she cared for you, even at the end."

"She did?" Penelope managed a tremulous smile, her face awash with hope.

Hallie nodded and returned the girl's smile. "During several of her more lucid moments, she spoke of your wonderful voice. She was so terribly proud of you. She used to say that her talented little sister was going to be the most celebrated singer of the century."

"She said that?" Penelope's smooth brow furrowed with bewilderment.

"More than once."

"Why didn't she ever say those things to me? Why did she let me think that I was a horrible person who was no longer worthy of her friendship?"

"Because she loved you and no longer thought *herself* worthy of *your* friendship."

"But why?" Penelope looked flabbergasted. "I never said or did anything to indicate that I wanted to end the friendship."

Hallie shook her head and trapped Penelope's gaze with hers, wanting to make sure that the girl understood what she was about to tell her. "Serena pushed you away because she didn't want to expose you to the depravity of her addiction. She knew how much you admired her and was afraid that you might suffer from her influence. She turned you away because she cared."

"Truly?"

"Cross my heart and hope to die."

Penelope drew in a shuddering breath and closed her eyes, as if absorbing Hallie's words. Hallie simply sat by her side, still holding her hand and stroking her cheek.

The healing balm had been applied to the poor child's lacerated soul and scarred heart. Given time, patience, and love, she would heal. And perhaps someday she would even learn to trust again.

After a long while, Hallie murmured, "Penelope?"

The girl opened her eyes and looked up at the woman by her side. For the first time since their acquaintance, her gaze was unclouded by wariness.

"I heard Jenny Lind sing. Her voice couldn't hold a candle to yours."

Penelope's face flushed pink with pleasure. "Honestly?"

"I never lie," Hallie vowed solemnly. "And you know what else?"

Penelope shook her head.

"I intend to do everything in my power to help you realize your dream, just like my mother did for me."

"Do you really think that it's possible? My singing on the stage, I mean?"

"With your beauty and talent, you'll be the toast of two continents." Upon delivering that vote of confidence, Hallie gave Penelope's cheek a pat and her hand a squeeze, and then rose to her feet. "I'll leave you to your rest now. If you need me for anything, I'll be in the library going over the plans for the new infirmary."

Before she could move away from the bed, Penelope latched on to her arm. "I-I do need y-your help." The girl bit her lower lip and turned a dull crimson. Fidgeting with the lace edging on the coverlet, she confessed, "I-It's my m-monthly flow."

Hallie nodded solemnly and sat back down on the edge of the bed. "Lots of women have problems with their monthlies. What seems to be wrong?"

"I hurt." Penelope gingerly patted her lower abdomen. "Here. Low in my belly. My insides feel as if they're falling out . . . and the muscles in my thighs ache. My back hurts too." She turned on her side and patted her lower back. "Here."

"Is this the first time you've had this pain?" Hallie asked, going over the girl's symptoms in her mind.

"Oh, no. I've had it during my monthlies since they started five years ago." She threaded a corner of the coverlet between her fingers, not meeting Hallie's eyes. "It's not always this bad, though."

"But it's been this bad before?" prodded Hallie gently.

"Sometimes better, sometimes worse. I told Dr. Barnes about it two years ago." Penelope's face turned a livid shade of purple. "He insisted on examining me i-intimately. It was awful. I've never been so embarrassed in my life."

"I know," Hallie commiserated. "All women are discomforted by such examinations. Especially the first time. What did Dr. Barnes tell you?"

"That I was perfectly healthy and that I was imagining my pain." Penelope's features contorted into a mask of indignation. "But I'm not!" she protested. "I really do hurt!"

"Of course you hurt, dear," Hallie reassured her, mentally damning Dr. Barnes for so callously disregarding the girl's pain. "And any doctor who would say such a thing is an insensitive clod. Lots of women have pain with their monthly flow, especially young ones. It's just an unfortunate part of being a woman. And though I doubt that your discomfort is due to any sort of serious condition, I would like to examine you to make certain."

When Penelope flushed again at her suggestion, Hallie hastily clarified her intent. "I don't need to make the same kind of examination as Dr. Barnes made. At least, not now. All I need to do is feel your belly and make sure that everything feels normal."

The girl chewed her lower lip with indecision, her gaze anxiously searching Hallie's face. Apparently what she saw met with her approval, because she managed a wan smile and nodded.

After Hallie had examined Penelope and had satisfied herself that the girl was normal, she set about to ease her pain.

Normally she recommended a small draught of laudanum to ease menstrual discomfort. However, knowing the Parrish family's understandable aversion to the drug, she decided it might be best to give Hop Yung's "No-Mean Head, No-Pain" concoction another try. After all, it had certainly worked wonders on Jake after he had been shot.

Once Hallie had coaxed Penelope to drink the Chinese herbal brew, to which a dollop of honey had been added to improve the taste, she placed a stoneware hot water bottle on the girl's abdomen, and another at the small of her back, and then tucked her securely beneath her blankets. That task completed, she sat next to her patient and rubbed her shoulders until she slept.

As Hallie tiptoed from the room, satisfied that Hop's potion had worked its magic, she was stopped by Penelope's drowsy voice. "Hallie?"

"Yes, dear?" Hallie paused, doorknob in hand.

"About my dream?"

Hallie smiled. "You mean to sing on the stage?"

"Well—" Penelope yawned. "—actually, I have two dreams."

"Good. Everyone needs lots of dreams. And when you're feeling better, we'll figure out how to make your second dream come true as well."

Chapter 24

"What do you say, Jake?" asked Judge Eustace Dorner, taking another sip of champagne from his glass.

No reply.

Eustace chuckled to himself. The boy was gawking at his new bride again and hadn't heard a word he'd said. Clearing his throat loudly, he prompted, "Jake?"

Reluctantly, Jake shifted his gaze away from Hallie, who was being spun across the dance floor in a quadrille, and looked back at Judge Dorner. "Sorry, Eustace," he murmured.

"I was asking if you were the one responsible for thrashing Nick Connelly? The man's pointing his finger in your direction and whining for justice."

"Er-yes." Like a hummingbird to nectar, Jake's gaze was drawn back to his wife. She looked beautiful tonight. Seductive. The lady's maid he'd hired had done wonders with her hair, drawing it softly away from her face and arranging it down her back in a cascade of molten curls. And her gown . . . !

For a moment Jake almost regretted selecting the ball gown she was wearing. Made of bronze tissue silk shot with burnished gold, the garment hugged every luscious curve of her body.

His eyes narrowed dangerously. *Curves which that young fool Michael Robbins was holding much too closely.*

"Can't wait to get the little woman alone, eh?" Eustace commiserated. "I remember when I was first married to my Maudie, thought my manly anatomy would be permanently blue from wanting her all the time."

That observation got Jake's attention, and he had the good grace to flush a dull red. Personally, his own manly parts felt as if they had gone beyond the blue stage and were now a shade painfully akin to deep purple. Acutely aware of his need, Jake let his gaze drift back to Hallie.

This time she was staring back at him over her partner's shoulder. As she trapped his hungry gaze with her sultry one, desire, intense and unbearably erotic, heated Jake's loins. For one libidinous instant, he was tempted to spirit her away to a place of shadowy seclusion, toss up her skirts and bury his throbbing flesh into her welcoming folds.

He almost groaned aloud at the thought. Knowing his passionate Mission Lady, she would probably enjoy such an impromptu rendezvous every bit as much as he would. At that moment he felt truly blessed. Not only was his wife beautiful, intelligent, and kind, but she possessed a rare sensuality that enslaved a man. Gratefully, Jake gave thanks for the precious gift of his Hallie.

Hallie smiled at her husband, eagerly accepting the sensual promise in his eyes. Lord! She was hot and flushed all over, and in a way that had nothing to do with the temperature of the room or her exertion from dancing. Distracted, she missed a step and trod on Michael's toes.

Heaven help her! She was burning up . . . feverish with the desire to feel every inch of Jake's body pressed close to hers, flesh against bare flesh, his muscles hard against her yielding softness. She was delirious with her longing to hear him groan as he quivered beneath her caresses, to know the thrill of feminine victory as he cried out in his masculine surrender.

Hungrily, she let her gaze slide down Jake's body, picturing in her mind what lay beneath his superbly tailored suit. Even after four months of marriage, she still found it impossible to believe that this magnificent man was her husband. Proudly, she noted the way his dark formal attire emphasized his powerful physique and how, as usual, his manly beauty made the rest of the men present pale to insignificance. Obviously the other ladies had noticed him as well, for Hallie hadn't missed the way their longing gazes followed him as he sauntered about the ballroom.

Especially that blasted Arabella Dunlap, she observed

jealously. Jake hadn't taken more than two steps away from Judge Dorner before the woman had waylaid him. The flirtatious baggage had been hanging on him all evening long, staring up at him with those dark, slanting eyes of hers and whispering intimately into his ear. It was maddening enough to make Hallie's hands itch to rip out the woman's hair.

Just as Hallie was picturing Arabella bald and resembling a shaved rat, the music ended. Stuttering his thanks, the enamored Michael Robbins escorted Hallie from the dance floor.

"Will you look at that?" hissed Miranda Wiley, inclining her stiffly coiffed blonde head toward Jake and Arabella, who stood against the opposite wall. They appeared to be embroiled in a very intimate sort of discussion.

Lavinia Donahue glanced over at the pair with a sniff. "Well, I can't say that I'm surprised. I knew it wouldn't take Jake Parrish long to tire of his drab doctor wife. Rumor has it that the man's been seen leaving Arabella's house quite frequently of late. Maggie Kemp saw him there just yesterday, and she said that he looked as if he'd been indulging in some fairly—ah—strenuous activities." She pursed her lips disapprovingly. "We all know that the only kind of exercise Arabella gets is the kind she can get in bed."

Standing unnoticed on the fringe of the group, Hallie overheard every word of gossip, and her heart seemed to freeze in her chest. Miserably, she glanced back over toward Jake and Arabella, but they had vanished.

"Ignore the old cats, dear." It was Davinia, who had also overheard the women's prattle. Slipping her arm around Hallie's waist, she gave her friend a reassuring hug.

"My sister and her clan are malicious fools. They're so jealous of your happiness that they're all about to split a gut."

Hallie looked at her friend doubtfully. "Jake and Arabella did look to be having a rather . . . friendly discussion."

"Durned woman's always throwing herself at the boy. He was probably just trying to fend her off in a gentlemanly fashion."

When Hallie didn't look convinced, Davinia snorted, "Everyone knows that Jake's had plenty of opportunities at Arabella over the years. If he'd wanted a piece of that tart, he'd have taken a bite long before now." She gave her friend a naughty wink. "Guess he likes his sweets a mite fresher."

Hallie laughed feebly at that. "I suppose you're right. It's just that I love Jake so much. The thought of losing him scares me to death."

"Well, of course you love him. The man's more perfect than a maiden's dream. And anyone with half a brain can see that he's equally besotted with you. Why, he hasn't stopped staring at you all evening. Been looking at you like a bear at a hive of honey that's just out of reach."

"Really?" Hallie stared at her friend hopefully.

Davinia nodded. "Besides, do you think it's fair to doubt Jake just because a pack of bored old biddies have nothing better to do than to cast aspersions on innocent folks? Hell and damnation, Hallie! I hadn't taken you for such a blubber brain!"

Hallie flushed, suddenly feeling very much the blubber brain. Davinia did have a point. Jake had never given her any reason to doubt him.

"Have you ever known me to be wrong?"

Hallie shook her head.

"Of course not." Davinia patted Hallie's cheek fondly. "Never fear, your husband knows what a thoroughbred he's married and he's not about to take up with a nag like Arabella. Jake might be a bit mule-headed at times, as are all men, but he's not stupid. Especially where women are concerned."

There was an amused chuckle from behind Hallie. "It's nice to know that I'm not stupid, for all that I'm mule-headed," Jake quipped, wrapping his arms around Hallie's waist and drawing her back up against his chest. "I could feel my ears burning from clear across the room."

"As well you should, my boy," scolded Davinia. "May I remind you that you're a married man now and, as such, should take pains to avoid Arabella's calf-eyed fawning? It's causing talk."

Jake lightly traced the shape of Hallie's jaw with his

fingertip, enjoying the feel of her backside pressing against his groin. "Believe me, Davinia," he purred. "I'm well aware that I'm a married man." Subtly he rubbed the evidence of his desire against Hallie's rounded buttocks. "Pleasantly so."

Hallie gave him a furtive thrust back and it was all Jake could do not to groan. Good God! You would've thought that his manhood would have learned to behave itself by now—or at least would've been too worn out from their constant lovemaking to plague him so. But he was finding his passion for his Mission Lady insatiable and even now, only several hours after loving her, he found himself aching to take her again.

"As for Arabella," he stifled a moan as Hallie moved against him again. "Perhaps if my beautiful wife wasn't so busy flirting with all of her admirers and deigned to spare me a glance once in a while, Arabella wouldn't feel so free to exercise her wiles." As soon as the words were out, he regretted them, for he had been unable to keep the resentment from his voice.

It was true. It *was* hard to stand on the sidelines knowing that he was unable to dance with his own wife. It pained him to watch while other men held his Hallie in their arms and brought a glow of pleasure to her face, pleasure which he was unable to share with her. Yet, he would never dream of denying her anything that made her smile and he was ashamed of his jealousy.

"I'm sorry, love," Hallie whispered. "You know that I wouldn't neglect you for anything in the world. If I had my way, I'd stitch you to my side and never let you out of my sight."

"Of course you don't neglect me. It's just that I'm possessive where you're concerned." Bending close to her ear, he whispered, "And I might consider sitting still for those stitches. However, might I suggest sewing us more . . ."

"Jake!" Hallie knew exactly what he was about to suggest and promptly turned as red as the Dorners' ballroom curtains.

Davinia let out an unladylike guffaw at the pair's antics. Lucky Hallie, to have such a lusty husband! From the way the rascal was looking down at her, it was clear that her friend had nothing to fear from Arabella or from any other woman.

And from the look on the Parrishes' faces, it was obvious that they needed a few moments to themselves. "Excuse me," she mumbled. "I need to speak to Marius."

Jake and Hallie nodded politely. As soon as Davinia had disappeared into the crowd, Jake pulled his wife down the hall and into the Dorners' deserted library. Without ceremony, he claimed her lips with his. As usual, he was stunned by the intensity of her answering passion.

God! What she did to him! The sweetness of her tongue as she teased the sensitive recesses of his mouth was enough to make him long to take her then and there, up against the wall. Jake groaned into her mouth. He could imagine how she would feel, his sex tightly sheathed in hers, her body held immobile between the hard surface of the wall and his own thrusting pelvis. He had never made love standing up, and the idea maddened him.

"Poor, poor darling," Hallie murmured, breaking off their kiss and boldly plunging her hand down the front of his trousers. Firmly, she grasped his rigid manhood. "It seems as if you're infected with lust again." She lightly caressed his length.

"Hallie. Don't—" he moaned, feeling as if he was about to explode at any moment. Damnation! She knew how it inflamed him when she stroked him like that. "Sweetheart . . ."

Hallie let her hand slide to his firm masculine sac. "Hush now." She kissed him into silence. "You know that I need to make an *intimate examination* if I'm to relieve your suffering." She lightly prodded at the tender flesh cradled in her palm. "Oh, dear. It seems as if you're badly in need of some of my care."

"Hallie!" His pelvis jerked against her hand in response. The woman was shameless . . . and he loved it. When Jake felt Hallie move lower to stroke the sensitive flesh behind his sac, he was sure he would lose control right then and there.

So caught up were they in their impassioned tryst that they didn't hear the door behind them swing open.

"Aha! There you are!" It was Eustace and his wife, Maud. They were standing on the threshold, beaming fondly at the embracing couple. "We were wondering where our guests of honor were hiding. Davinia said she'd seen you headed in this direction."

Smothering a frustrated oath, Jake hauled Hallie against him, effectively disguising the fact that her hand was still trapped down his trousers.

Maud moved into the room to peer at Hallie's highly colored face. "Are you quite all right, dear? You look terribly flushed." She glanced up at Jake. "Don't you think she looks flushed?"

"Very," he agreed, studying his wife's face with mock concern. "She was just complaining about feeling overly warm—hot, actually—and I—" He jumped as Hallie gave his sex a tweak that almost sent him over the edge.

Crushing his errant wife against his chest, Jake mumbled. "Sorry. I thought the little woman was about to faint. As I was saying, Hallie's a bit overheated and has expressed a need to retire early this evening."

Eustace let loose a snort of amusement. "Needs an evening in bed, eh? Come to think of it, you look a bit flushed yourself, my boy. You could probably use some bed rest as well." He winked at his friend meaningfully.

Jake grinned back over Hallie's head.

And Maud missed the whole point of the exchange. Standing on her tiptoes, she reached up to feel Jake's forehead. "I do hope you're not coming down with the grippe. It has been going around, you know. Make sure you both take a spoonful of quinine."

As Hallie opened her mouth to reassure the woman of the soundness of their health, she was cut off by Jake's reply.

"We haven't contracted anything that can't be cured by an evening in bed." His lips twisted roguishly. "My poor wife especially has been plagued by this ailment of late."

"Of late, yes," Hallie purred, stroking the length of Jake's hardness. To her satisfaction, his pelvis gave a violent jerk and she could hear his breath catch as he stifled a moan. She'd show him who needed an evening between the sheets.

"Well, then, you two run along," boomed Eustace, nodding sympathetically at Jake's pained expression. The boy looked to be in a hell of a heat. He cackled to himself, remembering how it had felt to be young and constantly in need. "I'm sure Maudie will be glad to serve as Penelope's chaperon for the rest of the evening, and I'll personally see to it that the girl gets home at a decent hour. That sister of yours has become quite the rage these days. Couldn't disappoint all the young pups by letting her leave now."

"That would be most generous of you, Eustace." Jake paused to glance down at his wife. Wicked baggage! Her expression was as prim as if she had been at a Sunday meeting, and all the while she continued to bedevil his male member.

"And, yes, I do believe we will retire early. I'm finding myself in desperate need of my bed as well." Silently he vowed to seek retribution from his wife for her merciless teasing.

It was during the short carriage ride home that Jake deftly turned the tables on Hallie.

As soon as the carriage door had clicked shut, Jake snaked his hand beneath his wife's skirts and loosened her drawers. Seductively, he trailed his fingertips up her inner thigh, smiling with satisfaction as she began to groan with yearning.

"Jake!" Hallie gasped as he parted her damp folds and lightly stroked the bud of her desire. Ruthlessly he teased her, stimulating her until she squirmed with passion beneath his fingers.

As she felt a rush of delicious sensations sweep through her body, she begged, "P-Please, darling. Now!" The humming deep in her belly had intensified to a frenzied pitch, singing for release. Whimpering with urgency, she thrust against his hand.

"Oh, no, Mission Lady." Jake chuckled, thoroughly enjoying his revenge. "You're going to pay for torturing my poor manhood in front of the Dorners."

With excruciating slowness, he eased his finger inside the sheath of her womanhood, moaning with her as she arched and gyrated against him. She felt so warm and wet clamped around his index finger, her thighs straining apart in her need as he flicked his thumb over her sensitive woman's nub.

Again and again he brought her just to the brink of ecstasy, only to pull her back at the last moment. When the carriage finally came to a rattling stop in front of the house, Hallie's urgency had become such an all-consuming fever that she was certain she'd succumb from the heat. Desperate to relieve the throbbing ache between her legs, she rubbed against Jake's fingers, moaning for her release.

From outside the carriage, they could hear the servants shout to one another as they prepared to open the doors. Hastily, Jake replaced Hallie's drawers and smoothed down her skirts. She groaned her disappointment.

"Remember, Mission Lady. Patience is a virtue," he teased, adjusting his dress coat over the straining bulge in his trousers. "And virtue is always handsomely rewarded."

The rogue. Hallie smiled demurely as the carriage door was opened. *She would give him a lesson in patience.*

She waited until she'd been handed out of the carriage and Jake was in the process of stepping down, and then she murmured seductively, "You'll have to catch me if you want your reward." With that she lifted her skirts and fled into the house.

Though Jake's leg was much stronger these days, thanks to Hallie's nightly massages and poultices, it still wasn't strong enough to allow him to run up the stairs, and he was forced to pursue his wife at a more sedate pace. Nonetheless, he had an easy enough time following her.

Like Hansel marking his way through the forest with bread crumbs, Hallie blazed a trail through the house with her clothing. There were a fan and gloves in the foyer, and a shawl on the stairs. Shoes, stockings, petticoats, and her bodice, all strewn down the hallways . . . all leading him to paradise. Jake's grin broadened as he picked up the chemise lying at the junction of the upstairs corridor. His Mission Lady was truly shameless—and almost naked at this point. Except for . . .

. . . Her drawers. Which were lying in a heap of fine

white batiste in front of the door of the bedroom adjoining his. With a chuckle, he picked them up. Waving them in the air like a white flag of surrender, he pushed open the door and stepped inside.

"Sweetheart?"

Silence. The room was empty. Jake grinned as he made his way to the door leading into his own chambers. He could already picture his Mission Lady lounging naked on his velvet coverlet, eager to feel him, hungry to feast upon his passion.

Just when he was about to open the adjoining door, a naked Hallie slipped from behind the curtains and pounced on him. Giggling, she began to pull off his clothes.

Piece by piece, Hallie undressed him, slapping his hands away when he tried to help.

"Oh, no. Tonight you're my gift and I intend to unwrap you all by myself." As she eased his shirt from his broad shoulders, she paused to kiss the scar at the base of his throat and then moved lower to lick at his nipples, knowing how much he liked it.

Jake groaned and returned the favor, enjoying the way hers turned pebble-hard beneath his tongue. Hunger sluiced through his veins as he molded the shape of her breasts with his hands, his blood quickening at the feel of her feminine softness.

"Oh, no, you don't!" she gasped, as his hands skimmed the contours of her waist and eased inward to draw circles around her navel. Firmly, she pushed his hands to his sides. "Not until your trousers are off and I can touch you just as freely."

Dropping to her knees in front of him, her face mere inches from his groin, Hallie began the tantalizing process of unbuttoning his pants. As each fastening was sprung from its moorings, she gently kissed the exposed expanse of his belly, her breath stirring the inky strip of hair that led down to his most intimate parts. Parts that she alone was free to touch.

At that moment, Jake was sure that if his manly parts could truly change colors, they would be the color of an eggplant. Briefly, he wondered if she ached as badly as he did. Then her knuckles grazed his arousal, and his mind went blank to everything but his own agonizing need.

When, at last, his member sprang loose, Hallie pulled her hands away and sat still, pausing to admire his beauty.

But that moment was one too many for Jake. With a growl, he impatiently ripped off the rest of his clothing himself. Pulling his laughing wife up into his arms, he wrestled her to the lace-decked bed, unable to wait another second to possess her. As their bodies sank into the mattress, the sweet, unmistakable scent of roses wafted up from the coverings.

Roses. It was as if someone had thrown a pail of icy water over Jake's body. Serena had always insisted that rose petals be scattered in her freshly made bed to scent the sheets. Apparently the servants were still indulging in the practice.

Jake shuddered. He could almost hear Serena's mocking laughter as he lay before her, flaccid and unable to perform his manly duty. *Impotent. Half a man.*

Shaking violently, Jake buried his face between Hallie's breasts and deeply inhaled her womanly scent, desperate to banish the cloying scent of roses from his nostrils.

"What's wrong, darling?" Hallie whispered, feeling his hardness begin to shrivel against her belly.

Jake groaned and rolled off her.

Perplexed, Hallie stared down at her husband's naked form. He was lying on his back with one arm thrown over his eyes, almost as if he couldn't bear to look at her. Every powerful muscle in his body was sharply delineated in his tension, and his chest was heaving as he choked in ragged gasps of air.

"Are you sick?" she asked, concerned by the way he was trembling beneath her hand.

Sick, yes. Soul sick. Jake felt Hallie move on the bed beside him, sending another whiff of roses swirling into the air. As he lay choking on the scent, he felt her cup his limp sex in her palm.

With a virulent curse, he pushed her hands away. "Don't touch me there," he growled, rolling to his side and pulling his knees protectively to his belly, hiding his shame from her.

Serena had touched him like that as he'd lain in this very spot, and when he'd been unable to rise, she'd laughed at him. To his humiliation, her laughter had made him shrivel even more. *Half a man. Impotent.*

And now he'd withered up in front of Hallie. Damn thing was cringing between his legs like a coward hiding from retribution. All because of the smell of roses.

"Jake," Hallie cried, frightened by his violent reaction to her touch. "Please. Tell me what I did wrong." A sob caught in her throat. Desperate to make everything right again, she lay down beside him and pulled him into her embrace.

He stiffened in her arms. Was she going to try to make him rise again? A cold sweat wreathed Jake's forehead. What if he failed? Would she too laugh at him?

But Hallie didn't try to coax him the way Serena had, nor did she mock him. She didn't even touch him like that. She simply held him. Jake slowly let his body relax against her warmth.

"I love you, darling," he heard her whisper.

And he knew it was true. Just as he knew he could trust his Hallie to understand about Serena and the roses.

"I'm sorry, sweetheart," Jake murmured after a long silence. "It's not your fault I can't . . ." he choked on the words. It was difficult to talk about his failure.

"Hush, Jake," Hallie whispered, aching at the pain she heard in his voice. "We don't have to do anything. I'm happy just holding you."

He lifted her hand from where it was resting against his chest and kissed the palm. "Sweet Hallie. And I'm happy being held. But I want you to understand . . . something." He shifted in her embrace until he could look into her eyes. The tenderness in her gaze made him long to confide in her.

"You see, I *want* to love you. Very badly." He swallowed hard. "But I can't."

Hallie's heart bled at the self-loathing on his face as he stared down at his flaccid sex. Cupping his chin in her palm, she forced him to look back into her eyes. "You're probably just tired," she said gently. "And no wonder, considering how much we've made love during the last few months."

"It's not that." Jake glanced around the room. Everything from the roses bordering the walls to the rose trellis pattern in the carpet recalled Serena and his shame. He shook his head. "It's the room. The scent of roses. They bring back memories."

Hallie tightened her arms around him, cursing herself for a fool. Whatever had she been thinking, to lure him in here? Of course, Jake wouldn't want to make love in Serena's old room.

"I wasn't thinking when I led you in here," she whispered. "I'm sorry. There's so much I don't know about you, I'm bound to make stupid mistakes."

Jake rolled out of Hallie's arms and sat up, his back braced against the rosewood headboard. Reaching down, he pulled her back into his embrace, murmuring, "Don't blame yourself. You've done nothing except try to please me. And you've succeeded."

"How?" she asked incredulously, resting her chin on his chest and staring up into his tip-tilted green eyes.

Jake kissed the tip of her nose. "By just being you. By being sweet and understanding, and by not laughing at my failure to perform my manly duty."

"I would never laugh at something like that!" She reached up and caressed his lean cheek. "I can't imagine anyone doing anything so unfeeling."

"Serena did. Cruelly so." He shifted his eyes from hers to stare into the fire. Hallie sometimes dressed in this room, and Celine always made sure the fire was lit.

"It happened right after I'd come back from the war. You see, Hallie, I hadn't gone to war because of any noble ideals or burning desire to fight for the cause. I was running away from the battle raging within my own marriage. In my own cowardly way I deserted Serena. I couldn't face the fact that she hated me."

He looked down at Hallie, locking her gaze with his, wanting to make sure she understood what he was about to tell her. "During the war, I became obsessed with the idea of making Serena love me again. I was so tired of all the hate and violence that I would have done anything to restore the peace in my marriage."

Jake paused for a moment, drawing strength from Hallie's loving gaze. She was looking at him with such compassion, such tenderness; somehow she always made everything seem better.

Laying his cheek against her hair, he continued. "Facing death day in and day out makes a man value the love of his woman and the tranquillity of his home above all else. Like a fool, I believed that I could recapture both. It was that belief that kept me alive after I'd been wounded.

Gently cupping his wife's chin in his hand and tilting her face up to stare into the tawny warmth of her eyes, he said, "You'll understand, then, how delighted I was when Serena tried to seduce me a few days after I'd returned from the war."

Jake could see Serena as vividly as if she stood by his side. She'd been naked that night, save for her silvery curtain of hair. Her skin had been ghostly white, unhealthy in its pallor, almost translucent in its delicacy, with the network of blue veins faintly visible beneath the surface.

He shook his head to chase away the disturbing specter. "When she lured me in here that last time, desperate to make love to me, to blame the child she was carrying on me, she had covered herself with rose oil. It was her favorite scent and she knew how much I'd once loved it. I thought everything was going to be all right. And it was . . . until she kissed me. Instead of purity, I tasted the depravity of her opium, and beneath the sweetness of the roses, I could smell the sickly odor of the drug clinging to her skin. She'd obviously had to use a great deal of the stuff in order to be able to stomach my touch."

Jake hugged Hallie close to his heart, needing the reassurance of her nearness. "My sex fell limp . . . and stayed limp, though she worked hard to make it rise. When she finally used her mouth on me, remembering how much I enjoyed being pleasured like that, my manhood shriveled up completely. I hated her for coaxing me like that . . . hated her persistence.'

He buried his face in Hallie's hair for a moment. With his voice half-muffled, he confessed, "When it became obvious that I was unable to get an erection, she laughed at me. She called me impotent. Half a man."

A sob escaped Jake's lips. "She was right. After that,

I was incapable of performing. Not even when Seth took me to Coralie's and treated me to her best whore. I didn't dare try again after I failed with her as well. I was too afraid to face the humiliating truth that I was no longer able to function as a man."

"That's all over now, darling," Hallie whispered, kissing his chest just over where his heart beat. If Serena hadn't already been dead, she would have strangled her for hurting Jake.

"You're right. It is over." He rubbed his cheek against her hair. Sitting up like this, he could no longer smell the roses. There was only Hallie. Fresh, womanly Hallie.

Reassured by her familiar scent, he confessed, "It was over the first moment I met you. You were honest and good, and I wanted you. You showed me you cared and I needed you. And when you came to love me, you healed the wounds of my shame. You gave me back my manhood."

"I love you, Jake Parrish," Hallie whispered, his words making her feel breathless with emotion. "That's all that matters now. We have a lifetime to make our own memories, and I intend to make sure they're all proud, happy ones."

Jake groaned and crushed her against his chest. "Sweet Jesus! I love you, too!" And then he claimed her lips with a kiss that gave truth to his words.

Coiling her arms around his neck, Hallie returned his kiss—with a kiss that clearly expressed her love and compassion, a healing kiss. One that made Serena's hovering ghost dissolve and put all the destructive memories where they belonged—in the past.

As Hallie parted her lips, responding like a spark to kindling beneath the probing heat of his tongue, her hand slipped downward and came to rest on his manhood.

Jake gasped as fire flared through his loins and he hardened completely. "No, Hallie," he murmured, pushing her out of his embrace and rising from the bed. "Not here. I want our new memories to be free from the taint of the past."

Then he reached down and scooped her up into his arms. For the first time since the war, Jake's leg was

Chapter 25

Hallie sat cross-legged on the floor, carefully removing the contents from the bottom drawer of Serena's dressing table. In the months following the first Mrs. Parrish's death no one had thought to clear away her personal effects, and the room had stood virtually untouched.

Even Hallie, who sometimes used the room for undressing after returning home from late-night emergency calls, had never spared the Rose Room more than a passing thought.

But that had been before last night, before she'd seen how devastated Jake was by the memories of the room. It was in the early hours of the morning, after her husband had finally drifted off to sleep, that Hallie had vowed to sweep away the pain of yesterday and turn the rose-decked room into a haven where her love could at last find peace.

As she lifted the last of Serena's possessions, the final sum of a wasted young life, Hallie caught glimpses of the once happy, carefree girl whose life had turned out so tragically.

It was the seemingly insignificant tokens, such as the bundles of yellowed letters, tattered dance cards, and faded ribbons that spoke most eloquently of a treasured past. With a surge of bittersweet longing, Hallie wondered what it would have been like to have childhood memories worth cherishing.

"Mrs. Parrish?"

Hallie glanced up as a contingent of footmen carrying an old sleigh bed stopped just inside the door to await her orders.

"Over there." She pointed to the wall opposite an enormous bay window. Serena's gilt bed had stood across the room by the fireplace, and Hallie wanted the room to be as different as possible. Nodding her head with satisfaction, she quickly finished clearing the remaining items from the drawer. Someday Ariel would wonder about the mother she'd never known, and these tokens might provide her with some insight.

"You can take the dressing table up the attic now," Hallie told the footmen, giving the drawer a push to close it. It stuck. She gave it another shove. Still it refused to close. With a sigh of exasperation, she removed the drawer and searched for the obstruction. As she gingerly poked into the dark corners of the drawer's slot, Hallie's hand brushed against something soft.

She could only stare, aghast, at what she found. Wrapped in one of Serena's handkerchiefs was a pessary. Hallie's forehead creased into a frown. If Serena had been using a pessary, then . . .

Joy, fierce and exultant, swelled in her heart: *Jake's seed wasn't fruitless. Serena had been using this device to prevent conception.* Hallie hugged herself. She couldn't wait to see the happiness on her husband's face when she told him the news.

Though he seldom mentioned it, Hallie knew how much Jake's fruitless state pained him. Once, while lying in each other's arms, they had each confessed their most secret yearnings. Jake's had been for a family of his own, and it had broken her heart knowing that it was the one thing he would never have.

That night she'd prayed for a miracle, the miracle of a child with Jake's stunning good looks and his loving ways. And now, with the discovery of this device, came the hope that her miracle might be possible after all.

Hallie let her hands slide to her belly with a sigh. Perhaps even now Jake's child grew within her. That thought made her heart surge with longing.

All through the afternoon Hallie worked, whisking away all traces of Serena's presence and transforming the room into one that suited her own, simpler tastes.

The furnishings, which she had discovered in the attic, were of the style of the French Empire which had been popular earlier in the century. The plain sleigh bed was of mahogany, as were the rest of the furniture pieces, all of which had been polished to a mirror shine by Celine and Hallie. Simple yellow-and-blue-patterned muslin drapes replaced the flounced pink silk ones, and the bed was covered with a yellow satin coverlet. On the floor was a soft blue carpet woven with accents of yellow, colors which reminded Hallie of the sun glinting off the bay on a spring day.

As she stood arranging daisies and lily of the valley in a vase, pausing now and again to survey her handiwork with satisfaction, the door opened.

Standing stock-still on the threshold, Jake quietly took in every detail of the room's metamorphosis. With pleasure, he noted Hallie's choice of furnishings. This had been his mother's furniture, and though Serena had banished it to the attic, pronouncing it old-fashioned, he'd always loved it. He could almost picture his beautiful mother turning from the dressing table mirror and holding out her arms to him, arms that had always been ready to embrace him.

A knot formed in Jake's throat as he crossed the room to the bed and traced the contours of the headboard with his fingertips. Looking over to where Hallie stood, a stalk of lily of the valley clutched in her hand, he murmured, "I like this furniture."

And he liked the way she looked, too. Dressed in a flattering gown of leaf green India cotton, with her hair pulled away from her face in a matching ribbon, his wife was the most beautiful sight Jake Parrish had ever seen.

Their gazes met, and held, as he closed the distance between them. Though his limp was still pronounced, and always would be, he now walked with a confidence he had previously lacked.

As Jake stopped before her, a smile tugging at his lips, Hallie thought that she'd never seen him look so wonderful. He had spent the day at the wharf seeing to his ships, and his face had a healthy, sun-kissed glow which she found irresistible.

Gently, Jake took the flowers from Hallie's hand and inhaled their perfume, his gaze capturing hers over the delicate blooms. "I've heard that lily of the valley symbolizes a return to happiness," he murmured, breaking off a small sprig and tucking it behind her ear. "The flower suits you, for you've returned me to happiness."

Jake's heart was filled with joy as he stared down at

his wife. She was everything to him. She made him eager to start every new day and gave him a reason to cherish the nights he had once dreaded. And now she was making his house into a home.

Tenderly, he pressed a kiss to her lips. "Thank you," he whispered, nodding at the room.

"I'm glad you approve." Smiling, she wrapped her arms around his taut waist to pull him near. He had been riding hard, and as Hallie pressed her face against his chest she could smell the musky scent of his sweat. She inhaled deeply, finding his masculine scent as seductive as an aphrodisiac.

"Want me to show you how much I approve?" He chuckled as he began unhooking the back of her dress.

Reaching up to remove his tie, she replied, "Only if you let me show you how much I love you in return."

"You already have," he pointed out, helping her remove his jacket and in turn easing her bodice off. "Now it's my turn to pay you back."

Hallie smiled wickedly as she tugged off his shirt. "I'll collect the debt later." She paused to nip at his broad shoulder. "Right now, I have special plans for you, Mr. Parrish."

With that, she blazed a path of sucking kisses from the scar at his throat all the way down to his navel, stopping in between to tease his flat nipples with her tongue. It excited her to feel him quiver beneath the tender assault of her lips.

With a low growl, Jake untied the ribbons of Hallie's chemise and slipped the flimsy garment to her waist. Then he bent down to return her sensual favor.

Leisurely, he kissed down the length of her torso, pausing to bite at the waistband of her skirt before nibbling his way back up to her breasts.

"That feels . . . wonderful," she sighed, arching against him as he traced slow circles around her nipples with his tongue.

"How wonderful?" he murmured, capturing one of the hardened peaks between his lips, alternately sucking and licking in turn until her sighs of desire quickened to pants of lust.

Her body trembled and with a whimper she strained her pelvis against his groin, crushing herself against the evidence of his need. "Too wonderful!" she gasped as the secret place between her legs began to tingle with delicious yearning.

Moaning with his own urgency, Jake let his hands slide down the narrow curve of Hallie's waist and in one fluid motion, he unhooked her skirts. With a soft *whoosh!* her garments slipped down her hips to pool around her ankles, leaving her clad only in her almost transparent drawers and silk stockings.

"Jake!" Hallie cried, as he fondled her heated woman's flesh through the thin cotton of her drawers. Oh! How he teased her . . . tormented her, his touch making her body quiver out of control.

A smile of anticipation curled Jake's lips as he explored the thinly veiled recesses of Hallie's womanhood. "Do you like it when I touch you here?" he whispered, sliding his fingers between her moist folds.

"Yes!" she whimpered, as he found the hardened nub of her pleasure. A rush of moisture soaked through the fabric of her drawers, landing proof to her declaration.

With maddening gentleness, he stroked her, his skilled hands ravishing her most sensitive place until she moaned her urgent need. Breathlessly, she pulsed against him, the answering thrusts of her pelvis keeping perfect time to the erotic motion of his fingers.

"Jake! I need . . ." Frantically, she increased the tempo of her hips, rubbing her swollen flesh hard against his hand. His intimate caresses sent her soaring toward heaven, straining for rapture, her body screaming for the climax just out of her reach.

"Tell me what you need, Mission Lady," he purred. God! How he loved the feel of her, so sweet and yielding. It took all his control not to plunge into her warmth and spend himself in one violent stroke.

"Paradise!" Hallie whimpered. "Take me to paradise!" And as his stroking became more insistent, more coaxing, the coiling heat in her belly exploded, and with a shuddering cry she found her paradise. Over and over again, her pleasure peaked, forcing her to grasp his shoulders for support beneath the soul-shattering intensity of her release.

As the last thundering crash of her ecstasy subsided,

Hallie's knees buckled and she would have collapsed if Jake hadn't caught her.

Almost frantic with his own aching need, Jake swept his wife into his arms and carried her to the bed. In one quick motion, he divested her of her drawers.

He hesitated for a moment as his hands hovered over her white silk stockings. He liked the way they clung to the slender contours of her legs and with a roguish grin, he decided to leave them. It made his groin surge with excitement to imagine those silk-clad legs wrapped around his hips as he took her. Experimentally, he ran his hand down the length of her thigh, enjoying the way she moaned in response.

Still moaning, Hallie reached up and unbuttoned Jake's trousers. His arousal was so intense that his sex was straining hard against his muscular belly. As she slipped his pants down to his knees, she pulled him onto the bed and then rolled over on top of him, straddling his thighs. Impatiently, she tugged off his boots, tossing them across the room. With a kick, Jake sent his trousers flying after his boots.

"Oh, no," Hallie murmured, trying to wrestle his hands to the mattress as he reached up to touch her. "It's my turn now, and I expect you to lie still while I have my way with you." Lightly, she teased the hair on his belly, tickling lower and lower until she touched the thatch of dark hair at the apex of his thighs.

With a primitive half-growl, half-groan, Jake surrendered to Hallie's loving ministrations. Down her fingers slipped, stroking his groin and lightly tracing the junction of his thighs. He gasped and squirmed uncontrollably, sobbing as she teased the flesh of his inner thigh, maddened with urgency as she touched him everywhere except where he ached the most.

"Touch me!" he begged, as she spread his legs wide apart and lay on her belly between them, tenderly kissing the scar on his thigh. Dear God! He'd die if she didn't relieve him soon. He ached worse than when he'd been a youth and had snuck into a bawdy show with two of his friends.

Jake groaned and thrashed his hips. "Sweetheart, please!" he cried hoarsely. She was lying between his legs, her chin propped up on his thigh, staring at his hardness.

"Please, what?" she prompted. "Tell me what you want."

He jerked his pelvis frantically. "Touch me! Please . . . release me."

Her hand traveled inward. "Touch you . . . like this?" He cried out as her fingers encircled his shaft. Lightly, she traced his length with her thumb, studying his frenzied response.

He gasped and moved against her. This was worse, far worse. She was tormenting him, touching him like that!

Suddenly Jake felt her move nearer, felt her warm breath fan across his inflamed sex and he knew what she meant to do. The thought made him freeze.

"No!' he choked, as she tentatively tasted him. "Don't! I can't . . ." He tried to squirm away, certain that his sex would shrivel, terrified that any moment he would hear Serena's cruel taunts and mocking laughter.

"Relax, darling," Hallie murmured, firmly bracing his hips between her hands, steadying him.

"Hallie . . ." He couldn't bear it. He tried to shrink from her, to escape, but she merely clutched his hips tighter.

"I want to taste you. To give you the same pleasure you give me when you use your mouth." Boldly, she nipped at his silky tip. "I love you, Jake." She nipped him again.

A sob escaped him as Jake felt his manhood surge beneath her exquisite probing, and his back arched involuntarily in response. He trusted Hallie and to his astonishment, he liked what she was doing to him. It felt . . . wonderful.

Then her lips encircled him, fully engulfing him.

"Hallie!" he screamed, thrusting his pelvis up to meet her. And as she moved down his shaft, Jake's groin muscles tightened and he lost himself in the violence of his release. Never had his man's flesh felt so deliciously sensitive as it did at that moment, never had his climax been so blinding in its intensity.

Every fiber of his body was alive with pleasure and his blood pounded in his head. Mindlessly, he was caught up in the whirling vortex of his all-consuming passion.

And his cries resounded through the room, cries of victory as he conquered the last of his crippling demons.

Jake groaned one last time as he collapsed against the mattress. Spent, he surrendered to his delicious lethargy.

"Hallie?" Drowsily, he opened one eye to watch as she cleansed him of his spilled seed. "I never thought I'd be able to bear being pleasured like that again. But I liked the way it felt when *you* did it to me."

"And I liked doing it to you."

"I'll never be able to look at this bed again without thinking about how good you made me feel. Thank you."

Hallie set aside the towel and stared down at the magnificent man stretched before her. As impossible as it seemed, he had grown even handsomer during the months they'd been married. She reached down and rubbed her hand against his sculpted chest. He smiled and drew her into his arms.

Contentedly, she curled up next to him.

"I was born in this bed, as was my mother," Jake explained, coiling one of Hallie's bright curls around his finger. "This furniture is one of the few things I have left to remember her by. She gave it to me when I came to California, saying that I'd need a proper bed if I found a bride out here. Most of our keepsakes were destroyed when our New York house burned." His voice caught. "It was the same fire that killed my parents."

Hallie's heart went out to him. She knew how wrenching it was to lose everything, and she said as much.

"Poor Mission Lady," he murmured, kissing the top of her head. "You truly did lose all your keepsakes. At least I still have my mother's furniture and my father's watch."

"The musical watch?"

"Yes." With a contented smile, Jake rested his cheek against his wife's hair. "On my parents' wedding trip to Vienna, they became enamored of the waltzing gardens. They claimed they spent every evening dancing beneath the stars. Their favorite waltz was "Invitation to the Dance." So for their first anniversary, my mother commissioned a watch that played the tune. She said that every time my father opened the case, he would be reminded that he was on her mind."

"They must have been very much in love," Hallie whispered, glancing up at her husband's handsome face. By his expression she could see that his thoughts were a million miles away.

"Yes. My parents had a very happy marriage. My father would open the watch case and dance my mother around the room to the melody. As I got older, I remember hoping that someday I too would find such joy with a woman." He looked down into Hallie's upturned face. "This time, I think I've succeeded."

"We'll find our joy together," she declared, lightly kissing his lips.

His expression grew tender as he returned her kiss. "And what about you, sweetheart? Surely you have some happy memories?"

She glanced away from his loving gaze with a shrug. "Very few. Every time my mother tried to do something special for me, my father ruined it."

"I can't imagine what possessed your mother to marry such an unfeeling beast. I remember her as being an intelligent woman."

"He was handsome and my mother fell in love with his pretty face. I suppose he was charming enough when he courted her. After all, he was penniless and she was a wealthy heiress." Hallie sighed. "He detested me from the beginning, saying that with my whey-faced looks he'd be saddled with me for the rest of his life. He made me feel worthless . . . unlovable. The only reason he let me go to medical school was because he saw it as a chance to get rid of me."

"Miserable bastard! I'm half tempted to go to Philadelphia and wring his neck."

"He *was* a miserable bastard. Still, he was right about my not being beautiful. I've seen myself in the mirror."

Jake raised his brows in wonder. "And what did you see?"

"My nose is too long."

"Ridiculous," he protested. "It's just the right length for about—" he kissed down her nose. "Three kisses. In my opinion, a three-kiss nose is perfect."

She smiled at his fanciful remark. "My hair is too red and too curly."

He twisted his hands through the coppery length and squinted at it, his expression serious. "I happen to like your hair. It reminds me of the autumn leaves, warm and vibrant. Besides," he pressed her curls to his nose and sniffed, "it smells good."

"My jaw is too square."

"Stubborn, maybe. But then, I like a woman with a mind of her own."

"My mouth is too wide."

"Your mouth is amazing, as you so recently proved. And beautiful too." Jake gave her lips a lingering kiss. "And sweet. I'm a lucky devil to have a wife with such an excellent mouth."

Hallie shook her head, giggling. "Now I know you're teasing me. Excellent mouth, indeed!"

"Look at me, Sweetheart." He cupped her chin in his hand and forced her to look at him. "Do I strike you as the type of man who would settle for anything less than the best?"

That was true. Jake did have high standards in everything. "No. But—"

"No 'buts' about it," he interjected, shaking his head. "You are the best and I'm lucky to have you. Don't you know that I grow breathless every time I look at you? That I'm dumbfounded by your beauty? Your kindness warms me and your intelligence pleases me. You're the most worthwhile person in the world, and I'm proud to call you wife."

"Not nearly as proud as I am to claim you as my husband," she whispered, wrapping her arms around his torso in a fierce hug. "I'm almost glad my father was such a beast. If he hadn't moved his mistress into my mother's house, I never would have answered Davinia's advertisement for a lady doctor. And if I hadn't come to San Francisco, I never would have met you. I can't imagine what it would have been like living without your love."

Jake crushed Hallie close and kissed the top of her head. For a long moment he just held her, enjoying her closeness. He couldn't imagine living without her love either. Finally he asked. "Is there anything you want from your Philadelphia home? Something special you had to leave behind?"

She toyed with his chest hair as she considered his question. "My dowry," she finally answered. "Right after we were married, I wrote a letter to my father's solicitor informing him that I'd married and requesting my dowry." Hallie shook her head. "I received a reply just this morning. It seems my father told him that I'd been murdered here in San Francisco and claimed Sinclair Mines for his own. The man thinks I'm a fraud."

"Sinclair Mines are your dowry?" Jake choked out. If that was true, he had married a very wealthy heiress.

She nodded. "And the foundries as well. My great-grandmother, Jane Sinclair, who founded the operation, decreed that they were to be passed from mother to daughter upon the death of the former. She said that every woman deserved to have something of her own, some kind of security."

"Freethinking woman, wasn't she?" chuckled Jake. "Just like her marvelous great-granddaughter."

"As are all the women in my family," Hallie replied impishly. "And we all love those mines. In my case, since my mother died so young, the mines were to be passed to me upon my marriage or my thirtieth birthday, whichever came first. It's all stated in the will. Unfortunately, my father has different plans. You see, my mother was an only child, as am I, and if I were to die, the mines would revert to him. And since no one has seen me in almost a year, well, everyone believes my father's claims."

"I'm happy to have you with or without the mines, sweetheart." It was true, for she was his greatest treasure. Jake stared down into his wife's eyes. They were the color of fine cognac, and their expression of love warmed him inside every bit as much as drinking a snifter of the potent liquor. "I have plenty of money for both of us, and it pleases me to take care of you. However, seeing how much the mines mean to you, I'll see to it that you get your dowry. All the monies will be yours to spend as you see fit."

"I love you, Jake Parrish!" Hallie exclaimed, covering his face with kisses. "Thank you! The mines have been in the family for three generations, and it would break my heart to see them fall into uncaring hands."

Jake caught her face between his hands, studying it intently. "I'm sorry that I'll never be able to give you a daughter to inherit your mines."

"Perhaps you will."

He stared at her bleakly. How he wished that was true. Not a day went by that he didn't bitterly curse his inability to plant a child in her womb. Sometimes, when he saw Hallie frolicking with Ariel, he wondered if he'd been fair in marrying her. It cut him deeply, knowing what she'd sacrificed for him.

With a heavy sigh, he looked away. "You know I can't—"

"—perhaps you can," she interjected. Reaching beneath the pillow, she pulled out the pessary. Her eyes glowed with anticipation as she explained the purpose of the device.

Jake took the contraceptive from her and stared at it for a moment, his emotions warring within him. With a vile curse, he flung it across the room.

"Damn her! All these years of hating myself for my inadequacies, feeling emasculated . . ." He sprang from the bed and began to pace the length of the room, the muscles bunching and releasing beneath his skin like those of a restless panther ready to pounce.

"How she must have hated me!" he ground out. "And what a fool I was! I actually believed that she loved me once, that she wanted my child." Jake smashed his fist against the marble mantle, painfully splitting his knuckles. Drawing a ragged breath, he buried his face in his hands.

"But she did love you," Hallie whispered, moving over to where he stood. Twining her arms around his waist and drawing him close, she added, "Don't you know how impossible it is not to love you?" She rubbed her cheek against his chest.

"I would hardly call letting me believe that I was inadequate a gesture of love," he snorted. "Do you know how demoralizing it's been, thinking that my seed was worthless? That I was less than a man?"

"Poor love. Of course, it's been awful," she cooed, forcing his anger-stiffened body closer. "But I don't think she prevented conception out of a sense of spite or cruelty. Not at first."

"Really?" He snorted again. "What's your theory, pray tell?"

"She was afraid."

"Of what, for God's sake?"

"Of dying in childbirth." Hallie felt Jake's muscles flex slightly at her pronouncement. Soothingly, she stroked the long line of his back. "During one of her bad spells, Serena believed that she was a child again. She huddled in her bed crying and clasping her hands to her ears, begging me to make her mother stop screaming. After she regained her lucidity, she explained that her mother had died trying to give birth to a stillborn baby. She told me she'd always feared giving birth, afraid that she too would die."

Jake pulled away from Hallie's comforting embrace and walked over to the bay window. Silently, he stared into the lengthening shadows of the coming night. At long last he spoke "If only she'd trusted me enough to confess her fears. I would have understood. I knew how her mother had died, but when I mentioned a child of our own, she seemed pleased by the idea."

"I think she truly wanted your child, but was too afraid to take the risk." Hallie moved to stand beside her husband. Taking his hands in hers, she whispered, "Perhaps in time, she would have let herself conceive. Or at least confessed her fears."

Jake gave the hands holding his a squeeze. Looking deeply into Hallie's eyes, he asked, "And do you have any such fears?"

"My only fear is that someday you might cease to love me."

"Never!" he growled, yanking her down onto the wide window seat and holding her close.

"Good," she murmured. "Because there's nothing I want more than to give you children. At least a dozen, which should be plenty to breathe life into this big house."

"And I'll enjoy making every one of them." Jake laughed, kissing the tip of her nose.

Hallie moved to straddle Jake's lap and twined her

arms around his neck. Moving her face close to his, she whispered, "I love you, Jake."

Jake stared into her eyes, mesmerized by the emotion blazing in their depths. "And you are, indeed, the woman of my heart." Then he claimed her lips in a sweeping kiss.

As their kiss deepened, Hallie could feel his manhood stiffen against her woman's flesh. Gently, she rubbed against him in response.

Groaning, Jake undulated his pelvis in sensual reply. He found the idea of taking his wife while she sat straddled across his lap highly provocative.

Hallie broke off the kiss as he tried to penetrate her. "What's this? Randy again already?" she murmured, reaching down to position his sex at her feminine opening.

Inflamed by Hallie's touch, Jake thrust his pelvis upward and impaled her. "Just thought we should get a start on those twelve children," he replied wickedly.

Chapter 26

"Fair as the moon, clear as the sun," the man murmured, his gaze leisurely sweeping the length of the woman's nude body. "Thy neck is as a tower of ivory; thine eyes like the fishpools in Heshbon. Thy two breasts," his lips curved into a sensual smile, "are like young roes that are twins, which feed among the lilies."

He leaned back against the Venetian dressing table and shifted his gaze downward to contemplate the woman's softly rounded belly. Inspired by its perfection, he lifted his glass in salute, quoting, "Thy navel is like a round goblet which wanteth not liquor." As he took a sip of strong claret, he looked yet lower, letting his gaze caress the voluptuous curve of her hips and skim the satiny length of her thighs. They too were flawless. With a rapturous sigh, he added, "The joints of thy thighs are like jewels, the work of the hands of a cunning workman."

Lying there in the middle of the bedroom floor, her skin moonlight pale and gleaming with the waxen sheen of a newly opened calla lily, Arabella Dunlap was so very beautiful in death.

The man tapped his thumb spasmodically against the delicate stem of his glass and tilted his head to one side, critically surveying his latest victim.

With her shapely legs carelessly thrown apart and her head pillowed on the ebony silk of her unbound hair, she reminded him of an erotic carved-ivory figurine he'd once seen in a Chinese curiosity shop.

Just remembering that figurine was enough to make his pulse quicken and his breath come out in shallow gusts. Sweet, shameless Arabella! She had been his living incarnation of the lewdly posed ivory lady . . . so wanton, so exquisite in her wickedness. A temptress with the flesh of an angel and the soul of a whore.

Lust not after her beauty in thine heart, he cautioned himself, shuddering at the sudden, fierce clenching of his loins. *For he that committeth fornication sinneth against his own body.*

Emitting a tormented moan, he pushed away from the dressing table and stalked over to the prone figure on the floor. With glass still in hand, he knelt by her side. It was such a pity he'd had to kill her. In his own way, he had loved her. Trembling with something strangely akin to grief, he reached out and gently traced the shape of her parted lips.

Shall I come unto you with a rod, or in love? she had purred, pursing those red lips with seductive query.

Bowing his head in shame, his reply had never varied. *A rod is for the back of him that is void of understanding. Thou shalt beat me with the rod, and shalt deliver my soul from hell.*

Grief choked the man like a fist to the throat, and the forgotten glass of claret slipped from his now slack fingers. The wine, expensive and darkly garnet in hue, splashed across the bright vermilion carpet, a monochromatic contrast to the drying crimson of Arabella's spilled blood.

How he would miss her ministrations, miss the bite of the switch and his own glorious response. How he would miss the feel of her silk-clad hands coaxing him to his final release.

Unlike the other women he'd been with, Arabella had understood his special needs. She had understood that the flaccidity of his sex stemmed not from a lack of desire, but from the shame and guilt he felt over his own carnal appetites. Most important, she had understood his need to be punished for the weakness of his flesh.

But it was necessary to kill her, he reminded himself. Her death was the final sacrifice in his crusade to right the terrible wrong done to him. And soon, very soon, sweet vengeance would be his. The reminder of his imminent victory was enough to chase away the sting of his regret.

With the reverence of a knight paying homage to his liege, the man lifted Arabella's scarlet-gloved hand to his lips and kissed her palm, unmindful that the fabric was sticky with his own spilled seed. He remained in that position for a very long time, safe in the knowledge that he had slipped into the house unnoticed, and aware that the servants knew better than to invade the sanctity of their mistress's bedroom unbidden.

It wasn't until after he'd whispered a lengthy benediction that he gently dropped her hand back to the floor and started to rise. Then he stopped abruptly, half crouched over her lifeless body. In one smooth motion he stripped off her soiled glove.

It bore the shameful testimony of his lust, it bespoke of sin. It was an abomination before the eyes of God, and therefore must be destroyed.

It was a beautiful afternoon, with the sun beaming down like a cheerful smile and the breeze as gentle as the stirring from a butterfly's wings. Colors, more vivid and prismatic than the paint on an artist's palette, surrounded Hallie, mingling to create a collage of striking splendor.

During the months since her marriage, Hallie had taken pleasure in restoring Serena's garden, and now, on the last day of May, her efforts were gloriously apparent.

Deep pink Sweetbriar roses nestled against creamy white Damasks, while pale yellow English Ramblers wept cascades of blossoms, creating a muted backdrop for the riotously blushed crimson Chinas. Centifolias of pale pink and Mosses tinted a rare deep purple merged amidst a hundred different varieties of roses, all abloom in a blaze of color.

Wielding a pair of clippers, Hallie now busied herself with the taming of an errant rosebush which was threatening to obscure the garden path. Today, however, her mind wasn't on her gardening. It was on one of her patients, a prostitute who had been viciously beaten and almost strangled.

The woman lay near death, her once pretty face savaged beyond recognition and her throat ringed with bruises—bruises that mirrored the unique, pendantlike configuration found on the necks of both Cissy and Serena after they'd been attacked.

Hallie tossed aside a bush clipping with a shudder.

What had shocked her most were the woman's gloves. They had been perfect replicas of the red silk ones Serena had so loved, identical right down to the faux diamond buttons at the wrist closures.

Cissy had also identified them as being like the ones she'd been asked to wear by her attacker, as had several of the other girls who had also serviced the depraved stranger.

Yet no one had seen hide nor hair of the man in question since the night Cissy was beaten, and the police, who shrugged him off as just another dissatisfied customer, had never bothered to investigate the incident. However, when this latest victim had turned up in a respectable part of town, lying half dead in the gutter, they had been forced to take an interest.

Jake, too, had taken notice. After being told about the gloves, he began to suspect, as did Hallie, that the same fiend who had assaulted the prostitutes had killed Serena.

So strong were his suspicions that he now accompanied Hallie on her rounds to the brothels, questioning the madames and the girls, searching for the clues which had evaded him for almost a year. Not surprisingly, the women were more willing to talk to the handsome Jake Parrish than to the police.

Despite the prostitutes' help, Jake was still no closer to discovering the identity of the killer than he had been at the time of Serena's death. There simply seemed to be no connection between her and the other two victims.

At first Jake had thought that Serena's opium addiction might in itself be a clue. After all, somebody had introduced her to the vice, for Jake had known Serena to be surprisingly naive about the darker aspects of life.

Yet everyone close to the other victims had vehemently denied his suggestion that the women had had a weakness for the drug. It appeared that despite their unsavory profession, the prostitutes who had been assaulted were a surprisingly clean-living pair. Both were said to be teetotalers and regular attendees of the Ascension Tabernacle. Of course, as Coralie LaFlume had observed wryly, the women's piety stemmed more from their fascination with Reverend DeYoung than with any real desire for redemption.

"Damn!" Hallie swore as she pricked her thumb on a thorn. Sucking on her finger to ease the pain, she stood back to survey her handiwork.

"Hallie!"

Hallie looked up to see Penelope scampering down the garden path, the laughing Ariel bouncing in her arms. Both woman and child wore straw hats which were extravagantly trimmed with a bounty of silk flowers. Jake had brought the hats home as May Day tokens, one each for Hallie and Penelope, and a miniature version for the baby.

"Celine said you needed to speak with me?" Penelope was panting, breathless from having run across the wide lawn.

"Yes," Hallie replied, taking Ariel from Penelope. After depositing a kiss on the baby's cheek, she set her on a soft patch of grass to play. "I thought you might be interested in hearing about my morning medical call."

Penelope dropped to the ground next to Ariel. "Not another one of those prostitutes? I do wish you'd be more careful where you go. I worry about you going to those wretched areas of town at all hours of the day and night."

"I'm safe enough. Jake or one of the footmen always accompanies me." Hallie smiled, touched by the girl's concern. She'd become quite fond of her beautiful sister-in-law during the last few months, and the women were now fast friends. Because of their friendship, Penelope had taken an interest in the new Mission House that Jake had built, and she now spent two afternoons a week teaching the Chinese girls deportment.

"I did check on the girl who was beaten two nights ago," Hallie added as an afterthought. "But she still hasn't regained consciousness."

"It must be awful to lead such a sordid life," Penelope murmured, gently wrestling a rose from Ariel's hand. The baby was attempting to stuff the whole flower into her mouth.

Immediately, Ariel's fair skin flushed poppy red and her lips began to quiver with anger. She opened and closed her mouth soundlessly a few times before releasing an earsplitting howl.

"Poor Sprite," Penelope cooed, lightly tickling the

baby's stomach. "It must be a trial to have such a horrid Auntie." She pulled a silly face and made a growling noise, comically pretending to be the mean auntie in question.

Ariel stared up at her aunt with surprise, her shrieks momentarily reduced to a mewling whimper. Growling again, Penelope swooped down and covered the baby's small face with kisses, not stopping until her sounds of distress had dissolved into chortles of delight.

"If only the proper Princess P's beaux could see her now," chuckled Jake, pausing just beneath the arched opening of the garden to stare at his sister.

It was hard to believe that this charming hoyden, her hair tumbling down her back and her white muslin gown grass-stained from playing with his daughter, was the same waspish girl of just four months ago. Yet Penelope seemed truly happy these days, something she hadn't been since their parents had died. Her happiness, like his own, had blossomed in the sunshine of Hallie's caring presence.

At the sound of her father's voice, Ariel held out her arms, squealing her delight. It was obvious that she adored her father, a feeling which was returned tenfold. Hallie smiled as Jake strode over to the baby. She couldn't recall the last time she had seen a man as crazy about an infant as Jake was about his daughter.

Sweeping Ariel up into his arms, Jake tossed her in the air, quipping, "What have we here?" Catching her tiny form easily, he held the baby high above his head, peering into her smiling face with mock suspicion. "Why, I do believe I've captured myself a garden sprite!"

With that, Jake swung her around in the air like a flying fairy, eliciting screams of laughter from Ariel. It was one of their favorite games, and neither ever tired of it.

Finally settling the infant in the crook of his arm, he declared, "Everyone knows that to give a fairy sugar is to ensure good luck for the whole year." He fumbled in his pocket and produced a stick of molasses candy.

"Jake!" Hallie protested, as he stuck the treat into the baby's mouth. "You're going to ruin her teeth giving her sweets."

"All three of them," Penelope added with a giggle, holding up her arms to take Ariel from her brother.

Grinning wickedly, Jake turned to his wife and planted a kiss on her lips. "Jealous, are you?" he teased, enjoying the way Hallie was frowning at his battered face. He'd just returned from boxing with Seth and was looking forward to having his wife fuss over his scrapes. Invariably, her innocent examinations turned into the intimate ones he so enjoyed.

"Never fear." He laughed. "I've got molasses sticks for all my girls." He playfully shoved a candy stick in Hallie's mouth and then bent low to do the same to his sister.

"You're in a happy mood," Penelope observed, daintily licking at her treat. "Considering that your eye and cheek are starting to swell and you've got a nasty cut on your lower lip."

With a raucous whoop, Jake lifted Hallie into the air, sending her candy stick tumbling from her mouth. "That's because I won the boxing match!" Twirling her around, he shouted, "I pummeled Seth from one end of the ring to the other!"

"Poor Seth!" Hallie laughed. Wrapping her arms around Jake's neck, she gave him a gentle kiss, careful not to hurt his torn lip. This was the first time since her husband had been wounded that he'd been able to best Seth in the ring. It was, indeed, a victory to be savored.

"And what would the champion like for a prize?" she whispered, staring into his sparkling green eyes.

Jake arched one dark eyebrow as he returned her gaze. "Perhaps an examination would be in order?" he purred, his meaning abundantly clear.

"For you or for Seth?" Hallie giggled. "It sounds as if you left poor Seth in dire need of medical care."

"Seth can find his own lady doctor," Jake growled, nipping suggestively at her earlobe. "Mine is going to be occupied for the rest of the afternoon."

Penelope cleared her throat, coyly reminding the pair of her presence. Jake and Hallie were always touching and kissing, and though it warmed her heart to see the two people she loved most so happy, she sometimes found their behavior a bit embarrassing.

"Jake!" Penelope admonished, shaking a finger at her

grinning brother. "Hallie wanted to tell me something important."

"Oh, yes! I was going to . . . Jake!" Hallie squealed, pushing her husband's roving hands away from her waist. "Behave yourself! I need to tell Penelope about my morning call."

Jake groaned. "Appetizing thought! Did you do some particularly fancy suturing? Or did you cut into some poor wretch's body?"

"Neither." Hallie laughed and gave her husband's backside a playful swat. He jumped and let out an exaggerated yelp, pretending he'd been gravely wounded by her blow.

Hallie smiled at his lighthearted antics before turning her attention back to Penelope. "Madame de Sonennes tripped over a sandbag while she was rehearsing for this evening's performance. She hurt her ankle, and in order to preserve her modesty, the theater owner contacted me to tend her."

"Madeleine de Sonennes? The singer?" Penelope choked. The world-famous Madame de Sonennes was in San Francisco to perform in a musical production titled *Gold Rush Nell*. Penelope practically worshiped the singer and had already been to see the operetta twice.

"The very same," Hallie replied, grinning at the girl's moonstruck expression. "She told me that the girl singing the ingenue's part is leaving the company to get married and they're frantic to find a replacement. I suggested you."

Penelope's mouth dropped open. "M-Me?"

"Yes. You. She'll hear you sing tomorrow if you're interested. And if she likes you, which I'm sure she will, she'll train you for the role herself."

"Interested!" Penelope screamed, hurling herself into Hallie's arms to give her a hug. "Of course I'm interested! Oh, Hallie! I do love you! Did you hear that, Jake?"

"I couldn't help but hear," Jake chuckled, jokingly rubbing his ears as if Penelope's shrieks had impaired his hearing. Giving his sister an affectionate squeeze, he murmured, "I'll look forward to bragging about my sister, the famous singer."

Suddenly everyone was talking at once, making plans

for Penelope's future and speculating on the scope of her coming fame. Even Ariel got into the act, chortling and waving her chubby fists in the air.

"Mister Jake! Mister Jake!" Hop Yung came tearing around the corner at breakneck speed. "Lawmen here—*pant*—say they take Mister Jake to jail." He skidded to a stop in front of his employer, his chest heaving from exertion.

"What the hell?" Jake expelled, shaking his head at Hallie's questioning stare.

Struggling to catch his breath, Hop merely nodded.

"Darling?"

"Don't worry," Jake murmured, tenderly stroking his wife's cheek. "It's got to be some sort of mistake." Turning back to Hop, he demanded, "Where are the police now?"

Breathlessly, Hop pointed behind him, just as four policemen poured through the small garden gate.

"Mr. Parrish?" snapped a middle-aged officer with steel gray hair and paunchy midsection. "We're here to arrest you for the murder of Arabella Dunlap."

Hallie gasped with shock, while Penelope stared at Jake, dumbfounded. Hop Yung, who had snatched up the now squalling Ariel, scowled at the policemen belligerently.

"On what basis?" Jake asked, taking Hallie's cold hand in his and giving it a reassuring squeeze.

"You were seen leaving Mrs. Dunlap's house this morning shortly before she was discovered dead. She'd been beaten and strangled. She was buck naked except for one red glove." The policeman gave a short laugh. "But you already know the details. By the looks of your face, she must've put up quite a fight."

"Ridiculous!" snorted Penelope, hovering protectively by her brother's side.

Jake stared at the man through narrowed eyes. "And just who are my accusers?"

The officer took out his tablet and shuffled through the pages. "You were seen by two witnesses. A Mr. Cyrus King and a Mrs. Lavinia Donahue. The latter claims that you were a frequent—ahem—visitor of the Widow Dunlap."

"I was at Arabella's this morning," Jake confessed,

aching as Hallie pulled her hand from his and moved away, staring at him with a wounded expression. He took a step toward her, "Hallie—"

"Aha!" interjected the policeman, signaling for his companions to surround their suspect. "So you confess?"

Jake forced his gaze away from his wife's and glared at the officer. "Of course, I didn't kill Arabella! She was very much alive when I left her. Reverend DeYoung can attest to that fact. And you can ask Judge Dorner about my whereabouts the rest of the day. You'll find him at the athletic club having a drink with Seth Tyler, the man who did this to my face."

"Well, until we've spoken to—," The officer paused to look down at his hastily scribbled notes. "Reverend DeYoung, Judge Dorner, and Seth Taylor?"

"Tyler."

"Tyler." The man made the correction. "Well, until we've questioned these men, we'll have to hold you at the jail." He nodded at his companions, who swarmed in and seized their prisoner.

As one of the men clamped irons on his wrists, Jake's gaze sought Hallie's, mutely begging her to have faith in him. But her face was carefully averted, and she refused to look at him.

"Hallie?" he whispered, suddenly terrified, not of the charges brought against him but of the way Hallie had turned away from him. "I—"

His words were cut off as the policemen pushed him toward the gate. Firmly holding his ground, Jake rounded on his captors, snarling, "For God's sake! Have the decency to let me say good-bye to my wife."

The men looked toward their superior, who shrugged and nodded. "One minute."

Yanking himself from the officers' restraint, Jake closed the distance between himself and Hallie in several long strides. She didn't move a muscle, nor did she acknowledge his presence as he reached out to touch her.

"Sweetheart," he murmured, grasping her chin in his palm and forcing her head up.

Hallie focused her gaze on the iron fetters at his wrists, unwilling to look into his eyes. She was numb, frozen inside. *Jake had admitted to seeing Arabella. Her husband had tired of her already.* With a sob, she jerked her face from his hands.

"Fine. Don't look at me," he sighed, hating the way the tears coursed down her cheeks, despising himself for causing them to fall. "Will you just listen to me, then?"

After a moment, she nodded.

It was a start. "First of all, I didn't kill Arabella."

Fixing her gaze on the toes of his boots, Hallie nodded.

"Good," he murmured. "Second. Though I was at her house this morning and have been several times during the last couple of months, there was nothing between us. Not like you're thinking. It was all perfectly innocent. I—"

One of the policemen grabbed Jake's arm and gave it a tug. "Enough. It's time to go now."

"Damn it! I'm not finished!" Jake ground out.

"Hurry it up, then," snapped the superior officer. "We can't wait all day while you try to make up with your missus."

Jake gave the man restraining him a hard shove and pulled himself free. Bending close to Hallie's ear, he whispered, "I love you. Don't you know that I'd never do anything to jeopardize our marriage? I'd kill myself before I'd hurt you."

No reply.

"Sweetheart—" He sighed heavily. His words were falling on deaf ears. "All right. If you won't listen to me, then ask Seth or Marius what I was doing at Arabella's. They'll explain everything. Please ... do it. I love you."

The desperate plea in his voice tore at Hallie's heart. She wanted so badly to believe him. With a sob, she glanced up at him and for a split second, their eyes met. But that second was long enough for Hallie to read the truth. Jake was looking at her with such hurt, such despair, that all her doubts melted away. Only a man truly in love could be so wounded by his woman's abandonment.

As Jake was being escorted through the garden gate, Hallie picked up her skirts and ran to his side. Throwing her arms around her husband's neck, she exclaimed, "I do trust you, darling." With that, she gave him a swift, hard kiss, ignoring the way the pressure of her mouth against his split lip made him wince. "And I love you, too."

"Good," Jake murmured, relief flooding through him. Tenderly, he returned her kiss.

"Enough!" snapped one of the policemen, pushing Hallie aside and giving his prisoner a shove that almost sent him sprawling.

Penelope shrieked her outrage at seeing her brother treated in such a manner and turned to give the man who had pushed him a severe tongue-lashing.

"I'm coming with you!" Hallie shouted above the chaos.

Jake, whose bad leg was beginning to give way from the policemen's constant prodding, was now fighting to keep his balance. He looked over at his wife, and her expression of mulish determination made him smile. How could anything go wrong with Hallie in his corner? Especially when she was looking so hell-bent on fighting for him?

Giving his head a decisive shake, he shouted back, "No. Go find Marius and bring him to the jail." He then turned to the houseboy, who was hovering close to his other side. "Hop! Go to my club and fetch Judge Dorner and Seth."

The little man bobbed his head and raced off across the lawn, Ariel in his arms.

"Penelope?"

Penelope broke off her berating of the policeman long enough to look up at her brother.

"Tell Celine to bake me one of her rhubarb pies. I'm innocent, and I intend to be home in time for dinner."

Chapter 27

The setting sun glimmered through the stained-glass windows, unfurling ribbons of colored light across the pulpit of the Ascension Tabernacle. It was a new church, immense in its proportions and magnificent in its gothic splendor. Even though Hallie had attended services here for months, the grandeur of the sanctuary never failed to take her breath away.

But today, as she rushed down the aisle toward the vestry, she barely spared her surroundings more than a cursory glance.

"Marius!" She knocked once on the office door before pushing it open and entering the room. Like the rest of the church, it was deserted. Snorting her frustration, she walked over to the cluttered desk, hoping to find a clue as to the preacher's whereabouts.

He had obviously left in a hurry, for the ink bottle was uncorked and his pen was lying next to a piece of parchment partially covered with neat writing. Hallie picked up the paper and quickly scanned its contents.

The mean man shall be brought down, and the mighty man shall be humbled.

Sermon notes. It appeared that humility was to be the topic of Sunday's lecture. With a shrug, Hallie let the paper drop from her hand. The parchment rustled softly as it drifted past the edge of the desk, spiraling downward until it came to rest at the corner of the autumn-hued carpet. As she bent forward to retrieve it, the wide expanse of her skirts belled out behind her, upsetting the dustbin beside the desk.

Bang! Whoosh! Rubbish scattered everywhere. Cursing the impracticality of crinolines, Hallie knelt down and began to clean up the mess. As she pitched a sheath of parchments back into the bin, a colorful piece of cloth slipped free. Hallie reached for the scrape and then froze, her hand poised in midair.

It was a scarlet silk glove, rusty with dried blood. Gingerly, she picked it up, grasping an unsoiled edge between her thumb and index finger. Two faux diamond buttons twinkled at the wrist closure, and Hallie could see a small rent in the fabric where the third had been torn away.

She gasped in horror as comprehension dawned. It all made terrible sense now. The common denominator among the murdered women was their interest in Reverend DeYoung. Serena and Arabella had both spent a great deal of time with him, heading up this committee or leading that fund-raiser, and the prostitutes had been openly enamored of the man himself.

Why someone at the church had felt compelled to kill the women was a question Hallie couldn't begin to fathom. She shook her head and hastily stuffed the glove into her reticule. Perhaps the police could figure it out.

As she made to rise to her feet, she heard a creaking sound directly behind her, followed by a soft scraping. With a startled gasp, she swung her head around. But before she could identify the dark figure hovering over her, pain exploded through her head. Then everything went black.

When Hallie regained consciousness, she found herself lying face down on a hard wood-planked floor. Her hands were numb from being tied behind her back, and the corners of her mouth ached from being stretched by the too-tight gag.

Moaning, she rolled onto her side, trying to peer around her. Except for a faint glimmer of light shining beneath a door, she was completely engulfed in darkness. There was a familiar musty smell permeating the space, and as her eyes adjusted to the dimness, she was able to make out the outlines of flat items piled in towering stacks on either side of her.

Hallie sighed. She had no idea where she was. All she knew was that she was cold and stiff, and her legs hurt. Groaning into the gag, she stretched her bound legs, trying to ease the cramps. She succeeded only in toppling one of the piles.

Books, she thought, wincing as she was repeatedly bombarded by falling volumes. Lying half buried beneath what felt like the entire literary collection from the San Francisco library, Hallie now realized where she was. She was in the small room behind the altar where the extra hymnals and seasonal decorations were stored.

"Hallie!"

Hallie's breath caught in her throat as she heard the barely audible syllables of her name penetrating through the door.

"Hallie!"

This time the voice was louder . . . nearer. A whimper escaped her lips.

"Hallie!"

Jake. Hallie's heart surged with relief. Somehow he'd gotten himself released from jail and had known to come for her. Desperately she tried to answer him, to call out, but the gag between her teeth muffled her voice.

"Hallie?"

Jake's voice seemed to be moving away now. *She had to do something . . . give him a sign . . . alert him.*

Panicked, Hallie kicked at the stack of books closest to her feet. Like the walls of Jericho, they came tumbling down, burying her beneath an avalanche of leather and parchment. Stunned and too sore to move, Hallie lay beneath the pile of books, listening.

There was the sound of footsteps hurrying up the altar steps, followed by a rattling at the door. "Sweetheart?"

Hallie gave the fallen books on top of her a violent kick, an act which was duly rewarded with a loud thump.

"Move away from the door and lie flat on the floor," she heard Jake yell. "I'm going to shoot the lock off."

Hallie did as instructed, curling into a tight ball and carefully tucking her face against her chest. After a long moment, she heard the discharge from a gun, and with a splintering crash the lock exploded inward.

Throwing his weight against the door, Jake burst into the room. Wildly he scanned the shadowy cubicle for his wife and when he spied her, an anguished cry escaped his lips.

There, circled in a shaft of light from the open door, was Hallie's still figure. Except for a length of bright hair and a tangle of blue skirts, she was almost completely buried beneath a pile of books. Jake fell to his knees and began to push the books off her body, terrified that she'd been badly injured.

"Sweetheart?" he gently touched her shoulder. To his relief, she raised her head to look back at him, sobbing into the gag.

"Don't cry, Mission Lady. I'm here," he crooned, deftly removing the filthy cloth from between her teeth. Sweeping the rest of the hymnals aside, Jake gathered Hallie into his arms, cradling her close. "Are you hurt anywhere?"

"I hurt everywhere," she replied with a sound halfway between a sob and a hiccup. "But I'll be all right."

Jake crushed her against his chest, groaning. "God! I've never been so afraid in my life as when I returned home from the jail and found you missing."

"Not nearly as afraid as I was when you were arrested. How did you get out of jail?"

"Arabella's cook told the police that he'd spoken to her shortly after I left." Jake turned Hallie onto her belly and draped her across his knees. "The parlor maid confirmed the story. They had no choice but to release me." He gave the knotted rope at her wrists a tug. It loosened slightly.

"When I arrived home, Coralie LaFlume was at the house. The prostitute who was beaten finally regained consciousness, and she was able to identify her attacker." Jake pulled out the last of the knots. "It was Marius."

Hallie lay still for a moment, absorbing the news. "I found the mate to Arabella's glove in Marius's trash bin, but before I could take it to the police, someone hit me from behind." She pointed to the sore spot at the back of her head. "I was knocked unconscious. When I woke up, I was in the closet, tied up."

"Poor sweetheart," Jake whispered, kissing the injured place. "Hop and Coralie have gone for the police. After you've spoken with them, I'm going to take you home and tuck you into bed with a warm brick at your feet." He helped her sit up and then began to untie her ankles.

"I'd rather have you warm me," she murmured, closing her eyes with a sigh as the ropes dropped away.

"And I'd like to warm you," he replied, drawing her back into his embrace. With that, he tipped his head forward and hungrily captured her lips with his. For one brief moment, Jake let himself savor the sweetness of Hallie's kiss, relieved to have her safe and in his arms once again.

Hallie eagerly returned his kiss, a kiss that, in her opinion, was much too brief.

Smiling tenderly at his wife's disappointed expression, Jake explained, "Marius has fled, and I need to help the police find him. I don't want him to have another chance to hurt you."

Hallie curled up in Jake's lap, her head resting on his shoulder. She felt so warm and safe nestled against the muscular strength of his body. "No one can hurt me while I'm in your arms," she sighed, snuggling closer.

"Such a touching display of faith," Marius observed, leveling his pistol at the embracing couple. He didn't miss the way Jake tightened his grip on his wife, nor did he fail to note the man's protective demeanor. *Good. Then the gossip was true. Jake Parrish was madly in love with his wife.* Marius smiled with satisfaction. *It would devastate him to watch her die.*

"Where did you come from, DeYoung?" Jake snapped, glancing around for his gun. "I searched the church thoroughly." Damn! He'd set his pistol by the door when he found Hallie, and it lay just out of his reach.

"Obviously not thoroughly enough," Marius replied coolly.

"Why, Marius?" Hallie whispered, staring up at the man who had always seemed to be the personification of the word "goodness." "I thought we were friends."

"Sometimes friends get in one's way."

Jake subtly shifted Hallie on his lap as he inched toward his gun. Her voluminous skirts camouflaged his motions, and he thanked God for crinoline skirts.

"What do you want, DeYoung?" he ground out, giving Hallie a furtive nudge in the side. She seemed to sense what he was about and moved accordingly.

"Thou shalt give life for life, eye for eye, tooth for tooth, hand for hand, foot for foot, burning for burning, wound for wound, stripe for stripe."

"Stop speaking in riddles."

"Hardly a riddle. But, of course, if you had spent more time at church and less time sniffing after Dr. Gardiner's skirts, you would understand exactly what I mean." The preacher advanced one step forward. "The translation is quite simple: vengeance. I mean to bring you down. To punish you. To make you suffer for the crimes of your blood."

"And what exactly have I done to deserve punishment?"

"He walked in all the sins of his father," quoted Marius, idly tapping his finger against the trigger of the gun. "Are you not the son of Reed Parrish?"

"What has my father got to do with anything?" Jake snaked his hand beneath the fabric of Hallie's outspread skirts, effectively disguising his movement as he reached for his pistol.

"Your father . . . and mine."

That brought Jake up short.

Marius laughed at Jake's shocked expression. "Oh, yes. It's true . . . *brother.* Not that our father ever acknowledged me." His voice seethed with venom. "After all, my mother was just a housemaid, and I was nothing more than the unfortunate result of a youthful indiscretion."

Hallie opened her mouth to speak, but quickly clamped it shut again as Jake gave her a warning squeeze. The way Marius was waving the gun at them terrified her.

"Our grandfather sent his randy son on a grand tour of Europe as *punishment* for his dalliance," the preacher rasped, his handsome face twisting into a mask of bitterness. "As for my mother, she was turned out without a reference."

His voice began to rise, taking on the booming, sonorous quality he used during his most inspirational sermons. "I was born in a New York tenement to a mother forced into prostitution to keep food in her mouth. *You* were born in a mansion to a mother from a wealthy family."

Marius's eyes narrowed as he studied his half brother. "I used to see you riding with your parents in their carriage. You inherited your mother's beauty and our father's arrogance. How I hated you." His voice was soft now. Chillingly so. "Nothing was too good for the mighty Parrish heir . . . the Parrish son. While you spent your early years being loved and coddled, I spent mine in a one-room hellhole trying to make myself invisible while my mother entertained her *friends*."

The sight of his mother pleasuring those men, her hands always clad in scarlet silk gloves, was indelibly etched into his brain. The darker scenes, those filled with horror and degradation, had been ruthlessly locked away in the deepest dungeons of his memory. Memories to be hidden but not forgotten, shackled to his subconscious by his shame.

"By the time I was seven, I knew every perverse sexual act by heart. I'd even experienced a few myself, seeing as how some of the men preferred young boys."

Hallie gasped. "Your mother let them use you so?"

"Gladly," he snapped. "After all, the price for young boys far exceeded that for wornout whores. The money she made from allowing some old reprobate to use me was enough to support her opium habit for a month." He shifted his gaze from Hallie's compassion-filled face to stare down at the gun in his hand. "When I was nine, my mother was murdered. Strangled by a dissatisfied customer."

And he'd felt nothing when he'd found her. By the time he was eight, Marius had taken to roaming the city streets, picking pockets, sometimes staying away from the tenement for days on end. She had been killed during the hottest part of the summer and had lain there for several days before he'd discovered her.

Marius almost gagged as he remembered the smell. Her face had been bloated beyond all recognition, her peeling skin a deep angry purple. On her hands had been the tattered remains of the red gloves with their faux diamond buttons, gloves which had been a gift from his father nine years earlier.

She had been his mother and he'd felt nothing.

After his mother's death, he'd been claimed by his only living relative, an itinerant street preacher by the name of Uriah DeYoung. For the next eight years, young Marius was dragged from town to town, spending his days listening while his uncle preached hellfire and redemption to unrepentant sinners. Marius had quickly learned that the word "hell" was synonymous with night, for it was then that Uriah had turned his attention to the redemption of his nephew's soul, a soul tainted almost beyond salvation by the stain of his bastardy.

In sin did thy mother conceive thee! He that hath suffered in the flesh hath ceased from sin!

Marius's body still bore the scars from his uncle's whip. When he was seventeen, he killed the preacher and escaped back to New York. It was then that he took an interest in seeking vengeance against the mighty Parrish family, intent on making them suffer as he'd suffered. Especially Jake, the favored son.

"Fine," Jake snorted. "You think you have reason to hate me." He was now close enough to the gun for his fingers to graze the handle. "But what reason did you have to kill Serena and Arabella?" His hand brushed against the pistol again, this time it moved, making a loud scraping sound against the wood floor.

That noise was enough to draw Marius's attention. With a bellow of fury, he pulled the trigger of his gun. The crash of the explosion reverberated through the sanctuary, it's deafening roar almost drowning out Jake's cry of pain.

"Jake!" Hallie screamed as she felt her husband's body jerk with the impact of the bullet.

As quick as the lash from a whip, Marius grabbed Jake's gun. Before Hallie could react, she was pulled up against the preacher's body, where he held her immobile, the barrel of Jake's pistol pressed against her temple.

"Damn it, Marius!" Jake shouted, clutching at his wounded shoulder as he struggled to his knees. Luckily, the bullet had merely grazed the upper part of his shoulder. "This is between you and me. Hallie isn't a part of this. Let her go."

"But she's part of you. As were your parents, as was Serena." The preacher cocked his head to one side, his finger tapping spasmodically on the trigger of the pistol. "Killing you outright was never my intention. That would have been too easy. I wanted to make you suffer first. I wanted to rob you of your friends and family, and then strip you of your honor. I started my vengeance by killing your parents . . . my father."

Jake felt as if someone had stabbed him in his belly and was turning the blade with agonizing slowness. His sweet mother and jovial father had been killed because of Marius's misguided sense of vengeance.

"I used dynamite to start the fire, just like I used it on the Mission House. Hallie was supposed to die in the flames." Marius looked down at the woman in his arms and shook his head regretfully. "I hated the idea of killing you, my dear. I actually felt real fondness for you. But you'd had the poor judgment to become enamored with Jake and he with you, so you had to die. I even hit you over the head to ensure that you wouldn't escape. I hadn't counted on your lover's heroics."

"You could have killed everyone in the house!" Hallie gasped.

"Whores." He shrugged dismissively.

"Like the two women you beat and left for dead?" Jake asked, trying to buy time while his mind scrambled for a plan. He had to get that pistol away from Marius. He knew the weapon to have a hair trigger, and it was only a matter of time before the preacher's habit of tapping his finger would discharge it.

Marius smiled coldly. "Cissy was a fool. She didn't know how to satisfy my, shall we say, unique sexual tastes, and therefore she was punished. As for the other woman, she recognized my voice and tried to blackmail me. The greedy bitch said she would tell everyone about my predilection for red silk gloves . . . and other things, if I didn't pay her off. Her, I meant to kill."

"Red gloves? Like the ones found on Arabella and Serena's hands?" Jake narrowed his eyes as he studied Marius's stance. Perhaps he could throw the man off balance and wrest Hallie away. Then he discarded the idea. Marius's finger was too tautly flexed on the gun's trigger to risk it.

"Ah, yes. Sweet Arabella. Now she knew how to satisfy a man." Marius closed his eyes for a moment, remembering how wonderfully deft she had been with a switch. "But, of course, you wouldn't know anything about that, would you?"

Hallie drew in her breath sharply at his words.

"It's true, my dear." The preacher nodded. "Your husband never did anything more provocative with Arabella than dance. She was helping him learn to dance on that gimp leg of his. He wanted to surprise you."

Hallie's heart surged with tenderness at the revelation and, despite the gravity of their situation, she smiled at Jake. Silently, she mouthed the words, "I love you."

Jake nodded, one corner of his mouth curling up at her soundless proclamation. *He loved her, too—too much to let her die at Marius's hands.*

"So sad about Arabella." The preacher sighed as he shifted his attention back to Jake. "But don't you see? I had to kill her. Everyone knew that you were visiting her, and it was assumed that the two of you were having . . . relations. I was presented with the perfect opportunity to bring you down. I tried to make it look like you'd had a lovers' quarrel and that you'd killed her. You would have hung for sure. How I relished the thought of the high and mighty Parrish heir coming to such an ignoble end!"

He tightened his grip on Hallie with a nasty laugh. "Do you want to know what brought me the most pleasure in all of this?"

When Marius received no reply, he laughed again. "Planting a child in Serena's belly. In one of her drug-induced states, she confessed how she'd been preventing the conception of your child. I knew you'd believe that your seed was fruitless when you found her pregnant by another man, and I exalted in your humiliation."

"Damn you to hell, DeYoung!" Jake expelled, his hands curling into fists. If it hadn't been for the gun pressed against Hallie's temple, he'd have killed the man with his bare hands. "I assume it was you who introduced Serena to opium?"

"And morphine as well," chuckled Marius. "I used to make her perform like the lowest of whores to earn her drugs. She became quite adept at satisfying my special needs."

Jake noted then, that in his preoccupation, Marius had let the barrel of the gun slip away from Hallie's head.

"You killed Serena," Jake stated with deadly calm. His muscles tensed as he prepared to spring.

"I destroyed Serena's mind and, yes, then I killed her.

In her half-witted state, she'd become dangerous. She talked too freely. Now you're going to watch while I kill Hallie."

With a feral growl, Jake lunged forward, hurling himself against Hallie. Just as she was thrown to the floor, the report of a gun roared through the sanctuary.

"Jake!" Hallie screamed, as a spray of gore splattered everywhere. In one frantic motion, she rolled onto her back, only to find Marius looming over her. She stared up at him for a second, too horrified to move. Then something deep inside of her snapped, and she began to scream uncontrollably.

Torrents of crimson blood streamed over bone fragments of gleaming white, springing like a fountainhead from the gaping wound in the center of the preacher's forehead. His mouth, drawn into a twisted smile, was opening and closing as if he was trying to speak. For a long moment, his wrathful gaze bore into hers. Then his eyes rolled up, and there was a hideous *thump! thump!* as his body tumbled backward down the altar stairs.

"Hush, sweetheart," Jake whispered, pulling her into his arms. He winced violently at the pain from his wounded shoulder, but no amount of pain was going to make him release his Hallie.

Hugging his wife protectively, Jake focused his attention on the tattered-looking man standing at the bottom of the stairs. For a moment, the man seemed frozen in place. Then he shifted his grief-filled gaze from the corpse at his feet and stared back at Jake. Neither man spoke.

Serena's eyes, Jake thought, noting the intense cerulean hue of the man's eyes. Poor Serena. She had been an instrument of Marius's vengeance, a victim to be pitied and forgiven. And in his heart, he did forgive her.

Slowly Jake nodded his thanks to Serena's father. "We owe you our lives, King."

"All these months of hating you . . . watching and waiting for the opportunity to avenge my daughter's death. I followed you here to kill you. And now . . ." with a sob, Cyrus dropped his spent pistol and buried his face in his hands. "Dear God! I almost killed an innocent man."

"That's all in the past now," Jake said. "It's over."

Cyrus took out a grubby cloth and wiped his eyes. "Yes. Over," he repeated, giving his head a rueful shake. "When I think of how I've wasted the last few years . . . hating you . . . making Serena hate you as well." He let his gaze drift to the preacher's body. "Perhaps if I hadn't poisoned her against you, she wouldn't have fallen prey to DeYoung's evil. Perhaps—"

"Perhaps," Jake interjected gently, "it's time to start your life anew. I have." He nodded meaningfully down at Hallie, who was busy frowning at his wounded shoulder.

"But how? My whole purpose in life was to take care of Serena. After she died, that purpose shifted to killing you. There's nothing left for me."

"There's your granddaughter. She's very like Serena."

"Yes. I've seen her." Cyrus's eyes took on a faraway look. "She's beautiful. How I've longed to dandle her on my knee."

"Then why don't you?"

Cyrus's mouth dropped open. "You'd let me?"

"Ariel is quite the little glutton when it comes to attention." Jake chuckled. "I'm sure she'd love having a doting grandfather. And if you'll let me, I'd like to help you start your life over again. I think we owe it to Serena's memory, and to your granddaughter—*ouch*!"

Hallie momentarily ceased prodding at her husband's wound to meet his resentful stare. "I know it hurts, darling," she scolded in her no-nonsense doctor's voice. "But the wound is nasty and it needs tending. It should be cleaned and stit—"

But before she could finish uttering the dreaded word, Jake clamped his lips over hers and kissed her, effectively banishing all thoughts of medicine from her mind.

Epilogue

I'm going to miss her." Hallie nodded toward Penelope, who stood surrounded by a bevy of admirers. As she had predicted, Madame de Sonennes had been enchanted by the girl and had given her the ingenue's role in *Gold Rush Nell.* The theatrical troupe was leaving San Francisco at the end of the week, and a ball was being held in Penelope's honor.

"It seems as if you're not alone in that sentiment," Seth replied, staring moodily at Jake's little sister. "The girl's leaving half the pups in San Francisco brokenhearted."

"And how's your heart doing?" Hallie inquired gently. She hadn't missed the way Seth had taken to lingering around the Parrish house, anxiously trying to catch a glimpse of Penelope, nor had she failed to note the way his face lit up when the girl finally appeared.

Her observation startled Seth's gaze away from Penelope. Grinning sheepishly, he asked, "Is it that obvious?"

"Only to those who care to notice." She laughed, giving his arm a gentle pinch. "Have you told her of your feelings yet?"

"No. It wouldn't be fair to burden her so, especially since she's leaving in a few days." He paused to scowl at a youth who had seized the laughing Penelope's hand and was playfully kissing her palm. It took all his willpower not to grab the young fool by the scruff of his neck and drag him outside to teach him a much-needed lesson in manners.

When had he become so possessive toward Jake's sister? he wondered. For the first time in his life, Seth Tyler felt jealousy over a woman, and he didn't like the feeling one bit.

"I'll speak to her when she returns home," he promised, more to himself than to Hallie.

If she returns home, Hallie added silently. If Madame Sonennes could be believed, Penelope had a bright future on the stage. Depending on the success of her first tour, it could be months, or even years, before the girl returned to San Francisco.

Seth and Hallie stood in companionable silence for a few minutes watching the colorful swirl of dancers glide by, both deep in thought. He, wondering if Penelope's lips tasted as sweet as they looked; she, looking forward to sitting at Jake's feet while he gently brushed her hair; both beginning to feel the fatigue from the long evening. It was past midnight, and thankfully the ball was drawing to an end.

"Wonderful party, my dear," boomed Davinia, moving to stand between Hallie and Seth. Looping her arms through theirs, she nodded at Penelope. "Going to miss that girl. She's become quite popular at the Mission House, you know." She slanted a knowing look up at Seth. "Bet I'm not the only one who's going to miss her, eh, Seth?"

Seth groaned. "Is there anyone who hasn't noticed?"

Davinia screwed up her face in an expression of fierce concentration as she considered the question. "Well. I doubt if old Elias Winthrop has noticed. Of course, he *is* blind and deaf."

Seth groaned again as he flushed a brilliant shade of crimson. Focusing his gaze on the floor, he mumbled something about needing a drink and wandered off in the general direction of the buffet table.

"Good-looking fellow, that Seth," mused Davinia, letting her gaze slide down Seth's retreating back to stare at his hindquarters. Damn those tailcoats anyways! They concealed far too much of a man's finest physical attribute.

Sighing her disappointment, Davinia turned her attention back to Hallie. "Not as handsome as that husband of yours, mind you, but then, it wouldn't be fair to compare any man with him."

Hallie glanced at Jake, who was talking to several of his business associates on the other side of the room. Davinia was right, he was impossibly handsome. So much so that she often felt drab in comparison—rather like a peahen next to a peacock.

Yes. But he's my peacock, she told herself, grinning wickedly as she eyed his expensive suit. And she was looking forward to plucking those fine feathers off his magnificent body!

As if he had sensed his wife's naughty thoughts, Jake looked up. For a moment, their eyes met, his smoldering gaze full of sensual promise. Very slowly, his lips curved into a smile, and even across the distance she could feel the impact of his magnetism.

What he did to her! Her heart was turning crazy flip-flops in her chest, and just looking at him filled her mind full of unladylike notions. Hallie snapped open her fan and began to fan herself frantically. Had the room suddenly grown warm?

Hope no one lights a match. Davinia chuckled to herself. Not with the way the sparks were flying between the Parrishes. There was enough heat in their gazes to catch a flame and burn the house to a cinder.

Clearing her throat to draw Hallie's attention, Davinia commented, "The new preacher for the Ascension Tabernacle is supposed to arrive next week. Bringing a wife and nine children with him. Solid sort of man."

"Um . . . yes." Hallie reluctantly drew her gaze away from her husband to glance at Davinia. "Uh—I hear his background is impeccable. He spent seven years . . ."

But her friend no longer appeared interested in discussing the new preacher. She was staring at something across the room, her eyes bulging slightly beneath her glasses, her expression dreamy. Curiously, Hallie followed her gaze. One of the gentlemen had bent over to retrieve a lady's glove, thus presenting a good view of his well-rounded, wool-clad buttocks.

"Durn fine backside," Davinia mumbled to herself. From the posterior view, the man reminded her of her dear departed husband, John. How she missed him!

As the man straightened up, and presented the woman with her glove, Hallie saw that it was Cyrus King. "You remember Serena's father, don't you?" she asked, grinning at her friend's besotted expression.

"That's Cyrus King?" exclaimed Davinia so loudly that several people turned to stare. "Hell and damnation! I never would've guessed that the man would clean up so well."

Hallie nodded her agreement. "He's working for Jake now. Jake says he's got a wonderful head for the shipping business." Neatly dressed in evening attire, Cyrus did look quite distinguished.

"If you don't mind, I think I'll go reacquaint myself with Mr. King."

And as Davinia moved toward Cyrus, who was standing awkwardly against the far wall, Hallie could have sworn she heard her friend mumble something about being able to judge the nobility of a man's character by the shape of his backside.

Perhaps there is some truth to that, she thought wickedly. After all, Jake *did* have a particularly nice backside and his character *was* noble. Smiling to herself, Hallie looked back to where her husband had been standing.

He was gone. She scanned the crowds, looking for him, but he was nowhere in sight. The orchestra was beginning to play the last dance of the evening, a waltz, and Hallie sighed when she heard the selection.

"Invitation to the Dance."

"Mrs. Parrish?" It was Teddy Carruthers. "May I have this dance?"

Hallie nodded and presented him with her hand.

"Excuse me." Jake sketched an elegant bow and took his wife's hand from Teddy's. "I believe this last dance is mine."

Teddy bowed and moved away, smiling.

"Are you sure, darling?" Hallie whispered, anxiously staring up into her husband's handsome face.

"Never surer," he replied, leading her out to the dance floor. As he placed one hand on his wife's waist and then took her hand in his other one, Jake forced himself to take a deep breath. It was now or never.

His first steps were stiff, self-conscious, and to his frustration, he stumbled twice. Then he felt Hallie give his hand a reassuring squeeze. Reluctantly, he forced his gaze away from his feet to look into her eyes. She was looking at him with such pride, such admiration, that his self-consciousness melted away.

"You're doing wonderfully," she said, bringing the hand holding hers up to her lips and kissing it. True, he wasn't the most graceful partner she'd ever had. Yet she couldn't remember ever enjoying a dance quite as much as she was enjoying this one. She gladly would have waltzed with her Jake forever.

Relaxed now, and moving automatically to the music, Jake whispered, "Have I told you how beautiful you look tonight?"

"Only about a hundred times."

"Then consider this one hundred and one," he murmured, drawing her nearer.

Hallie slanted him a seductive look from beneath her lashes. "You're holding me much too close, Mr. Parrish," she purred. "We must look terribly scandalous."

"Not nearly as scandalous as we'll look when I get you alone." Jake missed a couple of steps as he gave her a kiss, the pause almost sending the following dancers hurling into them.

"Wicked man!" Hallie giggled, returning his kiss fervently.

"I've got to get in my wickedness while I can."

"Whatever do you mean by that?"

"Well. Between your medical practice and the managing of your mines, I doubt if you'll have much time left for me."

"My mines?" Hallie stopped in midstep. "You got my mines for me?"

He nodded.

With a squeal of delight, she threw herself into his arms and proceeded to cover his face with kisses. "I do love you, Mr. Parrish!"

"Something which can't be said for your father." He laughed, tossing the couples behind them an apologetic look. Their abrupt stop had sent several of the dancers colliding into one another, leaving one couple lying in a tangled heap of petticoats and dark coattails. "He and his solicitor put up quite a fight."

"I don't doubt it." Giggling, Hallie fell into step as he resumed dancing. "I can't imagine how he'll be able to support all his mistresses without the profits from the mines."

"I guess he'll have to settle for just one. I could tell him from experience that it's wonderfully satisfying to devote oneself to one very special woman."

"And this particular woman will always have time for your wickedness, mines or no mines," she whispered, warmed by the sincerity of his words.

In silence, they took several more turns around the room, each contemplating their good fortune in finding the other.

"What?" Jake laughed, seeing Hallie studying him intently.

"Oh. I was just wondering something."

"Indeed?"

"Yes," she murmured, furrowing her brow in mock puzzlement. "I was wondering if the baby I'm carrying will be a boy to inherit his father's pretty face, or a girl to inherit Sinclair Mines."

That stopped Jake in his tracks, and for the first time in his life, he was struck speechless.

"You mean . . .?" He finally managed to croak. His voice drifted off as he stepped back and stared at his wife's still trim waistline, oblivious to the fact that they had again caused chaos among the other dancers.

"I mean you're going to be a papa."

"A-are you s-sure?"

"I'm a doctor, aren't I?"

Jake let out a loud whoop as he drew Hallie into his arms. Spinning her around he shouted, "We're going to have a baby!"

All around them, there were cheers and applause.

"When?" he whispered, hugging her close.

"December. Around Christmas, I think."

A Christmas baby. The child from his loins.

Jake threw back his head, howling his victory. And like yesterday's roses, the last of his doubts withered and crumbled, blowing away like petals on the autumn wind.

She had given him her love, and now their child. With a sob, Jake lifted his wife into his arms, cradling her close. As his lips claimed hers, contentment such as he had never known before bloomed in his heart, unfurling like the eternal, life-affirming buds of spring.

His Hallie had given him the most precious gifts of all.

The Young Midas's touch was truly golden at last.